SYBILLE

BOOKS BY MARION MEADE

Sybille

Madame Blavatsky:
The Woman Behind the Myth

Stealing Heaven

Eleanor of Aquitaine

Free Woman:
The Life and Times of Victoria Woodhull

SYBILLE

by Marion Meade

WILLIAM MORROW AND COMPANY, INC.
NEW YORK•1983

Copyright © 1983 by Marion Meade

All rights reserved. No part of this book may be reproduced
or utilized in any form or by any means, electronic or mechanical,
including photocopying, recording or by any information storage
and retrieval system, without permission in writing from the
Publisher. Inquiries should be addressed to William Morrow and
Company, Inc., 105 Madison Avenue, New York, N.Y. 10016.

Library of Congress Cataloging in Publication Data

Meade, Marion, 1934-
 Sybille.

 I. Title.
PS3563.E1685S84   1983   813'.54   82-18758
ISBN 0-688-00808-9

Printed in the United States of America

First Edition

1 2 3 4 5 6 7 8 9 10

BOOK DESIGN BY HARRY BROCKE

Note

I do not know how the Cathar religion originated. It is believed to have started in Bulgaria, probably during the tenth century, and to have spread rapidly westward along the rim of the Mediterranean. By the year 1200, perhaps half the population of what is now southern France had rejected Catholicism for the rival faith. To reclaim its own, the Catholic Church made war, unsuccessfully, with fire and sword. Then came organized psychological violence—the Inquisition.

The sect was known by several names—Cathars (Pure Ones) or Albigensians—but most often they were referred to as "the heretics." They themselves did not give any special name to their own church, only calling themselves Christians who were trying to follow the plain, unadulterated, and undeniably radical teachings of Jesus. It was the Church of Rome, the Cathars insisted, which had deviated so greatly from Christ's original ideas that *it* deserved to be called heretical.

While my narrative ends with the capture of Montségur, the Cathar church was not completely destroyed until the fourteenth century. Efforts were made to eradicate every trace of its doctrines and rituals, including any clues that might explain the religion's enormous popularity. Readers wishing to know more about the history and politics of these events are referred to Emmanuel Le Roy Ladurie's *Montaillou* and Zoé Oldenbourg's masterful *Massacre at Montségur*.

M.M.

And I looked, and behold a pale horse: and his name that sat on him was Death, and Hell followed with him. And power was given unto them over the fourth part of the earth, to kill with sword, and with hunger, and with death, and with the beasts of the earth.

—Revelation 6:8

Chapter One

"Stop jabbering, child. You're giving me an earache."

The small girl halted midsentence and clamped her lips. Her eyes closed, and she began to rock unsteadily from side to side, each swing of her body releasing a cataract of restlessness.

"Sybille." Again the silken voice sighed. "Please try to be still for once."

She struggled to hold back her tears and cast a wounded gaze down at the marble tiles, then up at the tapestry showing the Resurrection. When deprived of all other alternatives, she could express mood with her chin: chin defiant, chin meditative, although the latter was rarely to be seen. Now she muscled an apologetic chin, as if to say, "Forgive me, Lady Mother." But Douce d'Astarac's attention had moved on already.

Some hours earlier the child had tottered into her mother's bedchamber and planted herself, belly down. It was cool and sweet there on the rug. She lay still and watched the cat sleeping. Soon the door would open and her mother would glide in on waves of lavender. At her heels would tramp a servingwoman, arms lumped with bundles, the harvest of a morning's shopping in the bazaars of Rue de la Pourpointerie. "No need to visit Damascus or Constantinople," Douce would say. "The best comes to Toulouse." Douce knew about the best.

The bells of Saint-Sernin signaled noon. Within the child's head there was a silence ticking. After a while she began to hear sounds, not real words but a pulse that seemed more solid to her than words. *Fast*-slow, *fast*-slow. There was almost a kind of trot to them, she discovered. Forgetting her mother's absence, she played with the silence, with the sounds that were not yet words, and then at last with the words themselves. She thought:

Think of a word
to go with
ardit:
Valiant.
Maybe strong and valiant.
One Gawain
Two brave Charlemagnes
Three valiant courtly Tristrams.
A Roland
A Roland
A Roland calling Olivier.
Ardit e poissan.
Ai!

Then, quite excited, she added a dragon. Very large, very ugly, and he breathed fire. But when she tried saying that line aloud, it was too long and she ran out of breath. The sounds inside her head did not match those on her tongue, alas. And then Douce returned, and the child rattled out her poem, which grew longer and more meaningless until she found herself yawing in a labyrinth of words. At last her mother had silenced her.

From her place on the floor, Sybille could see nothing but her mother's feet. The rest of her had vanished among the cushions on the big featherbed. The servingwoman took away Douce's gloves and alms purse; she returned to tug off the riding boots, which she replaced with a pair of brocade slippers.

Precious objects abounded in her mother's room. Sybille knew each one of them: the prie-dieu with its crucifix of gilded brass in which the figure of Christ had been inlaid, the crystal scent boxes with their lids of gold and rubies, the chased goblet made by a goldsmith monk of Limoges. Nearby hung the cittern, its wood spangled by bars of sunlight. Every object was extraordinary. Like my mama, Sybille thought.

"Wine, Na Douce?" the servant was murmuring.

"Please."

Familiar sounds moved like psalms above Sybille's head. She could hear the tinkle of the goblet, the swooshing of ostrich feathers as the woman fanned her mistress.

"Mama," Sybille called out hoarsely. "May I come up?"

"Don't be silly. When did I ever say you couldn't? You won't believe the splendid things I found."

With a running leap she catapulted herself onto the bed and plopped headfirst into a cave of grass-green silk. The bed was mounded with silks, brocades, and taffetas in shades that would shame a rainbow. Her mother held up the green cloth. "From Persia," she crowed. Along its edges shimmered bands of gold embroidery, worked with violet silk into a vine pattern of nightingales and griffins. Douce had never heard of the word "simplicity"; but then nobody had ever brought it to her attention.

"Was it costly?"

Douce shrugged her shoulders. "Costly? Everything is costly. Look at this one." She unfurled a length of white samite interwoven with gold and silver threads. "From the shores of the Nile. Or so that pig of a Genoan told me."

Beside her, Sybille leaned on one elbow. She had discovered a bag of crystal buttons and began lining them in rows.

"Now tell me what my baby did today," Douce said, yawning.

"I'm not a baby."

"Nonsense." Douce pinned her down until she shrieked with laughter, and then she moistened her mouth and neck with splinters of little kisses. "My fat little girl." A hailstorm of buttons rattled to the floor. "My baby cake, sweet as new butter."

"Mama, stop!" She squealed and thrashed her legs, full of pleasure. "It tickles." After a while Douce tired of the game, and Sybille butted gently against her side, breathing in the fragrance of lavender. I want to stay here all day, she thought. Seconds later she was bouncing on her knees. "I made a poem while you were gone."

"Very nice. Make another tomorrow."

"But Mama, don't you remember? It displeased you."

"What an idea. It was charming. But Sybille, my dear, it rambled a bit. Verse must be tidy and fall sweetly upon the ear."

Sybille opened her mouth to offer excuses but grunted instead. The only person who took her compositions seriously was her mother, but then Douce was the only one who mattered anyway. She was acknowledged as an authority on poetical literature. Not that she herself wrote, indeed she had difficulty spelling her name, nor did she read. But shortly after the birth of her second son, at a tournament near Albi, she had caught the eye of a famous troubadour, who had composed a three-stanza tribute to her beauty.

This Folquet de Marseille, of course, had honored a score of ladies with similar impromptu ditties, a fact Douce had no trouble ignoring; she had wrapped the manuscript in silk and given it a place of honor on her chest. Occasionally Sybille was allowed to approach this shrine and view the parchment, but never actually to touch it. It made no difference that Folquet had abandoned poetry, and the fashionable ladies who had inspired it, to enter the monastery of Le Thoronet. The honor, bloated by now into the status of family mythology, could not be disputed.

That Douce would bother to discuss poetry with a child never ceased to amaze and thrill Sybille. "When I grow up," she told her mother, "I'll be a troubadour and write *cansos* like La Comtessa de Dia."

"*Trobairitz,*" Douce corrected her. "Not troubadour. Use the feminine. Now, what was I just saying? Oh, yes. The last words of lines must rhyme. I think I've mentioned that. Surely I said that before. Rhyme your lines."

"I know."

"It's the sounds of the words that matter. And don't forget adjectives. You want plenty of adjectives."

"God's teeth," Sybille broke in loudly. "You told me."

"Shh. Don't shout in my ear." She turned her head away and closed her eyes. "A love song without adjectives is like a sky without stars."

Sybille said quietly, like an adult, "But I don't like adjectives."

"Of course you do," Douce insisted. Her voice washed out to a mumble.

"They're stupid." To tell the truth, she was angry because she had more or less forgotten what an adjective was. From somewhere below came a racket of high-pitched voices and then the cook, shouting. Her brothers must have thieved something from the oven. Sybille studied her mother's face. "Mama?"

Just when she decided her mother was asleep, Douce murmured, "I bought you something. In my purse."

Sybille jiggled down and went to find the purse. There were a few coins and a length of pale-blue ribbon embroidered with seed pearls the color of clouds. She turned to the bed and said politely, "Mama, thank you." She couldn't help thinking the ribbon was pretty but not the nicest she had ever seen. No matter what God or Douce gave her, she always wanted more.

She lingered on the floor, feeling the smoothness of the pearls with her fingertips, until her sister came and took her down to the courtyard. It was hot and noisy, the sun bobbling high up in the sky like a double-yolked egg. They stopped in a vein of shade under the wall where the cobbles were coolest, and sat with their legs stretched out as stiff as sticks. Sybille thought her sister might feel bad because their lady mother had brought her nothing, but her sister said she did not care, truly, about ribbons. She had a box of them. Sybille knew that was true.

"Fabrisse."

Her sister was watching their brothers chip at each other's shoulders with wooden swords.

"Listen to my *canso*." She hunched up her knees and spread the ribbon across them. "It's about a frightful battle up in the mountains. This brave knight has a magic sword. He and his friend kill a whole bunch of infidels at Roncevaux. All by themselves."

Fabrisse rolled up her eyes.

"Listen, they both die at the end. Isn't that wonderful?"

"I've heard it." Fabrisse smiled in her superior way. "It's called *Chanson de Roland.*"

That was true. "No," she said stubbornly. "I made it up this morning, so help me God."

"Hush," Fabrisse said. "It's wicked to tell lies."

She searched for a persuasive detail. "They chopped off everybody's heads. A hundred thousand bloody heads."

"Disgusting."

"Why won't you believe me? Why?" She laced grimy fingers around the ribbon. "There was so much blood it ran down the sides of the mountain and drowned a whole village. I swear it." She smiled, delighted with herself.

"You really are revolting." Fabrisse grimaced. "If I were you, I'd make a song about something beautiful."

But you're not me, Sybille thought. Out loud, she said, "Like what?" Half turning, she tried to lock her arm through Fabrisse's.

Her sister wrenched away. "Look," she said, jerking her arm toward the corner of the yard. "There."

Blinking, Sybille followed the direction of Fabrisse's arm. All she

13

could see was the sunlight lifting out of a rosebush. They were only flowers. "A rose is nothing," she protested.

She fell silent then, picking at the pearls with her thumbnail. Across the yard Pierre and Mathieu sprawled under an olive tree. They looked sweaty and out of breath. She tried to imagine her brothers with their heads chopped off and shivered. She thought of petals of every rose on every bush in the world, petals without number bleeding into the earth; of every woman and every man who had breathed, or would breathe, and then had stopped breathing. She began to cry, because living was ugly and beautiful, because each thing lived only to die, because she would die. It was the one promise never broken.

She squeezed shut her eyes and asked Our Lady to make her a good person, like Fabrisse. For several minutes she sat there praying in the fiery blear behind her eyelids, before her chin thumped on her chest and the blue ribbon slipped down into a muddy crack between two cobblestones. She pretended to be asleep until she slept.

This day, in the spring of 1198, would remain her earliest memory. Later, when all those voices were stilled forever, she would sift her recollections in bursts of frustration. Surely her beginnings were marked by something more consequential than hair ribbons and squabbles with Fabrisse; events of importance must have taken place, if only she could remember them. But time had scrubbed memory clean, the way a tearing stream grinds smooth a boulder. It would eventually occur to her that the days of her childhood had been stained by a sameness and that this absence of turbulence was what is called peace.

Before the beginning of the new century Sybille had never known any other life existed but the one she was living. The Astarac mansion behind Saint-Sernin square, in the faubourg of Toulouse, had been built of the same ruddy-red brick as the city walls and was undeniably impressive. True, it was not quite as large as the neighboring Maurand house, which, before Sybille's birth, had had a fortified tower on its roof. But things had gotten hot between Pierre Maurand and the Church, and he had been forced to remove the tower. In any case, the fortifications had been nothing but a conceit, and a rather silly one at that. When had a burgher's home been in danger of a siege?

Sybille's father was not a native Toulousan. His youth had been spent on his father's lands in Astarac, or at the smaller but more comfortable castle inherited by his mother in the district of Fanjeaux. There was other ancestral property as well: villages and vineyards and fields, acre upon acre planted with grape and olive, all scattered piecemeal within a fifteen-league radius of the city, but these holdings held small interest for William d'Astarac. Twice each year, at Candlemas and Michaelmas, he toured his lands, more from a sense of duty than necessity, and every summer he escorted his family to the castle at Fanjeaux.

This annual exodus to Cantal had its practical side, for William was above all a practical man. It gave a good deal of pleasure to his aging mother; it excited his sons, who spent their every waking moment on horseback; and it offered an opportunity to have the house in Rue St. Bernard whitewashed. As for himself, William d'Astarac bore his ennui with rural life as best he could and hurried back to the city well before the first frost. He was a burgher, he said proudly. Not a farmer. Three times he had been appointed a consul, and even now it was politics and his precious library of leatherbound books that occupied his time. These two activities were, he always said, the only suitable occupations for a civilized man, and he could be very testy with anyone who disagreed.

The Astaracs were Catholics. But Sybille's grandmother had abandoned the old faith. She had become intrigued, almost obsessed, by new ideas, new ways of thinking about God that seemed closer to the original teachings of Jesus. The adherents of the new faith were known as Cathars, or "the others," but they referred to themselves as "the Good Christians." How these unorthodoxies had traveled over twelve centuries from Nazareth to southern Europe was not particularly clear. In those days the southerners never thought to question where an idea had come from. It was interesting, or it was not. If it possessed beauty and charm, so much the better. Many of them accepted the two gods of the heretical Good Christians. Just as many did not. There was little competition between the two faiths. Both were careful to respect, both were careful to tolerate each other because to do otherwise would have been discourteous.

Sybille could not remember a time when her family had not been powerful, when people as far distant as Avignon had not been honored to receive invitations to their banquets. The Astarac reputation for hospitality was legendary. In the courtyard torches would smoke fitfully, thrusting aside the darkness; the chandeliers in the great hall cast coppery nimbi upon white tablecloths and whiter bosoms. Pages would strut between kitchen and hall parading roast peacocks whose iridescent feathers had been reattached. Later, once Count Raymond had appeared, the dais would be commandeered by jongleurs and vielle players, the drone of their songs washing across the rooftops. Even the priests of Saint-Sernin, people said, interrupted their chess games to hum a *canso*. Sometimes a troubadour would come to perform his work for the assembled ladies and lords and depart in the gathering dawn with a stallion for his night's work.

This was the way it had always been for the Astaracs. There was no reason to imagine it would change.

"Is there a reason we're attending this thing?" William d'Astarac asked his mother. "I mean, a good reason."

Na Beatritz squeezed out a crusty smile to show his grumbling was not being taken seriously. "For the good of your soul, my dear boy. Though I don't suppose you would call that a sufficiently good reason."

"Lady Mother," he rumbled, "we are not of one mind in this matter."

It was the Sunday morning before St. John's Day. The family was on its way to Montréal, to a meadow just outside the town walls, where representatives of the rival faiths were going to have a debate. There were many of these occasions in the summer. People enjoyed listening—it was good entertainment—but they also had an opportunity to socialize with their friends. Directly behind William and Beatritz, Sybille jogged along on her white mare, listening to them bicker and scratching the mosquito bites on her neck. By now the sun was up and pumping down June heat on the olive groves and almost frying the rose-tiled roofs of the manor houses.

Beatritz gave a loud sniff. "I have no wish to quarrel with you, son. Let us drop the subject."

"Are those Spaniards still hanging about?"

"If you mean the bishop of Osma, yes. And Brother Dominic. He preaches quite often."

"I can't imagine why," William said heatedly. "Now, what does Rome stand to gain from two Spanish monks wandering barefoot around the Lauraguais and sleeping in ditches? Nothing. That's what the pope doesn't understand. The Good Christians worship the Almighty in their way and we Catholics in ours. And all of us are going to keep right on doing it. So what's the point of making a fuss?" He blotted his brow with the back of his hand. "Missionaries indeed. Aren't there any heathen left in Russia?"

"How you do get yourself worked up," Na Beatritz shouted. "And then you miss the point entirely."

"The point is—"

"—that the pope regards all of us as pagans." She looked across with a peppery smile.

"Rubbish."

"All right, all right. You say rubbish. Of course it's not my place to contradict you. You're a grown man." Actually she still thought of him as a small boy who required constant instruction. "But you're unfamiliar with the situation in this district. I'm only trying to explain the thing to you." Her face cracked into a glare. "For your own enlightenment."

"Thunder! But you haven't explained a damned thing so far."

"You're hopeless," hooted Beatritz.

William groaned. "Mother."

Sybille smiled into her sleeve. Fearful lest she miss the old lady's next bolt, she nudged the mare's nose level with her grandmother's elbow. But Beatritz had snapped shut her jaw and was staring down the narrow strip of road; William had turned away to study a mule wandering through some peasant's young vines. In Na Beatritz's presence her father's dignity, worn like a cloak in all weathers, swiftly disintegrated. Sometimes Sybille felt sorry for him, because in these scuffles with her grandmother, he won seldom. No, never.

Far across the fields Sybille could see Montréal humped on the crest of a hill. Its slopes shivered with almond blossoms. The fortified town cut off the road and peered out over the valley like a gargantuan watchdog hunkered on its hind legs.

"Na Beatritz," she called out. "Do you think there will be any fiddlers there?"

Beatritz shook her head. "What an idea. I've told you. The Spaniards are going to present their views on God. And then we Christians will have a chance to give our side."

Debating about God sounded quite ridiculous to Sybille. Ridiculous and boring. Everybody praying. She hoped there would be at least one fiddler. Even a bad sackbut player would do.

"Then," Na Beatritz was saying, "it will be decided who has won."

Sybille's brothers pounded by in a torrent of hoofbeats, whooping and dumping a cloud of dirt in their wakes. Sybille closed her eyes and tried not to breathe for a moment. She expected her grandmother to yell after them, but she did not. Sybille asked, "Oh, like a tourney?"

"I suppose."

"But who picks the winner?"

"Don't know. Someone."

"I don't see who could decide such a thing." She shuffled forward in the saddle.

"The judges."

Sybille gave a cackle of laughter. Almost all the noble families in these parts were Good Christians. If local people were going to judge the contest, there could be little doubt of the outcome. "That's stupid. I think—"

"Damn it," Beatritz said, "go back and ride with your mother. You're a pest."

Sybille looked over her shoulder. A hundred paces back, Douce was swaying along beside Fabrisse, and they were smiling and nodding. She swiveled forward again. "You mean," she said, chin shaking with laughter, "if the goodmen win, I won't have to go to mass anymore?"

Beatritz gave her a sharp look. "You are not amusing."

Rebuffed, Sybille dropped back and scratched her bites furiously. She heard her father cough and say, "Lady Mother, don't you find it demeaning? Catholics should not be obliged to defend the superior faith as if it were invented last week."

Beatritz said, "You've got it all wrong—"

Abruptly Sybille kicked up her mare and swerved around them. She whisked down the road in pursuit of Pierre and Mathieu.

The meadow was thronged. On the far side of the field a platform had been erected for the speakers. The scorched grass had been crushed down and food stalls thrown up; smoke and fat from roasting meat spattered in the noon air. Farther back, in a grove of cork oaks, swayed the pavilions of the noble families, the Tonneins, the Mazerolles, the Durforts. Sybille stamped about impatiently as her grandmother's servants raised the Astarac tent and spread tapestries and cushions on the ground; already the place was crowded with visitors. She itched to get away.

Douce slouched in a nest of cushions, whispering to one of the Durfort women. When she caught sight of Sybille, she feigned a half-scowl. "Sweet heart, that bliaut is filthy. Ask Fabrisse to help you change."

"I like it filthy."

"Go on. Be a good girl."

She started across the pavilion. Near the opening stood Fabrisse, her face arranged into a self-satisfied smirk. In a high-pitched voice she was talking to a knight who had attached himself, leechlike, to one of her sleeves. All the men Fabrisse attracted seemed to be bald-ing. This one, Sybille decided, must be at least thirty. She veered around them and loped up to her father. He was facing the wall, his arm crooked over the shoulder of his boyhood friend, Jordan de Villeneuve.

"Papa, buy me a cheese pasty," she wheedled. "Buy me marzi-pan."

William held out a goblet to Jordan de Villeneuve. "The Church," he spat. "Rome has no respect for deviant beliefs. Make no mistake about that."

"Papa—"

William never looked in her direction. He reached into his girdle and fished out a handful of deniers. Sybille picked out three. Then she clicked them all into her fist.

"Your daughter is high-spirited, William."

"My daughter is spoiled." William shook his head with a smile.

Over her shoulder, Sybille yelled, "Thank you, Papa."

Ahead, through the trees, she could see people hurrying forward, and she stumbled after them. The air in the meadow smelled like clo-ver and stale wine and burning grease. Her ears were straining for the sounds of music, but she could hear nothing, only people shouting and laughing and a wine crier trying to hawk a tun of claret that was overpriced by half. Everybody was in a hurry to spend money. They stampeded the merchants' tents, shoved themselves up to the food stalls, had no patience about waiting for anything.

Sybille bought a chunk of roast pork, charred black on the out-side, and two cheese pasties. The meat must have just come from the fire because it burned her tongue. She gulped it down quickly and then bit into a pasty. Cobwebs of whitish cheese oozed down the front of her bliaut. The pasty man was handing pies to a man standing behind her and roaring for service. "Wait your turn, son of a bitch. Do you think I have six hands?"

Sybille hung around a few minutes because she could not decide what to do. The heat was burning a jig on her shoulders. She elbowed forward into a crowd, noticed her brothers, hastily retreated. By craning her neck she could see an old man with matted hair and beard down to his waist. Somebody must have hoisted him onto a barrel because his face, withered as a dried goatskin, suddenly popped up above the heads. Even from that distance Sybille could imagine the tunic seething with vermin. Goggling, she crumbled the last of the pasty into her mouth. The old man began speaking in jerks. He told them he conversed with God, and God said He had not created the world. It was hard for Sybille to hear over the spittles of laughter. God only took credit for making the archangels—it was these beings who had created the sun and the moon.

"That's nice," someone bawled. "What else did He tell you?"

The man picked out a woman eating an onion. "You there! Do you know how the world was made?" He did not wait for an answer. "From the sun's piss. And humans were made from the moon's shit. Aye, by God. It has been revealed to me."

The crowd whistled with guffaws, which did not seem to anger the man a bit. "You are shit, I am shit." He was smiling and hopping about unsteadily on the barrel, like a small, loud wren.

Ringside, a woman cackled, "But what about Christ? What was He?"

"Shit," replied the old man promptly. "Mahomet too."

Sybille laughed out loud. The world was full of lunatics. More than she had imagined. Feeling a hand jostle her elbow, she whirled around. "Oh," she said. "It's you."

"Aren't you going to say hello?"

"Hello," she said pleasantly. She had not noticed Jordan de Villeneuve's son in the tent. Obviously he had grown; there was an orderly band of fuzz over his upper lip.

"Nice weather for this," he said, smiling.

She nodded.

"What's going on?"

"Nothing." She turned away. "I've got to go."

"Where? The debate hasn't begun yet."

"Have you seen any fiddlers? I want to find the fiddlers." She quickened her step, not waiting to see if he was following. She hoped he was not; she didn't much like the idea of Pons de Villeneuve's company. She bumped against bodies. From the tail of her eye she could see him lumbering along behind her.

"Have you written any new poems since last summer?" he yelled.

She gave a laugh. "New poems? I should say. Dozens." She hesitated. "All trash. I'll never be a writer."

"Sure you will. You'll just be a writer of trash."

She gave him a piercing look to see if he were being mean. Why, she would rather be no poet at all than a bad one. He caught her arm, made a face, then grinned. "Who's your favorite troubadour?" she demanded.

"Never thought about it. I like them all."

Ahead, two or three men had blocked the way to give the customary three bows to a heretic woman preacher and to ask for her blessing. When the goodwoman drew abreast of Sybille and Pons, Pons stepped into her path and bowed. Remembering her manners, Sybille hastily jerked out three bobs of the head. Then she slapped Pons on the shoulder. "Don't be silly. You must have a favorite."

"All right." His mouth curled down thoughtfully. "Then, Bernart de Ventadorn."

She regretted asking and grimaced. "God, if He'll forgive me saying so, should have given you better taste."

He shrugged and laughed. "Who do you like?"

"Peire Vidal."

"That buffoon!" he hooted. "He's crazy."

She puffed out her cheeks, indignant. "That's why I like him." She bristled. Of course Vidal was mad. But he was also a genius, no one could deny that.

Finally, Sybille spotted a fiddler she knew sitting beneath a carob tree and fingering the strings of a vielle.

"Hie, Blondel!" she cried.

He looked up, bowed from the waist, and flashed her a toothy grin. Spindle-legged, he had pimples on his chin and a mushroom cap of straw-colored hair that grew in six directions at once. "Have you a new song for me, lady?" he called out.

She shook her head at him. "What are you going to play? Play something gay."

"Lady, would you care to sing with me?" He scooped up a pair of cymbals from the grass and thrust them at her.

She did not like her voice. It was rich and strong but throaty, filamented with growls. It lacked the sweetness of a woman's voice. Once Mathieu had called her a frog singing in a well, and she had never forgiven him. Since then she felt self-conscious about her voice. Not that it prevented her from singing, and lustily too. "If my grandmother finds out—" she mumbled hoarsely to Blondel.

Glancing around furtively, she noticed a crowd gathering. That morning Na Beatritz had been specific about the sort of behavior expected of her. No consorting with idlers, jongleurs, or riffraff. Sit still at the debate and no whistling during prayers. Sybille scanned the faces and noticed Pons, arms folded, staring at her with amusement. She gave the cymbals a tentative jangle, grinned at Blondel, and cleared her throat. "How about this one? *The other day I was in paradise—*"

Quickly he took up the Monk of Montauban's tune. *"And that's why I'm feeling so gay."* The bow raking the strings threw up a sharp trickle of sound into the hot air.

She shouted the next line. *"Lord, I said, You're making a big mistake—"* A chuckle went up from the onlookers.

Sybille, happy, slapped her foot against the hard-packed dirt.

An hour later, full of guilt, she raced toward the speakers' platform and tumbled, panting, into a vacant spot next to Fabrisse.

Her sister looked disapproving. She started to speak, then only hissed, "Brother Dominic preached."

She followed Fabrisse's glance. A man in dark blue was making his way to the center of the platform. It was Arnaud Othon, the deacon who frequently visited her grandmother. Arnaud began to speak in an absentminded voice. One might have thought he was remarking on the weather. "The Roman Church," he began. "The Roman Church is not holy. She is not the bride of Christ."

Someone croaked, "Alas!" There was a rumble of polite laughter.

Arnaud smiled professionally. "On the contrary. She is the church of the Devil. Her doctrines are demoniacal." He stopped and squinted at the faces below. "My good friends, I'll tell you what she is. She is that very Babylon that John, in the Apocalypse, called the mother of fornication."

The face of the sun leaned down. A ceiling of heat quivered over the meadow. I must not fall asleep, Sybille thought, and aimed her gaze at Brother Dominic. He was a smallish man who reeked of weariness and was dressed in sandals and a dust-stained cowl. Against the orange light, his pallor was pasty and unhealthy. Sybille recalled hearing that once he had come to a village near Laurac and some hooligan children had thrown manure at him. Perhaps the story was not true.

Dominic did not appear to have the slightest interest in Arnaud Othon, who was walking up and down, still smiling, mouth opening and shutting. Sybille forced her attention on his words, just in case Na Beatritz should quiz her later on. "The Lord Jesus Christ," he was saying, "did not invent the mass as it exists now. Neither did His apostles."

She did not believe him. She did not disbelieve him either. She did not care who had invented the mass, any more than she thought it worthwhile to ponder the identity of the inventor of the wheel. Several minutes went by. The deacon was taking his time. No telling how long he might stay up there. She yawned and thought enviously of Blondel. It would be cool under the carob tree. She could imagine him sitting in the spongy grass, counting the coins that had been tossed into his cap. Then, vielle slung over his shoulder, he would start down the road toward Fanjeaux. She rolled on her back and listened to time swimming with songs.

Daylight fled the sky in a great hurry. Between one breath and the next, like the plummeting of a portcullis, the rose stain had plunged to blackness. Cressets dipped from the lowest branches of the trees, and the Astarac tent blazed with enough candles to light a Christmas mass. On the white-clothed trestles had been laid platters of roast meat, fruit, and cheese. Beatritz d'Astarac's seneschal was busy filling platters and rushing them, one by one, over to the ladies; a page floated around swinging a silver censer.

Sybille grabbed a goblet and slipped outside. The breeze hissing among the leaves made a sound like rain.

"Please." The man's voice was coming from the far side of an oak tree, directly behind her head. "You promised."

"Don't. You'll crumple my gown."

"But you said—"

"I didn't say tonight."

Ordinarily Sybille took pleasure in spying on Fabrisse and her fumbling suitors, and then teasing her afterward. Tonight she did not care. Her head felt thick from the sun and the brief nap she had snatched during the speeches. She saw Pons coming toward her.

"The Christians won this afternoon," he said. "Isn't that wonderful?"

She did not think so.

"Don't you like them?" He swiped at his shaggy hair.

"Not much." She felt annoyed. All day long she had heard nothing but God, God. "Oh, I really don't care one way or another."

She had known Pons de Villeneuve all her eleven years, could remember playing with him every summer at Cantal and once visiting his father's mansion at Carcassonne, and she was too well-bred to have purposely offended him. Of course, her brothers had never liked him, nor had they bothered to hide their feelings. That was understandable.

Pons, as a young child, had possessed only a single remarkable feature. He had been very fat, clumsy in movement, ponderous in thought and speech, in any game puffing to finish last. He could not pass a table without knocking off half the goblets. Now he was no longer fat but merely stocky and solid, and he made her think of an affable bear, half grown.

Pons, unlike the boys of his age, was never interested in getting his nose bloodied and proving his manliness. He was therefore an outsider. One summer the children had discovered a cliff beyond the oak forest. In a reckless mood, they decided to jump off, into the dried-up creek bed below. Everybody in turn had crept quaking to the edge and gone off—everybody but Pons. How they had taunted him! Afterward, Sybille had questioned him, and he answered without hesitation, "I was afraid."

Sybille had been appalled. To admit cowardice was something only a fool would do, and she told him so.

"I'm not a coward," he protested. "But why take stupid chances?"

Why, indeed. A few days later, by no surprising coincidence, Pierre had broken his ankle badly at the cliff and spent the rest of that summer confined to the hall. After that, Sybille eyed Pons with a kind of grudging respect; all the same she never felt completely comfortable with him.

But now she forced herself to go to him. Uneasily she said, "What's gotten into you?"

Pons said, "Don't you wonder why my mother isn't here?"

His mother was not beautiful like Douce. His mother was a whiner, endlessly bleating about headaches and constipation. She had puggish lips, like a dog Sybille had once seen in a juggler's act. "No, where is she? Did you leave her home?"

"Yes." He gave her a sideways stare, eyes smoky as rain. "She's dead."

For a moment she said nothing. She could not imagine Na Raymonde dead. People were always dying, but she had never remarked it particularly; it had never happened to anyone she knew. She stared stupidly at Pons. The thought of Douce pounded into her head. "I'm sorry," she mumbled. "Truly I am. Nobody told me."

Pons gazed at the ground.

Tears, hot, salty, itched at her eyes. Claps of laughter rocketed from the pavilion. She did not want to think about Na Raymonde. She hated her for dying. In her throat a sob flowered, fragile as a bud, and she pressed her fist over her mouth and wept.

Her mother came out and folded her arms tight around her head and hustled her to bed. That night, lullabied by the scent of lavender, she slept on Douce's pallet.

She did not see Pons again for two or three years. The next summer the whole family was involved with her brothers, who left to begin their knighthood training with the count of Foix. The way they strutted and showed off, anyone would have assumed they expected to be dubbed in a month, when actually they were only going to be squires, along with fifty or sixty other lads.

And the following year all the attention was on her sister. That was the year of Fabrisse's wedding, and nobody talked of anything else.

Their father complained, happily, that after paying for his daughter's dowry and for the cost of the nuptial feast he would end a poor man. Sybille got used to hearing him rant for whole evenings about the villages and vineyards Fabrisse would have and the wedding guests he planned to invite. He would sit at a table in his library, account books and lists spread under his elbows, and throw back his head in frustration, swearing that he refused to spend one more sou, even if Fabrisse remained unwed forever.

Douce whirled through each day in purposeful agitation. Her trips to the bazaars became more frequent, more frantic. She would buy a silk one day, decide it was not good enough for Fabrisse, and return it the next. Even so, she managed to keep a dozen seamstresses occupied.

In the midst of this Sybille could not help feeling half superfluous, half in exile. Fabrisse was living; she was not. Douce was sensitive enough to notice this, because one afternoon at the end of Lent, she came to Sybille's room. She sat on the edge of the bed and Sybille climbed into her lap. Finally Douce said, "Why don't you write a *canso* in honor of Fabrisse's marriage? That would please her."

Sybille sighed. Fabrisse was not musical. She would not care.

"We could hire a jongleur to compose the music," her mother suggested. "Have it sung at the wedding. You want to, don't you?"

The last thing she wanted to do was write a song for Fabrisse. "Yes," she lied. "I'll try."

So far as technique went, Sybille was developing into a fairly competent poet. She had easily mastered the metrical schemes for *canso, sirventes, alba,* and *tenso,* and could produce a well-rhymed song for almost any occasion. She thought about things more deeply now, or imagined she did, but she had yet to find a style of her own. Her verse sounded like copies of Cercamon's or Peire Vidal's. She was a mimic of hand-me-down voices.

A *canso* for the bridal couple would be no easy matter. The subject failed to inspire her, especially her sister's betrothed. Contrary to tradition and custom, Fabrisse herself had selected him, and William, always indulgent, had let her have her way. Andrew Fauré was nothing special. He was neither tall nor good-looking, and he was old, sufficiently old enough to be Fabrisse's father, and had in fact a son two years her elder. For nearly a decade he had been a widower, and he devoted his time entirely to tournaments. Fighting in these events was a passion, virtually his only one, and if he did not ride he came to bet. For this reason he was rarely at home, which, Sybille pointed out to her sister, was not exactly a hopeful omen. But Fabrisse did not seem worried; after they were wed he would stay home. She would see to it.

Worse than all this, Andrew Fauré came from Béziers. How did that old joke go? "As crazy as the Biterrois." Poor Fabrisse, thought Sybille, how unpoetic, how crass.

She wrote an eight-stanza love song in the mewling style of Bernart de Ventadorn.

Before she opened her eyes, Sybille could hear her sister sobbing and the sound of their mother's slippers padding swiftly along the passageway. A door opened. "It's raining!" Fabrisse wailed. "Mama, why is it raining? Why?" The door closed. But after prime the sky began to lighten, and by midmorning the sun was scorching, and Fabrisse complained of sweating to death before she reached Saint-Etienne.

The house was packed. For days each featherbed had been holding twice its usual number of occupants, and some of the wedding guests were obliged to sleep on pallets in the great hall. Upstairs, Fabrisse's chamber hummed with giggling, chattering girls who clustered around the finery Douce had labored to collect these past months. Special hooks had been nailed up to hang the gowns and fur-lined cloaks. Seventeen pairs of slippers stood in rows beside a chest that held twice that number of lace-trimmed chemises and stockings embroidered with tulips and lilies of the valley.

All that morning Fabrisse stood near the window, straight as a beech. Around her knelt and stood half a dozen maids, expertly flitting their hands over her pale body like confectioners decorating a plain cake. The bride was bathed with scented soap, and then oil was rubbed into every inch of her skin. Sodden towels lay in crumpled heaps at her feet. The first layer was applied: a chemise of fine linen, its sleeves worked in gold thread. Then over her head went the bliaut, flaming-red silk cut around the bottom into girons and edged with emerald embroidery set with pearls. Low on her hips was wound a braided cord of pale-green silk, each of its ends studded with a carbuncle. And finally a sleeveless mantle of garnet brocade, lined with delicate emerald silk. Fabrisse was standing because it was impossible to sit.

Douce appeared in the doorway and gave her eldest daughter a bruised look. "Fabrisse, my love, you look like a queen. So now you're going to leave me! I can't believe it. Just think of it, my first baby is going away." Oval tears were spilling out of her eyes. "Oh, if I ever manage to live through this day. I don't know what I'm going to do."

Fabrisse's face wrinkled like a cucumber pickled in strong brine. "Really now, Mama. Stop before you make me cry."

"I tell you, I can't stand it." Douce rushed away.

The maids twisted Fabrisse's hair into braids and tied the ends with ribbons. One of the women climbed onto a stool; with a small brush she started to comb each hair of Fabrisse's eyebrows in the same direction. This was her special task, and she had waited all morning to do it. Sybille was tiptoeing just outside the circle of maids, making a nuisance of herself and not caring how mischievous she was. To keep her occupied, somebody handed her the circlet to hold; she ran her fingertips over the diamonds and gold-beaten eglantines. Her sister, frozen-lipped, did not seem to be breathing.

Sybille edged closer, balancing the circlet in both palms. "Fabrisse," she teased, "I'll bet you're sorry now."

Fabrisse's eyes did not appear to focus. There was no reply, and Sybille was about to repeat the taunt when her sister said, sniffing, "Sorry about what?"

"Having to be wed." The circlet was taken from her and planted on the bride's head.

"I'm not having to be anything. Nobody forced me." She stared at the end of her nose. "I'm very happy, thank you."

The Château Narbonnais, built into the city wall alongside the Narbonne gate, was the home of the counts of Toulouse. Its present occupant was Raymond, the sixth of that name, who lived there with his ten-year-old son, also called Raymond. At the moment Count Raymond had no wife; there had been four of them, all dead or repudiated, and there would be a fifth, but for the present he had no pressing need of a new political alliance. Raymond was a happy man. The land of the *langue d'oc*—his land—swept from the Rhone to the Pyrenees and luxuriated in a sweetness, an ease of living, found nowhere else in Europe.

From outside the great portcullis, Raymond's palace looked like a forbidding fortress. The guardroom and servants' hall were clamorous with the hubbub of people coming and going and soldiers dicing and swearing; the rat-infested cellars held dungeons where one would not have willingly passed a single hour. But the ground floor was given over to a gold and marble hall encircled by rooms tapestried with color and by shade-combed little gardens rivaling in splendor anything yet devised by the caliphs of Baghdad. The frail songs of nightingales, the water plashing velvety into tiled pools, and now and then the muffled wail of flutes threaded through the château like the surf.

Unlike some other princes, the count was immensely popular

with all his subjects. He was a good deal like them. Indeed, it could be said he embodied the national virtues as well as its vices: love of pleasure, mercurial temperament, indolence, tolerance. Courtesy and good manners demanded he respect the beliefs of everyone, whether they be Catholic or Good Christian, Jew or Arab. His second wife had been a Good Christian, but now Beatrix of Béziers lived in the heretical convent at Termes, where she practiced asceticism and ate boiled vegetables. These habits held no temptation for Raymond, who was a lover of sensual women and sensual poetry, although he often told his friends he knew of no more noble philosophy than that of the Good Christians.

His subjects praised him as an extraordinarily democratic overlord. It was true. His cities and towns ruled themselves by councils, and he took no step before consulting them. He enjoyed visiting the burghers' homes and would ride through the streets alone and without fear; and he liked to help the gentry celebrate the important occasions of life by holding feasts at the Château Narbonnais. Just such a banquet he arranged for William d'Astarac's daughter on the day following her marriage.

Sybille was sitting beside her grandmother, not far from the high table where Raymond presided over the festivities dressed in an indigo-colored tunic dotted with silver stars. A jongleur, waiting for the cittern, started to sing one of Arnaut Daniel's most erotic sestinas. It was appropriate because Raymond used to be the great master's patron, but, Sybille thought, too solemn for a wedding. Before it had ended, some of the guests were whispering and shuffling their feet. Soon it was time for the jongleur engaged by Na Douce to come forward and sing Sybille's *canso*.

She shut her eyes because people were staring at her. The song was dreadful. Not because the jongleur didn't have a good, thundering voice. It was bad because the verse was banal. Sybille would have liked to poke her fingers in both ears. After he had finished and everybody clapped and shouted, Sybille's face remained rigid with embarrassment.

"The count is shaking his finger at you," Na Beatritz said. She pushed her arm. "Go along."

She stamped up to the dais, where the count was beaming at her.

He said, "I want to have a word with you, sweet heart." He gripped her waist and pulled her down on his lap.

"About what?" She struggled to keep from blushing. This was

not the first time Raymond had dandled her on his knee, but then she had been smaller.

"That was splendid." He kissed her several times on the side of the cheek. "Reminds me of Jaufré Rudel."

Sybille ducked her head. "Thank you, my lord." She could feel his fingers against her thigh, squeezing heat through the brocade. She sat stiffly upright.

"Pity you're not a man."

"My lord?" she breathed, avoiding his eyes. The closeness of his mouth, his heavy perfume, was making her feel queer.

"I might have been your patron," he said.

She wiggled out of his grasp and stood up, searching for something courteous to say. Finally she located her voice. "My mother wants me," she squeaked and leaped off the dais. Behind her, she could hear him laughing.

Feverishly she edged along the wall, dove out a side door, and ran blindly along the corridor, past statues of plump, naked women, until she saw light ahead. Breathless, she stepped out into a rose-trellised balcony. Beyond, a garden wavered among violet shadows and apple trees. She edged forward, touching her thigh where the count's fingers had been and wondering why it had bothered her.

Abruptly, to the side of the fountain, something vaulted down from a tree. Startled, she leaned forward and put the tip of her nose through the ropes of thorns. It was a boy, scarcely older than herself. He began arching one arm, straining for something concealed in the branches. Then he gyrated on the balls of his feet, jumped, caught an object in his hand, and began to tug, like a fisherman hammering in his line. After a moment he lowered his arm and walked around behind the tree.

During these antics Sybille had waited, wondering what the boy would do next. He was strange. When he returned she saw he was carrying a stool, which he carefully staked in the pebbles. She watched him walking around the stool, coolly shifting it a few inches this way and that. Once, when he stepped out into a patch of light, she got a full glimpse of pale cheeks beneath a bonnet of honey-colored curls.

The ripening sun began to fan the shadows of the apple tree. The boy hoisted himself onto the stool and pirouetted to get his footing. From the depths of the branches a bird honked into the stillness. He stretched up his hand and pulled down a rope whose end was looped into a noose. Sybille's tongue started to shape a scream, but the sound burst far down in her throat.

He gave a sudden yank.

A minute later it was over. In a tangle of arms and legs on the gravel, he clutched the broken end of rope in his fist. Slowly he sat up and stared at the frayed pieces, and then he spit out a croaky laugh.

"Olivier!"

From the back of the garden came the sound of running footsteps and a boy's voice calling, "Olivier!"

Count Raymond's son stood there, waving at the boy. "Hurry," he panted. "The dancing is about to start."

The boy sprang up. With a flick of his wrist, he hurled the rope into the bushes before racing inside.

Sybille tasted salty relief. After a while she shuffled slowly back to the hall, temples throbbing. Couples were lining up for a quadrille. A man in long-pointed crimson shoes grabbed her hand. The horns brayed an ear-splitting smear before settling down to the formal measures of the dance.

Later that evening Sybille caught sight of the boy again. He gave no sign of unhappiness. He was partnering a dark-haired girl, and he was shaking with laughter. Sybille thought, surely he did not seriously intend to take his own life. It must have been a jest, some obscure game played only by the sons of royal fathers. All the same, she could not rid herself of the worrying suspicion that had the rope not snapped, he might be dead now. He was beautiful, with a face an archangel might have envied. She did not understand what could have made him so life-sickened.

In the morning Fabrisse and Andrew left for Béziers, and everyone crowded into the courtyard for the farewells. Five mules were cascaded with wedding gifts and Fabrisse's coffers. Fabrisse sat very stiff on her mare, her face wearing a pasted-on smile.

Douce held up both hands, like a bishop about to deliver a blessing. "My beloved daughter Fabrisse, my beloved son-in-law Andrew. May God shine His light upon your union. May Lord Jesus Christ and Queen Mary and all the saints give you years of blessed happiness and children and grandchildren down to the seventh generation." Her voice was turning scratchy. "Fabrisse, Fabrisse, my precious, don't forget your mother. My God, I can't bear seeing you go. What did you say, William? Yes, I know she'll come back to visit. But . . .

Fabrisse, I beg you, write to me. *Have a joyous life, darling. Fabrisse!*"

The caravan heaved through the gate and made a serpentine turn into Rue St. Bernard. Douce was still waving. At last she dropped her arm and stood there, trembling so that her teeth chattered. The tears welled up. William plucked her off the cobbles and cradled her against his chest. "There, my heart," he murmured. "Don't cry, my nightingale." He carried her toward the steps.

Sybille walked jerkily behind them.

On a foggy morning in January, 1208, a small party of men, the pope's men, appeared on the western bank of the Rhone, south of Beaucaire. At the quay, three ferrymen were squatting quietly near their barges, eating bread and drinking wine that one of the men's daughters had brought. It was not yet prime, too early for customers. The oldest man was chewing on his right side where he still had several teeth. The girl just stood there pulling on her lip, mooning before she returned to her mother. The wind creaked above their heads. The Rhone, mouse-gray, sucked sleepily at the tethered barges. And then suddenly the air was full of commotion. The girl dropped her basket. The ferrymen stopped chewing, spittle and bread wadded immobile in their cheeks. Like spectators at a play, they squinted in silence at the riders in their expensive cloaks who were jolting closer to the quay, then at the lone hooded man whose mount burst from a clump of frosty hazel trees and streaked headlong toward the horsemen. The boat people gaped. The hooded rider plunged a dagger into the chest of one of the pope's men, wheeled sharply, and was lost in the murk. Within the space of a paternoster it was over. Were it not for the unholy dagger rooted in the victim's cloak, it might have been a dream. The wounded man, without uttering a sound, dropped the reins; after a moment his body rolled sideways in the saddle.

Chapter Two

Two weeks after Pierre de Castelnau's murder, Sybille was formally betrothed to Pons de Villeneuve. One event had nothing to do with the other.

For several years William d'Astarac had been chewing on the idea of a match between his daughter and his old friend's son. There was the future and grandsons to think of, and he knew of no other family with which he so greatly desired to mix his blood. The girl was handsome and strong, a bit more willful than he thought desirable in a woman, but she would outgrow that. As for the boy, he had watched him grow from infancy and knew him as a steady lad, intelligent and pleasant of temper.

Granted, William had put off broaching the subject because over the years he had watched Jordan inching away from the Church. This he had attributed to the influence of Jordan's dead wife, a woman who had been hereticated on her deathbed. But no, he must not blame Raymonde. He was forgetting the whole city of Carcassonne had a great liking for the inferior faith. How could it be otherwise when their young viscount had been tutored by a heretic like Bertrand de Saissac? When the bishop of Carcassonne, after threatening his parishioners with hellfire for their toleration of heresy, had been escorted to the city gate by indignant burghers and locked out? No, it was only to be expected that his friend would favor the other faith. In any case, when finally he did mention the betrothal, it was Jordan himself who had been the one to bring up religion and to assure him Pons had been raised a Catholic.

"You don't suppose," William wondered aloud, "the murder of the ambassador is going to stir up trouble."

"I should think not," Jordan said, frowning. "It isn't as if the count doesn't know who's responsible. En Bernard blabbed enough about wanting to kill Castelnau."

"He and a hundred others," William said with a little grimace. "When a man is so greatly hated—"

"My dear friend," Jordan broke in, "all the count must do is hang somebody and the thing will be forgotten."

With this, William was obliged to agree.

But Count Raymond hanged no one. He did not in fact even trouble to investigate the crime, since he was due to depart on a hunting trip and had more pleasant matters to occupy his thoughts.

"I assure you," William said, "En Jordan could not have been more pleased. He was about to suggest it himself. No trouble about the dowry. A Christmas wedding and in nine months—"

"He's got flappy ears," Sybille said.

"Who does?"

"Pons."

The long smile drained off William's face. They were in his bed-chamber, splinters of winter sun wedging in at the shutters. William, in his shirt, was sitting in bed chewing on a piece of gentian. He rubbed it methodically over each of his front teeth. "I thought you'd be pleased. What do you have against the boy?"

"Papa, you wouldn't understand."

He was watching her from the corners of his eyes. "I might."

She jerked back and forth on the balls of her feet. The squire detoured around her, holding William's hooded mantle and mumbling about the time. The cloak smelled strongly of violet perfume. Sybille sneezed.

"I don't want to go away," she said hoarsely. "Mama will be unhappy."

"You're right," William grunted. "You mother will be troubled." He got up and tugged the mantle over his head.

"Papa, can't I—"

"Come here."

She went to stand next to him, hands trembling at her hips.

"Give me your hand. Sybille, my sweet, you are nearly fifteen. If I waited until you were thirty for this, Douce would still be upset. It's only natural."

She nodded reluctantly.

"So we must not distress her more than necessary. Now, here's an idea. What you must do is go to her chamber and say, 'Mama, I'm going to marry Pons de Villeneuve and I'm very happy about it.'" He pulled her face up to kiss. "You'll see, she'll be all right."

"Yes, Papa," Sybille said and ran out.

Douce's door was shut. Sybille pressed her ear against the crack, heard no sound, and turned away. She hurried down the passageway and took the steps two at a time. In the kitchen her mother's maid was smearing butter on a crust of bread.

"Why isn't Mama up yet?" Sybille demanded.

"Because she isn't—that's why." She pushed a pitcher toward Sybille.

"I never drink ale in the morning." She snatched up an unbaked honey bun in each hand and stuffed them into both cheeks. Behind her back Cook shook her head. "I'm going to be wed."

"We heard," said the maid. "Good news travels fast." She winked.

"What's good about it?" growled Sybille. She grabbed an apple and headed for the door leading out to the yard.

"If you're going to mass," the maid called, "get your cloak. It's raw out."

Sybille went down Rue St. Bernard, bent forward against the wind. By the time she reached the corner, her teeth were chattering and she had to tuck her hands deep into her sleeves. Cutting diagonally through Saint-Sernin square, she ran along Rue Lauzimes, then down Rue Palmade toward the river. Beyond Saint-Pierre de Cuisines, where her mother's maid went to mass every Sunday, she could see the topsails of masts in the harbor.

God's teeth, she should have seen it coming. Why did it have to be Pons de Villeneuve?

Near Saint-Pierre people were rushing about, and she narrowly missed colliding with a white-bearded man, his arms full of bread. Immediately recognizing the face of the heretic bishop, she whipped around and gave him an embarrassed smile.

"Excuse me, please."

Guilhabert de Castres smiled at her with tired eyes. "You need a cloak, child. You'll take ill."

"I'm not cold." She looked at him, slightly curious. It was rumored he had once been Countess Beatrix's lover.

"How's your lord father, Fabrisse?"

"Sybille. Fabrisse is the other one."

He nodded. "God's greetings to your father."

She bowed low, for the sake of being respectful, and hurried on.

Inside Saint-Pierre the air was stale but not much warmer. She leaned against a chipped pillar, crossing herself from habit and remembering a remark Fabrisse had made once about not being surprised should one of them end up with Pons, and she prayed God it wouldn't be herself. Sybille had laughed. Nor me, she had thought.

And now look what had happened.

All along she had been pushing aside the idea of a husband, dreaming a thousand hungers and thinking vaguely that someday she would meet a man she loved and then, like Fabrisse, beg her father to let her have him. True, she had not searched for him. There was the squire she had kissed at the De Perellas' last Michaelmas; she had even permitted him to reach his boyish hands into her bliaut and stroke her nipples. But she had never considered him as a possible husband. Now she had waited too long. God! It was a nightmare. Now she would have to let Pons see her naked and poke his prick between her thighs. She pulled out the apple and savagely gouged a bite.

At this late date there was no point in arguing with her father, because she could not think of a single logical objection to Pons. He had no obvious defects, unless it was his lack of enthusiasm for music, no offensive habits save his occasional odd behavior. She would be wasting her time trying to get out of it. She stood up and socked the apple core toward the alms box, surprised when she made a direct hit.

"Tch, tch," said a voice from behind the altar. "Now see what you've done. I'm going to have to unlock the box and fish out that garbage."

With a start she whirled to meet the eyes of a burly priest, his tonsure half grown in. "Oh, it's you." She grinned. "There's no money in there anyway. Who would leave alms for this stinking hole?"

He clacked down the choir steps, dragging a broom behind him. "Perhaps you've forgotten," he said mildly. "You're standing in the temple of God. Don't they teach you manners at home?"

Sybille giggled. "Father Jacob—is it still Father? I'm surprised to see you in that." She pointed to his chasuble. "Didn't you give up the Church to become a jongleur?" The question was rhetorical, because not two weeks earlier she had seen him in a feathered orange cap, strumming a cittern on Daurade bridge.

"That's no business of yours." He sniffed.

"Oh come. I've heard you. That's not a bad voice you have."

He beamed. "Thank you, thank you. I appreciate your saying so." At the center of the crossing he stopped and began swiping the broom along the pavement, absentmindedly brushing bones, mouse droppings, and clumps of mud into a heap. He said in a low voice, "I only sing at private affairs. Reasonable rates. Pass it along to your friends, if you wish."

"Maybe I'll hire you for my wedding," she said jokingly. "I'm getting married, you know."

"That's nice. Local boy?"

"The son of Jordan de Villeneuve. His father's a consul at Carcassonne."

"Heretic, isn't he?"

She waggled her head. "That's no crime."

Father Jacob shrugged his shoulders. "Didn't say it was. Of course the pope might feel differently. I wish people wouldn't bring their dogs in here." He stepped over a hill of dried feces.

Sybille sauntered to the pulpit steps and scrambled up. She clenched her hands on the railing, frowning down at the priest's back. "The pope," she said loudly. "What could the pope do?"

The priest rolled back his head with a sneer. "Get up an army and—"

"Against our land," she hooted.

"—and burn up all the buggers. Your fancy man will go up in smoke probably." With a twist of the wrists he swept the congregation of garbage behind an ugly statue of the Virgin. He sidled back toward the choir, grinning maliciously at her.

Sybille said, "Why don't you get rid of that filth instead of polluting the Holy Mother? This place stinks."

The priest's lips tightened into a glare. "Get down from there. I've got this whole nave to clean this morning."

She jumped to the pavement and thrust out her chin at him. "About the pope. You're full of muleshit."

"Go on, get out."

"Frog throat." She turned and stumped slowly through the nave without glancing back.

* * *

For the rest of that year the man most frequently spoken of in Languedoc was Pope Innocent. He was, rumor said, displeased with them. More than displeased, he was furious. Immediately after the murder of his ambassador, he excommunicated Count Raymond, which surprised no one. It did not distress them unduly either. But on the tenth of March he canonized Pierre de Castelnau, and on the very same day urged all nations of Christendom to launch a holy war against Languedoc, whose inhabitants, Catholic and heretic, he called "worse than the Saracens." If the wheat could not be distinguished from the tares, uproot both. From a standpoint of legal precedent, this crusade was an astounding innovation. Never before had Christians been called upon to wage war against their fellow Christians.

The idea of the people of Languedoc becoming the target of a crusade was so absurd that it was only too easy for most of them to dismiss it with a shake of the head and a smile. If, to give an example often mentioned that summer, if some person like the king of Aragon had declared war on them, that would be different. Then the knights of Languedoc would be rushing to place orders with their armorers.

But the pope? The Church had no armies on its payroll. All the campaigns Rome had mounted against the infidels had been fought by volunteers. Did Innocent imagine any right-thinking Christian would willingly take up arms against his own kind?

One could only regret, Douce remarked to her husband, that the pope was growing senile and he not yet fifty years of age.

"What have we done?" she asked in bewilderment. "That's what I can't understand."

"Nothing at all," William reassured her. This conversation was taking place in Douce's chamber and William did not like to discuss politics in female surroundings. "My dear one, there is absolutely nothing to worry about."

Douce gazed out the window. "It's a scandal," she sighed gravely.

By the first week in December the Astarac mansion was given over wholly to preparations for Sybille's Christmas wedding.

Each morning when she pulled aside her bed curtains, the sun flowed over the coverlet in long yellow waves. She sat in bed dreaming until noon, pulling melodies out of a lute. Two days before Christmas, at twilight, Fabrisse arrived with one of her husband's squires. Andrew, she said, had been detained.

"Will he be coming tomorrow?" Sybille demanded a bit huffily. "The wedding is Friday. Surely he'll be here by Friday."

Her sister shrugged, tense eyes cast down at the rings studding her left hand. Clumsily she began to polish an emerald with the end of her sleeve.

Suddenly furious, Sybille cried, "That's just wonderful. You couldn't be bothered visiting Mama and now your husband doesn't have the courtesy to see me wed. I can't imagine why you've come. What a great inconvenience for you."

"Oh, Sybille." She brushed past. "Don't be tiresome."

Sybille darted after her, palms moist. "I didn't want to see his stupid face anyway. Or yours."

At the doorway of her own chamber, Fabrisse stopped and wheeled. "When will you learn to shut your mouth? You know nothing about nothing."

"That is incorrect usage. One should say 'Nothing about anything.'" She examined Fabrisse's belly, hunting for a sign of roundness, but her sister was flat, bonier than on the day she had ridden away to Béziers. She had prinked herself up with a wimple of the latest fashion, and the skin on her cheeks was tinted pinkish, like two ripening peaches.

Fabrisse asked quietly, "What's gotten into you?"

Sybille hung her head. "Sorry," she murmured. It was her old refrain. How many arguments had they had? Thousands. And always they had ended with her asking forgiveness. Now her tongue moved automatically. "I beg your pardon, sister." Then: "Fabrisse, how are you?"

"Not so bad."

"You don't look happy."

Fabrisse straightened her back. "Suppose I'm not. Is it any business of yours?"

"I guess not," she said slowly because she could think of no good reason to insist it was. Her sister went into her room and Sybille followed. "Oh, Fabrisse, listen. Did you know we're having four troubadours at the feast? Just think, four! And Fabrisse, did you see my gifts? There's this long silver stick with prongs at one end. Pons de Capdenier sent it. You'll never guess what it's for."

"What?"

"Eating. You spear a piece of meat with it and carry it to your mouth."

"Instead of fingers?" Fabrisse shook her head in disbelief. "What a useless invention."

"Utterly." She grinned. "Oh, Fabrisse, we'll have fun. It's going to be a lovely wedding."

In the Astarac hall, yew trees, hacked from the slopes of the Pyrenees, swayed in barrels of water; needles carpeted the floor, spiking the ladies' slippers. With the dark-blue silk glazing the walls, the hundreds of fire-pointed candles, the hall dazzled like a forest glade illuminated by the lights of night. Pons was conversing loudly in French with an elderly woman. At least he was trying to. Sybille could hear him lunging at the harsh consonants, shouting to make himself heard over the racket. There was scarcely room to turn around in the hall. The music was starting up again, two fiddlers and a jongleur with castanets.

Sybille crossed to a trestle, stuffed a cake into her mouth, and washed it down with a goblet of chilled wine. At once a page refilled it. Nearby she heard her father-in-law arguing with Pons de Capdenier, the richest man in Toulouse. The man was saying indignantly, "The pope is a patient man."

"He's an idiot."

"You people deny the Incarnation—you say Christ came into the world by way of Mary's ear."

Jordan de Villeneuve smiled with amused benevolence.

"You scoff at the Old Testament—"

"Because it's full of false doctrines, dear sir."

"—and you take stock in neither purgatory nor hell."

Jordan said mildly, "Isn't the world hell enough?"

"Well," Pons de Capdenier boomed, "it's paradise compared to what's going to happen when the crusaders land on us. Innocent folk are going to get hurt because of you people. And think what it will do to business. Right off they'll burn the vines. There won't be a decent tun of wine in Toulouse next year."

Douce's head popped up alongside his shoulder. "My lord," she said, all honey, "calm yourself. We are all Christians here."

"Madam, with all due respect, you are badly misinformed. The pope intends to cleanse this land of heresy, one way or another. He's given us plenty of warnings but nobody paid attention. What else can the poor man do?"

"Oh, En Pons," Douce sighed impatiently. "All this talk of war is so boring. I'm sure it will blow over."

"And if it should not," he murmured, "the good God help us."

Sybille wondered if Pons de Capdenier's "us" included the Good Christians. She rather doubted it.

Sybille and Pons went up to a chamber on the top floor, where Douce had draped the bed with silk curtains and sprinkled dried rose petals between the sheets. Sybille stood by the hearth watching the firelight dance reddish on the crystal goblets and on a bowl of pomegranates. Did her mother imagine they would be eating fruit?

"Well," Pons drawled, "shall we have a cup of wine?"

Sybille leaned forward until the flames began to scorch her nose. Without turning her head, she said, "If you like." Is he innocent? she wondered. This had not occurred to her before, but now it seemed terribly important. Why hadn't she married an older man who had been with a woman before? Pons, she thought, I hope you know what you're doing.

She arranged herself on a stool. Pons presented the wine with a bow and a little flourish. Glancing swiftly at his face, she saw his eyes were sleepy. Perhaps he would fall asleep and this could be postponed until another night. Since midday she had been drinking, and her tongue felt furry. She drained the goblet in one gulp and set it on the tiles.

Pons slid to the floor next to her and stretched his legs toward the fire. Then he scratched the back of his neck. He said at last, "Do you dislike me?"

"What?" she said, startled. "In God's name, why do you ask that?"

"Because I want to know."

She chose her words carefully. "We are husband and wife."

"Yes, but you could still dislike me."

"I suppose." Sybille shrugged. "No, I don't dislike you. Do you dislike me?"

"No."

After that, neither of them could think of anything more to say. Sybille heaved herself up and began perambulating nervously around the room. From the hall below rose the muffled screech of a vielle, and she could hear people laughing. She made sure the door was locked, blew out the candle, lit it again. Wobbling on one leg like a stork, she broke apart a pomegranate and began to crunch the seeds between her teeth, one by one.

Pons stared at the juice staining her fingers. "Lady, will you do me the honor of lying with me tonight?"

"I have to." She flushed dark red.

"Not if you don't want to."

Her eyes widened. What was he talking about? "Of course I must. My mama would be angry."

"She won't know."

"She will." With her chin thrust forward, she started pacing between the bed and the hearth. "That fire is nearly out."

He jumped up. "I'll fix it," he offered.

"Never mind." Didn't he want to lie with her? She threw the rest of the pomegranate into the embers. He seized both her hands roughly in his large ones. She said to him, "Blow out the candle."

The sad chimes of Saint-Sernin threaded midnight into the room. Somewhere in the street below, the watchman was thrashing over the cobblestones. In one movement Sybille rolled on her side and pulled up her knees. Pons lay motionless beside her, not speaking. Perhaps he was asleep. She hoped he was.

He whispered, "I beg your pardon, my lady."

"What did you say?" she asked over her shoulder.

"I'm sorry." Suddenly he was rearing up on one elbow.

She did not reply immediately. Finally, more than a little annoyed, she said, "Did you have no pleasure then?"

At once he began to protest. It was all he had expected. More, in fact. But he worried he may have hurt her. He was not an animal; his pleasure was not worth an oyster if it meant causing her pain. Would to heaven there were something he might have done differently. His big hands began fluffing her hair.

With a grimace Sybille squirmed her nose into the pillow. She had heard Douce's friends describe their wedding nights. Remembering, she decided hers had not been so frightful. But it was not good either. In truth, she was disappointed and she thought, Is this all it is?

"Ah no," she told him. "There is no reason to apologize. What makes you speak of hurting me? I never said that. Don't interrupt, please. As usual you're exaggerating the whole thing. I liked it as much as you. It's true, you know. I do wish you'd stop fussing with my hair." She jerked her head away and sat up.

"You know very well," he flared, "you hated it. Well, maybe that's an exaggeration. But telling me you liked it is a lie."

"Indeed."

"And saying I didn't hurt you is another lie. What kind of a person do you take me for? Do you imagine I have no eyes or ears?"

With a quick movement she swiveled to squint at his face. "Don't you dare call me a liar!" she shouted. "Whether you hurt me or not is none of your business."

"But it is! I'm your husband."

In a fury, she mimicked, "I'm your husband. That doesn't give you the right to know what I'm thinking." He caught her arm and she snatched it away. "I don't know where you get a stupid idea like that. You know the trouble with you? You don't understand anything about being married."

Pons snorted.

"It's true. Undoubtedly you've not noticed how men treat their wives. A courteous husband doesn't ask embarrassing questions. He doesn't pry."

"He doesn't?"

"No."

"All right. Then I don't want to be your husband."

She gave a cry of astonishment. What does he propose to do? she wondered, give me back after deflowering me? She would die of shame. Damn him. Why couldn't he fall asleep like a man was supposed to do?

In the shadows Pons said softly, "Forgive me, lady. I meant no offense."

She stared straight ahead, blinking back tears. "You said you don't want me."

"I said I didn't want to be your husband."

"I heard that."

"I would rather be your friend."

She scowled. What an insane remark! A man and a woman could be friends—did the troubadours sing of anything else?—but friendship was for lovers. Not for husbands and wives. Scooping the coverlet around her shoulders, she said, "How is that possible?"

"Don't know." He shrugged.

It struck her she had never had a real friend, aside from Douce. Very likely mothers did not count. She forced out a smile. "If you want the truth, I didn't much care for—it."

"I know," he said.

"Is that so terrible?" She glanced at Pons, who was lying on his back, hands crossed under his head. "Is it?"

He was silent a minute. "The pleasures of the flesh," he said slowly, "are of no importance. Some say."

Some also said the world was an evil place, created by Satan. "Some" were heretics. She decided to feign ignorance. "Which means what?"

"That I wouldn't worry about it." He crawled against her and tethered his arm around her neck. "Probably it will get better. By and by."

Sybille said, very softly, "I want my mama."

The city in which Sybille began her marriage sat on a shelf of rock high above the Aude river. Its citizens bragged it was the most highly fortified town in Europe, and this was not an exaggeration. With a cool eye to the latest in urban planning—not even mentioning the most up-to-date advances in military technology—the viscounts of Trencavel had transformed their ancestral home into a model city. Girdling Carcassonne was a thick wall punctuated by fifty jutting watchtowers designed for easy firing of missiles. Outside the wall the ground had been cleared for a space of fifty yards, and then there rose, cunningly, still a second wall. Beyond that spread the suburbs, which were also fortified. Not even a mouse could have crept into Carcassonne unobserved.

But this was a time of peace. The watchtowers housed granaries and the city's treasury and private residences. Finally the snow had come, and a milky robe was beginning to thicken the shape of the battlements and stifle every sound. Now, on the Feast of Epiphany, the Villeneuve party surged up the hill. Once inside the Aude gate, they trotted down a roofed avenue, passed the château of the viscounts, and a few minutes later reined up at the gate of an imposing villa. A dozen servants hurried into the courtyard, sending dried rose petals shivering against the snowflakes. Behind them skidded a procession of flute players.

Sybille gorged herself, both on the attention and later, at table, on garlic snails and fried Valencia oranges. "Marvelous," she kept saying, "marvelous." She dozed off in her chair before the feast had ended.

Early next morning Pons insisted they hear mass at Saint-Nazaire. The church did not compare with Saint-Sernin, but Sybille kept her mouth shut and murmured appropriately admiring remarks. She did not wish to hurt Pons's feelings. Inside she counted ten worshipers, which may have accounted for the priest tearing through the service at top speed. After a time Sybille forgot about praying and concentrated on smothering her giggles. The man spoke as if his chasuble were on fire.

Afterward, on the porch, she laughed and said to Pons, "That was awful."

He gave an embarrassed sigh. "Well, Father Gauthier is a jackass, everybody knows that."

"You mean this happens every morning?"

"Only if he's late to open his business. He's the proprietor of the tavern near the Tour des Prisons."

She stepped off the path into a snowdrift. The powdery flakes squeaked under her boots. "Did you ever go there?"

"I'm acquainted with it," he allowed. "But there are better places, believe me."

"Take me to one," she demanded suddenly. "And don't tell me ladies don't go into taverns. I don't care."

Pons gripped her arm. "Don't be so sure of what I'm going to say before I say it. If you want to go, we'll go." He smacked a cold kiss on the side of her cheek.

The streets in the business district were jammed. Merchants were lighting bonfires outside their doors. A tangle of women with baskets pelted along the narrow paths where the snow had been cleared. Sybille and Pons looped around and cut through the drifts piled against the buildings. At the corner of Rue Petite they ducked under a sign that said Pig's Trough. A fireplace across the far wall belched heat and more smoke than was necessary.

"Interesting," Sybille remarked, because she was unsure how to behave in a tavern. She thrust out her neck to scan the wall drawings, all of human shapes with pigs' heads eating, weaving, fornicating. There was a pig pope pronouncing a blessing.

"Shut the damned door!" a voice bellowed from the kitchen. "I can't afford to heat the whole town."

They pushed in, dropping puddles of slush, and flopped near the fire. Pons pointed to the wall behind her head. An obese sow was smiling coyly at a svelte pig jongleur on bended knee. They doubled over the trestle, laughing.

A woman came toward them and stood by the table, scratching her chin. "It's too early. I don't—Oh, it's you, En Pons. God give you good day, master. I thought you had gone off to Toulouse for a wife."

"That's right. Here she is."

Startled, the woman's eyes veered from Pons to Sybille and back again. Quickly she began grumbling about having nothing in the place to set before a lady.

Pons said, "What do you have?"

"You must be daft to— Only a pot of stew."

"That will suit us perfectly," Sybille assured her.

It was an eel stew, peppery and so thick that a shepherd's crook could have stood upright in the bowl. "This is wonderful," Sybille cried. Among the jars of ale and empty crockery and bread crumbs, they reminisced about the days of their childhood, those summers at Fanjeaux when it would be getting on vespers and they would hide in the woods until her grandmother had to send men with torches to chase them home. And then they repeated all the lewd jokes they had ever heard, mostly about the Church. Then Sybille began a story about a heretic blacksmith who died and got to the portals of heaven, where he saw a big cross on the gate and said to himself this could not possibly be the right place. Suddenly she looked over at Pons, noticed his expression, and stopped.

"That's not funny," he said in a low voice.

"Well," Sybille said uneasily, "it gets funnier."

"I don't want to hear it."

She took a breath. "Very well."

In the silence that followed, she stroked all the crumbs on her side of the table to the edge, ladled them into her palm, and dumped them into a bowl of congealed stew. Then she said carefully, "With all respect for the Good Christians, it seems odd that it's all right to tease Catholics but not the others. They're not sacred."

Pons did not reply.

She asked, "You don't believe that garbage about two gods, do you?"

Quickly he said, "There can only be one true God. But on the other hand—"

46

But on the other hand. In the months ahead she would hear those words often. This was the first time, however, and she listened with ill-concealed impatience. He reminded her of the unexplained suffering in the world. Terrible things happened to people who seemed completely undeserving of misfortune. Didn't it seem strange that a loving God should visit these woes upon the innocent? he asked. Sybille snorted. He was mouthing heretic rhetoric, saying the goodmen were not entirely wrong to call this world an evil place.

She waited, eager to correct him. "The world is no such thing," she finally shouted. "On the contrary. The world is beautiful. You have only to look around."

But what about women raped during war? Pons said. What about peasant children who were starving? How did she explain those things?

By God, if he were going to bring up atrocities, it really was not fair. "It's quite simple." She glared at him. "If there is sin, it is sinful people who are responsible. Not an evil god." She squirmed on the bench, dismayed by the turn their conversation had taken. Let's find a more pleasant subject, she pleaded.

He nodded, contrite. This talk, he said, was spoiling a beautiful morning. He yawned, pushed back from the table, and threw down a handful of coins.

In the street the melting snow cascaded between the cobbles like furious waterfalls.

"I've been thinking of growing a beard," he said.

Still, the conversation stuck in her mind because the following week, in bed, she suddenly said, "Don't answer this if you don't want to. But I'm curious. Are you a heretic?"

He raised drowsy eyes from the volume of Virgil on his lap. "My mother adored the Christians. The night she died, Bishop de Simorre himself came to give her the *consolamentum.*" It did not seem as if her question offended him. "My father, well, you can see for yourself."

Thinking him evasive, she went back to tuning her lute. "I didn't ask about them."

"I know. I'm telling you anyway." He brought up his hand to cover a yawn. "I can't say whether or not I'm a heretic."

"If you can't say," Sybille said, smiling, "who can?" She plucked out a chord with her fingers.

"You talk about realism, Sybille. Take a good look around. Look at the Good Christians—not necessarily at the preachers but at the ordinary folk. Then look at the Catholic priests. Now who suggests Christ? You'd have to be as blind as a plough not to draw a few conclusions."

She stared ahead. The whole wall opposite the bed was painted over with a mural. Snowcapped mountains overvaulted a village with red roofs, twisted cypresses, sunlight. Nothing startling about it except for the large number of doves. She said aloud, "Whoever did that must like doves."

"I did it."

"Oh." She hesitated. "I understand what you're saying. But there are bound to be some corrupt priests. Remember, I was raised in the Catholic faith and I—"

"Where do you think I was raised? I'm only suggesting someday we may not be able to rely on faith."

"On what then?" she demanded.

He shrugged. "I don't know. Reason maybe. We might have to forget everything we've been taught. If the French mobilize, there will be war."

"The French!" she rasped. "Philippe Auguste won't fight us." Pons was talking nonsense.

"Philippe Auguste," Pons said impatiently, "told the pope he personally wouldn't lead a crusade against us. He did not say he would forbid someone else doing it."

"Oh, Pons. Really. The French are a bit provincial, but I wouldn't call them stupid. And they are an honorable people. It would be a sin to come down here and kill Catholics." She gulped noisily. "And suppose a few do come. What's the worst that can happen? They'll hang around for a couple of weeks and then go home. I'll wager they don't capture one town."

"Yes, it would be a sin. But"—he was shouting—"a sin that is not a sin. A sin blessed by the pope. Think about it from a Frenchman's point of view. Innocent is asking him to take the cross against us. No big trip to Jerusalem. Just a short summer holiday down the Rhone. Forty days in Languedoc and all the plunder he can cart home. And, pif-paf, all his sins are instantly wiped out. Big sins, little sins, even the sin of killing Christians. Was there ever such a bargain?"

She did not answer but only shrugged.

"There has never been a bargain like that one," he repeated. "Never."

Her chin sagged against her chest. At last she mumbled, "A man would have to be very evil to accept it, I think."

"Yes. So everything depends on how many evil men there are in France. Pray God not many."

That's finished, she said to herself. She rolled to the edge of the bed and leaned over to lay the lute on the floor, making a mental note not to step on it in the morning. Yawning, she glanced back at Pons. "I need Carenza to braid my hair."

"I'll do it," he offered.

She backed up to him and folded her knees against her breasts. His hands began clutching at masses of hair, twisting the strands clumsily between his big-boned fingers. She said, "About being a heretic. You didn't answer."

"I did," he said, close to her ear. "I said I don't know." He told her it would be worthwhile to study their philosophy. He had heard that the New Testament did not contain all the gospels. There were others that had been condemned by the Church. They had been well hidden. In Castile there were a few men, not more than three or four, who had memorized these secret writings, passed on by word of mouth from generation to generation. So Pons had heard.

"Oh," Sybille said blankly. "What sort of secrets?"

"New facts about Jesus' ministry."

She said, puzzled, "I can't imagine what could be so dangerous about that."

"They prove the so-called heretics are not heretical." He paused, fingers tangled in her hair, and his next words floated into her ear like a feather in the wind. "Rome is."

A shiver rocked Sybille. She felt Pons's eyes on the nape of her neck, and she held her breath, waiting to hear what he would say next.

The winter rains came. For three weeks the walls and roof peaks of Carcassonne dripped. Inside the Villeneuve mansion, where hearths and braziers blazed in every room, Sybille hardly noticed the damp, and she had few complaints. The Villeneuves knew how to live well. She was accustomed to a household many would consider greatly privileged. Still, it amazed her to notice how the really wealthy found ways to spend their money. Jordan de Villeneuve behaved as though money did not exist. He was a genuinely kind man, a devout Good Christian who had not made the conversion lightly, and he tried to model himself on Jesus. The whole effect was startling, Sybille decided. Something like Jesus living in the style of the emperor Augustus.

As for Jordan's son, Sybille told herself that here was a complex young man, and she spent the early weeks of her marriage learning just how complex. In Pons there was a joyous good humor, as safe and nourishing as bread. But suddenly, when she least expected it, the pendulum would take a wild swing.

He had a disturbing habit of posing questions she could not answer, that nobody could answer. He wondered why, now of all times, Rome had become so incensed against Languedoc. After all, there had been Good Christians in these parts for more than a century. "What do you think it means?" he would ask.

Then he liked to maunder on about the meaning of life. "What is the purpose?" he would wonder aloud. "Do you believe there's a reason for our existence?"

At these moments she found him truly irritating. Finally she would reply, "Why, to live. To enjoy. That's all." And she added automatically, "And to do God's will of course." She tried to jolly him out of these eccentric flights. The way he fussed about meanings, she said, was perfectly silly and only could lead to nervous headaches.

Then he would grin and say he loved her good sense. She was not a brooder like himself. She was not the sort to break her head turning ideas inside out and picking them apart like a moldy cheese. He admired her attitude.

But a few days later he would start fishing for alternatives again. Perhaps life had no meaning at all, maybe the point was there was no point. And so forth, until she would have liked to throttle him. After a while she stopped responding, and finally she stopped listening. If he wanted to work himself into a state over the meaning of life, he could do it without her help.

Sunday evenings never varied. Shortly after compline, the courtyard would begin to fill. Ladies and gentlemen, cloaked and hooded, would mount the steps into the hall, and then En Jordan would usher them upstairs to his bedchamber. There the group would wait for the coming of the goodman. The preacher was not always the same man;

sometimes it was not a man at all. The sight of a woman leading prayers and reading from the New Testament never ceased to horrify Sybille. She wondered if the pope knew about the women preachers. He must. No doubt that had helped to kindle his rage.

Beaming, the blue-robed preacher would stand behind a table and wash her hands. A white cloth would be spread, candles lit, the Scriptures opened. No incense, no Latin. Everything plain and simple and one-dimensional. God without trimmings, Sybille thought.

"Bless us." The worshipers joined hands and bowed three times in unison. "Pray God that He may make and keep us good Christians and bring us to a good end."

"May God bless you," came the preacher's friendly response, "and snatch your soul from evil death and bring you to a good end."

All this had been explained to Sybille. An evil death meant dying in the faith of the Roman Catholic Church. A good end meant the *consolamentum* with its assured entry into the true church of Jesus Christ. It was very important to have the *consolamentum* before you died.

After the kiss of peace, the preacher would linger to chat. Small gifts emerged from the worshipers' cloaks. A shirt, a gourd of wine, sometimes smoked fish. Never anything of worth, never meat or eggs. The goodmen and women would not touch flesh.

Sybille did not menstruate in February, nor the following month. To her parents she wrote:

"We feel sure now that I have conceived and the seed is well and truly set. Around Ladies' Day I felt sickish upon awakening but now that has passed and I could not be better. I think Pons is slightly disappointed because there is no longer any need for him to mix his herb possets. With his gift for herbals, he would make a good physician.

"My pregnancy has not prevented me from having a marvelous time. Nearly every week we are invited to the viscount's for feasting and music. I can see why everyone here adores Raymond-Roger. He is wonderfully well read for his twenty-three years, very lively and gay, and terribly, *terribly* good-looking. I like him because he's not at all stuck-up like Viscountess Agnes. Here's who (or should it be whom, Mama?) I've met: Bertrand de Saissac (important but dull); a grand-niece of La Comtessa de Dia (she claims); a sweet old man who's the heretic bishop in this district—can't recall his name; a jongleur who told me he once sang at our house about seven years ago; and William Augier. This last is a very talented troubadour from Valence and I know Mama would adore him.

"Mama, I want to ask your forgiveness. Remember one day we were in your room, and I said awful things about what lay ahead of me. And you said I shouldn't worry because it would come out all right. Well, you were right.

"About going home to Toulouse—you can expect us a fortnight after Easter for a fairly long visit and I will be counting the days until I can kiss Mama's sweet face again. Pons has been talking about the two of us traveling to Castile in the autumn, maybe even going on to Compostela. But of course the baby has made that impossible this year. Perhaps next spring.

"I have begun to write again."

But before the letter reached Toulouse, Sybille's stomach suddenly began to cramp one evening after supper, and she bled into her slippers. By midnight it was finished.

Throughout the night she wept bitterly, tortured by her glimpse of the pulpy red ball the servingwoman had hastily wrapped in a cloth and taken away. They did not tell her where, and she did not ask. Too gruesome for a proper burial, too ugly to acknowledge as hers, it was part of her nonetheless. She would accept no comfort and called the thing "my child" and loved it as if it had had breath and eyes.

Next morning Jordan de Villeneuve sent for a priest. He sat by Sybille's bed, tranquilized banalities cascading from his tongue, and explained it had been God's desire. She must stop crying before she made herself truly ill. "Love God," he told her. "Accept His will."

"Yes, Father."

"God grant you conceive again soon."

"Thank you, Father. You're very kind." She closed her eyes. He went out and immediately she heard his voice rising angrily in the passageway. She asked her maid what was wrong.

"Nothing, lady," Carenza said. "He wants two sous for coming."

En Jordan must have paid, for soon it was quiet again.

During Easter Week Sybille had a visit from her brothers. She had not seen them for three years and did not recognize them at once. It was hard to believe this pair of towering youths, all spit and swagger, were the sons of William and Douce d'Astarac.

There was no doubting Pierre and Mathieu were brothers. Some-times people took them for twins. The tousled black curls, the long legs and narrow hips, made them seem as alike as two sides of a wild colt. Otherwise there was little resemblance. Pierre led, Mathieu followed; Pierre decided, Mathieu agreed. They had worked it out long ago.

A month earlier they had left Foix and slowly made their way north, although apparently their travels had not included their native city. Sybille suspected they had deliberately avoided Toulouse. Their conversation was limited to the war, and on this subject they delivered geysers of reckless opinion.

"The pope," Pierre announced, "made a bargain with the French. Any of our cities they can grab, they get to keep."

Sybille laughed. "I don't believe that. Rome can't give away our cities. Anyone who told you that has to be joking."

Pierre did not answer, and after a moment's silence, Mathieu said, "So, little sister, your lord husband—I trust he's in good health."

"Yes. Excellent health." Remembering their aversion to Pons, she did not want to go into detail.

"Do you still sing?"

"Now and then." She smiled crookedly at Mathieu.

"Voice improved any?" Before she could respond, he flashed her an impish grin.

"Cut it out," Pierre growled. "She wasn't so bad."

Footsteps thumped in the passage, and a procession of serving-men rattled in and began uncovering dishes. Within minutes the table was set with an abbreviated banquet. The boys ate rapidly with both hands, and for five minutes nobody spoke.

Sybille watched them fill their stomachs. "Mathieu," she said, "you haven't mentioned why you're here."

Mathieu looked surprised. "Why, to take service with some lord. Why else? We figured the viscount—"

"He means," Pierre broke in, "with somebody who's hot to kill a few Frenchies." He poured wine into a goblet and took it down fast. The dark wine splashed onto his tunic and the trestle top.

Both their voices oozed with a lust for calamity that gave Sybille a disagreeable tingle. She struggled to speak in a casual tone. "What makes you think there will be war? Isn't it likely this crusade won't happen?"

Pierre glanced up sharply. "Ah, sister," he said in mild disgust, "the muster has been called for the end of June. You think they'd go to all that trouble for nothing?"

"A lot can happen between now and June," she murmured.

Hunched over a platter of roast quail, Pierre ripped off a leg, bit, and rushed on with a full mouth, just as if she had not spoken. "Here's how we see it. Now that we're free-lancers, we can pick and choose. It's no sense serving somebody who's going to sit on his ass and miss the action." He was looking past her, at the Seven Deadly Sins mural.

Sybille watched their faces and listened.

"So we came here thinking Trencavel is sure to be in the thick of it. But no such thing. 'Sorry, lads, we have enough men.'"

"The sergeant was damned snippy about it, too," Mathieu added.

"Fuck the sergeant," said Pierre hotly.

"Raymond-Roger will fight," Sybille said with confidence. "But only if he has to."

Pierre sighed and shook his head at her. "Don't be so sure. I'll bet you ten livres you didn't know something. Count Raymond invited your viscount to Toulouse last month."

"I hadn't heard."

"The count said to him, 'Nephew, we may be of different faiths, but we're of the same blood. Let's forget our differences and stand together against these bloody bastards.'" Pierre began to wipe his mouth against his sleeve, and Sybille pushed a napkin over to him. He raised his voice. "And do you know what *your* viscount said?"

She gave a little shrug. The way he kept repeating *"your* viscount" was forcing up her temper.

"No." He drummed his fist on the trestle dramatically. "Your viscount said, 'No thanks.' What do you make of that?"

"Mysterious," Sybille grunted and locked her lips. It's no mystery, she said to herself. Young Trencavel disliked his uncle. Why should he hurry to make an alliance when there might not be an enemy to fight? Of course he had said no. She decided to change the subject. "Well," she said brightly, "I guess you're going home now."

Across the trestle neither brother spoke. Then Mathieu pushed his platter away and mumbled, "Brother has a girl at Bram. Maybe we'll go back there."

"Oh, Pierre! You're going to marry?"

Pierre kept his eyes lowered. "Not that kind of girl," he said quickly. "Anyway, there's nothing going on in Toulouse. The count isn't arming either."

"Papa would want you to come home," Sybille reminded him. "And I know Mama has missed you terribly."

His head rose. "That's just the point. Holy Jesus, if we go home now, we'll miss everything. Maybe the garrison at Bram has a place for us."

Mathieu lifted his head to grin and he said, "It's going to be a glorious summer."

"Is it?" Sybille could not resist adding, "The crusade may be called off."

"Not a chance," Pierre replied carelessly. He stood and picked up his cloak.

They swung down the hall and out into the April sun. In the courtyard the air was damp with the scent of acacias. While they waited for the stableboys to bring their mounts, Pierre described a jet stallion, twenty hands, he had seen at Limoux. If he could bargain down the owner just ten more sous, he planned to buy it. Sybille kissed them goodbye with a smile.

Chapter Three

"This sword has a matching dagger," Sybille said. She closed her fist around the cross-shaped hilt. "You grip it with your right hand and use your left to—"

"Gentlemen's jewelry." William d'Astarac sniffed. "While you fuss with the knife, somebody slips a blade between your ribs."

"You won't be using it anyway."

She put the sword back, careful not to nick herself. Her eye jerked to a pommel studded with pearls and crystal, and she stopped to admire it. She had always had a weakness for gaudy weapons. Across the table a knight in mauve velvet was examining a pair of spurs. Sybille elbowed people aside and went around to get a better look at them. One of the leather straps was inscribed DOMNA JAUZIONDA. Joyful Lady. She could not make out the lettering on the other.

"Sybille," her father shouted. "What do you think of this?" He was holding up a shield painted with a black and gold checkerboard pattern.

"Dreadful. Papa, please get something nice." Before leaving the house, Douce had given her instructions. Under no circumstances must William be permitted his usual conservative selections. He was still waving the shield at Sybille. "Put it back," she mouthed at him. "I hate it."

The knight in mauve sidled closer. "Do you like this?" he asked, low. The Joyful Lady spur clinked between his fingers.

"Very nice." She glanced down sideways.

"And this?" He tilted the mate so she could read its inscription: CON JAUZIONDA. His voice was vulgarly expressionless.

At the sight of the obscenity, Sybille reared back. She was tempted to slap the fellow.

The armorer's shop was packed. Shields hung along the walls on pegs, and the customers clanged them free and thumped and banged, their knuckles clanking out a charivari of steel. At the rear, old Barthélemy Marty was toting up numbers on a big wax tablet. Yes, he told a knight, it was true, the price of helmets *had* doubled since February. If he didn't like it, he knew what he could do.

Sybille began squeezing her way toward the spot where she had last seen her father. It was too hot that morning. The noise and heat and the spicy smell of sweat made her feel dizzy. Men bawled questions at the apprentices, and some spat abuse and stalked out. Most of them stayed and paid, not cheerfully. Sybille gave up seeking her father and slumped against the wall.

A boy came toward her, a blond cherub of a youth, freckled, blue-eyed, choirboyish—which had been the case until his voice had changed. Frowning slightly, he stopped and stared at her.

"Lady, are you ill?" he said. When she did not reply, he caught her hand and led her to a bench. As Sybille was about to speak and dismiss him, he turned and scurried away. Almost at once he was back with a cup of water.

Without warning, he dropped on the far edge of the bench, mouth curled into a beatific smile. "This is a hellish place," he said. "You can bet my head is pounding by closing time."

Sybille clamped on a disposable expression, sympathetic but not encouraging of confidences. She drained the cup and handed it back to him.

"My father won't let me out. Business is too good." And he added, "You wouldn't believe how much he took in this month."

"Daniel!" Barthélemy Marty's grizzled head shoved through the crowd. "What the hell are you doing?"

"Nothing," the boy mumbled.

"Get me a shirt, bastard! Size large." Daniel swooped away. The armorer twitched his head. The good Lord had seen fit to give him only one son, a lazy, good-for-nothing turd. What could a man do? He ranted on to no one in particular.

After that, Sybille's father stepped up. Marty forgot about his son and started to huckster William with a sales talk. Holding up a mail shirt that must have weighed close to twenty-five pounds, he said, "You won't find higher quality than this."

William said, "I don't need one."

Marty said, "Quarter of a million rings."

"Nothing special."

"That's where you're wrong." He thumbed a silver seal dangling from one of the links. "Armorer's Guild of Toledo. Guaranteed."

"Let's see it."

Marty said, "The king of Aragon has one. For you I'll make a special price."

On the bench Sybille began to yawn. She was miserable and bored, and she was hoping William would finish soon, when a heavy knight by the name of Hursio joined the two men and began spewing unkind remarks about Count Raymond. In no time a crowd gathered. Hursio claimed the count was an asskisser among other things. The more he talked, the angrier he seemed to get. It did not take long for the armorer's shop to heat up. Sybille put her face down on her hands. She was so sick of war fights.

"God's balls!" Marty shouted to make himself heard. "It's not fair blaming Raymond. Any man in his position—"

"No, no!" boomed Hursio. "I beg to differ. No man of honor would crawl on his belly to the enemies of Languedoc. The count—"

"Sir," William broke in politely, "I can assure you, Raymond has no intention of crawling anywhere."

The man turned and swayed toward William. "Oh?" he said. "So a man who joins his enemy isn't a traitor. Since when?"

William replied stiffly, "Don't forget—the count is an excommunicate. He plans to make peace with the Church next week. I happen to know he will allow the pope's ambassador to whip him publicly. Now, what more can he possibly do?"

Marty added hastily, "You can't blame him for making peace with God."

"That's not what I'm talking about," said the heavy knight, still puffing mad. "I'm talking about the count joining the crusaders."

"What?" William said. His eyebrows arched.

"Raymond is taking the cross," Hursio said dramatically.

Sybille looked up and blinked. Her attention snapped to the knight. What on earth was the man saying? Now everybody was yelling at once. Barthélemy Marty flung down the mail shirt. She heard him scream, "Move your lying ass out of here!"

William was shaking his head at Marty, silencing him. He took a step toward the knight and said, still polite, "You've made a serious accusation."

"It's true, don't worry."

Round-eyed, Sybille sat up straight on the bench.

"I think you're mistaken," her father said to Hursio. He circled behind Marty and went over to stand next to the man. Suddenly the crowd hushed. Hesitating, William stared at Hursio. Then he asked, "Why would Raymond join the crusade?"

The knight's lips jerked into a smile. "A crusader's property can't be touched. It's the law, isn't it?" He scratched the underside of his chin. "If Count Numbskull is one of them, the crusaders can't attack Toulouse." At once the shop erupted in a chorus of whistles.

The difficulty, when Sybille tried to sort things out, was in deciding the significance of this information. Raymond's submission, if he had truly made one, sounded despicable. Then she saw she had got it all wrong. By taking the cross he cleverly would be placing their land under the Church's protection. She had not credited him with the capacity for such deviousness, and she almost smiled.

Marty exclaimed, "If this is true, the count's crazy. Because it won't work." He glanced at William d'Astarac for confirmation, but William was standing with his head bowed.

When he finally looked up, his expression was not quite so calm. Sybille could see beads of perspiration gathering on his upper lip. To Marty he said, "It may be a ruse, some sort of strategy."

"Strategy," somebody called out mockingly. "Yes, a coward's strategy."

William shook his head. "Nothing of the sort," he said between his teeth. "After all, a man in his position has to be cautious. Sometimes it's best to bow before a storm. Perhaps the count is hoping to get through this sorry business with as little loss as possible."

"That's right," Hursio agreed. "By whoring among the ranks of his enemy." The remark got a big laugh, and Sybille saw the color drain out of William's cheeks.

She got up quickly, dragged herself toward the entrance, and then stopped. It was definitely getting hotter. She heard her father insist, "I still think this is gossip."

Ugliness hung in the air like small black flies netted over carrion. Sybille pushed open the door and stumbled into the sunlight. Opposite, a dairyman was wrapping yellow cheese for a customer, who was herself chromed the same shade of gold. There was not an object, living or otherwise, that did not appear gilded. It was one of those exceptionally bright middays when you could not imagine any better place than this earth and hoped you would remain here a good long while, in spite of the heat. Sybille walked aimlessly toward the river. It was cool and sad alongside the dirty water. She watched a boy glutting himself on the mouth of his lover, who traced discreetly appreciative circles in the air with his fingertips.

When she returned to the armorer's a half hour later, her father was waiting outside, the mail shirt slung over his shoulder.

"Is it true? Did the count take the cross?"

"Yes."

All the way back to the faubourg, William spoke not a word.

The following week, on St. John's Day, twenty thousand men began moving out of Lyons. On foot and on horse, the army of God rolled down the Rhone valley, and strings of barges covered the river from bank to bank. In the castles along the way, sentries high in the watchtowers stared down, stupefied, at the endless flow of packhorses and siege engines and summer pilgrims eager to unload their sins and be home in time for the haying. Exactly where these streams of humanity were going, and what they would do once they arrived, was a mystery. It was said that even their leaders themselves—the abbot of Cîteaux, the count of Nevers, the duke of Burgundy—did not know. Once they reached the Midi, God would show them what to do.

The weather was fine and the moors a mass of bee orchids and yellow broom. By the time the army halted at Montpellier in the second week of July, its ranks had already been joined by a composed and cooperative count of Toulouse, former enemy of the faith. Although the count had recently topped the list of victims marked for destruction, his name had been removed now.

Still, the crusaders had not gone to all this trouble for nothing and certainly they did not lack targets. The most logical was Raymond-Roger Trencavel, viscount of Carcassonne and Béziers, a young man whose provinces were notorious as a heretics' Garden of Eden.

Raymond-Roger and his barons lost no time in preparing to rush themselves to Montpellier. Why was the Church picking on him? the viscount wondered. Wasn't he a Catholic? Perhaps once there had been heretics in his lands, but that had been during his childhood. The Church could hardly hold him responsible for evils that had taken place while he was a babe in the cradle. In pleading his case, he planned to bring up some of these points. The crusaders were, he said, gentlemen. He would reason with them.

Once during the night, Sybille was jolted into consciousness. For several seconds she lay still, listening to hooves clattering in the yard and then to a man's voice giving commands. Jordan, she thought, but could not hold on to the sounds. Shadows surrounded her and she dreamed of eating artichokes. She woke, stiff-necked and in a bad mood. Otherwise it was like every other morning. The sun shook white-hot on the shutters, and down in the street the fishmongers were hawking young carp they had pulled from the Aude before dawn.

She poked her head into the passage and yelled for Carenza. The girl was never near when she needed her. Unplaiting her hair, she thought of the crusaders and how they had spit on Raymond-Roger. At once they set off to snatch his city of Béziers. Fools, Sybille snorted under her breath. Béziers had thick walls and plenty of food. It could hold out forty days. Even longer. Which meant the crusaders would have to go home with nothing to show for their trouble.

A good five minutes passed before Carenza came in lugging a basin of water. Without turning, Sybille grunted, "Is Master Pons home?"

"He's not here, lady." Her voice suddenly began to squeal. "There must be bad trouble. At mass people were saying the crusaders have left Béziers."

Sybille plunged her face into the water. She hoped it was true. Very likely the army had given up the idea of tarrying outside Béziers. The city wasn't going to unlock its gates just because the abbot of Cîteaux knocked. Who was the abbot anyway? She waved an arm at the maid.

Carenza stuffed a towel into her hand and broke into a wail. "They're coming this way! Lady, we've got to escape—we'll all be murdered."

"Don't be ridiculous," Sybille snorted into the towel. "They know Carcassonne can never be taken. And if they want to try, good luck to them." She straightened. The maid's broad face was creased with fear. "Dump that dirty water and bring some clean. My hair needs washing."

"I can't," Carenza said, sullen. "Steward says that's all he can spare."

Sybille threw down the towel, horror-struck. "He says what!"

"The well is low. Lady, if the crusaders aren't at Béziers and if they aren't coming here, where are they going?"

Damn the well! Did the steward suppose she would allow her hair to be washed in used water? She must speak with him. She said roughly to the girl, "How should I know? Albi maybe. Or Narbonne." Narbonne had flimsy walls. A cow could knock them over.

"But Na Sybille, my mother's sister is in Narbonne—"

The girl was beginning to make her edgy. She finished washing and then dressed herself. Carenza remained in the middle of the room, with her thumb wedged between her teeth. Sybille longed to swat her.

"By St. Martial!" she finally exploded. "Are you going to stand there all day? Tell Cook I want fried mullet and some of her raisin cakes. And Steward must speak to Gauzia or whatever her name is, she's using too much soap in Master Pons's laundry. His shirts are stiff."

"There are no raisin cakes," Carenza whined, "because we have no eggs or milk. Cook said the dairywoman didn't show up this morning."

"Go on. And take care not to spill that water all over my floor." Gracelessly she crouched on one knee and mouthed a quick paternoster, all the while debating whether or not she should send a squire to the château for word of her husband. It was discourteous of him to stay away. She wondered if he might have spent the night with a woman. It seemed unlikely, but one could not know for certain.

She grabbed her key ring and clanked downstairs. There was an odd silence in the hall; the pages and servingmen who normally congregated near the kitchen door were absent. Then she noticed the marble tiles had not been scrubbed. Muddy footprints could be seen clearly. She sat down at the end of the trestle and tapped her keys against the wood. "Hello!" she called loudly. Where the devil was everybody hiding? Footsteps approached and the steward trotted in at a fast clip, balancing a tray. He was a man of about forty, fat but not too fat. "Madam—"

"Isarn, is something wrong?"

"God is out of sorts today," he announced. "In the first place, we have not a single egg in the kitchen. And less than five pounds of goat cheese left." He was bustling from side to side, huffing, transferring dishes so carelessly to the table that a capon slid to the floor. He boomed, "I told you that woman was unreliable. She lives too far out along the Roman road to make deliveries at a reasonable hour. There are better dairy people in Le Castellar." The tufts of hair growing from his nostrils began to twitch.

"Why are you speaking like that?" Sybille asked.

"Like what?"

"So loud."

Isarn clamped his mouth shut.

Sybille said crisply, "Today is the feast day of St. Mary-Magdalene. Probably she's a Catholic. In fact I know she's a Catholic. We can live without eggs for one day." She began to tick off a marketing list: two dozen ducklings, ten rabbits, a lean pig for making jelly. From the spicer, five pounds each of cloves and galingale. As she was talking, she surveyed the platters, hunting the fish she had ordered. "Where's my mullet?"

Isarn only shrugged and went hastily toward the kitchen.

She waited two or three minutes. He did not return. Disgusted, she ate a handful of olives and gulped down two cups of ale. There was a full day's work ahead—they needed to make candles, six dozen at least. She got up and went to find the housekeeper. Midmorning she dispatched a squire to hunt for Pons. It was almost nones before the boy returned, his breeches sagging and his breath smelling unpleasantly of sour wine.

She looked up from her account ledger. "Did you find him?"

"No, lady. And then I was delayed by a fire. The empty house where—'"

Sybille broke in, "Any news from Béziers?"

He shook his head. "But they say the Roman road from the east is jammed. People from Capestang wanting to shelter in the city. En Pierre Borrel said there isn't a villein left in his vineyards." The boy shuffled his feet importantly.

Uneasy, Sybille turned back to the column of figures she had been adding. If the villagers beyond Minerve were abandoning their homes, there must be a good reason. They must have seen crusaders. She threw down her pen and decided to hunt Pons herself.

The squire said, "Someone is asking for you in the yard."

"Have my mare saddled. I'm going out."

In the courtyard, sitting in the shade of the chestnut tree, waited a woman flanked by two girls of ten or twelve, who were asleep on their stomachs. When the woman saw Sybille, she got up and stared blindly, shading her eyes with one hand. "Sybille d'Astarac?" she called softly.

"That's right."

She swayed closer, and then Sybille noticed her white face and the dark-blue gown scummed with dust. With an apologetic smile, she bowed three times to the goodwoman, who was fumbling in her sleeve.

"I come from Béziers," she murmured and did not smile. "Madam your sister sends a message." She held out a letter.

"Fabrisse!" That was unusual, for Fabrisse seldom wrote. She slit open the parchment with her thumbnail and saw the purple-ink scribbles in her sister's peculiar sideways handwriting.

"From Béziers, this twenty-first day of July in the year of our Lord Twelve Hundred and Nine—"

"She wrote this yesterday," Sybille said aloud. For a moment she glanced at the goodwoman, wondering how she had managed to get through the crusaders' lines in her blue robe. Probably the French were so ignorant they didn't know how a heretic dressed. Then she began to read again, struggling to decipher Fabrisse's misspellings.

"Well, the crusaders have come, but I must say they look a sorry lot. Andrew is commanding the St. Jacques gate. Yesterday he took me up on the wall to look at the camp. Sister, there are *hordes* of them! Andrew says that's good—they will run short of food by the weekend. They are sitting around doing nothing. The tents are splendid—the fanciest belongs to the abbot of Cîteaux. It is terribly amusing to see the banners of Count Raymond and all the flags from Toulouse. Poor Raymond, having to fraternize with all those dreary bishops and northerners."

Sybille smiled. The sun was burning her face, and she moved into the shadow of the chestnut; the goodwoman followed. Fabrisse did not sound frightened but seemed to regard the crusade as a diversion in an otherwise dull summer. Sybille remarked to the goodwoman, "My sister sounds in good spirits, don't you think?"

"I didn't see her, lady. The letter was entrusted to me by a knight on the St. Jacques gate."

Sybille's eyes flicked to the bottom of the page. Fabrisse was talking about an ultimatum and asking Sybille to inform their parents there was no danger.

"Pardon me, but what does this ultimatum mean?" she asked the goodwoman. "What do the crusaders want?"

In a flat voice the woman said, "The abbot of Cîteaux gave our consuls a list. Over two hundred names. If we hand over these people, the abbot promises to go away."

Under the wimple Sybille could feel beads of sweat trickling down her throat. She stretched her neck, gazing up at the sky. Dark clouds were gathering beyond the faubourg. She smiled, thinking how relieved she would be to feel rain again. She said absently, "What people do they want?"

The goodwoman clasped and unclasped her hands, but she made no response. Then she said, "Our people." She meant the heretics.

"Your consuls refused, didn't they?"

"Oh yes. They refused."

"I should think so," she trilled sympathetically. With one hand she tucked the letter into her waistband, with the other pulled out her purse.

At the sight of the purse, the goodwoman shook her head. She glanced down at the children who had awakened and were staring and now turned their eyes away. After a pause she said to Sybille, "You could give us shelter for a few days. We're able to work, we're weavers."

"As you wish," said Sybille. "Stay as long as you like." She put the coins away and steered them to the kitchen, where Cook began ladling out lentil stew.

Sybille, hurrying back toward the yard, heard a horse nicker and then Pons's voice grating orders to one of the grooms. She relaxed, steadying herself at the top of the steps until she saw him springing toward her, his beard dripping sweat. "Pons." She clicked her teeth impatiently. "Where have you been?"

Grunting, he slapped her lightly on the shoulder as he swept by, and she wheeled around and went after him. She was reluctant to scold him about last evening. He lumbered across the hall at top speed and burst into his father's library. The room was dim and silent. The shutters were locked against the sun, and Pons's brow and cheeks, wreathed in shadows, looked mottled, as if he had contracted some disfiguring disease. He unlocked the chest by the window, drew out a leather pouch, and tilted it onto a table so that a trail of livres spilled across the wood.

Sybille came up behind him. "The whole town's gone crazy," she sighed. "Everybody's flapping about like it was Doomsday. The traffic is awful—" She was going to ask him why he needed money when she realized something was wrong and she stopped chattering. In the half-light, his lips were sagging.

"Béziers is gone," he said, and Sybille laughed.

"Gone," she repeated and laughed again. "Did somebody thieve it? Who would steal a stupid town like Béziers?"

"They're all dead," he answered slowly. He was fingering six coins at a time and lining them up in uneven little mounds. "Or they were burned."

Her eyes bored into him and she smiled. It was absurd. The town of Béziers was not a crossroads village. Thousands of people lived there, perhaps as many as ten thousand. She told him that and then she said, "I beg your pardon, but I don't believe you."

He shook his head. "At daybreak some men from the city rode out to look at the camp." His fingers went on stroking the coins. "When they tried to get back, the French gave chase."

But that sort of horseplay was common at the outset of any siege. A few claustrophobic burghers always dashed out to annoy the besiegers. And after the ritual insults had been exchanged, they always retreated inside their gates, and then both sides would settle down to boredom. Still, the smile had drained from Sybille's mouth. She circled around the table, watching him.

"Apparently one of the French captains took it upon himself to attack," he said to the coins. "His men weren't even dressed yet."

Did he mean everyone got to the gate at the same time? Is that what happened?

"The French pushed their way in and now everyone is dead." He snatched the bag of coins from the table and lunged for the door, tripping over her feet.

Sybille plowed after him. He must be exaggerating. "Didn't they fight? Didn't people defend themselves?"

He ignored her questions. So violently did he take the steps going down to the yard that he nearly dropped the coins. "All dead before noon," he cried without turning to look at her. "It's the truth, lady. Don't expect to see me for a while."

A gray gelding danced in the yard, tail fluffing off flies. A groom was lengthening the stirrups, and when he saw Pons he nodded and went back into the dark stable. Sybille leaned against the saddle rack. Her wimple had bunched into a sodden ball at the nape of her neck. She pulled it off and draped it over the rack. She said, still arguing, "But a whole city can't be destroyed in one day."

"One morning," he corrected her calmly. "People hid in Sainte-Madeleine and Saint-Felix. There must have been thousands in the churches."

Sybille stood up, rigid. She willed her ears shut.

"They burned the churches," he whispered.

"And the others?" She brought out the words with difficulty. "The ones not in the churches?"

"Killed. And the whole town set to the torch."

"Killed. Even the Catholics?"

"All." He looked away. "Every living—"

Surely not all.

From the stable doorway, a hound appeared and strolled toward them, slapping her tail. Pons sank on his heels and reached for the dog's head. He fondled an ear. The dog nuzzled against his knee. Sybille watched him roll back his head and look up at the sky, and she followed his gaze, squinting a little. The rain clouds she had noticed earlier snaked directly overhead and were hanging between Carcassonne and the sun. She let out her breath in a gasp and clutched Pons's shoulder. No rain would descend from those clouds. They were the work of the Devil.

"They say it was God's will," he said evenly.

"Who says?"

They stayed motionless in the yard, hardly breathing, and studied the smudged clouds rolling and rolling in the sky like dirty stains that would not scrub clean. If the clouds disappeared, she could pretend nothing had happened.

She could think of nothing to say. After a while Pons got up and they stood face to face. The dog peered up at them, expectant. "My father needs me at the château," he said. He rolled into the saddle and reached for the reins. Not knowing what else to do, she patted his knee as he nudged the gelding toward the gate. Suddenly she ran after him. Outside, a clump of women had planted themselves in the middle of the street, all shoves and shouts, their market baskets dangling watercresses and fat gray mullets. They were oblivious to the clouds, or were ignoring them.

"Pons!" Sybille shouted. But he had disappeared around the corner.

Upstairs in the hall, Carenza pounced on her, wild-eyed. "Lady," she shrieked, "what did young master say?" Her rosary clattered to the floor.

"Nothing of importance."

The girl shoved herself closer. "In the kitchen they're saying Béziers has been taken. Is that true?"

"Leave me alone," Sybille said harshly. She turned and hurried down the passageway leading to the garden. She wandered up and down under the chestnuts, past the yellow pea bushes and some dead roses, and finally threw herself on a bench. The temptation to look up at the sky burned like an itch in her mind. God could not have willed the deaths of ten thousand souls on one particular morning. But—there was no denying it—He had permitted it. All? she wondered. Even the children? A dragonfly with gauzy azure wings hummed past her nose. Once she had tried to write a song about dragonflies, but it had come out badly. Hunching her shoulders, she pitched forward until her forehead touched her knees. Her waistband crackled. She brushed her fingertips against her girdle, groping for Fabrisse's letter through the fabric.

After darkness had smutted the cloud of Béziers, Sybille went down to the yard and slipped out the gate. Everyone in Carcassonne seemed to be in the streets, dark shapes flailing their arms and buzzing in shrill voices. They were all drunk or drinking. The flames of torches and bonfires turned the gray walls to orange. Sybille plunged into the mob.

Halfway down Rue Château, a wine jug sailed from an upper story and smashed at her feet. Frightened, she hugged closer to the sides of the houses, running breathlessly. To her dismay, the palace gate was shut and barred. At the postern door a sentry was clutching an ax. She lurched forward and said loudly, "I want to see the viscount."

He flashed her a contemptuous look. "Go home," he croaked. "Do you think Raymond-Roger has time for stinking sluts?"

Sybille stared at him, indignant. She planted her thumbs on her hips and shouted, "By God, I'm Sybille de Villeneuve! How dare you speak to me like that!"

Instantly the sentry's eyebrows rose. He gave a half-bow.

"Mark me, I carry an urgent message for the viscount." Over his shoulder she could see horses and men milling around in the yard. "Let me in, boy."

He scratched his ear. After a moment, he muttered, "It's against orders," but shifted sideways an arm's breadth. Before he could change his mind, she slithered by.

The courtyard echoed with the sounds of men screeching at the tops of their voices. Under Sybille's slippers the cobbles were slimy with ale and urine. She ran up to the first man she saw. "I'm looking for the viscount," she burst out.

He laughed, but it was more a cackle than a laugh. "You and forty thousand crusaders," he said. He laughed again. "Come here." Dropping to his knees, he flung out both arms as though he meant to lock them around her hips.

She backed off, sliding on the cobbles.

He said, "I'll pay—I have money."

Color rushed to her cheeks. Lifting one foot, she suddenly kicked him square in the middle of his chest.

He tumbled over and sprawled on the slippery cobbles. *"Con!"* he shouted at her. *"Putana!"*

These men have become beasts, she thought. Trembling, she turned and fought her way toward a long flight of stairs leading up to the great hall. Only a few weeks earlier, she and Pons had climbed these steps, and at the top Raymond-Roger Trencavel had waited, a careless smile on his sunburned face. A very fine troubadour sang that night, and there had been cherry sherbets and a sky icy with stars.

There were no songs now. Upstairs, the entrance to the hall was clumped with men cursing the people of Béziers. "What else can you expect!" somebody cried. "Those fool Biterrois! Whooping and whistling and waving their flags—"

"Like they were scaring crows in a fucking wheat field. Jackasses!"

They did not pity the dead burghers; on the contrary, they blamed them, saying they had got what they deserved, and Sybille felt fury rise in her throat. She forced herself to call out to them, pushing close but careful to stand beyond their reach. At the sound of her voice, one of the knights spun around toward her.

"My lord, is the viscount within?"

He thrust out a thumb, indicating the passage that led to Raymond-Roger's apartments. Sybille turned away and began to run, skirts swooping like wings. Some ten yards ahead, she saw a guard and lunged toward him. "The viscount," she blurted out, "let me see him."

"Busy," he barked, barely glancing at her.

"Please, I must talk to him." Her voice rose. "I must."

He shook his head.

"I'm Sybille de Villeneuve, I swear it. Just tell him my name then, that's all I ask."

He looked at her. He was a country lout, not terribly bright, she guessed, but he recognized her father-in-law's name. Grumbling, he stamped to a carved door and disappeared. Sybille slumped against the wall, shivering under her gown. Everyone could not have been slain. Peasants maybe. Shopkeepers and vagrants. Heretics advertising themselves with long pale faces and blue robes. But not the daughter of William d'Astarac. The crusaders would not have dared to kill a Catholic noblewoman.

Minutes went by. A dozen times she glanced at the door. When it finally opened, a man walked out unhurriedly, and she stepped forward. He was not Raymond-Roger but his chief minister, Bertrand de Saissac. Without preamble, he said, "You ought not to be here."

Sybille did not bother to listen. "En Bertrand," she said, "I beg you, give me the truth. My sister lives in Béziers."

Bertrand de Saissac appeared composed. His silver hair was combed and perfumed and his tunic uncreased. There was an air of cool assurance, even indifference, about him. He jangled a little cough in his throat but did not reply.

"Some escaped, didn't they?" Sybille insisted. "You must know."

He said briskly, "The reports are incomplete."

"Her name is Fabrisse, Fabrisse Fauré. Just tell me, is she dead or alive?" Her heart was thumping so loudly she wondered if her chest would burst. "She's the daughter of William d'Astarac of Toulouse."

Saissac nodded, acknowledging her father's name. "A few people may have left the city last night. Before—" He cleared his throat. "But there's no confirmation."

"What people?"

He made a helpless gesture with his shoulders. "Oh—Jews, I believe." The Jews were Raymond-Roger's bankers.

Sybille held her breath, waiting for more names. The conversation seemed intolerably slow, but it was all taking place in a matter of seconds.

The chief minister put back his head and sighed loudly. "It's a terrible business. According to our preliminary reports, there is not a single survivor. I would be misleading you if—"

She flung out her hands. "What about Count Raymond? There are men from Toulouse in the crusaders' camp." The sound of her voice throbbed angrily in the passage. "Do you mean they did nothing? Didn't they try to help the Catholics inside Béziers?"

"Ah well. How could they? They took the cross, didn't they?"

Bertrand de Saissac was a heretic, one of the most fanatic. It was to kill men like him that the crusaders had come. Instead, Fabrisse was dead. Sybille stared at the wall behind his head.

"I'll have someone take you home," he said softly. "The streets aren't safe."

Raymond-Roger Trencavel took the precaution of doubling the guards in his fifty watchtowers, but the abbot of Cîteaux hustled his army along the Roman road, and three days later the crusaders were assembling siege engines and laying mines, and suddenly people in Carcassonne did not talk about Béziers. Raymond-Roger laughed. When the abbot sent a courier offering Raymond-Roger permission to leave the city before it was too late, the viscount hooted out loud, "That will happen when an ass flies to heaven," and other boasts. But then he got serious and composed a formal reply using more temperate language. "Rather than desert my people," he wrote the abbot, "I would be skinned alive."

Sybille was told of these remarks by the refugees who had poured into Carcassonne like dying leaves blown by a gale wind, dragging with them their children and featherbeds, their sheep, pigs, and goats. More than twenty thousand had crammed into the city, and about two hundred settled in the Villeneuve mansion. All day long they scuttled about, quarreling, weeping, getting under each other's feet. The roar of their voices—the baas, clucks, and squeals of their animals—was earsplitting, and the only lull came when darkness fell. Then, exhausted, they collapsed in every room of the house with their arms, legs, and heads jumbled together at random. You could not see the marble floors.

The hot blue sky stood overhead. With all those wretched ani-

71

mals, no one was hard up for a meal. But the wells and cisterns dried up, and people bartered their pigs and chickens for a half-cup of water, then for a spoonful. It was pointless to ask for more.

By the beginning of the second week, after the faubourg had fallen, dysentery gusted through the city, and Sybille turned Jordan's library into a hospital. In spite of strict sanitary measures, the stench was ghastly. Sybille worked with her nostrils pinched together and a heavy cloth wound around her face. When she would step into the hall for a deep breath, someone was always sure to bless her for doing God's work and say that not every noble lady would submit herself to such disgusting tasks. "Oh," she would reply cheerfully, "you get used to it after a while." But it was untrue, and the stink of death, the flies, seemed to be everywhere. Down in the yard, Cook screamed at two knights from Cruza who were trying to lop off each other's heads with her meat cleavers. Children, straddling the water trough, giggled. From the top of the yard steps, Sybille yelled at the knights. Blades flickered in the afternoon sun. She forced herself to go down calmly into the tangled yard.

"Lady," Cook sputtered, "those are stolen knives. Let them have their fun with their own knives."

The knights, eyes red and bulging, had separated and stood there panting.

Sybille walked over to them and said casually, "Good afternoon, friends." They lowered their eyes. "You have abused my hospitality. I must ask you to leave my house."

"You heard her," Cook said. "Clear out."

Without a word, both men obediently dropped the cleavers and slunk toward the stable.

"Water?" Sybille asked Cook. Not a day passed without quarrels over the water ration.

"Not this time, lady. The puny one says we're going to surrender—the viscount made a bargain with the French. He says the heretics will be handed over tomorrow."

Tomorrow. She had not thought of the morrow in the last two weeks. If her mind flew forward to tomorrow, it could just as easily skitter back to yesterday, and then she would have to think of her sister. Where Fabrisse once had been in her head was now a churning void. She would not think of her, not now. She said aloud to Cook, "Rumors."

Cook, breasts as loose as pudding, stooped to collect the knives. Straightening, she said in a quiet voice, "I've heard it a dozen times since prime. It must be true."

If a surrender was being considered, Sybille thought, Pons surely would have sent word. Still, she was alarmed. Starting for the steps, she called back to Cook, "Send the Baralher boy to me. I'm going out."

With the squire riding pillion, she went to the wall behind Saint-Nazaire, where Pons was stationed. Together they climbed up to the top story of the watchtower and went out into the air and stood alongside a stone-gun. Up there, the flies were not so frightful. Sybille rested her arms along the edge of the rampart and leaned out. Through a pale-yellow haze she could see the countryside spread before her like a vandalized tapestry. Once there had been terraced vineyards and the green minarets of cypresses. Now she saw only stumps and fallen tree trunks and an anthill of tents and banners splashed with rosy crosses. She watched the tiny figures scrambling around on the slope beyond the outer wall. Flights of Greek fire were soaring toward the walls, leaving red-gold and plum-colored trails behind them in the air.

"Friend," she said, "there is gossip about Raymond-Roger surrendering. That's not true, is it?"

"God, no!" But then Pons fell silent, pulled at his lower lip, and added, "The siege might be over soon. But not because we surrender."

Sybille raised her eyebrows.

"The abbot has asked for a peace parley. They want to go home and I guess he'd like some concession to take back north with him. Some little scrap to make the pope happy." He scratched the back of his head vigorously.

"Who told you this?"

"Raymond-Roger. He's agreed to go out and talk to the crusaders tonight."

"*Kyrie Eleison!* Not alone?"

"With an escort." He gazed over the battlement. "Father and I are going and about a hundred others."

"No!" she said sharply. "I don't want you to." Oh Lord, what had made him volunteer?

Pons said, "Surely God will watch over us. We've done nothing wrong."

She did not want him to go. She struggled to tell him so, but in the end she did not. He would not listen to her. "Well," she sighed. "Very well," and she shut her eyes.

"Do you love me?" he said and sounded happy.

She opened her eyes and grinned at him. They went down the steep stairs and out into the street. The squire bounced to his feet and said to Pons, "Sire, I want to fight. Let me stay with you."

Pons slapped an arm around his shoulder. "Not today, boy—see that my lady gets home safely."

Without looking back, Sybille crossed to the mare, who looked as if she would fall dead of thirst. It would have been kinder to come on foot, but she could not bear walking through the streets. She slung herself into the hot saddle; the boy stood on one leg, sulking. She sidestepped the mare over to Pons and leaned down to crush her face against his neck. Wrenching herself upright again, she called to the squire, "Hurry up, the answer was no."

As they jolted down the street, the boy said, "Did Master Pons say we're going to surrender?"

"No," she grunted. She thought of Pons and Jordan going out to the French camp. Somehow the crusaders had obtained the names of the heretics living in Béziers; they might have a similar list for Carcassonne. Jordan was one of the city's most well-known heretics. What was to prevent them from seizing him? Her stomach began to cramp.

The squire could not stop squirming. "Why can't I be a soldier?" he pestered. "Why?" He tugged at her sleeve.

"Because you're a child. You haven't even got a beard yet." Full of impatience, she longed to kick the mare into a gallop, anything to feel coolness rushing against her skin. In Saint-Nazaire square, waves of heat rippled up from the rutted cobbles. Children no older than two or three clung to her stirrups, their scabby mouths begging water. At the corner of Rue Porte d'Aude a dozen dead horses, already sizzling with clouds of flies, had been stacked against the wall, and as she scuttled past, the flies swooped down on her. Swollen with blood, they clung to her clothing and skin; they burrowed under the wimple, into her braids, and even prowled across her mouth, until it was all she could do to keep from swallowing them. She coughed and coughed, thinking her lungs would surely come up.

The Villeneuve yard was thick with people eating. The smell of pork lay in the air. The squire slid to the ground and helped Sybille dismount. Isarn strutted up.

"Madam," he wheezed. "What is it? What did Master Pons say?"

Sybille said, "I'm going out of my mind. These cursed flies!"

Isarn lowered his voice to a whisper. "I can keep a secret."

She plucked off her wimple, to shake out the flies. "The French have asked for a parley."

The steward stared at her. "God have mercy. Surrender?"

"Peace treaty. Both masters are going with the viscount. But hold your tongue about this."

"I promise."

There was no need for promises, however, since the whole town knew about the parley by vespers. All over Carcassonne that evening, people talked only of the meeting. Surely God would take pity on them and send the crusaders home. They were going mad with thirst and the flies. Just after the sun had gone down, Raymond-Roger and his men cantered out the Razès gate and disappeared down the slope into the darkness.

In the watchtowers, where the torches had been extinguished, you could look up and see the tails of shooting stars wheeling against a dome of pure black. But no one was looking up. Leaning on their elbows, people stared uneasily into the distance where the plain danced with lights, and they tried to imagine the French sitting around their fires. Just inside the Razès gate stood a column of boy drummers waiting to hail a triumphant Raymond-Roger Trencavel. All night long they fidgeted in formation. Toward morning they were dismissed to have their breakfasts. A half hour later the drummers tramped back to their posts, ready to start banging at a moment's notice.

The bells in the church of Saint-Nazaire tolled noon.

Then nones.

Then vespers.

The sun, incredibly, began to sink.

By now people were kneeling in all the churches and beseeching Jesus Christ and Queen Mary to return their brave young viscount. Even those who no longer subscribed to the Roman faith—who in fact spat upon it—hurried to church. The vigil went on. Periodically the bells of Saint-Nazaire punched dark craters in the air. Nobody thought of sleeping. God knows, they said, we can sleep tomorrow or the next day, when all this madness is over.

At dawn the long thuds of the French artillery started up again, and a company of screaming Brabantines tried to scale the eastern wall but were beaten off. Then the defenders of Carcassonne knew that Raymond-Roger would not be coming back that day, prayers or no prayers.

The crier stood on a barrel in the square near the faubourg gate. He held up his arms and smiled, all gums. "Citizens," he shouted. "Lord God has sent us a miracle. We cried out for deliverance and God, in His grace, has answered. Everyone's life is to be spared. All? Yes, all will be safe." He stopped to gather his breath. "But to win this concession from the French, our leaders were forced to pay a price: We must leave our homes. It's not a bad bargain when you think of it."

Sybille stood as still as a gargoyle. Leave home and go where? Carenza clutched her sleeve and whimpered, but Sybille pretended not to notice.

The crier shouted louder. At noon, he said, they must start lining up at the gates. Order and discipline would be strictly enforced during the evacuation. "Alas, good people, you must go empty-handed. Take no belongings with you. Nothing. My friends, the crusaders wanted us to walk out naked, as naked as God made us, but our leaders refused. Women will be permitted to wear shifts, men, shirts and breeches. All other clothing is strictly forbidden."

Such a roar rose from the crowd that it sounded like a thousand mongrel dogs snarling at once. When the yelling had subsided a little, a child piped, "Can I take my pillow?"

No—not a pillow. Not even a poge.

Farther back someone yelled, "But when do we return? Tomorrow? When?"

The crier stared at his feet. After a while he lifted his head and said in a cracked voice that the crusaders wanted this place for their headquarters. The city's wealth would be used for the furtherance of God's work. "My neighbors, truly we should be thankful to have our lives—we could not expect to take along our gold and silks." He had no more information to give.

One of the crowd, Sybille straggled home with her head down.

Chapter Four

The count of Toulouse's troops were stationed about a half-mile from the Aude gate. The place had been an orchard of peach trees two weeks earlier. Now the trees were gone, but the smell of rotting fruit hung over the dusty earth.

The Toulousans were observing the evacuation with as much in-difference as they could manage. They had been instructed to offer no assistance whatever and to encourage the refugees to disperse. Opposite a field kitchen, men were eating without haste; some had already finished with their stew, others were just stabbing bread into their bowls, and it was impossible to distinguish them from the Burgundians Sybille had passed a hundred yards back.

She rushed across the road, brushing people aside, and cried out, "Friends, tell me when the viscount will be released. My husband is with them. Is everyone safe?"

At the sound of her voice, several of the men looked up.

She scanned their faces, to see if she knew anyone. When she realized they were not going to reply, she added, "I'm Sybille d'Astarac."

They squinted blankly, as if they were half-wits. They had round, bristly faces. Their jaws, opening and closing on the bread, made them look like hedgehogs, Sybille thought. After a long hesitation, one of them said, "What makes you think we know anything?"

Rooted to the ground, she stared with wide-open eyes. "Have you seen them?"

"Not really."

"But you must know if they're alive."

He shrugged.

"You must know," she repeated. "You must. They were taken prisoner four days ago. Listen, if they were killed, tell me. You needn't spare my feelings."

One of the knights said, "Judge for yourself—do we look like the abbot's confidants?" All of them burst out laughing at once.

Sybille clenched her fists at her sides. She had been so sure they would help her, but when she heard their laughter and saw their bitter expressions, she knew they were as ignorant as she was. She gulped a mouthful of gritty saliva and made an effort to collect herself. It was important to think calmly now. She looked around. Beyond the men, on a barrel, sat a knight chewing a turnip and watching her. Automatically she folded both arms across her chest.

"Hello there," he drawled. "Are you a Toulousan?"

She nodded.

"What street?" He got up and began to walk to her.

"Rue St. Bernard," she said. "You?"

He hesitated. "Well," he said, "here and there. Are you looking for someone? Who?"

She thought she recognized him, although there was no good reason to connect this tall knight in the grimy surcoat and the boy she had seen years ago at Fabrisse's wedding feast. Both had masses of fair curls and faces that pleased her. That was all. "My husband," she told him. "Can you give me news of Raymond-Roger? My husband is with him."

"They're under guard, girl," he said. "When the army moves into the city, no doubt they will be taken along." He added hastily, "That's a reasonable guess. I wouldn't swear to it."

Mechanically Sybille pulled up the neckline of her shift. "You don't know when they'll be set free, do you?"

"Not today. The Frenchies are going to be busy inventorying the viscount's treasury." He laughed. "No, certainly not today."

Sybille said, "I'll wait."

He said quietly, "Don't be a booby." With a rolling thrust of his chin he gestured at the crowds moving by. "Where are the rest of your kin?"

She pointed dumbly with her thumb. "I can't leave without Pons."

He went on as if he had not heard her. "Now listen carefully. Hurry and catch up with them. If you stay with a big group, no harm should come to you. Hold on." He spun around and went toward a white stallion tethered near the kitchen. Unstrapping a saddlebag, he pulled out something. The men sitting on the ground began to make loud, rude noises.

"Hie, Olivier!" one of them teased. "Hie, lover!"

He paid no attention to the catcalls, but brought a shirt, none too clean, and thrust it at Sybille.

She wanted to tell him she had seen him before, many summers ago in the count's garden, then reminded herself that possibly she was mistaken, it may not have been the same person. Then she remembered the noose hanging shamelessly from the tree, and she avoided his eyes. "Thank you," she said gruffly, "but you needn't have bothered. I can take care of myself."

He stuffed the shirt into her hand. "You'll be cold later."

She turned and stumbled toward the road. She was thinking of Pons and where he would be imprisoned, not about the knight and his shirt. Behind her, he called in a low voice. Without turning, she stopped and waited. He came around and caught her free hand and rolled four dried olives into the palm. "Bye-bye," he said to her and was gone before she could speak.

She dropped one of the olives onto her tongue and walked on.

Fabrisse d'Astarac had not been fated to die in Béziers. At the eleventh hour, Andrew Fauré had sent her away with a convoy of Jews going to Pamiers. At first Fabrisse had refused, since her safety had not been the issue. Andrew wished to remove a prize gelding from the city and mistrusted the Jews not to sell it along the way. Fabrisse objected furiously to acting as custodian for a horse, but Andrew would not listen to her.

In the autumn after the surrender of Carcassonne, Sybille slept in her bedchamber next to her mother's, and Fabrisse slept down the passageway. All day long Sybille talked, nervously, incessantly. Words spun from her mouth like a volcano scattering particles of ash. Afterward she could not remember what she had said.

Michaelmas passed, with day after day of torrential rains. William rode to the château each morning, asking for news. As the crusaders began to leave, Sybille believed it only a matter of days before her husband would return. She ordered a half-dozen linen shirts in the shade of blue he liked. One afternoon, while she was embroidering a floral design on one of the collars, Carenza came to say William was asking for her. She jabbed the needle into the center of a tulip and ran down, Carenza flapping at her heels. Her father stood at the bottom of the steps in a soggy cloak, his face turned into the shadows. He did not speak until Carenza had come all the way down and disappeared into the servants' passage. "You won't want to hear this. We have a new viscount."

She waited.

He turned to her. "This Simon de Montfort. He's been elected viscount of Carcassonne. *Elected.* Béziers, too, much good that will do him."

She was watching his face. Angry lines bulged around his mouth. "Papa, where's Pons? Where is Raymond-Roger? Are they dead?"

William said, "Holy God, so now the Church can elect princes. What a farce."

"Papa—"

"They say De Montfort refused at first." He turned and strode into the hall, leaving wet, muddy tracks. Blindly Sybille followed. "Then he agreed. When he sobers up, he'll regret it." He sent a page for ale.

"Please," Sybille said. She watched him shrug off the wet cloak and sling it over the trestle. If there is a new viscount, she thought, there can be no old one, can there? She sat down opposite her father. The page came back with cups and a pitcher.

Sybille lifted her cup. The ale rushed down her throat. William mumbled something, but she did not catch it. Pons was not yet seventeen. He had no sins. I did not love him enough, she thought. That is my sin and this is my punishment. When she looked over, she saw William staring at the wall mural.

"These people," he murmured, "lack courtesy. They have no notion of decency." He spoke as if these ideas were occurring to him for the first time. "Wild dogs. What can one do against wild dogs?"

Leaning forward, Sybille rested her head on her arms. There was silence, and then William went on, "These people must be—demons."

When she sat up her father was still staring at the wall. "Papa, Pons is dead, isn't he?"

"I don't know." He kept his eyes averted. "I've tried to find out and they say—they say everyone has been hanged. It may not be true."

"Do you think it's true?" Sybille asked.

Abruptly he put down his cup half finished, and pushed to his feet. "Don't say anything to your mother. Not yet." From the corner of her eye, Sybille watched him thump down the hall.

Her mother hurried in, keys jingling on her hip. "Cook says it can't be done." Douce smiled. "But what does Cook know?"

Sybille struggled to appear interested. In recent days Douce had become obsessed with the idea of installing flush toilets in the house. She kept talking about a monastery in the Alps that had had them for hundreds of years.

Douce said, "If the monks at Saint-Gall can pass water into running water, I don't see why we can't. Do you?"

"No, Mama." She forced herself to utter the words like a normal person.

Douce swung down the trestle, moving each napkin a half-inch to the left. Her glance flickered over her daughter. "Why so quiet?" she asked when she came to the end of the trestle. "You aren't ill, are you?"

"No." Sybille shrugged.

"Good," Douce said. "It's a simple matter of laying in a few pipes. It works like a fountain."

Sybille nodded.

"I'm surprised the count hasn't thought of toilets. It would make such a difference. Was your father just here?" Douce brushed away a loose strand escaping from her wimple.

"A few minutes ago," Sybille answered. "Papa was here."

Douce frowned. "Did he mention the toilets?"

William d'Astarac was in the habit of denying nothing to his wife. But he was drawing the line at toilets. "No," Sybille said, "he did not."

Douce's mouth puckered into a determined line. "It isn't as if he can't afford it."

Sybille tucked trembling hands under her skirt and listened to her mother talking.

Douce summoned an engineer to inspect the house. He was more experienced in designing fortifications than sanitary systems, but he thought something might be done. Sybille folded the half-embroidered shirts in a chest. Fabrisse said she ought to be ashamed of herself, since there were plenty of refugees who would be grateful for a shirt. Sybille had difficulty speaking to her sister. In early November when Raymond-Roger Trencavel was reported dead of dysentery, Fabrisse merely nodded knowingly.

"I don't believe it!" Sybille cried. "He was murdered."

Fabrisse, in bed, squirmed deeper in the pillows. "Murder or dysentery, what's the difference? You knew they wouldn't set him free. I don't know why you kept pretending."

From the tower of Saint-Sernin, the bells sprayed sound. Sybille said, "Don't be cruel. I loved Pons."

Fabrisse jammed the coverlet under her chin. "Love," she muttered. "It's completely meaningless."

"It means something to me."

Fabrisse smiled, not pleasantly. "You've heard too many troubadours."

During Advent the Astaracs went to Fanjeaux to visit Na Beatritz. The woodland around the castle of Cantal was seared with frost in the mornings. Sybille stumped slowly through the trees until she found the cliff from which Pons would not jump. The wind rattled the top branches of the oaks, and she did not linger. She did not know what she was seeking there, or what she had expected to feel. Being there did not make her feel bad. Or good. She walked quickly back along the trail and across the drawbridge.

Upstairs in the hall, beside the hearth, her grandmother was having breakfast. Sybille hopped up and down behind her canopied chair.

"Sit down, you're making me nervous," Beatritz said sharply. "Where have you been? If you're going to roam the woods, take a horse."

"Why, do you think Simon de Montfort will get me?" She climbed over a bench and sprawled opposite her grandmother.

Beatritz looked up from her porridge, beady-eyed. "Don't be sarcastic with me."

"I was only trying to make conversation." Sybille tore off a hunk of bread and smeared a thin film of butter on both sides.

Abruptly Beatritz said, "Your sister has the right idea. She did her mourning and then put it behind her."

"She never loved her husband," Sybille replied hotly.

Beatritz tapped her spoon on the table. "There are all kinds of love." She glared. "Just tend to your own business and don't make assumptions about others."

Sybille drank cider. She took another piece of bread and a slice of lamb and looked sideways at the fire. Her grandmother's kitchen boys were crouching on their haunches, turning birds on a spit. Fat dripped and crackled. She thought of Pons. Something had been lacking in her. She had found no pleasure in sleeping with him until he noticed and stopped suggesting it. Unloving wife, she thought. It was I who rejected him.

Beatritz was talking. Changing her tone, she said placidly to Sybille, "He came here, you know."

"Who?"

"De Montfort." She wiped her mouth on the end of a sleeve. "Sat right where you are and drank red wine. Talked sweet about his wife. Alice, her name is. He wanted to go home to Alice."

Sybille straightened up and began listening carefully. "Nobody is forcing him to stay here," she said hoarsely. Then: "What else did he say?"

"I don't know," Beatritz said. "Oh yes. God. It's his destiny to serve God. He blabbed for a long while about God. And Lady Alice."

"But what did he want from you?"

"What he wants from everybody. Homage. And he wanted to know if there were any heretics living here. Asked me straight out, 'Are there any heretics on your domain? People who worship the goodmen?' "

Sybille laughed and rocked forward on her elbows. "What did you tell him?"

"I said certainly not. I know when to lie." Her grin was spicy with pride. "What a fool. The hall was full of believers but he didn't know it."

Doubling over, Sybille let loose a peal of laughter.

The old woman flashed her a feisty stare. "What's the matter with you, missy?"

"Nothing. Lady, you have nerve." She was still smiling.

Sybille tramped across the hall to the circular staircase, crunching reeds under her boots, and scrambled up to the bedchamber. It was dim and stuffy up there, and the hanging tapestries separating the featherbeds were stiff with years of dirt and smoke. "Fabrisse—" She pushed aside a curtain.

"Shh. I'm reading."

She flopped, lumpish, on the bed beside her sister. "Would you like to go riding? We could go into town. Come on, let's do something." She poked Fabrisse with her toe.

"Don't."

Moving away, she stared at the tapestry. When she had first slept in this bed, next to Fabrisse, she had been a baby. The colors had once been brighter, the knight's surcoat a dull blue and the woman's gown a muddy shade of red. Now everything was veiled over with a rusty blur. Sybille began to hum under her breath.

Fabrisse looked up and frowned. She laid the book flat on the coverlet. "What are you so happy about?"

"Na Beatritz tricked De Montfort."

"Is that all?" Fabrisse said. "Watch where you're putting your feet."

Sybille propped herself on one elbow and glanced down. The book was bound in leather but badly stitched. "What's that? A romance?"

"The Bible," Fabrisse said, sounding angry. "I'm reading the Bible."

"Whatever for?" Full of curiosity, Sybille sat up to take a look. It was the Gospel of St. Luke, written in their language. "Where did you get this thing?"

"Arnaud Othon."

"The goodman?" She smiled, feeling mischievous. "Is he trying for another convert?" She reached for the volume, but Fabrisse snatched it away.

"Perhaps," Fabrisse said, her face giving nothing away.

"Think twice before you take that road," Sybille said. "Are you thinking twice?"

"No. I'm reading the Bible."

"But I'll bet you're thinking of converting." She squirmed around to peer at Fabrisse's face."

"That's none of your business."

"It sounds like you are," she teased.

Fabrisse glanced up, fierce. "Answer me this, sister. How could a loving, intelligent deity be responsible for a world full of pissing brats, bad breath, stupidity, and husbands who fart in bed?"

"And jongleurs with croaky voices. How?"

"He isn't."

"Muleshit!" Sybille whooped.

"What a fool you are," Fabrisse said heatedly. "Well, here's something else to think about. Why is it Catholics turn heretic but heretics never become Catholics?"

Never at a loss for an answer, Sybille shot back, "Why does good wine turn to vinegar but never contrariwise?" and she grinned. She refused to take Fabrisse seriously. Her sister was one of those who dabbled in heresy because they had nothing better to do. Her interest would not hold.

Fabrisse went back to Arnaud Othon's Bible, and Sybille lay on the coverlet, staring at the tapestry. With difficulty she could still make out the lion on the knight's shield. Fabrisse, she said silently, isn't it stupid to become a heretic, now of all times? Mama won't be happy to know of this. She stared at her sister a long time, but Fabrisse would not look up, and finally, bored, Sybille went down to the yard. She had a mare saddled and set off at a canter toward Fanjeaux.

Dirty, wool-colored clouds gusted over the rocky slopes. The deserted road was windy and smelled of dead leaves. Sybille's wimple snapped at her throat. Outside Gaillarde Seguier's alehouse, a crowd had gathered and people were talking in excited voices. But there was always a crowd there, and Sybille paid no attention. Men in leather jerkins were loading crates of chickens into a wagon. Feathers dusted the cobbles. Sybille heard her name being called, drew rein, and glanced around.

Blondel Puy scooted toward her from across the square, munching some kind of pie. He twisted his face into a grin. She had not seen the fiddler since her wedding. If he mentions Pons, she thought, I'll cry. "God's greetings," she said, leaning out of the saddle. "Well, where's your fiddle?"

He touched cold lips to her fingers, then fastened his eyes on her face. "Lady, you must be feeling very joyous. God gave you a lucky star."

Bewildered, she recoiled in the saddle. "What are you saying?" she cried. "Listen, my husband is dead. Joy is not what I'm feeling."

Blondel said, "But, lady, how could he be dead? He was in Prouille last week."

She narrowed her eyes. "Your jokes aren't funny."

"The smithy saw him. He was on his way to Toulouse."

Sybille stared over his head. The alewife opened her door and came out, looked up at the sky, blew her nose, and went in again.

In a bewildered tone, Blondel said, "I thought you knew."

She watched him brushing his tongue busily across his upper lip, then suck it inside the slit. All her hopes abstracted to one wet mouth.

"Four escaped," he said. "I was sure you knew."

Two days later, in the courtyard in Rue St. Bernard, Sybille was reunited with her husband. Had the gatekeeper not pointed and called him by name, she would not have recognized him. After five months in the dungeons of Raymond-Roger Trencavel's château, his head was skull-shaped, like a dead man's. Shivering, Sybille forced herself into his arms.

Later in their chamber, she said to him, "When I believed you dead, I was full of remorse. And do you know why? Because I never gave you my body as a wife should. That was all I could think of."

There was silence. Then Pons laughed. "Do you suppose that mattered to me? Sybille, the flesh is unreal. It has nothing to do with our love for each other."

"Then you didn't care?"

"No," he said. "There are more important things to worry about." He rolled back among the pillows and stretched out his legs. "You should take a lover. That would be the sensible thing to do."

"No." She saw that his eyes were closed. She said loudly, "The only man I want is you," but he was asleep.

The terrible year had ended and now summer was coming again. The southern sun was as brilliant as new glass. In the Astarac garden the May light looked lime-green. These were the weeks when the apple trees were laced with white blossoms and girls in filmy dresses went out riding beyond St. Cyprien with falcons on their wrists and returned with bouquets of rock roses and hangman's orchids. And it was the time of year when the burghers who owned farms and vineyards worried about hiring extra men and women for the weeding. It was as if the Toulousans had slept straight through a bad dream and, awake now, had lost all memory of unpleasantness.

The city, of course, was jammed with families who not so long ago had lived in Carcassonne and Albi and Castres. More than a dozen towns had fallen to the crusaders the previous autumn. Simon de Montfort had appeared and demanded a levy of ten sous—for the pope, he said—and sometimes left behind a token garrison in their castles. Ten sous were cheap enough to rid themselves of the man, and some lords even contributed a horse or a sack of meal, as they might toss a bone to a ravenous dog.

The people who had taken the precaution of fleeing their homes were the heretics; they had streamed into Toulouse to winter in their town houses or to spend an extended holiday with relatives. Understandably some were hard up now.

All over the city people were avoiding the subject of the future. Unlike many others, Sybille had been personally touched by the crusade, which she had come to regard as a fistful of catastrophes narrowly averted. She kept shuffling her blessings and misfortunes. Pons's father was dead, but Pons had come home safely; Béziers was destroyed, but Fabrisse had magically survived. The crusaders had come and gone, but the world was still whole and turning. Don't look back, she warned herself. Don't ruin this day with hideous thoughts. How happy it is possible to be. And she pumped herself up, approximating the idea of joy as if she were ripening a theme for a *canso*.

The Astarac household had become a family of two religions. Douce and William went to mass and made confession, as they had done all their lives. For Fabrisse and Pons, the faith of Rome had been poisoned forever by the crusade. They could not forget what had happened and who had caused it, and they turned their backs on the old Church. The genuine church of Jesus Christ was open to all who had eyes to see and ears to hear. It was the only faith left, the true pulley to the Almighty, in their opinion. Sybille stood between these two camps, uncomfortable with the fervor of the Good Christians and filled with vague distrust for the priests at Saint-Sernin. She continued to go down Rue St. Bernard to the church but less frequently.

One morning, leaving the house with her rosary, she heard Fabrisse come up behind her and say, "How can you go near that vulgar place?" She meant Saint-Sernin.

"I like it," Sybille said stiffly.

"Churches should be destroyed," Fabrisse announced. "There's no need for them. God is everywhere."

Fingering the rosary, Sybille said nothing.

"It's a sin to worship rotting bones and wood. The cross should be despised, not worshiped. It was the instrument of Christ's suffering."

"Leave me be!" Sybille shouted, out of temper. "If I wanted to convert, I would. It's irritating the way you keep saying hateful things about Rome. It's petty."

"It's clear you prefer to wear a sack on your head," Fabrisse snorted and walked away.

Aside from these rare scuffles, the two faiths coexisted. William uttered no objections to goodmen preaching in his hall, while Douce's tolerance of differences went even further. She determined to help the heretics. Now that a toilet had been installed, she sought new projects and decided to hold a feast to raise money for those who had been made widows and orphans by the surrender of Carcassonne. Meetings were held to determine the exact financial need of these unfortunate families. Menus, availability of certain jongleurs, lists of guests and the amounts they might contribute were carefully worked out in advance.

On the evening of the feast, Sybille waited in the empty yard by the olive tree where her brothers once had played. Pierre and Mathieu had been home at Easter, but Sybille had not known what to think of them. Once she had loved them. Why did they now behave like strangers? Their eyes were wild and angry, and when they returned to Bram after three days, Douce wept bitterly.

Sybille hoped the guests would not come too soon—it was peaceful standing there in the shadows, looking up at the branches and thinking of nothing much. The sky was low over the rooftops and a darkish pink, and the grooms had not yet begun to light the torches. Through the open gate came sounds from Rue St. Bernard, hoofbeats on the cobbles, and in the distance the priests of Saint-Sernin neighing the evening psalms.

Suddenly the yard was full of horses and guests: Helis and Pierre Baragnon, the abbot of Saint-Sernin, Pons de Capdenier, who had more money than God. Behind them came Raymond and Corba de Perella with their small daughter, Philippa. Sybille stepped forward, waving to Corba. "I thought you might have left for the Ariège already," she said.

"We're going next week."

Raymond said, "You can visit us." He was a tall knight with an intelligent smile, and he always smelled of soap and something sweet that Sybille could never quite determine.

"You mean Montségur?" She went over and kissed his cheek. "That heap of rocks. No, thank you." Raymond and Corba had acquired a mountain near Lavelanet, how Sybille did not know. Once there had been a castle on the summit, but it had fallen down long ago. For the past several years Raymond had been gradually rebuilding the place. But hauling stones up that slope was no easy proposition. "Is there a roof on it?" She smiled.

"Not yet." Raymond's mouth curled sheepishly into a grin. "But there will be, God willing. I'm hoping for money from the church."

They started up the stairs to the hall, Philippa puffing on short, fat legs. Sybille thought the heretic church must have money to waste if they were investing in the De Perellas' castle. The place was miles from anywhere.

At the top of the stairs, Corba said, "You ought to see it. Once you get up there it's really marvelous. Windy but very peaceful."

"Mmmm. I suppose." Corba's idea of marvelous did not match hers. "What does the church want with Montségur?"

Behind her, Raymond said, "They need a headquarters."

"Like the pope?" She laughed.

"Not exactly. Well, maybe."

She turned to him. "Nobody would go there," she said. "It's too far away."

"Yes. It's a two-day journey from Pamiers."

"And they say the mountain is haunted."

"Oh, Sybille!" Corba hooted. "Don't be silly."

Sybille looked down into the yard. A mob of people, richly gotten up, had jogged in, and the space was filled with horses, grooms, and seven scents of perfume. In the hall a fiddler had begun, then a bagpipe squealed. Douce came glimmering through the crowd, carrying Philippa in her arms. Slivers of candlelight rimmed the edge of her head. The child hung down and lunged for her mother's sleeve, and Douce reluctantly handed her over. Sybille could not bear watching Douce watch the De Perella child.

Her mother could hope for no grandchildren from her own children. None of them would bring her a baby to dandle, not Fabrisse, not her sons who lusted after blood and garrison whores. Not Pons, who had been heard to insist that only a boor would object to his wife's taking a lover. Not Sybille, who sometimes rubbed her husband's back at night before they faded into sleep. Innocents, side by side. Yes, what of it? Sybille thought. Is that a great sin? It is, it is. Turning, she walked toward the music.

"The sweetness of love"—the jongleur's voice struck her hard in the middle of her chest—*"in a garden or behind curtains. With—"* Her breath constricted. *"—a friend I desire."* Oh God, she thought. Jaufré Rudel, I wish I could write like you. Abruptly she laughed aloud. Jaufré Rudel wrote of love hunger so intense you could roll it on

your tongue. Because he was impotent, she thought. And so am I.

In the garden the men gathered around the count's son. Shouts—angry, leaking fear—rumbled into the darkness. When the men began to move back into the hall, Sybille ran to tug at her father's sleeve. "What did he say?" she asked. "What did young Raymond tell you?"

"Alice de Montfort is visiting Carcassonne."

"His wife?"

"The countess brought five hundred men with her. So now we shall have more trouble, more dying."

"Papa," she said. "Will they come to Toulouse?" When he did not answer, she repeated, "Will we have a siege?"

William shrugged. "Nothing like that. Not with so few men. Lucky for us Alice isn't a more efficient recruiter. There isn't a chance they'll come here."

At the end of June, Simon de Montfort took Alice's troops into the Minervois, not far from Béziers, to the city of Minerve and cut off its water supply. When Minerve surrendered De Montfort promised to spare the lives of all heretics who recanted.

On an afternoon in July, one hundred and forty ordained ministers, men and women, were burned outside the château. It was the first time Sybille had ever heard of mass incineration, and she refused to believe it was true.

The end of the summer brought home one brother, now suddenly riding alone because the other was dead.

For a month the Astaracs had known about the capture of Bram. One evening William had taken Sybille and her sister into the library and poured them wine, and he had told as much of the truth as he dared. The garrison had had their eyes gouged out—they also had their noses and upper lips slashed off, but he could not bring himself to mention that. They had been set on the road to Cabaret, a warning to Christ's enemies. The same words William repeated again and again to his daughters: Barbarians. Wild beasts. God forgive them. Fabrisse said nothing, and Sybille burst into tears. To shield his wife William made them promise to say nothing of this to Douce.

William was intending to ride down to Cabaret, to see for himself. So far, he had put off the trip and had disguised his suffering as best he could around his wife. Secretly he thought it would be better if his sons were sitting in heaven now. But he could not voice that hope either, and so he mourned, mute, in his library with the door bolted and wet the pages of Aristotle.

One morning Pierre rode into the courtyard and found his mother preparing to go to the bazaar. She was hurrying to make her purchases and be home before the rain began. Douce stared at the bearded man with one eye and half a face.

Shortly afterward Sybille left the house, to shut her eyes to the screaming. In the streaming rain she loitered around Saint-Sernin square among the beggars. When she returned late in the day, the house was graveyard-quiet. She guessed Douce had wept herself to sleep.

In the hall a pair of candles danced against the shadows. At the end of the trestle Pierre was drinking wine with his father. Eyes half closed, William rose finally and gripped Pierre's arm and then padded down the hall. He passed Sybille without a glance. She made herself walk over to Pierre.

"Mama will get over it. Tomorrow she won't be screaming."

"Won't she?"

"Stay with us." She knelt on the bench, in the place William had been sitting. "You can't go on fighting."

"I still have an eye." Pierre fingered his cup casually. The hall was too dark to see his face.

"Aren't you sick of killing?"

"I'm not sick of it," he said. His voice dripped through the pulpy flesh. "The killing time has not yet begun."

"Just don't go for a while. Please, brother."

"De Montfort left me sight. Only me. 'These pretty boys might lose their way,' he said. 'And what's more, they might walk straight over a cliff and never get to Cabaret. So let's give them one eye.'" His voice was careless. "Fool! Someday he'll be sorry, mark me."

The hall smelled of damp. Outside, raindrops swooped down the stained-glass windows. Sybille sat thinking of Mathieu, who had cried during thunderstorms and would be comforted only by his mother. "How many," she said, hoarse, "went to Cabaret?"

"About a hundred."

Her whole body was cold. "When did Mathieu—?"

Behind them a candle stirred and snuffed itself out. Quietly Pierre said, "Before. An arrow." He lifted his cup and drank deeply. "There's plenty to do. I can see as well as anybody. I can see to the ramparts of heaven."

The ramparts of heaven, Sybille repeated to herself; I can see to— It could be the first line of a *sirventes,* bitter as new red wine. She listened, hoping the next line would swim up. But nothing moved.

She said good night. Two days later her brother took a black stallion and went away down the road to Carcassonne.

Chapter Five

After that year, memory failed her. The summers came, two or three in a row, such sad, fiery summers that afterward they seemed as if they had been all one. Of course, there were certain ways to distinguish them. One year, four hundred people were burned at Lavaur. And there was the sweltering summer the crusaders had camped outside the walls of Toulouse and burned the olive trees. Some chronicler must have been recording these events in their correct sequence, but Sybille got them jumbled in her mind and only reminded herself that all those things that could not have happened took place before Muret.

There were people in Toulouse who believed Pope Innocent was Christ's vicar on earth, a little lower than God Himself. They crossed themselves and chose to live each day asleep, refusing to believe the soldiers of Christ had really burned living human beings.

Fabrisse, eyes wide open, her appetite for meaning fed as her mission in life grew clear, invented lies to account for her absences from the house. She came home late and ate in the kitchen after the servants were asleep. Sometimes Sybille went down to talk with her.

She said one night, "Mama was asking for you."

"Yes. Will Pons be home tonight?"

Sybille was the last person to know of her husband's whereabouts. She said to Fabrisse, "Well, he went to Comminges yesterday, if you want to know. But it's none of my business." Pons did not confide in her the details of his work for the church. She had come to think of him as a person who arranged things—lives, money, worship services.

Fabrisse carefully cut three slivers of yesterday's bread and poured herself a cup of water. Sybille left the table, looking for something to eat, and shuffled platters in the larder. When she returned with a sausage, Fabrisse was breaking the bread and taking it to her mouth in nibbles. Fabrisse glanced at the sausage and grimaced. "Disgusting. The flesh of unclean animals. How can you pollute your body that way?"

"Want some?" She cut a thick slice and stuffed it whole into her face.

"You know I never eat flesh." She reached for the water and sipped a mouse-mouthful.

"God's bones." Sybille sawed off another slice, licking greasy fingers. "Not everyone wants to live on bread and water. Have a decent meal. You're getting to look like a scarecrow."

"I cannot believe," Fabrisse said, "what an ordinary person you are. How unspiritual."

Sybille laughed. "Don't worry about it. I like being ordinary. Maybe I'll be like you in my next life." The heretic belief that the soul reincarnates in another body galled her, and she took childish pleasure in needling her sister about it. "Maybe I'll be reborn a hundred years from now and I'll pray a lot and give up meat. And God will say, Well, well, she's perfect. Just like her old sister, Fabrisse, who was high up on my list of perfects."

"If you come again, it will be as a toad."

"Ah-ah." She waggled her finger at Fabrisse's nose. "That's why I can't take you seriously. All your fasting and praying and what has it done for you? You're still mean to me."

"Sister," Fabrisse said, "I'm trying to love you. But it's not easy." She shook her head at Sybille. "I want you to know something."

"What?" She grinned at her.

Fabrisse stared away. "I'm thinking of taking the *consolamentum*. The De Perellas say they can get me into the women's seminary at Foix."

Sybille was shocked into fury. "Wonderful!" she exploded. "That's all we need. A goddam goodwoman in the family. What are you trying to do? Kill Mama?"

"Mama will make no objections," Fabrisse said. "She has nothing against the church. You're wrong, if you think she'd try to stop me."

"Mark me." Sybille leaned foward, eyes fastened on her sister's face. "She's not so stupid as you imagine. She hasn't minded yet, because what is there to mind. But it's one thing to be an ordinary believer and quite another to preach." Her voice rose. "They burn preachers, haven't you heard?"

"I've heard." Fabrisse laid a pellet of bread on her tongue delicately.

"She knows that, even though she pretends she doesn't. The count himself told her what the pope said. Clean out the heretics in Toulouse." She bounced to her feet, knocking over the stool, and tramped to the far end of the table.

"Oh well. What does that mean? The count won't do anything."

Sybille came back to stand beside Fabrisse. "No—there's not enough firewood to burn all the heretics in this city." She laughed. "But—" She plopped on the edge of the table. "But suppose you were a preacher. They're sent all over."

Fabrisse's nose puckered into a sniff. "I know that."

"Suppose they send you and a partner to Castelnaudary. And just suppose De Montfort decides to take Castelnaudary. Now I ask you, what's going to happen then?"

Fabrisse only smiled placidly. "I guess I'll have to burn." She gulped the rest of the water and pushed aside the cup.

"Oh?" Sybille stared, her upper lip sweaty with anger. "You have about as much sense as a bedbug. A small bedbug."

She took the sausage back to the pantry and looked for wine. Behind her, she could hear Fabrisse blubbering another prayer under her breath. Dear God up there, she thought, is this really what You expect from us? All this fasting and praying? It's not much fun, I'll tell you.

Footsteps banged in the passageway. Sybille filled both hands with crocks and carried them to the table. When Pons came in, she was uncovering a mutton stew.

His face was bronzed from the sun, and his eyes and mouth were exuberant. "My lady, are you still at your supper?" He bowed to Fabrisse.

Sybille said to him, "What happened at Comminges? You look very pleased about something."

He grinned, hair falling wild on his forehead, and sank on a stool opposite Fabrisse. His dark eyes were shining. Sybille watched him spoon cold stew over a chunk of bread. Thank God he had not become a crank like Fabrisse. As always, he ate whatever appeared before him.

Fabrisse grunted. "It's time I was abed." She did not stir from her seat.

Pons raised one hand, indicating she should stay. He looked over to Sybille, gravy dripping between his fingers. "Our trouble will be ended soon. De Montfort and his red crosses will be going back to France. This land is going to see joy and worth again. Lady, I need a cup for this wine."

Excited, she turned away. She brought a cup and napkin and hurled herself down next to him.

Fabrisse asked, "Pons, the pope is sending him home?"

"We're sending him home. He doesn't know it yet."

"We!" Sybille slapped her hand on the table impatiently. "We can't do anything."

Pons drank. He smiled over at Fabrisse for a moment, then said softly to Sybille, "Peter of Aragon is bringing twenty thousand knights over the mountains."

"*Ai!*" she gasped and could not close her mouth. Fabrisse clapped her hand over her chin.

"He said it's a matter of honor," Pons told them. "He said, when your neighbor's house is ablaze, your own property may burn too."

Fabrisse reached for the mutton stew.

"A matter of honor," Sybille repeated. "Oh God, king of Aragon, I adore you! Well, but Pons—remember. His sister is wed to the count. Naturally he would want to defend his own kin." She rattled on, teeth flashing, jabbering about the king, his sensitivity, his admiration for troubadour poetry, and so forth.

"Sister," Fabrisse broke in finally, "calm yourself. He's burned heretics in Aragon. He doesn't sound like any savior to me."

"Well," Sybille grunted uneasily, "he's a Catholic, isn't he?" God's ass, leave it to Fabrisse to spit cold water on good news. She glanced at Pons.

"She's right." He frowned. "The count swore there were no more heretics in Toulouse. I'm sorry to say Peter has no love for our faith."

"You think he'll betray us?" Sybille stood, hoping that nothing bad was coming.

"Not necessarily. No." He brushed his mouth against the napkin. "He despises De Montfort as a common adventurer. Thinks he fights Rome's battles only to line his own pockets." Abruptly he sprang up and headed for the cupboard. A minute later he was back, juggling three of Douce's best crystal goblets. He set them on the table and filled each to the brim with wine. Lifting his goblet, he smiled at Sybille. "Sweet heart, to whom would you drink?"

The sound of her laughter filled the kitchen. *"A parage!"* she cried. "To joy. To the king of Aragon! To the king!"

"To life," Pons called out.

Brune Maurand was paying her weekly call. She lived just opposite the Astaracs, but visited only on Thursday afternoons, by appointment. Informal calls she considered very poor manners.

"Read me something you've written." Brune turned her face toward Sybille. Over her coiled braids the sun was setting wreaths of lemon light.

"There is nothing to read," Sybille explained. "I've stopped writing verse."

Brune said, "Then you must start again." There was a tray of apricot cakes and fruited wine between them on the table. "A *trobairitz* must write."

Sybille forced herself to lean forward, casual, and dip two fingers into her goblet. She plucked out a strawberry and brought it to her lips. "Na Brune," she said carefully, "I'm not a *trobairitz."*

"Of course you are," Brune told her gently.

Sybille thought, Songs pour unending through my head but nothing more happens. All I ever get is a headache. She said aloud, "What's there to write about?"

"Love," Brune replied.

"I've never known true love."

"But what about a lark? A sunset?" Brune crumbled off a sliver of cake. "There are plenty of things to make songs about."

"I can't!" The words burst angrily from her mouth and she tried to retrieve them. "Beg pardon, lady. I mean, I'm not able to write now."

Brune nodded. "But someday you will. I feel confident. One day you will be a poet of great worth."

Sybille felt tears starting to gather in the corners of her eyes. She said, "That's very kind of you," and hurried to change the subject. When Douce came in, Brune Maurand was describing her new falcon and the apricot cakes were gone.

A loosened sky hurled rain deep into the earth, endlessly. All morning, after Pons had dressed and gone, she lay motionless in the center of the bed listening to the universe trying to unspring itself. It was late afternoon when the door opened and Carenza slipped in, carrying a tray piled with dishes. As Sybille sat up, she saw the maid clinking cutlery and looking at her in a peculiar way.

"How do you, madam?" Carenza asked politely.

Sybille bundled the coverlet around her neck. "Not hungry."

"Your lady mother wonders if you are ill. Are you ill?" She did not wait for Sybille to speak. "Why aren't you hungry?"

Sybille nodded at the tray. "Put it down and leave it. Or take it back to Cook. I don't care."

The girl approached the bed, deposited the tray near Sybille's elbow, and towered over her, staring.

"Carenza," Sybille said, "do you ever feel anything?"

The maid thought a minute. She said cautiously, "I don't think so," then corrected herself. "Madam, could you rephrase that question? I don't know what you mean."

"Pain. I mean do you ever feel love or hunger or pain?" She meant ecstasy.

"I am," Carenza said quickly, "an orphan," as if that constituted an appropriate reply.

Sybille nodded.

"May I go now?" the maid asked, without looking at Sybille.

"Have you ever enjoyed a man?"

Reddening, Carenza jumped back. "Madam, I've never sinned, I swear to you." She avoided her mistress's eyes.

"I'm sorry," Sybille said quickly. "I know you're a good girl. You can go."

Stumbling toward the door, Carenza said, "I hope you feel better, lady," and fled.

She stared at the tray. There was no point lingering there any longer. There were no answers in love spells self-cast under the rain-soft bedding. All the same, she did not move until Saint-Sernin announced vespers, and then she got up, with effort.

Dressing quickly, she ran downstairs to the courtyard and strode purposefully out the gate and down the street toward Saint-Sernin.

Inside the church she caught sight of a priest swagging toward the crossing. It was gloomy in the sanctuary, and the stale light from the candles hurt her eyelids. "Father? Wait, Father." She was on the brink of tears that would not flow.

"God's good evening, Na Sybille." He stopped. It was Father Bernart, with his long, stupid face.

"God's good evening, Father." She made an effort to sound normal. "I want to make my *confiteor*."

He clucked impatiently with his tongue. "Now? It's late. Come back tomorrow."

She touched his sleeve. "I can't wait. Please." She began to stammer. "My soul is in jeopardy."

"Oh well," he snorted. "If it's your soul—" He stared openly at the purse hanging from her girdle.

She fumbled for a coin and nuzzled it into his hand. The church was deserted, silent, while the Catholics of Toulouse spent this hour at their trestles. Sybille trotted along behind the priest, down the side of the nave toward the confessional. She slouched on her knees until he had settled himself behind the golden grille. "Well, speak up," she heard him say drily.

"Father," she whispered, crossing herself. "I have sinned most grievously. *Mea culpa.*"

"Yes, yes, sinned grievously," he repeated irritably. "What have you done?"

She could not think of any particular sin she had committed, of any name for the churnings she was experiencing, and after a moderate pause she finally said, "Nothing."

There was a disgusted sigh behind the grille. The priest offered no reproach though, having heard that reply before. Sybille stayed on her knees, head bowed. There was a clink of crockery and then the distinct aroma of garlic floated through the grille. The priest mumbled something.

"What did you say, Father?"

Chewing, he repeated, "I said God will not be mocked. Say what you have to say."

"I'm unhappy," she said promptly. "Some sickness of the soul."

"Everyone is unhappy. God has more important matters to attend to than your happiness."

"Demons are chasing me. They chew me." She could sense Father Bernart leaning forward, his nose pitched a few inches from her own. "They shoot hot flames at me. Do you think God is punishing me?"

"Shoot flames at what part of you?" he asked, suddenly interested.

Neck sagging, she sighed and whispered, "Private." She waited. There was a scraping sound, as if he were scouring the bottom of the bowl. He said rapidly, "All right. Tell me this, does your lord husband lie with you?"

"What do you mean?"

"What do I mean? How precise must I be?" He groaned. "I mean to say, do you sleep with your husband?"

She decided to get it over with. "No. Not anymore."

"Why not?"

She tried to see his face through the grillwork and could feel him staring at her. She forced herself to say, "He follows—the other religion."

"Oh," grunted the priest.

They waited through a long pause. The priest erupted in a belch, then scraped his feet against the paving stone. He cleared his throat several times. At last he said tautly, "Want my advice?"

No, she thought. I want God's advice. "Yes, Father. What should I do?"

"Sleep with your husband. It can be done if you go about it properly."

Quickly she got to her feet. "Thank you, Father."

She hurried through the nave, choking back a laugh. She thought, I paid a sou for that. That advice I could have given myself. Sleep with my husband. Well! Oh God, oh God, I'm down here in your Saint-Sernin. Are You smiling? I am.

In the Astarac courtyard grooms with elated faces were gathered near the stable door. A single torch glowed bronze. Noticing Pons, Sybille came up to the men, who were making a commotion about the king of Aragon and eating sausages.

Pons twisted around, smiling. "It won't be long now," he said, his mouth full. "They're mustering at Barcelona next week. Where have you been?"

They walked toward the olive tree, its tiny oval balls glittering bluish against the silvery leaves. Behind them, the grooms were making bets about how many knights Peter would bring.

"Over at Saint-Sernin having a laugh," Sybille said. "Oh gentle Jesus! Those priests must believe all Catholics are bloody fools." She growled in a voice brimming with disgust. "I made my *confiteor.*"

"Yes," he said, disinterested. He hooked one foot over the edge of a bench. His eyes were sleepy, half closed. Now she saw his thoughts were still on the news from Aragon, and she felt herself fluff up with irritation, wanting his attention for herself.

"Pons!" she exploded. "I'm trying to talk to you."

"I was listening. Speak."

Sybille turned her head away, suddenly self-conscious. She said, "I've been troubled lately. Lewd thoughts, you might call them." She laughed. "Father Bernart was not much help. He advised me to lie with you."

Pons made a noncommittal sound in his throat. His foot dropped to the cobbles abruptly.

Sybille noticed Douce standing at the top of the yard stairs, gazing anxiously into the yard. She waved to her mother. "I'm going up now," she said to Pons and started around the bench. She saw his eyes were open.

He said, speaking carefully, "You should pray. Say the Lord's Prayer eight times and then repeat it eight more times. Sixteen in all. Then you should say, 'I have the will—God give me the strength.' Go apart by yourself when you do this. And I'll pray for you as well."

She lowered her eyes, nodding slightly.

He went on. "Remember the words of St. John—the lust of the flesh is not of the Father, but of the world. The world passes away."

"Yes," she muttered politely, not wishing to listen.

"Lust passes away. But he that doeth the will of God abideth forever."

Sybille felt anger begin to flail her ears. He began quoting St. Luke now, reminding her the Lord had given man the power to tread on serpents and scorpions. She clenched her fingers behind the folds of her skirt.

Every day the sun sat fiery hot in the sky, even though it was September. Intoxication, rusty from disuse, convulsed the rhythms of life. Simon de Montfort and his knights were holed up a few leagues to the south in a castle near Muret. Toulouse forgot to sleep. Nights were given over to feasting and toasting Peter's assured victory, and everybody sang Raymond de Miraval's new *canso, "Then ladies and lovers will recover the joy they have lost."* When the king of Aragon finally rode into Toulouse, the ladies and lovers packed the streets to scream themselves voiceless.

Sybille stood opposite the château with Douce and William. They had been waiting two hours; soon it would be noon and Sybille, sweating, began to wonder if the king was coming after all. Her stomach was squeaking with hunger. The pink orchids in Douce's hair had withered in the heat. One of them sagged over her ear. The Aragonese army began to file along the street in straight columns, and the crowd gave a cheer. Here were the knights of the royal house of Aragon, more than two thousand on their war horses with plaited manes and their saddles tassled in green leather. And there were the waves of squires and pages leading destriers and palfreys and carrying silk banners embroidered in bright gold and scarlet. Each knight and his retinue got their share of cheering. The morning air churned with the sound of hooves clattering on the cobbles, and horses neighing, and men and women's voices singing and yelling. And then, riding alone at the end, came King Peter, and the uproar trebled.

"The king!" William called out to Douce. All around them people were shouting, *Parage! parage!*, as if they were possessed.

At William's shoulder Sybille jerked onto her toes and braced herself. She could see the king's white robes, his hand flung into a perpetual salute and the rubies and sapphires winking on his fingers. In his tanned face his dark eyes were shining like bits of glass. And then he had moved out of her line of vision, and Sybille let down her toes to the ground and turned to her mother.

"Wasn't he handsome, Mama? Did you see—?"

Douce was ecstatic. Rubbing the tears away, she hugged Sybille. "A real prince, a real prince," she singsonged. "That's it. That's the end of De Montfort. No, please, I'm all right. William, where is William? Oh, those poor crusaders. But that's what they get for coming down here without being invited."

The procession was over. The crowds began to disperse. Those who had been standing for many hours flooded out into the center of the street, running, hoping to get another glimpse of King Peter. The Astaracs slowly made their way across Rue du Château and went up along Rue d'Alfaro toward the Marty armory, where they had tethered their mounts. The sunlight fell diagonally on tile roofs and ruddy stone walls, and the whole city seemed to have been dipped in pinkish paint. William led Douce by the arm.

"Calm yourself, sweet heart," he murmured.

"This heat—I feel a bit dizzy."

At the armorer's Douce cooled down and allowed Barthélemy Marty to seat her formally in a high-backed chair near the entrance of the shop, where she could get fresh air, and she accepted a wet cloth for her temples.

There could be no doubt about the outcome of the battle. Everyone in the crowded shop said so. The men were impatient to spend money; they wanted new hauberks and shiny helmets and swords so they might look extraordinary on the battlefield. It would be good to fight again, especially when it was going to end in victory.

Barthélemy Marty was unusually talkative that afternoon. Smiling, he took William to the rear of the shop and unlocked a chest lined in red velvet, and he lifted out a sword with a watery pattern on its blade. Sybille, who had been trailing after her father, ran her finger politely over the wavy marks while William engaged Marty in a conversation about the manufacture of Damascus steel.

"How much carbon in this?" William asked the armorer.

"My lord, I can't reveal that. You know the guild won't permit it."

"Quite a bit, I'd imagine."

Marty shifted his feet uncomfortably. "My lord, I can tell you the secret isn't in the carbon content."

William said promptly, "That's right. It's in the cooling of the steel. No mystery about that."

Marty replaced the Damascus sword in the chest and lowered the lid. "My apologies, sire. I must tend to business now." He turned and headed for the front of the shop.

William and Sybille came after him. William called, "Where's your son? Haven't seen Daniel here lately."

"Daniel!" echoed Marty, immediately indignant. He whirled around. "That shit-nosed jackass. Do you know what he did? He's gone off to the Preaching Friars. Dominic and that bunch of nancies. Gone for good, that lazy—" He broke off, hissing spittle into the air.

"Oh well," William said sympathetically. "Perhaps it was God's will. The Church is still a reasonably honorable profession. You can't deny that."

"Well, yes. The Church. The Benedictines, even the Cistercians, are plenty respectable." Marty sniffed. "But Dominic, he's out of his mind. Filthy beggars, I tell you. Bums."

William laughed and said, "You know what they say. You can't get into the order if you've ever had a bath."

Sybille circled around Barthélemy Marty and William and went up to her mother. Douce was talking to Vigoros de Baconia about changing the colors of his coat of arms from green to blue. She suggested a white dove on a bright-blue background.

"You must be tired, my love," William said to his wife.

They rode home.

Sybille d'Astarac crouched at the window of her mother's chamber and watched the gauzed silhouette of Saint-Sernin strew twilight low across Rue St. Bernard. Never before had she kept vigil there at that hour, but now she watched, chin resting on folded arms. The street below was empty, the cobbles melted into a river of cinder darkness. The darkness surged on, straight to the corner of Saint-Sernin and then washed back through some subterranean tributary until she felt it coursing within her chest. She began to breathe rapidly.

Behind her, Douce snored as she slept, the tides of air sucking in and rushing out, her tears penned into some antechamber before gathering to break free again. Sybille heard the silence down in the street, and saw it burbling and writhing and knew it was speaking to her, its soundlessness more deadly than a scream.

There is nothing to fear, Sybille told herself. We will not lose. There is no more chance of our defeat than of a salamander burning, and in a few hours the couriers will ride through the Narbonne gate to announce victory. All the people now asleep behind shutters will run in the streets.

She saw two women come dragging down Rue St. Bernard, their pastel gowns hard-edged against the shadows. They moved slowly, shoulders touching, legs kicking forward in unison, a pair of wooden marionettes with their strings lost in the shadows of the belltower. One of them broke stride and stopped, as if she had wandered mistakenly into the wrong street and only now realized it. The other reeled on, almost up to the Astarac gate, before stopping. Then she went back and said something to her companion.

Sybille could not see their faces. If she could see their expressions she might know if salamanders burned. The women started forward, more briskly than before. They passed the gate, went directly under the window, and kept on. Sybille thought, They are only two tired women returning from vespers, and then she remembered she had been waiting there for several hours. The bells had not pealed for vespers that afternoon. Perhaps they had rung and she somehow had not heard.

She sat and waited for Saint-Sernin to sound compline, which it did not. Now the cobbles lay in blackness. After a while one of the grooms came out carrying torches and placed them in the rings on either side of the gate. Her legs had gone rigid. The sound of hooves smashed against the cobbles as a horseman tumbled through the twin pools of light outside the gate. Then she saw another horseman career down the street. She thought she could hear shouting from the square.

After the second rider had gone by, she heard the door open behind her and Carenza call her name. "Madam, Cook wants to know—"

Sybille spoke softly. "Be quiet, please. My lady mother is sleeping." She did not turn. "Go down to the yard and send out a groom to ask what's happening."

"But, lady, where should he go?"

"To the square," she hissed, furious at the girl's slow wit. "To the château." She rose heavily, steadying weightless legs against the edge of the stool, and leaned out the window. She had heard rightly. There was a mob in the square making plenty of noise. When she twisted around, Carenza was still in the doorway, clutching the stub of a candle. Sybille brushed past her.

"Where are you going?" the maid asked.

Sybille did not answer. Down in the yard the gatekeeper lurched up. "Bring a torch, Florent!" she shouted. She hurled herself toward the gate.

"Lady, what is it?"

Outside, she snatched a torch from the wall and ran in the direction of the square. Behind her, Florent was panting. She held the torch high. A man rattled toward her carrying a child in his arms. She shouted at him, "What news?"

"God help us," he cried and rushed on.

They won or we won. If God must help us, they won, and she tried not to think of what that meant. By the time she reached Saint-Sernin square, the heat of the torch was flecking her knuckles. Among the crowd outside the relics shop she recognized Peytavi Borsier, one of Mathieu's boyhood friends. He had an arm slung over the saddle of his gelding. A wineskin dangled from his hand.

"What's wrong, friend?" she called to him.

Peytavi straightened. Black stubble pebbled his cheeks. "Go

home, lady. The beast is coming." He jerked his head toward the portals of Saint-Sernin.

"Please—"

"Listen," he said to her. "I'll give you good advice. Go back home and lock the gate. De Montfort will be knocking in the morning."

He was drunk and feeling in the mood to make jokes. I'll have to ask someone else, she thought. But she went on staring at his face.

"*Havo,* you don't believe me," Peytavi Borsier said mildly. "No, I see she does not believe me."

"Where is King Peter?" Sybille demanded.

"You won't see him again. He's with the seraphim." He swaggered up to her. "Glad to see you, Sybille. Would you like to come home with me?"

"No, thank you," she said. "Where's our army?"

His lips fractured into a sottish line. "Sleeping. In the arms of undines. At the bottom of the Garonne." He rubbed his lips with the back of his hand.

"May the Devil piss in your ear!" she cried. "You lack courtesy."

Florent had come up and was standing silent at her elbow. Now he said to Peytavi, "Liar. The Aragonese wouldn't permit their king to be slain. God would not forsake the king."

"Good," Peytavi said. "I'm happy God would not. It must have been somebody else."

Sybille wheeled around. "Come on," she yelled to Florent. "Stay with me."

Now the square was so noisy she could hear only a single throat vomiting a stream of sound that dragged down the heavens. Listen, she thought. Listen well, for that is the death song of our land, an unsingable *planh* improvised by a dismembered jongleur. I must get to Mama before someone tells her.

As they ran toward Rue St. Bernard, the gatekeeper asked, "Why are we leaving, lady?"

"To eat," Sybille said. "We've not yet had our suppers and soon it will be matins."

"I had soup a while back," Florent said. "I'm not hungry."

"What kind of soup?"

"Bean. With some kind of meat. Lady, is the king of Aragon dead?"

"We must barricade the gate," Sybille answered.

"Someone is banging on the gate," Fabrisse said to Sybille. Since prime she had been stroking Douce's hand in the garden, insisting she knew nothing of what had happened at Muret, until Fabrisse had come and called her inside.

"The gatekeeper wants to know if he should open up."

"Who is it?"

"Florent doesn't recognize the name," Fabrisse said.

"A message from Papa perhaps."

"Perhaps," Fabrisse said. "We had better go down."

Florent was standing with his ear against the gate. On the other side someone was shivering the wood with a sword, perhaps a mace. The gatekeeper turned. "This person is tricky. When I ask who is it? he says, The master. But ladies, it is not En William's voice."

"Let me talk to him," Sybille said. She took Florent's place and listened. Only the sound of a horse's imperious snorting reached her ear. "This is Sybille d'Astarac," she shouted. "Who goes?"

"Tell that booby to open," a man called back.

Fabrisse shook her head.

"Excuse me, sir. State your business." The man did not reply, and finally Sybille called again, "Do you intend to do us harm?"

He cursed. Then: "No."

"Unlock it," she said to Florent.

She and Fabrisse writhed back toward the olive tree, clutching each other.

There were two horses but only one rider, a knight whose mail shirt was plastered with dried blood. A pair of bodies were trussed over a white stallion. Don't scream, Sybille warned herself. This is going to be bad. If you scream, Mama will hear. She started toward the knight, Fabrisse at her heels.

The knight dismounted. Without looking at the women, he walked slowly back to the white stallion and began to unknot the ropes. "This one is still all right. I hope." Roughly he scooped down one of the bodies and laid it face up on the cobbles, near the water trough. The man's face was smeared into a mask of dust and congealed blood. Before Sybille could move, her sister was screeching Pons's name and flinging herself past Sybille to the cobbles where Pons lay. "Is he dead?" Fabrisse asked the knight.

"Fainted. He's not badly hurt."

Sybille stayed where she was while her sister sent the grooms for wine. She looked at the knight, who was chewing his thumb, then at the body yet to be untied, then back to the knight. Finally he said, "There's no hurry."

"Please," she said, her voice low. "Can you take your mount into the stable? My mother—"

Nodding, he went around to unhook the white horse and led it out of the sunlight into the liquid coolness of the stable. Sybille trailed behind. Chin wobbling, she watched him loosen the ropes and lay William d'Astarac on the straw floor of the stable. She forced herself to stare at the brown holes embroidering his chest. Then she noticed one foot was missing. This is the worst I will ever have to see, she thought. No matter how long I live, nothing will be this bad.

"That is my lord father," she said to the knight.

He nodded. "May his soul fare well. And the other?"

"My husband."

"I thought he was her husband," the knight said, although there was no surprise in his voice.

She sank down cross-legged in the straw near her father's head and folded her hands in her lap. After a long while she whispered, "Do you know how he died?"

"No. He was dead when I met your husband. He was carrying him. I know nothing about it." He came around to stand opposite her. "Good. It's better to cry."

"I'm not crying," she said, tears spilling into her hands without making any sound. She did not want to see the knight, only to hear his tongue moving. "Is it true? Is the king dead? Is the count dead? Is there anyone alive?" How had this happened?

It was cool in the stable, and dim. The man slumped against a stall. He spoke reluctantly, as if he were annoyed. "After the king was slain, the cavalry began to flee. Then the foot soldiers. I can't say exactly how or when. But suddenly everyone was running." He moaned. "The Garonne. That is what destroyed us."

"Sir knight," Sybille said, grim. "How could the river do that?"

He shrugged. "The water was deep. The current swift. Those who were not already cut down were pushed back to the river. They drowned."

"How many?"

He lifted his shoulders again. "How should I know?" he said. "Thirty thousand, maybe forty. How should I know?"

"And the count?"

"Safe, God be thanked!"

Sybille kept her head down. Even though it was not yet terce, a whole day seemed to have passed; every minute had been lived that there was to live, and now she was ready for starlight and her nightmare bed. Outside in the sun-stained yard she could hear Fabrisse arguing with the kitchen boys, then there was silence. They must have carried Pons upstairs. She said, "De Montfort must be Satan."

"Or the executor of God's will." He laughed harshly. "They say he stopped to pray at Bolbonne Abbey before the battle. Consecrated his sword to God."

Sybille thought, God, must you elect barbarians to fight for you? She went on staring into her lap, listening to the knight yawning.

In the late afternoon the knight went down into the yard and called for his horse. Sybille came out and stood by the water trough.

"Your husband," he said, "has been asking for you."

"I'm going up now." Climbing the stairs would take quite a lot of strength. She did not want to go up. Coming across the yard the knight looked different to her. He was wearing a clean shirt, one of Pons's, and he must have shaved and washed his hair. She had seen him before. She had seen the crown of ringlets and the striking eyes, the color of water irises. He looked at her and went on talking for a while about Pons, and she looked back. It was uncanny how he had appeared twice now at particularly bad moments. Some guardian angel perhaps? She broke in, "You gave me a shirt at Carcassonne."

"No, I gave you olives."

"Both."

He did not say anything. Then he shrugged, as if to say, "All right, if you say so."

"Forgive me, I forgot to thank you. I was not thinking of my manners."

"You needn't thank me."

She ground one heel against a cobble. She wanted to find the right words. "Odd, isn't it? Do you suppose this is some sort of fate?" She laughed self-consciously.

He turned away and began lengthening a stirrup. "Well," he said over his shoulder, "the world is a small place."

Sybille could think of nothing more to say. She watched him mount the stallion.

He moved the horse around to face the gate. "I'd better go," he said.

"Where?" She smiled at him.

"Places."

"I don't know your name," she said. "You never told me your name. Isn't that funny?"

He gazed down at her, grave, indifferent. "Olivier. Olivier de Ferrand."

She watched the knight and the white horse go through the gate and turn into Rue St. Bernard.

Chapter Six

The gloom of another autumn grayed Toulouse. Scarcely one house did not have someone to mourn, a son, father, lover swept downstream, slumbering now in the bellies of sea beasts. The leaves on the carob trees yellowed, then sifted to the ground, and the dawns grew chilly. Surely Simon de Montfort would march on the city. But De Montfort crossed the Rhone, into Provence. The war was over, there was no doubt about that. When would he come back? How would they know when?

And yet why nip an overripe apple from its bough? It drops to the earth in God's good time. So people said in the shops along Rue de la Pourpointerie. No. It was over. See how certain of us he is, they told each other. He can take his time collecting his trophy. They smiled bitterly.

All the same, there was little to smile about. Each morning Douce d'Astarac would dress in black silk. Her maid opened the jewel box and lifted out a bracelet, a ring, one gem after another until the box was empty. Jangling like a goldsmith's shop, Douce would be carried in a litter up Rue St. Bernard and around to the porch of Saint-Sernin. After lighting colored candles to the Virgin, she was brought home, where she tottered upstairs and remained until the following morning.

Sybille and Fabrisse begged her to come downstairs for meals and she said, "No."

They said, "Why not, Mama?" and she said, "Because God does not wish it."

"Mama," Sybille told her, "we love you. Please come down to the hall."

And Douce told her, "It does not please me to argue with you, daughter."

The rents from the Astarac farms had not been collected at the fall quarterday, which failed to interest Sybille. Pons went to see the Astarac banker in Joux-Aigues. There was no cause for alarm, but it would be poor precedent to allow the rents to go unclaimed. Pons said they should go themselves, and around the middle of Advent they set out for Astarac. With them they took the sarcophagus of William d'Astarac.

The castle had been built in the tenth century by a knight from the Auvergne. The original keep had been torn down after the first crusade and replaced by a fancier one. Indeed, each generation of Astaracs had made improvements, so it was now almost impossible to know what the original had been like. Sybille thought the place a charmless pile of rocks. She could not imagine Na Beatritz living there as a young woman, could understand why she had fled once her husband was dead.

In the cavernous hall William's great-grandfather had hung mosaics he had ripped from the walls of a Saracen mosque in Jerusalem, and later someone had covered them with green paint. Now everything was old, scarred, crumbling. Backs to the hearth, Sybille and Pons sat at the head trestle flanked by the bailiff and the provost. Account ledgers lay open before Sybille, and the Astarac villeins, who had lined up on the side of the hall, came forward one at a time, clinking coins.

"This is something Pierre should be doing," she growled to Pons. "It is only proper that the eldest son take charge of these matters."

Pons shook his head. "Proper but not possible. You must do your duty."

"He was always irresponsible," she muttered sharply, unwilling to drop the subject. Nothing had been heard of Pierre since Muret. In all likelihood he was dead. But since Douce insisted otherwise, all of them went on thinking of Pierre as if he were a naughty boy hiding under the hedges. She hunched over the ledger, trying to decipher William's handwriting. "My brother's never thought about his duty."

The provost cleared his throat. "Lame Pathau—five acres." He pointed.

Sybille glanced up. At once, the peasant began howling about the departed soul of her father.

The provost roared, "Bow the head, swine!"

Lame Pathau jerked a quick bow to Sybille and went on talking.

He had barely half the rent due. The bishop's tithe collector had taken his pigs. "I had to pay God," he wailed, indignant. And if that were not bad enough, he had gone over to Auch on fair day and got his pockets picked on the church porch. He had burned a candle for the soul of En William.

The provost jetted a spray of curses, and after a while Sybille took Lame Pathau's four sous and entered the figure in the ledger, next to her father's last notation. Although the fire blazed, the hall was biting cold, and she muffled her fur cloak higher around her ears. The morning crept on. Few of the villeins could pay what they owed. All of them wept for her father. At noon she hauled herself up and shoved the ledger at Pons. Unsteady, she climbed the ladder to the empty solar and dropped on the first bed she saw.

After twenty or thirty minutes, Pons came up with ale and a platter of meat. Sybille said, "Why can't they stop talking about Papa?"

"Stop complaining," he said with annoyance. "He was their lord." He sat down on the bed.

She twisted to face him. His lips sagged into an uneven line. Rays of violence vibrated from his eyes. It had been like that since Muret, although she could not understand why his peevishness should be directed at her. Sitting up, she reached for the ale.

"Come down when you've finished eating," he said. He did not look at her.

"I can't. I don't want to." Why couldn't *he* do it? He never helped her, never protected her as William had her mother. "Why can't you be more like Papa? He wouldn't make me do it."

"Don't deify him," he shot back in a voice that made her tremble.

She whispered, "My lord father died to save our land. And don't you forget it."

"No," he said between his teeth. "I beg your pardon, but he threw himself on a French sword. When everyone was riding away, he turned around and waited for them. And he didn't even bother to lift his sword."

She stared at the bubbles in the ale. Her temples throbbed. She roared, "You ought to be killed for saying such lies!"

"I don't care if you believe me," he shouted. "He didn't want to live. You should know that."

"No—"

"Begging to be slain is the same as taking your own life. There's nothing wrong with that. I wish I'd thought of it. Who would want to live now? But just don't make him out to be a hero. Understand me?"

She sank back on the pillow, head buzzing. Through a long silence she and Pons avoided each other's eyes. Her father had been a patriot. But he was also a man who reasoned clearly and made decisions of wisdom, and if he had chosen the grave it was because he foresaw the south in ruin. She thought, the battle may have rattled his mind. The French cannot stay here forever. One day our land will belong to us again.

"My friend—"

"Damn you, I'm not your friend!" She rolled slowly to the edge of the bed and pulled herself upright. If it were true, he should not have told her. There was no reason for it but brutality. He stroked her elbow.

She wrenched aside. "Don't touch me!" she cried.

"I'm sorry." When he put his hand on her waist, she knocked it away.

Too angry to speak, she went down to the hall.

In the evening, Pons brought her a bowl of hot wine. Peace offering, Sybille thought, but she sat up and sipped the spicy liquid. She glanced at him over the edge of the bowl. By the candle's glow, his face looked thoughtful, almost severe.

"It's cold up here," he said.

"Yes."

"Do you want to talk?"

"No."

"Why are you looking at me like that?" he said in a dried-up voice. "Stop looking at me. I said I was sorry."

Tense, she answered, "I too am sorry." She felt bad tonight, sickened and bad, assaulted in some way she could not name. She said aloud, "Sorry neither of us has gotten any joy out of being wed."

"Don't presume to speak for me," he answered sharply. "You know nothing of what is in my heart."

"I'm stagnating," she said, but he ignored her. He took his bowl and went to sit on a chest, near the candle.

Pons said, "Don't talk to me of joy or love. You spurned my love." He twisted his face into the shadows. "A woman is supposed to love her lord, is she not? It was never anything but an ordeal for you. You should not have married me."

"What choice had I?" Sybille snapped. "I was raised to obey. It was not my choice."

"Come, lady. No one forced you. You might have said no."

"I should have," she muttered, draining the bowl.

He whacked his bowl against the chest. Leaning into the candle-light, he said, "Excuse me, it was you who would not lie with me."

Mine is the fault then, she thought.

"I wanted to give you pleasure. I tried, Sybille. You did not—react. Am I wrong?"

Which was true enough. She fell silent, thinking. Wanting to be fair, she grunted, "Well, I suppose I did not. What you say is correct, yes." No! some part of her screamed, not true.

He stood up and went around the chest to the shadows near the tapestry. She could hear him rustling; a boot dropped to the floor, then another. When he came back, he was wearing his nightshirt. He cuddled under the furs, staying at the far edge of the bed, and he said to her knowingly, "Sybille, I don't blame you. Some women—they are incapable of passion. Perhaps this occurs naturally in women born under the sign of the Virgin, I know not."

She believed not one word of it. "Aren't you going to blow out the candle?"

"It's about to gutter soon. Leave it."

"And so you think I'm one of those women? Is that what you're saying?" She squirmed to face him.

He said, "I believe so," and crossed his hands over his chest. "Obviously that is why it hasn't worked between us."

In the dark she felt her cheeks flush, felt something malignant swelling out of control inside her. She murmured very softly, very deliberately, "And yet I wonder, my lord. You speak of women who lack passion. What of men?" Her voice rose steadily. "What of those men who fail at being men? Mayhap that is true of males born under the sign of Scorpio. Men who act like wooden saints."

He shot upright.

"Or little stone gods. You preached to me. When I was in torment, when I would have fucked a goatherd, you said pray—"

"Lady, your language—"

She blasted over him. "—and you said everyone suffers. Wait until you die, it will get better." She was lying motionless on her back, yelling at the rafters. "I don't want a goddam god, I want—"

Pons's knuckles cracked.

"—a man!" She gasped for air. When next she peered at him, the corners of his mouth were defining reproach.

"Lady," he said stiffly, "that was discourteous."

Splendid. He could speak of discourtesy. After five years of wedded celibacy? She wanted to slap him. Instead, she repeated between her teeth, "I want a man."

Silence. The candle sucked itself out. Silence. In the blackness she turned away from him and burrowed her nose into the side of the pillow. Her feet were numb. Suddenly she heard him cry, "I love God! I love the sun and the trees. I love the stones!"

What of it, she spat silently. Am I less deserving than a stone? And what had he been doing all these years, Playing with it? Paying men to suck it behind the high hedges at Dalbade Church? She was not that ignorant, she knew about these things.

"I love the stars and the moon." He was whispering to himself on the other side of her pillow.

Oh, damn him. Why doesn't he stop? If he says one more word, she vowed, I will rise and move to another bed. But he did not speak again, and then he was snoring and the wind groaned around the roof of the keep. Once they had been friends, more than friends. When had that been?

In the morning Sybille sent for the village crier and gave him three sous to make the proclamation. Before he had yet crossed the moat, she could hear him singsonging, "William, lord of Astarac. Pray God for the dead—"

The sky was scummed the color of iron, and a forbidding wind hissed through the ward. Sick from lack of sleep, Sybille was still simmering over last night's quarrel, and later, when she went down to break her fast, she was relieved to find only two servingwomen.

One of them said to her, "Lord Pons told me to say he is in the chapel."

Sybille yawned. She took her bread and ale over to the hearth and listened to the women gossiping. Men had been summoned from the village to help rearrange the sarcophagi. It seemed there was a problem finding space for William. There are more Astaracs dead than alive, Sybille thought. The women were taking turns searching for nits. The older one began talking of De Montfort—he was marrying his eldest son, Amaury, to Beatritz of Burgundy, and now poor Beatritz must fornicate with a Frenchman. The other made a disgusted sound with her tongue. Sybille left and went out through the ward to the chapel.

For most of the morning she stood at the rear, watching the villeins sweat and shove the stone caskets around until her father's had been wedged into a space between his own father and his elder brother. At last the life-size marble effigy of William was levered over the casket. She swayed up to have a look. A stone man held a sword; a small dog curled at his feet. Choking back her dismay, she stared at the face. It might have been anyone. Pons came up to stand beside her.

Before she could speak, he said, "Lady, it's not a good likeness, is it?"

She kept her voice bland. "Wonderful likeness of the dog, whomever it may belong to. See what a mess. Hiring a local sculptor was stupid of me."

He patted her arm.

She smoothed a thumb slowly along the dog's back. Her father had detested small dogs of this kind. "Well," she said at last, "I suppose it's only fitting. He has no right to be here. God's little joke on secret suicides. Give them another man's face and a dog."

She could hear Pons sucking in his breath.

"Easy, lady—" he stammered. "I didn't say that."

She wheeled to face him. "No?" she hissed. "Either he took his life or he didn't. If he did, he's not entitled to lie in holy ground. Even a lapsed Catholic like you knows that." She was boiling.

Pons looked away. Finally he whispered, "To me this is not holy ground. No matter what he did he has a right to lie with his kin. So you had best keep your mouth shut."

She spun away and walked quickly to the back of the chapel.

The priest came. Gradually the chapel filled—neighboring castellans, villeins, the provost, William's rich nephew, Centulle. Pons came and escorted her up near the altar, where she stood, head bowed, staring at the dog. Midway through the prayers, her eyes began to tear from the incense. Good, she thought. People will think I'm weeping. Papa, forgive me. There's nothing I can do properly, remember?

Out in the ward, bonfires crackled and servants were thumping tuns of wine over the cobbles. After the mourners had filed outside, Sybille knelt at the head of the casket. When she got to her feet again, Pons was still there, his face sealed. They did not speak.

On the porch waited the priest, looking professionally sober. "My lady," he began sleekly, "let the lord of Astarac be received into paradise this day—"

She cut him off with an amen. The man's chasuble was dung-stained; she had not noticed it before.

"Begging your grace's pardon," the priest said, "but I was wondering, I've heard it said that Lord William left a legacy to our humble church. For a rose window, I believe."

"My lord priest," Pons replied quietly, "see the bailiff for your fee and get out of here."

Sybille and Pons moved down the passageway and slept together in William's big room. Douce had insisted, saying Pons was now lord of the house of Astarac.

"Fair son," she told him, "I consider you the legitimate heir of our domains. You are a fine lad and I can tell you candidly that I think of you as my own son. My lord whom I loved more than life itself has been called to the throne of heaven and rests in the arms of our Lord Jesus and Saint Peter and Saint—" Her small white hands fluttered at her throat. "God's will be done. The generations pass. I wish—I pray—our Lord grant my one desire before my heart stops beating. May I tell you frankly, my son, that I pray my daughter's womb be filled, so that our line will not die out."

This speech astonished Sybille. It was the first time Douce had acknowledged Pierre's death. And she would remember it for another reason, as the last words of any real sense that Douce spoke.

As for her mother's prayers, Pons did not misunderstand. Nor did Sybille. Of course, the houses of Astarac and Villeneuve must not end. Dynasties cannot be permitted to dribble away merely because a woman and a man do not desire one another. They had to lie together and make Douce happy.

One night, when Pons returned home long after darkness, Sybille was waiting in bed, determined. She got up and helped him pull off his boots. "Your toes are frozen," she said and began to massage them with both hands.

After a while he pulled off his clothes and she said quietly, "Have you had your supper?"

"Yes." He circled around and got under the coverlet, naked. She could feel his eyes on the back of her head. He said, "Blow out the candle."

In the dark the idea seemed possible.

"Do you love me?"

"Yes. Do you want to?"

"All right—if you want to."

"Kiss me."

She shut her eyes and turned toward him. When his mouth moved over hers, she tasted sour wine. He had been drinking. More than a little. She wound her arms around his back. There was nothing to this. In a few minutes it would be finished and the seed planted. Maybe. If nothing happens, she thought, I may have to do it again next month. A shutter banged somewhere below in the house. She thought of the pretty-faced knight she had passed in Rue des Nonnes that morning; he had stared, smiling, at her breasts, and she had turned away her face before she smiled back.

"Touch me."

The skin was silky, and she held it in one palm clumsily. Oh God, it's not supposed to be squashy. If it doesn't stand up stiff, all this is for naught. She held it against her thigh, brushing her fingertips up and down for a long time. What's wrong with him? she wondered.

He pushed her hand away and rolled on his back, and then abruptly he sat up.

"What—"

He said nothing, and then he said, "You were right. I can't please you."

She knew she should say something, but she did not know what. Eventually she put a smile in her voice. "Oh well," she said lightly, "it's just being churlish tonight. And that's that. It's got a mind of its own and—"

Pons made a sound in his nose.

"Corba once told me Raymond's gives him trouble some nights—it says neither boo nor bah. Well, there you are! No need to—"

"Stop it!"

She sat up and tried to peer into his face. "Pons, what's the matter?" The mattress shook under them. "Are you crying? Please don't cry, Pons."

He turned his face away.

"Let's go to sleep now. Please."

He whispered, sniffing, "I love your soul. God be my witness, I love your soul."

She rolled away. "My dear, I must sleep now," she told him. "I promised to go hawking with Corba in the morning." She sank into sleep and dreamed she was the third verse of a Bertran de Born song—she was a siege with lots of shields and crashing towers.

Before cockcrow she jerked awake because she sensed Pons bending over her. Startled, she opened her eyes.

"Sybille," Pons whispered, "I want you to have a lover. For your sake, find someone."

The room was black and shadowy with just a rim of light around the shutters. "What time is it?"

"Did you hear me?" he said. "That's what I want. I won't care. Do it." He began breathing faster. She closed her eyes, pretending she had not spoken.

"Take a lover," he repeated, pushing her shoulder. His voice was unfamiliar, and she breathed in his bitterness through every pore. "I'll help you. How about a priest or an abbot? A bishop? They are more lustful than other men. What do you say?"

Fully awake now, she hesitated. "Nothing. I say you're crazy." She added, hostile, "Go fuck a nun."

Silence. Then: "I have."

She could never have guessed that was coming, and she gasped. Was he joking? Lying? Somehow she did not think so. At last she said, "And anyone else?"

"Whores, a couple of villeins' daughters"—his tone was cold, flat, and it frightened her—"the cheesemaker at Blagnac, a widow in Pamiers who'd not had it for—" He went on, giving more examples, more details.

"Did you pay them?"

He paused before he answered, apparently wanting to be absolutely truthful. "Yes. Well, not the widow—Ava would have gladly paid me." He laughed.

Bit by bit the picture took shape. All these years he had been fucking fit to break his breeches. She told herself she did not care, she was past that. It was the ugliness of it that troubled her, the furtive, loveless mingling of genitals. Raising her voice, she said slowly, "I can't imagine the pleasure in that kind of dirty coupling with strangers."

"Dirty," he said. "No, I don't think so. It was pure, innocent. A business transaction that pleased both parties. I never removed my clothing."

Not even with the widow? She got out of bed and reached for her shift.

"Are you going to ring for Carenza?" he asked.

"In a minute." Suddenly she felt old and bitter-wise. In these days of upheaval people lacked honor. Even Pons. There was no one who would not betray you, given a chance. It was the invisible plague of her time.

"Please ask her to fetch me warm wine."

"Yes." She made herself turn toward the bed. He was lying on his side, eyes wide open. "This is what troubles me, my lord." She kept her voice level. "How is it that a Good Christian like yourself has committed the sin of the flesh so—promiscuously? Aren't you ashamed?"

He shrugged. "All fornicating is sin. With your wife, with a whore, it makes no difference. The sin is the same."

Indeed. His sophistry sickened her. Then sarcastically: "And on your deathbed the goodman will come and wipe out all those sins. So why worry about it?"

He did not answer.

Her burgundy gown was hanging on a wall hook near the door. She put it on, then slowly plaited her hair and fastened the ends with embroidered ribbons, without saying a word to Pons. She pulled open the door. "I'll send Carenza up."

"Warm wine."

"Warm wine," she echoed and went out.

"Lady Mother."

Douce's pale fingers teased nervously at the cittern on her knees.

"Mama, please listen."

Douce dipped her head, stubborn, and crashed out a furious chord. *"Love, have mercy! Let me not die so often—"*

Sybille got up and went over to the open window. "Come down to the garden. We can sit together under the cherry trees."

"For you could easily kill me outright, but instead—"

"Just this once," Sybille wheedled. "Spring has come. I promise you, you'll like it."

"For when my eyes laugh, my heart cries."

"Mama! Stop singing that song."

She spoke at last. "Why?"

Sybille turned and forced her voice to be patient. "I've told you. Nobody sings that anymore."

Sadness dewed Douce's eyes. She said, reproachful, "Folquet de Marseille is the greatest troubadour in the world and always will be."

"Folquet isn't a troubadour anymore, you know that."

"I know," she agreed. "He's a monk."

"No, Mama. He's bishop of Toulouse and he's a nasty man. Remember I explained it to you. He toadies to De Montfort."

Douce stared at her, aghast but adamant. "No, no." Her voice grew sulky. "I heard him sing at the château only the other day. He's the greatest—"

"Ai!" Sybille expelled a long sigh of agitation. Her mother had not stepped out of her room since the beginning of Lent, not even for mass. She said that whenever she crossed her threshold her head began to swim; surely she would fall down into a swoon. "Mama, come to the window and breathe. The air smells like flowers."

It was nearly nones. Clouds were piled soft in the sky, and along Rue St. Bernard the nectar of wild broom was blowing in the wind. At dawn she had smelled the scent of sweet springtime before she opened her eyes, and had guessed it was coming from beyond the Garonne, from St. Cyprien.

Douce tightened the string of her cittern. Without lifting her head, she said, "The count is a nice man. Only yesterday I heard him tell Lord Folquet—"

"No," Sybille broke in, "I doubt it was yesterday, Mama. The old count is at Narbonne."

"Eh?" Her mother was staring at her.

"Anyway, the old count is no longer count. The young count is." What was the good of explaining? She would not understand. "Raymond promised the pope's new ambassador he is giving up all his rights to young Raymond."

"Heavens," Douce murmured. "He's not yet fifty. Why did he do that?"

So that the pope would not hand over the county to De Montfort. But she did not say it because there was no point alarming her mother. She smiled. "Because he's a nice man, Mama."

Douce strummed her cittern and sang. *"When my eyes laugh—"*

Sybille glided out, closing the door gently behind her. She ran down to the yard and had Dolosa saddled. In Rue St. Bernard she turned right and right again, and rode out the Matabiau gate and past the leprosery, where she kicked the mare into a stiff canter. In the distance the spires of Saint-Etienne were snowcapped by clouds. In another month this road would be dust-dry.

The wind licking her face, she pounded by the Montgaillard gate and into the Count's Meadow. There were the fat green oaks where William had taken her and Fabrisse for their first riding lessons, where Pierre and Mathieu and another boy whose name she had forgotten had teased them and pelted pebbles to make their ponies bolt, until William had told them finally that was not intelligent behavior. Oh, Papa, not intelligent! Wherever you are now, Papa, I can tell you frankly, you should have beaten them.

At the Narbonne gate she reined Dolosa to a walk and started down the crowded Rue d'Alfaro, dodging pedestrians, going back toward the faubourg. Still thinking of her father, she smiled to remember a pasty shop beyond Saint-Geraud where he had always bought them treats. Surely, after so many years, it could not still be there. But if it is, she promised herself, I shall stop.

It was easy to miss, a tiny place squeezed in between an alehouse and a fancy shoemaker with boots displayed on racks. But there were the same trays of flaky dough, the same sign listing the twenty different fillings. Sybille jumped down and noosed the reins to a post. Mouth already watering, she smiled at the pasty girl and pointed. "One eel, one ham, two cheese and mushroom—"

Halfway through her ordering, she remembered she had no money. "Little friend," she called to the girl, "I've come away without my purse. Tell me how much I owe and I'll send my maid around tomorrow."

The girl hesitated. Finally she shook her head and spoke politely about her mother and the bad temper she had and of the beating she could anticipate.

Sybille frowned. It was only a few deniers, did the girl take her for a cheat? Behind her, a man's voice rumbled, "Go on, give them to her. I'll pay."

She swung around, preparing a grateful smile. She squinted, started, and then she said, "It's you."

He stared back, eyes remote, unsmiling. "Olivier is my name."

"Yes. Olivier. I remember."

He did not bow to her, merely dug into his girdle for the coins and flung them on the counter without saying a word. He was not the most courteous man she had ever met, she thought. Nevertheless, she looked up at him through her lashes, posturing, and said, "Permit me to thank you, fair knight. I see I must be in your debt once again." Even to herself she sounded fraudulent, and she bit hastily into a ham pasty.

"Your lord husband has recovered?" Olivier asked in his cool voice.

She leaned up against the counter, chewing nervously. "Yes. Of course. Are you wed?" The last words had sprung from nowhere, and she flushed beet-colored to the roots of her hair and cursed herself for having not thought before she spoke.

He laughed out loud.

"God's pardon," she stammered. "That was—I really don't know why I—" She could feel the pasty plummeting like an anchor stone to her stomach, and she stared down at her feet. When she lifted her head, he was still grinning broadly.

"Sweet Christ, not me. No, lady, I'm a bachelor." He laughed again, and all of a sudden he stopped and gazed down, meeting her eyes with a boldness that alarmed her.

"I wish," she said sharply, "that I had not said that."

"I'm sure you do."

She turned back to the counter and to eating the rest of the pasties. She did not want them; they were making her feel sick. The pasty girl wiped her hands on a red cloth. Two men with yellow skin, who looked like Arabs or Chinamen, stumbled out of the alehouse and stood there yawning before venturing into the stream of traffic. After several minutes had passed, she heard Olivier say, voice low, "Will your husband be home this evening?"

For a moment she hesitated. "I don't think so. Why?"

He said, "I want to come to your house."

Her throat tensed. "What do you want of me?"

"I like you. I want to sleep with you." His tone was steady, expressionless, and he rammed the words together, one close on the heels of the next. *Ilikeyouiwanttosleepwithyou.*

She turned slowly. He was rubbing his jaw with the back of his hand. She said, "All right," as if it were usual to hear a man say he wanted to sleep with her. She flapped over to her mare, mounted, and jolted off up the street without glancing back.

The hall was quiet now that Carenza had left the tray of wine and cakes, and they sat running their eyes over each other, alert and suspicious. Sybille was thinking, His eyes are magnificent. They are deep lavender-blue, almost as dark as grapes. And he has a fine voice, deep and sensual. I like listening to it.

But the beauty of his eyes and voice was not the whole of her attraction to the knight. It was at once more complicated and more simple than that. He was nothing less than dream made flesh, her picture of the completely masculine male. To her, he appeared to be every knight in every popular romance and *canso* she had ever heard or read. Even his name—Olivier—came straight from the *Chanson de Roland,* with its images of acceptably heroic men.

The sound of the knight's voice broke into her thoughts. "Lady," he said timidly, "I've never loved a woman. I'm—unable to love."

Impatient, she shrugged away his words. "It doesn't matter," she told him quickly. "I've never loved either. It doesn't happen every day, you know." When he did not respond, she grew a bit alarmed and demanded, "Do you mean you refuse to abide by the rules of chivalry? Do you object to placing your heart and soul in jeopardy for me?"

Olivier seemed to hesitate, but then he said, "I didn't say that."

The compline bell had rung. She worried lest Olivier still be there when Pons returned. She said to him, "Please say what you do think then."

He leaned forward in the high-backed chair. The firelight spilled a red-orange frost across the side of his face and the hand holding the goblet. "I'm not as backward as you seem to imagine," he said stiffly. "I understand the rules of courtly love. As I told you a few minutes ago, I'm willing to serve you in any way you wish. I'll do whatever you ask."

He went on, insisting that of course he would treat her with respect and adoration. But the faint playfulness of his voice disturbed her. He seemed to sense how irresistible she found him and how badly she wanted him as her lover.

"One more thing," he said. "What was that last rule you mentioned? It's left my memory already."

She groaned under her breath. Was he deliberately trying to exasperate her? She thought, This knight is shrewd. He guesses I won't refuse him, that I would throw away all the rules of love in order to have him. With an effort she said, "The last rule is that in no way shall you exceed my desires."

He nodded. Then he asked solemnly, "What does that mean?"

She was beginning to fume. "You may not do anything to me without my permission." She took a little breath and added, "No matter how much you want to. You may not so much as touch the hem of my gown if I do not see fit to grant it." She knew he was amused by the stern tone of her words. But he must be made to understand what was expected of him. Watching him gulp his wine, she quickly began to list the qualities of a true lover: fidelity, humility, discretion, patience. Above all, self-control. And of course on no account must she be dishonored or exposed to scandal.

He frowned. "I must keep this secret?"

"In God's name," she shouted, "have you forgotten I have a husband?" A man who could not keep a secret could not be a lover. She bounced to her feet and began shuttling between the hearth and the chairs. "And listen, my friend, have you had no mother to tell you these simple things?"

"I do not," Olivier growled, "have a mother."

"Well," she snapped, "you must have had one once." He looked down at his knees, and immediately she felt ashamed and softened her tone. "Who are your kin? Where is your father's fief?"

Olivier looked flustered. "I have no father," he said more brusquely than she thought necessary. "And he had no fief."

Sybille stopped and came over beside his chair. He smelled of soap. Come on, sir knight, she thought. Do you expect me to believe that? She waited, but he offered nothing more. She murmured, "If you truly desire me—"

"I do," he said, turning. "I'm sorry, lady. But there is nothing of interest to tell. I'm a ward of the count's. My lady mother died giving me life. She was one of Countess Joanna's ladies." Olivier's lips closed.

"All right," she said. "What happened to your father?"

"He died."

"How?"

"Dicing."

"I don't understand," Sybille said.

"You don't understand a man getting killed in a game of chance? It happens all the time."

"I suppose. It seems odd to me. But did he not—?"

"Nothing. Not one acre. You understand?"

"Yes," said Sybille. This man was hiding something. He donated information like a miser handed out alms. She went around behind his chair and got the dish of cakes and held it out. He shook his head. After she had taken the cakes back to the trestle, she walked over to her chair, nervous. The wine was making her head ache. She flopped down and said, "It's getting late."

His fingers twisted around the stem of the empty goblet. The nails were caked with dirt. "You agree to have me?" he asked abruptly.

Staring into the fire, she murmured, "Better no lover than one who scoffs at refined love."

He laughed. "But lady, haven't I agreed to every condition you set? I promised to worship you." His eyes were setting off sparks. "I told you I'm yours, to give away or sell or burn or hang. What more do you want?"

She began to breathe hard but said nothing. Your tongue agreed, she thought. Not your heart.

Olivier stretched back in the chair, as comfortable as though it were his own hall. "One further point," he said, conversational. "According to the rules of courtly love—"

Sybille nodded, grim.

"—when a woman freely loves a man, should she not ask of him exactly what she is willing to give?" He thrust out his jaw. "Between two friends, neither one should rule."

"What!" she flung into his face. "Don't you believe a lover should do his lady's bidding?"

"Absolutely," he said quickly and smiled. "But within the bounds of common sense. He should treat her as a friend. And she should behave likewise."

Sybille's lips ground into a frown. This was making her furious. What he argued was subtle, despicable.

In the street below, somebody began to bawl in a thin voice, "Alamanda, Ala—man—daaaa." After the second "Alamanda," Sybille set her teeth together and tried to shut her ears. Olivier was searching her face from the corner of his eye. The calling threaded away.

"Drunks," Sybille said. "There are drunks in Rue St. Bernard."

"There are drunks everywhere." Then he said, "Love should be one joy between two hearts. Don't you think it's unfair for the woman to be higher than the man?"

Sybille cupped her hand over her chin. She would think that when the Garonne flowed into the Rhine. Women were not equal to men. They were better. She said evenly, "Olivier de Ferrand, here's what I think. When a suitor seeks a lady's favor, he should get down on his knees and join together his hands and say, 'Grant that I may freely serve you as your man.' Those are the proper words. If a man is a woman's servant, how can he also be her equal?" She said to herself, Let him sift that over.

Olivier was silent, motionless. Then he lifted his head and he said, "Is that your answer?"

"I didn't seek you out," she said, unrelenting. "Did I tell you I like you? I want to— The choice is yours." She stood, wishing he would leave so she could go upstairs to cry.

Hauling himself to his feet, he came forward a little. Suddenly, like a cypress toppling indignant in a mistral, he crashed to the floor on one knee.

A tremor arced down Sybille's spine. At her feet she heard him muttering as if to himself, and she stared down.

"Very well then," he whispered and lowered his neck over his bended knee. "Let me serve and love you always. As your man." He raised his voice. "And may God hear me."

She smiled.

Sybille went the next morning to the town house of the De Perellas. Corba, pregnant again, was entertaining, and her bedchamber on the topmost floor was crowded with heretic women sipping sherbets and chattering of De Montfort and Rome. All morning long Sybille glued on a polite smile and waited, restless. Toward noon, after the door had shut on the last guest, she said to Corba, "Friend, I must seek your counsel in a matter of great importance."

Corba kept silent.

"A certain knight has shown his regard for me. What should I do? My thoughts are full of disorder and I want your advice."

Corba gave a smile of surprise. "I'll ask you this," she said. "Have you set your mind to loving this man?"

Sybille sat down on a cushioned bench at the window. Three stories below, she could see the cloister of Daurade, a bowl of velvety green. After a moment she said to Corba doubtfully, "I think so."

"I suppose he understands the laws of courtly love."

He did now. "Yes."

"And he will pledge himself to the cause of perfect love?" Corba leaned forward, looking moderately excited.

"Friend, he claims so but"—she sighed and clicked her teeth—"I greatly fear it is only lust speaking. He's not suffering, that is obvious. He does not die for love of me. He even told me he can't love."

Awkwardly Corba rose and came over to sit beside Sybille in the window. The two women fell silent, both watching a monk slowly pull weeds from the edge of a gravel path and lay them in a basket. Corba murmured, "They all say they can't love. From my knowledge of these matters, most men do not love at once. You must teach him to love you. Then he will want to suffer and die for you." She added with deliberate severity, "How can you train him if you yourself have not yet learned patience?"

Sybille hung on the words. Corba was right. Olivier had to be taught, and she would be his instructor. She must not expect miracles. But she sighed and sighed again until Corba could see she had already put herself in the fire.

"Describe him to me," she said gently.

"He is—his beauty is like the star that raises up the dawn."

"Naturally."

"And yet"—she looked away—"he is not free of imperfection. This one shall require a fair amount of effort." In truth, she was not as unhappy about Olivier's deficiencies as she sounded. An unflawed man would have bored her.

The door opened and a maid came in to clear away the sherbet cups. Sybille pivoted her neck and stared into the cloister. The monk, pate like polished stone, was still weeding. Corba said nothing more until the servant had gone out. Then she told Sybille, "Your knight has permission to call on me. Once I've spoken with him, I will give you my candid opinion as to whether he deserves the honor of your love."

Sybille glanced back, uncertain. And what, she wondered, if he is found wanting? For God's love, what will I do then? I will die. No, I will take him anyway. But she replied, "My friend, I will gladly abide by your judgment." She turned and sat with her head bent over the window ledge. The monk was getting to his feet. He snatched up the basket, walked a half-dozen paces up the path, and set it down. He knelt. Sybille cleared her throat. "Suppose this knight proves true and faithful."

Corba smoothed her gown over her rounding belly.

"And just suppose I decide he is worthy of me. I know of no private place where we might enjoy each other." God knew such a thing could never take place in Rue St. Bernard.

"Perhaps the knight has—"

"He owns no house of his own," she said, not turning.

Corba's voice was thoughtful. "I don't see why you couldn't come here. We will have left for Montségur by Lammas." She paused. "But three months is a long time to wait."

She nodded, although she was thinking it was plenty of time. It might take as long as six months before Olivier de Ferrand learned to love her. She said aloud, "Don't the monks mind people watching them?"

Chapter Seven

On Good Friday Beatritz d'Astarac died. A goodman traveling west from Fanjeaux delivered the news to Sybille, and he said her grandmother had asked for the *consolamentum*. Sybille wanted to tell her mother, but Pons and Fabrisse, even Corba, argued against it, and in the end she agreed not to speak of it. The truth was, she was as bare of grief as her naked hand and could think of nothing but Olivier de Ferrand. All during the first week of May, Olivier appeared in Rue St. Bernard. Each evening after compline, he stationed himself across the road near Brune Maurand's gate and squinted up as if he were waiting for rain. In her shift Sybille padded softly into Douce's darkened chamber and watched. She wanted him to stand there forever drenched in flakes of moonlight. Beautiful, she murmured, beautiful above the most beautiful are you. She wondered what he was thinking.

On the eighth night of his vigil, intrigued, she sent Carenza to ask how long he was going to keep this up. She stooped at Douce's casement and peered at them talking. The slant of Carenza's white gown blurred back and forth in the shadows a long time. When she saw the girl finally jogging across the road, she rushed downstairs, palms clammy.

"He says you've bewitched him." The girl was breathless with the excitement of it. "Lady, he wants you to come down and I told him I was sure you wouldn't and he said— He's pretty, isn't he?"

Sybille clutched her arm. "Blessed Mary's son! Stop gabbling and start at the start."

"Why are you yelling at me? I'm trying to tell you." Sybille pressed her lips. "He wants to speak with you. If you don't come down, tomorrow he's going to bring his lute and sing."

That might cause trouble, she thought. People in the street would not necessarily assume he was courting her. But they might.

"Lady, he said to tell you—he has no talent for singing. His voice cracks and he mangles even the simplest song. And besides he feels a head cold coming on."

Sybille asked sharply, "Was he smiling when he said that?"

"Smiling?" Carenza echoed gravely. "I don't think so. You wouldn't believe the questions he asked. He would have kept me there all night."

Next morning Sybille sent Carenza to the château. She was to give Olivier no particular message, but at some point she was to mention, as if accidentally, that her mistress might be praying in Saint-Etienne around terce. Sybille was careful to select a church where she was not known.

Midafternoon, she anointed herself with Douce's costliest lavender and rode into the city. She kept Dolosa to a slow walk, not wanting to get there too early, but all the same he was not there when she arrived. Inside the sanctuary the stone walls breathed mildew. Near the altar rail, a party of pilgrims was lighting candles and keeping up a noisy chatter about the reliquaries. Wearily, Sybille knelt and bowed her head, pretending to pray.

After five or six minutes, she heard boots clopping on the paving stones behind her; they moved closer, then stopped. I'm not going to turn around, she decided, and began a paternoster. She heard him pitch to the ground.

Suddenly, at her ear, he wheezed, fierce, "You have the heart of a dragon."

Her chin jerked up.

"It's clear enough," he said, "that you care nothing for me. For a fortnight you've made me hope and hang around that damned street liked a beggar." He was taking great gulping breaths.

"I don't know what you're talking about." She bristled at him over her shoulder. "I made you do no such thing." She eased back on her heels, uncertain whether to feel amused or annoyed. She detected, below the complaints, a swell of suffering in the gulping voice. Splendid, she thought. Tell me more.

"I promised to serve you with a faithful heart, but what have I had from you?" She heard him gather his breath. "A few minutes with your maid. That's what I've had of you and not another thing."

"After all—"

"Not even a bit of ribbon have you given me," he rasped.

"Ah, sir knight," she called softly, "you haven't learned your lessons." Her chin was shaking with laughter. "Remember patience? Remember self-restraint?"

He gave a choked curse. "Go on, laugh at me if it makes you feel good. You prove your cruelty."

"I wish you no harm," she said, taken back.

"You want to crucify me!" he cried.

Sybille faced him for the first time. His eyes were open wide, his mouth was clenching and unclenching, lunging at air. She saw he was afraid and swiveled her head forward again.

"Tell me what deeds will satisfy you, lady. What would you have me do?" The whistling of his breath scalded her ears. "Burn Avignon? Assassinate De Montfort? How about slaying a dragon? Name it."

She sat up straight and fixed her eyes on the altar candles. Finally she said, "Olivier de Ferrand, I will tell you what I want you to do, since you asked." She breathed deeply. "Love me."

For a little while they sat quietly in the semidark. The pilgrims were weaving up the side of the cathedral, gawking at the discolored saints. The hum of Olivier's painful breathing seemed to fill the nave; it sounded as though he were strangling. For a few moments Sybille tried breathing at his pace, until the effort made her chest burn and she had to slow down.

After some moments had passed, Olivier said, "You have beautiful eyes, Sybille."

"I get them from my mother."

"And your face too?"

"No." Not from my mother, she thought. No woman in the world could equal her beauty.

He reached out and touched her shoulder with his fingertips. She felt waves so innocent, so gentle, move unendingly through his flesh and blood into hers, and she sat very still. I want to hold him in my bare arms, she thought. My body I will give him for a pillow.

"I resemble my father," Olivier said. "Damn him."

Sybille stiffened. "Don't curse the dead."

"It doesn't bother him."

"He left you no portion," Sybille said. "Is that a reason to hate him?"

"What is hate, lady? I've hated you all week and you make me happy." She noticed he was breathing normally. The panting sound was gone.

Sybille groped around and caught his fingers and laced them, motherly. The pilgrims had gone and the shell of stone was silent except for the creaking of the spider webs.

He said, "What could he give me? He was a monk." She twisted, gaped, but he avoided her eyes. "It's true. But he had no taste for the cloister. His craving was for the illegal."

Sybille said, "And you are one of his crimes?"

"The hell with him," Olivier said to her and laughed unpleasantly. "I don't think of it. There is enough to cry about now without thinking of that booby." He laughed again.

Sybille let go his hand. His face had changed. She smoothed down the skirt of her gown. Eventually she said, "It's late."

Limbs numb, she labored up unsteadily, and Olivier scrambled after her. Their feet inched down the nave. Outside, in the sun, she peeked at him. His garments, she noticed, gave off a sense of disorder. The embroidered shirt was faded and soiled, the breeches wrinkled. The colors did not go well together. Olivier was talking about the old count. Raymond, sweet Raymond, had promised him a fief, some small spot in the world to call his own. He would have fresh air in summer, he told Sybille; in winter his fire would roar. He hated being poor, he had been poor too long—his mouth was so full of envy his breath stank. But now noble Raymond would sweeten everything.

She let him ramble on. He was full of hope and happiness and his mind was far away.

"To the Noble Lady Sybille d'Astarac, his dearly beloved lady, from Olivier de Ferrand, her true friend and vassal.

"I am bored to my very marrow here, even though I am surrounded by many comrades and friends and this is supposed to be a rich court. This morning it does not really seem like summer. It rains hard and everyone is quarreling worse than death, about nothing. We get meat cooked hard, almost cremated, and a lot of water drowned in a little bit of wine. And I will tell you what bothers me most: I am always sleepy and cannot sleep. Right now I can do nothing but recite complaints and get on everyone's nerves. Why? Do not ask.

"Sometimes I think about what I would tell you, if I were near enough. And sometimes the thought of you terrifies me, because you force me to suffer and you rob me of my reason. I walk around dying. Are you doing this to me for your pleasure or to torture me? Do you want me to give up?

"Tomorrow to Tarascon. They are going to teach me how to build a mangonel.

"My lady, it's been a good two months—a thousand thousand years to me—since you promised to consider giving me what I long for most. You can do as you please. But in God's name, I ask you for an answer to this: How will it all turn out?

"Fare you well. God bless you today and every day. Written at Foix this third day of June in the year of our Lord, 1214."

In the July heat no one cared to remain in Toulouse if they had some cooler place to go. The De Perellas left for their castle in the mountains, taking Fabrisse with them. Pons was making collections in Albi for the church, and once a week he came home with his saddlebags stuffed with sous and livres tournois. It worried Sybille that he carried so much money, that he seemed oblivious to the dangers of being murdered by some bandit who would not stop to distinguish between God's money and Pons's.

One day seemed little different than the next to her. The windows in the hall had to be kept closed because of the stench from the street, and each morning she had the servingwomen burn spices to perfume the air. The rest of the morning she drowsed away in Douce's room, listening to her play the cittern and talk idly of her girlhood in the Limousin when she had first met William d'Astarac. To this she was required to say nothing, only nod at appropriate intervals.

Sluggish, Sybille went into William's library and reread Olivier's letters. By now she knew them from memory. Progressively his tone had grown more anguished, more irritable, until she had stopped taking pleasure in his distress and began to worry. He sounded as if he were beginning to hate her. Finally, after a good deal of hesitation, she risked a stiff note, merely observing that he could not blame her for the fact of his being in Foix. If he were going mad to see her, as he claimed, he had only to ask the count's permission to leave.

She had no word after that. Perhaps Olivier was finished with her.

He might well have found a woman in Foix, the court must be swarming with them, and perhaps his vow of fidelity was worthless as a plucked chicken. She decided he did not love her, despite his piteous letters. Then, there was something else to consider: Did she love him? And that question made her even more uneasy.

What she liked about him were the things her eyes could see. And her ears could hear, because no man alive had a voice like his. Still, only a lunatic would love a man for his voice. She thought, Don't be so big a fool, Sybille, as to imagine that a woman's passion is anything more than the cry of the flesh. All you want of him is his body and that is exactly what he desires of you. So she told herself, but she did not entirely believe it. With these troublesome thoughts she struggled day after day, until she had exhausted herself.

Two days before Lammas, while she was coaxing her mother to eat a little of her dinner, Florent brought up a letter sealed with gobs of red wax. A boy waited in the yard for a reply. In the passageway she broke open the seal and read the spidery handwriting. Olivier's message could not have been more bloodless: He was home. He wished to see her, if she wished to see him. That was all. She went into her room, giddy, with Florent at her heels. On the parchment, below Olivier's words, she wrote: "I refuse to play this game any longer. Are you ready for the final test?" Florent stood gazing into the corner. She resealed the letter with purple wax and handed it to the gatekeeper without a word.

In Corba's chamber Sybille lay on the curtain-hung bed like cold marble. Olivier was talking in a deep, cool voice. On a chest a candle brooded; a light wind snapped the curtains and the sky outside the window was cracked with flashes of lightning. Neither restless nor impatient, he spoke quietly of a colt he had acquired in the mountains, of a Catalan troubadour he had heard sing at Pamiers. It seemed to Sybille he might have been speaking to anyone, to an abbess, so starchy was his manner.

She listened, smiled at his shadow swooping languidly on the wall, and thought he was taller than she remembered, and thinner.

After some fifteen minutes had gone by, he said abruptly, "What would you have me do?"

"I'll tell you," she answered promptly. "It's going to storm and anyway I must be home before matins." She patted the coverlet next to her side. "Poor Olivier. You look like you're about to be executed."

Quickly he came to her and knelt on the edge of the bed, facing her. His face was in shadow, but the candlelight slashed at his hair, a blizzard of filmy gold. He said, "I wish—" and stopped, looking down at her.

She lifted both arms and stretched him down until his lips were brushing her mouth, then she squeezed shut her eyes. Her fingers fluttered shyly on the nape of his neck. He clung to her mouth; she felt the flesh all over her body begin to hurl up dampness. Unable to help herself, she moaned against his tongue. Then she pushed him away, tingling, and opened her eyes. He was smiling.

"I would like to hold you," he said. "What do the rules of chivalry have to say about that?"

She swallowed, her mouth still full of the taste of his tongue. "You may lie next to me and hold me. But that's all. And don't try to kiss me again."

"Why?" he asked, stretching out comfortably. "Didn't you like it?"

She turned her head on the pillow to meet his eyes. "No," she lied.

Still smiling, he reached one arm lightly around her waist. "Your mouth gave a different answer." There was a touch of mockery in his voice that made her uneasy.

"If it did," she said quickly, "it would not be wise of you to mention it, would it?"

His smile blurred away and he nodded. "You're right. That was the wrong thing to say."

"And you were wrong about my liking it. I didn't." She could see he was already cocky and sure of her, and that was her fault. She thought, I must make more of an effort to cool myself. But, God knows, this is hard.

He lay silent a long while, covering his eyes with one fist, not moving.

She threw at him, challenging: "You may touch my breast, if you wish. But if you don't feel able—"

He groaned into the pillow. "Please, lady," he said, "this is agony." She could hardly hear him.

"It's not supposed to be easy. Try." She was afraid to push him beyond his limits and spoil everything. A moment later he was scrabbling with hungry fingertips and she twined her fingers over his, gentling him.

He stroked and stroked. Then, in a rush, he said, "When I was eight, my father got knifed down at Bazacle and they took his body back to Lézat and dumped it outside the gate. Because that was where he belonged, wasn't it? Yes, indeed it was. Rarely seen there, but that was where he belonged. Oh, what's this? Our old friend Brother Pierre. No, couldn't be Brother Pierre—he's busy diddling all the court ladies. Hold your noses, brothers. Because it was a hot summer, I mean very hot, and pretty soon Brother Pierre was not smelling like a rose. Smelling like other things, yes, but not a rose. One of the other pages—a real friend he was—he took me over to Lézat to see it. Hie, bastard-boy, have I got something to show you. Surprise, surprise. So I got sick and had nightmares and that is when I decided to— Lady—." He stopped.

She touched his cheek, not looking at him.

"Lady," he whispered, "we could give each other great joy."

"Yes."

"You can do whatever you want with me. Whatever pleases you. I promise."

"You swear it?" She raised up to face him. "Would you sleep with me naked but not touch me? Would you promise that if I asked it?"

He squinted at her, thinking it through. She waited. And then he shook his head. "Oaths," he said cautiously, "should have meaning. If I saw you naked, I wouldn't be able to keep from touching. Lady, I can't swear it. I know that's the wrong answer but—"

Deliberately she turned her face into the shadows. Oh no, my friend, she thought. That is the right answer. I do not want a lover whose oath is meaningless. He was watching her. She said, "Let's not mince words. If I were to mingle my body with yours—what shall I do if I become pregnant? I would be lost."

Olivier said, "I would not want to give you a baby. Not as long as your husband is alive. He would be shamed." He added, earnest, "If you had no husband, I'd be quite willing to give you one."

Sybille heaved her legs over the side of the bed and stood upright. "Olivier," she said over her shoulder, "do you know how not to give me a baby?" She went toward the door, knowing his answer before he spoke.

She heard him mutter, "No." He staggered to his feet. "Lady, you're going already?"

"Bring the candle," she instructed. "I don't want to break my legs on the stairs."

He picked up the taper and she followed. When they got down to the yard, she veiled her face with the edge of her wimple and ran toward Florent and the horses. The air was succulent with droplets of waterless rain, and by the wall the leaves of the pear trees were twisting their backs to the wind. Behind her, Olivier was breathing heavily. "But you've given me no answer!" he cried.

She frowned, angry that he should speak in front of Florent.

"Lady!" Anxiety seeded his voice.

She did not turn her head. As she rode out the gate, he was shouting, "Why are you crucifying me?" and his railing circled in her ears all the endless way home.

In Rue St. Bernard the torch outside the Astarac gate burned like a mirage. As she gave the reins to a groom, she heard him say quietly, "The master came in a little while ago." He said something else, but she could not hear the words for the taste of Olivier pounding in her blood.

When she opened the door of their chamber, Pons was sitting there against the bed cushions, writing on his knees. He tilted up his eyes at her. He said, "I've added these bloody numbers twice and can't get the same figure."

"Wait until morning," she told him. "Your head will be clearer. Did you ride far today?"

"No. From Grisolles. Should we put out the light? It's past matins."

"You aren't ready to sleep yet, are you?"

"I'm a little tired," he said.

"All right. Wait till I braid my hair."

She went alone to the midwife's, pulled her veil up over her nose, and sat down on a bench in the solar opposite another veiled customer whose eyes she avoided. Under the silk her face began to sweat. The woman said, "Has sext rung yet, do you know?"

Numbly Sybille shook her head. The air in the solar was stale and sweltering. She wanted a drink. The minutes crept by. Abruptly the other woman got to her feet and tottered to the door. When at last Na Jacotte came in, Sybille was alone in the room and stated her business without hesitation. The midwife nodded at once and disappeared into a back room. Sybille sat quietly. The smell of herbs stewing somewhere in the house sickened her.

Returning, the midwife showed Sybille a queerly shaped object dangling on the end of a string. Sybille held it in her palm, studying it from all angles. Then she brought it to her nose and sniffed, but through the veil got nothing. Some kind of poultice, she decided. Finally she said, "What's in it?"

"Secret herbs, lady. Gathered by the dark of the moon."

Sybille nodded. "What herbs?"

"Consecrated by Hecate, the dispenser of all justice."

"I will pay you double," she said smoothly, "if you name them."

Na Jacotte hesitated for only a moment. "Comfrey, yarrow, rennet of hare." She shrugged.

Satisfied, Sybille rolled the poultice over her palm. "And what," she asked briskly, "does one do with this magic?"

The midwife assumed a professional tone. "Before your lover lies upon you, you must tie it around your neck. Or—" With the end of her wimple she swiped the sweat from under her chin.

Sybille waited.

"Or you can place it in the opening of your womb."

"I see. Which is better? In your opinion."

Shrugging again, the midwife said, "Your grace, it does not much matter. Some say in the womb makes more powerful magic. But it makes no difference. I assure you, lady."

Rubbing her chin, Sybille said casually, "In case of failure, you know of—other remedies?"

"Of course, lady. Others."

Ah God, she thought, how easily I concoct my own sins. Hastily she stuffed the poultice into her girdle, paid, and walked home through the puddles. Sybille allowed two more days to pass before sending Carenza to the château with a note simply stating the De Perella house and giving a date and time.

In the cloister of Daurade, on a stone bench, sat an old monk turning soundlessly the pages of his psalter and waiting for the evening bell. Through the vespers air a scream suddenly drove down like a nail, penetrating through the emerald and sard stillness. The monk stopped midsentence and tipped up his head, aghast, listening to the earthbound walls reverberate.

Then he turned his face away. God had passed by.

Douce stroked her cittern and sang the songs of Bernart de Ventadorn. Each morning she dressed and then made music. At noon, limp, she fell back into her tented bed. The lazy afternoons spun themselves out, while Sybille watched her mother from the window seat and ate pears from a silver bowl. She imagined lying undressed with Olivier. Behind her head, the moted sunlight bleached to galaxies of shadow. There was no need to talk or think.

Those end-of-summer days bled away in remembrance and expectation. The only hours real to Sybille were the ones she spent with Olivier; the rest did not matter. Around her the life of the house went on as usual. Frequently Pons was away; Fabrisse studied the gospels and went off to prayer meetings with her heretic friends. Their comings and goings interested Sybille not at all. Those dreary people, she thought.

Nights were cooler now. The fall quarterday arrived, and the De Perellas were back from Montségur. Olivier moved out of the château and found a cottage across the river on St. Cyprien, just the other end of the Bazacle bridge. Sybille felt pleased because she had not suggested it.

Olivier's new home was a slapdash place with a miniature hall and a bedchamber barely large enough for the featherbed he never straightened. There was a small kitchen and a patch of garden at the back. He bought kettles and red napkins and mousetraps. Sometimes he prepared supper for the two of them. In the kitchen fragrant with oil, Sybille sat with folded hands and watched him chop garlic and tomatoes. The sight of her lover cooking for her filled her with delight.

"Lazy wretch," he called over his shoulder. "I slave like a woman while you watch."

She chuckled, never taking her eyes from his tall frame stooped over the fire. Hand on hip, he stirred and sniffed and tasted. When the stew was done, he carried it to the trestle and served her. After the first bite she would rush to praise him. "Very fine!" she cried, although Olivier did not cook all that well. "My lord, you're a superb cook."

"Yes, aren't I?" he would burst out boastfully when a simple "thank you" would have sufficed, and his whole face would flush rosy with pride.

Sybille could not help noticing that some of his habits were as coarse as a villein's. He ate too quickly—his bowl would be empty before she had taken three bites—and his table manners could only be called piggish. Which surprised her because he had been raised at court and obviously knew what good manners were.

Once when he belched noisily at table and did not apologize, she asked him why he had done that.

"Oh," Olivier answered gravely, "to annoy you."

Uneasy, she pushed away his words as if he had not spoken and got up to wash the bowls. In the kitchen she chattered exuberantly, told him he was exceptional, rattled on and on about his voice, the cleft in his chin, his unearthly eyes. He sat silent in the other room while she elevated him to godhood and beyond. "My sweet, my joy, angel mine," she called to him, as if she were God spattering raindrops. Such expressions did not flow easily from Olivier's tongue; they did not flow at all, actually. It was some time, however, before Sybille noticed. Why does he hold back? she wondered, and she teased him about the Almighty making tongues for talking.

"Do horses speak?" he grunted. "Do dogs? Tongues were made for lapping."

She frowned and made no answer. Olivier's unpredictable moods baffled her. Sometimes, animated, he would bring his helmet and shield into the hall and spend the afternoon polishing them and talking. Then he was almost incapable of being still, and when he did manage it for a few minutes would jump up again immediately.

In the other mood he drenched himself in inertia, almost a kind of paralysis, it seemed to Sybille. "It's time for a rest," was his way of announcing the onset of his malaise. Before the hearth he stretched out full-length on his back like a corpse and pulled up his shirt. One palm doming his eyes, he jabbed his right thumb into his navel. Sybille, entertained, asked him why, and he said he had to keep his belly button warm, didn't he? He lay there motionless for long hours. Sybille knew he was awake because he spoke to her occasionally. Time, he lamented, spins by so quickly and before he knew it he would be dead. Sybille sat meekly at his feet, singing *cansos* under her breath and pretending patience. She wondered if she bored him. After an hour she suggested it would be amusing to go hawking. "Yes," he groaned, eyes closed. "Let's do that." But he did not stir.

Sybille told herself she had small experience with men; she must consider herself an apprentice and learn about them, be tolerant of Olivier's odd ways. Even so, he was wholly unlike other men and she sensed it from the beginning. His low opinion of himself—she could have sworn he despised himself—she attributed to the fact of his being a bastard and an orphan. And that he resented terribly his lack of position and felt angry about it was also apparent to her. He whined and complained to excess, seemed chronically unhappy with his life. Poor sad-eyed Olivier, child of shame. I must be understanding, she decided. It's not his fault. She found herself constantly winnowing his miseries, scouring her brain for causes and cures. As the weeks went by, she grasped that saving his soul would be no easy trick. He successfully resisted salvation.

And yet all her strainings to enter him were predicated on simplistic interpretations. The truth was, he defied both entry and explanation, but this she was unwilling to acknowledge fully. She did not imagine either that in crusading for Olivier's soul she might misplace her own.

One night, full of missionary zeal, she said, "You know, I remember seeing you once when I was a girl."

"Yes."

"Trying to hang yourself."

"Oh." He shrugged as he spoke, as if neither the act nor the witnessing of it had been shameful in any way.

"Why?"

"You wouldn't understand."

She waited, playing the compassionate Sybille.

Finally he said, "The world had had enough of me." And then he added, "And I, likewise, enough of it." Then he glanced at her with such fierce reproach she almost felt his attempted suicide had been her fault.

She loved him with her whole heart. This man needed her, she decided, and even had he not, still she would have loved him. Or so she assured herself. The Wednesday before Allhallows, Olivier went off to Quercy with the count on some secret business. He was absent more than a week, their longest separation since becoming lovers.

The day after he had gone, she had the queer sensation of floating several inches above the ground. The familiar force that had once anchored her feet to earth seemed to be flaking off, and she felt herself drifting out of control. She rode out to the Count's Meadow and tied the mare to an oak. It was midafternoon and the sun shone wanly. She dropped on her stomach in the decaying October grass, nose grinding the moist sod. Behind her feet, flushing rose across the arched sky, the walls of Toulouse stared down.

She was dizzy with a feeling of something vast rushing at her from the outermost rim of the world. What this something might be, she had no idea. It was still a great distance away, but she sensed it coming closer, like rollers breaking and hissing. *Ieu sui,* it swelled in her ears, *I am.* She got up and rode back to Rue St. Bernard.

That evening in her bedchamber, the sensation grew more powerful until she recognized it as a song. At her writing table she lit an oil lamp and in the cave of light settled herself with parchment and quills. The structure of the thing came to her first, like the silhouette of some unfinished cathedral flying-buttressed against a chalk-white sky. Nothing more. She sat there stock-still, waiting, not moving even when the bells of Saint-Sernin boomed out their bronze lullaby into the smoky night. Then she imagined rectangles, eight of them, eight stanzas. Each line must rhyme with two other lines within each stanza. And the first line of one stanza had to rhyme with the first of the next. Why this particular arrangement felt compulsory she did not understand. But it was. Then she conjured images of water melting, of cool rivers and salt seas, which she had never seen, and then of beaches and tides and emerald-eyed dolphins. In the folds of her ears she could hear the moaning and swelling of waves. Sounds blurred into words. She listened.

Toward prime, she fell through empty space into sleep. A few hours later she woke with three words on her tongue: IEU SUI CYPRIA. Only then did the theme, full-blown, begin to surface. She was the sea. The sea was her. She flowed like water, curled herself into every bubble of foam, divided into myriads of Sybilles, and penetrated the depths of each atom until she was not writing the poem, it was writing her.

Sybille did not leave her chamber that day. Nor the next.

> *I am Cypria who love*
> *and sing as I flow on.*

144

Twice she lived through the going down and the rising up of the sun, noticing nothing, sleepless mind entranced. Wind lashed at the casements. It grew cold in the room and she relit the brazier. Once when Fabrisse again pounded on the door, threatening to have Florent break it down, she considered stopping to revise the six completed stanzas. She decided to push on to the end. Late in the evening on Saturday, she carefully printed the last lines.

> *I feel.*
> *I know.*
> *I am.*

And after she had written the final *Ieu sui,* she beached on the bed in her sweaty gown and thought for an instant of Olivier's blue-iris eyes before allowing oblivion to drown her at last. She dreamed she was a metaphor.

"You haven't said how you like it."

"Are you trying to embarrass me?" Olivier asked, folding the sheets of parchment. "Why do you show me this?"

"I wanted to," Sybille said happily. "It's about you."

"No, it's about you," he corrected, unsmiling. He slid *Ieu Sui* across the trestle and flexed his fingers, as if he had no further interest in it. While she watched him over her fist, he got up and walked past her into the kitchen. She could hear the rattle of cups. He returned with a wine gourd and the cups and knelt on the tiles before the fire.

Sybille wondered what it was about the verse that had displeased him. Something. It was fine verse, better than any La Comtessa de Dia had written for Raimbaut d'Orange. She went over to stand behind him and patted his head.

Olivier did not look up. He dug into his girdle, brought out a vial, and carefully tapped something into one of the cups. She leaned over his shoulder, trying to see.

"What's that?" she asked.

"Nothing." He shrugged. "I'm spicing my wine."

She went around and settled herself opposite him. Grayish feathers floated on the wine. "What is it?" she asked again.

Olivier raised the cup to his lips and took a long sip. "Hashish," he said at last.

"Oh God!" she cried. "Isn't that poison?"

"No." He drained the cup. "It makes me feel good."

Sybille stared at him. He appeared happy. She grabbed the other cup and held it out. He got out the vial, and all at once he was grinning and humming under his breath. She seized the cup in both hands. Tentative, she took a tiny swallow and gagged. He was watching her. She forced a second sip, trying to roll it past her tongue without tasting, and he laughed mockingly.

"Ah," he whooped, derisive. "Look at the dainty lady." Crooking one elbow, he lifted his empty cup and began to mimic her. He pursed clownish lips, coquettish as a woman. "Careful there, you're wasting it. Go on, drink."

His contemptuous tone made her go hot to the roots of her hair. Never before had she heard him speak in that tone, and she was shocked and bewildered. She tipped up the cup to drain it. She choked. Olivier reached for the cup.

"More?" He gave her a hard smile. Before she could shake her head, he said, "Forget it, you've had enough."

Drinking the wine had been a mistake. She did not feel good; she felt light-headed. Olivier was watching her, almost studying her face. The smile had evaporated.

"Clarity," he said, deep-voiced. His eyes were slits. "I can see you very, very clearly now." Sybille held her breath, alert. "You are sly."

"What do you mean?" She twisted the rings on her fingers.

"Cunning little fox. You steal a man's strength. You suck his blood and cook his brains. You're nothing but a thief in silk and lace, a sly little word-rhyming fox." He laughed.

"Stop it!" she shouted, indignant, and scrambled up.

Jerkily Olivier got to his feet. Avoiding her eyes, he brushed by and lurched into the bedchamber. She stared into the fire, arms wrapped protectively around her waist. After a few minutes she heard him call, querulous, "Sybille, aren't you coming?" She sucked in her breath and went to him. A candle smoked on the floor near Olivier's shirt and breeches. He was lying facedown on the bed with his head smothered by a pillow. She peeled off her gown and shift and stretched alongside him.

Hesitating, she put one hand on his shoulder. His skin was clammy. He jolted over on his back and let her work her fingers across his groin. She closed her eyes, stroking back and forth. "My love, my sweet—" she whispered.

"You talk too much," he muttered hoarsely.

Alarmed, she pressed her lips together. What is wrong with him? she wondered. He did not touch her. He lay beside her like a fallen log, and his penis crouched limp in her palm. After some minutes had passed, she said to him, "I'm sorry. If you would tell me what to do—"

"Whatever you do or don't do is irrelevant."

His face was hidden in shadow. One hand covered his eyes. She said, "I know you're upset but—"

Under his breath, he said, "Upset, that's a brilliant observation."

"Please, Olivier." A cart rutted down Rue du Crucifix, somewhere behind the cottage, and the shutters clacked. Her wrist began to ache. She shifted hands. The candle guttered.

Without warning he reached out both hands to catch her waist. Then he raised her off the bed and hauled her body on top of his, face up. Stupefied, she held her breath.

She felt him reach down to take his penis in his hand, as if he were alone. Olivier handled the soft stalk between his fingers, jiggling it rhythmically against her buttocks. On her back, she gaped straight up into the shadowy dark and forced back amazement and disgust. Who had ever heard of this method of coupling? The room stank of cooling wax. Olivier seemed to have forgotten her existence. Slowly she began to twitch her hips, trying to rub herself against him.

Behind her head, he said abruptly, "Stop jumping around."

She made herself go rigid. Her muscles knotted and unknotted in helpless humiliation. She wanted to cry. There was nothing else to do. He is using my body, she thought. Finally he groaned, a series of soft, whiny gasps. After he had stopped whimpering and lay quiet, she tumbled down sideways and sat up. His face was twisted away from her.

"Don't look at me," he mumbled. They stayed there among the tangled sheets until eventually he vaulted off the bed and thrashed around for his clothing. Behind him, Sybille stared at the wall. "We haven't eaten," Olivier said, in a muffled tone. He was pulling on his shirt.

"My lord," Sybille said in a tiny voice. "I feel bad." He ought to know that without her saying it.

"Let's eat," he replied, as if she had not spoken, and went out the door.

When Sybille came into the hall, he was shoveling bread into his mouth. Dazed, she sank down without looking at him and smeared cheese on a slice of ham. She did not feel hungry and finally took a bite without tasting it.

Half in tears, she bowed her head and stared into a bowl of olives. From the corner of her eye she could see him licking butter from his fingers. She swore she would not speak to him again. But a minute later: "Why are you acting this way? Please don't do this."

"I've done nothing to you!" He shot her a furious look. "The little fox is being provocative. But I hear that is common among wedded ladies who have lovers."

Obviously he wanted to punish her. But she did not understand why. Perhaps the hashish had caused his craziness. Even so. The knight was trying to kill her. Grimly, she got up to search for her slippers.

The fire was almost out. She trotted to the hearth and stepped into her shoes, intending to leave. There was no use trying to talk to him. As she started back toward the trestle, Olivier said, "Here she comes, marching along on her stumpy little legs."

She sank down on a stool beside him. Suddenly he closed his eyes and pitched forward into her lap. Without thinking, she wrapped her arms around his head and cradled him. Never have I loved anyone as I love you, she said silently. Not even Mama or Papa. He was rocking against her belly. He needs affection, she thought. He is only a little boy who wants cuddling. Words caught in her throat. After a while she cleared it. "My lord," she said, all gentleness, "I understand. You were distraught tonight."

"Oh, I'm distraught." He raised his head and wrenched up. "You're distraught yourself. What do you mean? Nervous?"

"Yes. Nervous." He was scaring her.

"People make me nervous." He put back his head and threw her a glance heavy with hostility. "You make me nervous."

Wild again, she yelled, "All evening you've been disgusting!"

"That's your side of it," he snapped. He got up and carried the platter of ham into the kitchen.

When he came back, Sybille said, "Take me home." She crossed to the door and waited. He was putting on his boots, neck bent to the ground. She said, truthfully, "When I got here, I was so happy—so glad to see you." He glowered at her over his shoulder. "And now I feel like my insides have been ripped out."

Olivier said, "Is that my fault?" and loped out.

In the street she stood shivering until he came up leading the stallion by the bridle. The sky was flaunting its stars. He mounted and pulled her up behind him. They trotted silently across the bridge. Beneath the stallion's hooves she could hear the dark water creaking toward Bordeaux. She felt desolate and could not bear it. Finally she called to Olivier, "This night has been unreal."

He made no reply.

Chapter Eight

At daybreak, before she opened her eyes, Sybille smelled his scent on her, among the strands of her hair and along the dune where upper arm sloped into shoulder. Her flesh sang of him, his sweat or the smell of sex maybe, she did not know which. She pinched her nostrils. The fragrance stabbed through her fingertips like shards of glass until she moaned in pain. He has invaded me, she cried to herself, he is pushing me out of my body.

"Madam?"

It was Carenza. Sybille opened her eyes. "Bring the tub," she told her and sat up. "Make sure the water is very hot."

Ten minutes later she was standing in the tub. On the water's surface she glimpsed her reflection, another Sybille rippled into the face of an old woman. She smeared herself with soap before settling into the hot water. Immediately she got up and began scraping viciously at her arms and thighs, so the skin turned fiery red. The room was thick with steam. She sank down to wet her hair. When she surfaced she sniffed her own familiar smell again. Olivier was gone; she had rinsed him away.

Midmorning, as Sybille was combing her mother's hair, Corba de Perella rode into the courtyard, and barely ten minutes later Pons arrived with Jean Maulen, a goodman from Gaillac. With unexpected guests to entertain, Sybille sailed down to the kitchen and instructed Cook to bring out the best wine and cook up some vegetables. She led the visitors into the hall, Corba in her velvet riding gown, the little bony-faced preacher in his crumpled blue robe. Pons followed, talking about the shortage of good smoked herring this season. He was smiling and speaking more loudly than usual, Sybille noticed.

"My beloved lady—" Jean Maulen said to Corba, for the De

Perellas were among the most important families in the Good Christian community. Taking her elbow, he settled her at the trestle as reverently as the pope handling a precious reliquary. He bowed his head and blessed the vegetables in a nasal voice. Mind wandering, Sybille thought of Olivier's wild eyes as he savaged her. "Stumpy little legs," he had said. They were not.

The preacher was saying, "We have two hundred new converts in Pamiers alone. By the end of the year—"

"The great beast is dead in our land," Corba interrupted.

Pons cried, "No, Na Corba, not dead. But Rome has suffered enough wounds to keep it abed a long while."

"Rome is a joke," Corba said.

They went on exchanging blasphemies against the Church and gossiping about prominent heretics. In the gaps in the conversation, Sybille smiled agreeably and refilled the wine goblets. The rest of the time she picked at her beets and kept still. Nothing they said made much sense to her. Even if every soul in Languedoc turned heretic, that would not make the pope turn his back on their land. Nor would it rid them of Simon de Montfort and his greedy crusaders, insatiable for the south's wealth. All the Good Christians were doing when they boasted of new converts was giving people false hopes. While she dished out the stewed pears, Sybille realized she had not thought of Olivier in nearly two hours; but once she had that thought he roamed in her head again and she could not chase him out.

"Na Sybille—" Corba was rising to take her leave and bowing three times to Jean Maulen. Sybille walked her down to the yard. Her shoulder blades were studded with tension. Corba said she looked unwell, was anything troubling her? Sybille lied that she was having her monthly flux and suffered pains in her stomach. She did not want to tell Corba about Olivier. She was ashamed.

But as though she had read Sybille's mind, Corba asked, "How is your knight? I saw him at the château the other day. He grunted at me."

Sybille waved at Florent to saddle Corba's palfrey. The autumn morning was heating up and the cobbles, already warm under her feet, would be hot by afternoon. It seemed unfair that the summer, having expired weeks ago, should return to flout them this way. She said to Corba, "It's over between the knight and me. Some demon has entered him."

"Has he been untrue?"

"No, he insulted me."

Corba studied Sybille's face.

"When we lie together," Sybille said, "he thinks only of his own pleasure."

Corba's eyebrows shot up sharply. She said, "He goes too quickly?"

Sybille could not begin to describe Olivier's antics—they were outrageous. She went on, "And he's mean to me. Calls me names and ridicules me."

Florent led up the palfrey and Corba went past him and took the halter. She stared into the horse's eyes. Without looking at Sybille, she said gravely, "And now what?"

Sybille stood there gnawing on her fist. Corba went around and mounted. Her brown ringlets swirled around her ears like fine mist. The knight would not return; he had as much as said so. If I were he, Sybille thought, I would be ashamed to face me again. No, Olivier de Ferrand has ridden out of my life for good. She looked up at Corba and shrugged.

"Rotten potato," Corba said. Her voice was ready with anger. "Throw him away like a rotten potato."

After a moment Sybille nodded. She said Corba was right, the knight was worthless. Any fool could see that. She did not confess she loved him and hungered for his return. Corba said if she were a man she would find Olivier and break his bones, and Sybille thanked her.

She went upstairs to her mother, thinking that Olivier's suffering must be very great to punish her and himself with such exquisite cruelty. She went around Douce's chamber collecting gowns that had been dropped on the floor and hung them on the wall hooks. Douce, propped against her pillows, watched her. Over her shoulder Sybille said, "When a man loves a woman, why would he dishonor her and flee? Do you understand what I'm saying, Mama?"

Douce sniffed. "Only a wicked man would do that," she said.

"But suppose he weren't wicked," she insisted. He was a monster, but he was not wicked.

"Then," Douce said, yawning, "it must be God's will."

"Yes."

"I plan to wear that red gown today." She pointed to the wall.

"I'll get it down again," Sybille said.

She went through the day making a pretense of listening to Pons and Jean Maulen. She could not bear thinking of the knight but found she couldn't stop. He seemed to have gotten trapped in some fold of her mind and would not budge. Sybille smiled too much, drank wine without watering it, and, without showing her irritation, told the goodman no, she had not given serious thought to leaving the Church. When Pons left the hall for a few minutes, she asked the goodman what made people behave crazily when they were not really crazy.

Jean Maulen did not answer at once, then he asked for further details. He was not exactly certain what she meant. "Obvious lunatics—"

"No, no," she broke in. "This is subtle. I know of a person who appears to be as sane as anyone else. But he suffers from strange humors."

Across the trestle the goodman studied her blandly. "Are you talking about some sickness of the mind?" he asked.

"I think so." She fingered her goblet. Olivier suffered more than any person she knew. She said to Jean Maulen, "He makes others miserable but his own suffering is greater. He is either being a monster or an angel. Why are such people so afflicted, do you think?"

"Why are they afflicted?" he repeated. "Why are the blind sightless?" He stared into his lap. After a while he said, "Mayhap he is paying for some sin committed in a former life."

"Oh," she replied. His answer dissatisfied her but she nodded politely. And if that should be true, she thought, what was my sin in a former life that I must love this damaged man? What is wrong with me, wanting him back despite the indignities he heaps on me? I must be crazy too. She smiled at the goodman, and when Pons returned to the hall, she bowed three times and excused herself.

That evening, after the compline bell had rung, Florent knocked on her door to say the knight was down in the yard. At the stable doorway, torches splashed thin beams of light diagonally across the front of the yard. There was no one in sight. Then, from the darkness by the olive tree, came a low whistle. Blinking, she walked slowly to the edge of the shadows. Olivier was sitting on the bench under the tree. She waited.

"Hello there," he said. "What's the matter? You look tired."

She stumbled forward and sat down, careful to keep the length of the bench between them. Florent crossed through the torchlight into the stable. He did not look back. Sybille sat with her hands folded in her lap. She allowed her eyes to adjust to the dark before turning to face Olivier, apprehensive.

"Lady," he said, "I have some walnut cakes for us. They're very tasty."

Full of bitchery, she snapped, "Oh, did you make them?" Now that he was there, she wanted to hurt him.

He gave an offended laugh. "Your tongue has a jagged edge. No, I got them at the château. Cook made them for a feast."

He unknotted a piece of cloth and laid it between them. Sybille took one of the cakes and ate it slowly. Olivier, as usual, gobbled, throwing down one cake after another. He seemed to be in an amiable mood.

"I had a dream last night," he said conversationally. "I dreamed I could see my whole back. It was covered with thousands of moles and pimples."

She licked crumbs from her fingers. Often he told her his dreams, but he was never clever enough to divine the slightest notion of their meanings.

"You're not listening. I'm trying to tell you—"

"Moles and pimples. Go on."

"—and leper sores. It was disgusting. So I went to Saint-Etienne and I said, 'Father William, get rid of this shit on my back.'" He stopped.

"And then?" Sybille prompted.

Olivier shook his head. "That's all. Does it mean I'm going to get leprosy?"

"No."

"Do you know what it means?" he asked earnestly.

"No." She stared up at a yellow moon. The meaning seemed clear enough, but she said nothing. A priest could not cure him of his woes, at least no priest she knew. Perhaps the Blessed Virgin, she thought, and she decided tomorrow she would light candles and pray for his soul.

After they had finished the cakes, Olivier told Sybille about visiting a castle at Queribus as a child. She asked him whose castle, but he did not remember. He had been touring with the Countess Joanna. He said passionately he would never forget the family who owned that castle. On the supper table there had been enormous platters of oysters and lobsters, sperlings and sea bream, and more kinds of drinks than he had ever seen—claret, cider, ale, pear wine, wine from the Auvergne, clove-spiced wine. He ticked them off, wide-eyed, and then he recalled they had a wall tapestry in their hall with portraits of each member of the family. That was a real family, it was what he had always imagined it would be like to have kin and his own fief.

Sybille said she hoped he would have it someday.

Afterward, when he had gone and she was in her chamber plaiting her hair, she remembered he had not apologized for the previous evening, had not even referred to it. She almost wondered if she had dreamed it.

She stood in William's library, his manuscripts of Plato and Aristotle yellowing in the cupboards all around her, and moaned softly behind one hand. A fire burned too hotly in the hearth; the glass in the casements sweated. A copy of *Ieu Sui* waited on the writing table for further refining. But anxiety hung in her chest like a gray haze, dread that Olivier might abandon her. He's making me edgy again, she thought. His very existence makes me edgy. Each time they met, he drew back in some way. Each time they parted, she feared never seeing him again. The library door creaked on its hinges.

"Lady." Pons put his head in, then cracked the doorway wider. "Am I disturbing you? I need my account lists."

"Come in."

He crossed to the table and began to fish through heaps of parchment, hurriedly picking up scraps, examining, turning them over into a pile. Sybille stared into the fire. Olivier complained she asked too much of him, wanted to own him like some captured Saracen slave. He was a free man, he said.

"This is your work?"

Glancing over, she saw Pons was staring down at *Ieu Sui*. She wanted to snatch it away. She took a step forward, then folded her arms around her waist. "Yes, mine. I've been writing again."

Pons picked up the pages. "May I read it?" he said absently.

For a moment she hesitated. She had only to make some excuse. He would not press her. She said, "All right," and stared into the fire.

He took the poem to the window, reading as he went. Neck bent, he ran his eyes down each sheet and made remarks as he went. "Fascinating." "Hmm." "Good metaphor." At the end, silent as light, he stood there holding the pages in his hands.

Sybille coughed.

He raised his head and looked at her.

She waited, scarcely breathing.

"I've known you have a lover." His voice was casual.

"Oh." Then: "How?"

"Oh, Sybille!" Pons laughed. "Do you imagine it isn't obvious?"

Sybille turned her back to the fire and faced him across the table. It had not occurred to her that anyone might know. Only Corba and Carenza, whom she trusted. She threw back her hair, wondering how she had been indiscreet, and she sighed loudly.

"Don't upset yourself." Pons laid the poem on the table in the exact spot he had found it. "I don't mind. Haven't I been telling you to do it? Good. You did it."

"Yes." She thought he sounded relieved, even pleased. "I did it." She laughed huskily.

He said, "Although I do think it would be courteous to tell me his name. We are civilized people, aren't we?"

She studied his face. He was slouching against the table, gazing at her as calmly as if he had just inquired about the weather.

"One of the count's knights," she said. "Olivier de Ferrand."

"Who?"

"Olivier de— I just told you."

"At Muret?" Pons was looking at her with astonishment. "That man who—?"

She nodded slightly. He was shaking his head from side to side, opening his mouth and closing it without speaking.

"Words fail me," he finally gasped. He slapped his hand on the tabletop. "This is about De Ferrand? I imagined some king. No less than a prince. Oh Jesus, De Ferrand." He laughed harshly.

Startled, Sybille reared back.

Pons shook his head again. "You amaze me," he sputtered.

She felt waves of rage sizzling up her spine. She said between her teeth, "You don't approve. That's too bad."

Pons pursed his lips. "Did he seek you out?"

"No."

"You sought him."

"No. We met by accident, in the street."

He laughed. "Fate. And he made love to you skillfully."

At the beginning, yes, he was skillful. Not now. "Yes," she said.

"I thought so. And you were swept away by the mere sound of his voice, which is"—he grabbed the parchment—"oh yes, like the wind penetrating the sea."

"Yes."

"Fine. The voice of Olivier de Ferrand. Glorious. What else? Ah, eyes the color of irises." He waved his arms. "Curls as radiant as light."

"This isn't necessary."

"This is—stupid. You chose a lover. Very good. But my dear lady, why this—this shit-nosed knight? This common adulterer who steals another man's wife. Where is the great virtue in that?"

"He didn't steal me—"

"And why do you write about fornication? Lust of the flesh is an animal appetite one tries to overcome. Oh God, why do you idealize fucking?"

"I'll idealize anything I wish," she hurled at him. "You don't tell me what to write." Her head was beginning to ache. Pons went on haranguing her about Olivier's eyes being blue, not lavender. She backed toward the door, opened it with sweating hands, and let herself out. Pons was still talking. She ran up the staircase to her chamber and drew the bolt. Minutes later, Sybille heard Pons bawling at Florent to open the gate. Then the sound of hooves crashed over the cobbles.

Toward the end of the week, Sybille received the briefest of letters from her husband: He was at Fanjeaux, at her grandmother's castle, where he planned to remain until Christmas. Perhaps longer. He hoped she was in good health.

Sybille met her sister on the stairs. "Pons isn't coming home for Christmas."

Fabrisse pushed her hair behind her ears. "Is he coming back ever?"

"Oh, I suppose." She grimaced.

"You're an imbecile," Fabrisse said sharply. "That knight has crazed you."

Surprised that she knew about Olivier, Sybille turned and went down the steps without answering.

Christmas came. She embroidered a shirt for Olivier.

"Sybille." She whispered her name to herself.
"Shhh. Shhh."

Already the flat blades of winter sun had flitted below the window; the shutter slits darkened. The walls gloomed to dust around the honeyed circle of candlelight. They lay together quietly like two sides of a denier, loin touching loin, arms and legs yoked, mouth locked to mouth. Sometimes she sensed she existed. Sometimes she felt her limbs dissolving and could not distinguish her body from his. She stared into his face and saw the mirror of her shattered self dancing deep in his eyes. Once she moaned aloud.

"What's wrong?"

She shook her head and attempted to look away. "Nothing," she said to him.

He held her in the palms of his hands, more gently than a baby. He said if that moan was nothing, he would hate to hear something.

Sybille squeezed shut her eyes. Rhythmically Olivier began to drink in her breath, pumping it up from deep within her lungs and then returning it mixed with his own. She had lost all sense of time grinding. He cleaved to her as a drowning man claws speechless at the sky; he clung and fed and drank, until she felt part of her self being devoured. The distant noises of the city had corroded away. There was no foot tread, no child's bleat or rasp of horse's hoof, not even the dying echo of wind or bird. She strained her ears but heard only the rumble of abandoned bodies fusing genderless ghost-breaths like incense burning in a closed tomb. And then the flailing of a heartbeat, hers or Olivier's, she did not care which.

He moaned he was not himself, he had become her. His tears pearled on her cheeks.

She said nothing.

Outside a dog barked. The sound penetrated the room like a spray of summer thunderbolts. Suddenly Olivier was himself again. He wrenched apart and sat bolt upright. After a moment he said, "It's late. Time for me to take you home." His voice had a gritting quality that made her go taut.

She forced open her eyelids and gazed at the back of his head. Incomplete, she fluttered shaking fingertips on the sleeve of his shirt. But he did not turn and she pulled back her hand.

"Come on." He laughed, irritable. "You're not moving."

She looked at him sitting there and struggled to stitch herself together.

"You're being quiet." He turned, without looking her in the

face, and scratched his forehead. He said to the far wall, "She's being quiet again."

She dragged herself to the edge of the bed. There was no sense trying to talk to him. He had bared himself to her. That person she had seen crying, it had been he. Now he had to tell her it was not. My God, she might have foreseen it. She reached down for her slippers.

Two days after that Epiphany arrived, cloudless and frosty as fine sugar. Down in the yard, the topmost branches of the olive tree were sparkling with silver rime. Olivier brought her an orange, which he said had been costly because it came from Valencia. His cheeks were dotted red from the cold and he cupped an open mouth against her lips. Sybille led him into the hall and drew up stools to the hearth. A kitchen boy heating wine took the bowl from the flames and cleared out in a hurry; no other servants appeared from the kitchen. Not speaking, they sat with their knees touching and stared at each other. He was grinning in a cocky way that disquieted her, but she could not have said why.

"I've been worried about you," he said.

She twisted away, surprised, because he did not look worried.

"Are you all right?" he asked.

She did not reply. Rolling the orange in one hand, she debated lying.

"You're not talking," Olivier said, unreasonably. "Come, lady, you can tell me."

She sniffed at the orange, still cautious. "Sometimes it is wise to keep one's thoughts to one's self."

She could sense his irritation. He said, "That's foolish. Why can't you trust me?" Sybille pulled in her chin. "Believe me, I'm your friend. It's best to be forthright."

Several minutes passed and when she finally spoke, she had to force her tongue to move. "I become more shredded every day. If you held me up to the sun, you could see straight through me."

He nodded, eyes as approving as a priest hearing a *confiteor*.

Encouraged, she stood up and began to pace before the hearth. She told him her husband was grossly jealous. Pons had no reason to play the cuckolded husband; he did not wish to lie with her himself, he never had. She could not count the times he had urged her to take a lover and now, when she had one, he was behaving badly. It did not make sense. She did not tell Olivier she wished to go away with him, to leave Toulouse and live together like an ordinary wife and husband. They might go to Lombardy or Castile. She said the other things, but these longings were left unspoken.

Behind her, Olivier grunted. "I had a terrible dream last night." She wheeled to face him. "I had three mothers. Two of them I murdered—and I stuffed their bodies into a well."

"Oh—a what? A well?" When she came over to press his arm sympathetically, she saw he seemed disturbed, and then she realized his usual melancholy was missing.

"I said I was sorry. I said I wanted the remaining mother, but nobody would trust me."

"What do you think it means?" she asked, dropping on the stool.

He shrugged. "How should I know? Sybille—"

She straightened her back. The flames were heating the side of her face.

"—you must not see me again. For your sake."

Her head jerked up. The orange plopped into her lap. "Beg pardon, my lord," she managed to blurt out. "What are you talking about?"

"It will only get worse, not better. End it now."

Her mind scummed with dread, she sat there and searched his eyes. She might just as well have been peering into dusty casements, for they veiled everything.

"Stop staring at me, will you?" He pushed back his stool. "I'm getting a stomachache. Conversations like this are bloody bad for me."

There was a long silence while she swiped at her nose with a fist.

"Listen to me, Sybille," he said, softening his tone. "All these months I've been playing. But now I can see you're not a woman to play with. It's too dangerous."

A word of his dislodged her daze. "Playing, you say?" She stammered a half-laugh, heavy with disbelief. "You were playing with me, as if I were a game of chess?"

"But isn't courtly love a game?" He put his head to one side, with a touch of coyness in his expression. "Games are to be played."

"I wasn't playing any game," she boomed, turning away.

Olivier said, "I understand that now. You lack the talent for it."

Beyond the passageway, in the kitchen, Cook was screaming at someone and pots rattled. If it had been a game at the start, it very quickly had ceased to be one for her. "I love you," she said desperately. "My feelings are real. I—"

"I know," he interrupted soothingly. "But you deserve better than a penniless knight. I'm not good enough for you."

"Do me no favors." She tossed her head angrily. "I am capable of deciding what I deserve."

From the kitchen Carenza came into the hall with Douce's tray, bowls sloshing. She walked quickly past them, not looking, and headed for the far door. Sybille could not look away from Olivier's face. She remembered a hearth rosy with fire, Olivier's head spangled bluish-orange against the flames. "I am unable to love," he had said, but she closed her ears to his words. Now the unthinkable edged into her head. If he leaves me, she thought, I am lost. "What are you trying to tell me?" she made herself ask. He sat motionless, and she said, "Olivier, is it your wish to leave me?"

"Leaving you would give me no great joy," he answered, too hastily.

She raked the orange skin with her nails to stop her fingers from trembling. "I want to go on seeing you," she said. "It is *not* my wish to stop."

She continued to watch him, wondering what had provoked this visit. It had been he who insisted she confide in him. If she had not spoken, would this have happened?

Olivier was smiling. He rose and went for his cloak, thrown over a trestle. Almost impishly, he hiked the cloak over one shoulder. "I have to run along," he said. "There's a horse fair at Malamique. I'm thinking of buying a palfrey."

"We're roasting a pig today," she said, for something to say. Deadly tired, she got up, and Olivier wrapped both arms around her back and hugged. She clutched the orange.

"God give you good day, lady. Till we meet again." He was decidedly merry, his eyes and mouth shining the relief he could not hide. He looked just like Mathieu when he was a boy and had escaped his lessons.

She watched him swing down the long, dark hall, head listing cockily. Already he seemed to have forgotten her. This was no chance visit, she thought. He had come there on the Feast of Epiphany purposely to cast her aside, and no action of hers would have stopped him. That made her drop back on the stool.

Alone in the hall, she gazed at the orange.

Gaudily colored, the orange sat on her writing table and observed her. A week passed. A speck of brown began to form on its topside. No word arrived from Olivier.

One afternoon, unexpectedly, she slithered free of the pain. Fool, she raged at herself. He told you he could not love. Could she now pretend those words had never been uttered? Or that her ears had not heard? But the truth was, he had loved. Perhaps in spite of himself, but he had loved. She sent Carenza to St. Cyprien, to the château, even to the taverns along the Garonne.

"Find him," she ordered.

The girl looked at Sybille as if she were witless. "Madam, I'm telling you—"

Sybille lashed out a fist and pounded the maid's shoulder. She wanted to kill her. "I don't care what you tell me. I want him. Now go!"

Not until vespers did Carenza come lagging in the gate. Olivier de Ferrand had left Toulouse three days earlier with a company of knights. As for their destination or date of return, one might ask such questions but it was an idiot who expected answers. The men had gone to fight. That was all. Every day men left the city to fight.

Time did not heal, it merely masked the wounds. There were plenty of hours to brood and reconstruct the psyche of Olivier de Ferrand, and she reminded herself that she had learned from him. But what? That the human spirit is capable of giving and getting infinite mutilation?

Was this worth knowing?

In the end all she understood for certain was that never again could she eat an orange.

He had been a mischief-maker, a man born to create trouble for himself and others, and the depth of her bitterness about the knight who had run away awed her a little.

It was around this time that a Church council at Montpellier decided that neither Raymond, old or young, was fit to rule Toulouse. The prelates unanimously awarded the land to Simon de Montfort, but they dared not give him the title of count. *Dominus et monarcha,* they called him, which meant little more than a warden responsible for policing a conquered land. The already battered Toulousans took this abstract news for what it was worth and no more, and they joked about how unhappy poor Simon must be. No one actually believed the Church had a right to dispossess their counts, nor did Raymond himself believe it. He planned to take his son to Rome, to visit the pope and straighten out this mistake.

Under the jests festered waves of fear and suppressed rage. People could not keep rein on their tempers. The slightest annoyance, an overcharge for a loaf of bread, would spark fights and drawn swords. In the Astarac house, most everyone was at someone else's throat, and the noise of quarreling became so commonplace that nobody bothered to take it seriously.

Every Sunday in February, cold rain fell steadily. Sybille would sleep until midmorning and then doze through the gray afternoon until it was time to sleep at night. In her waking hours she cursed Olivier, calling him useless prick and son of a leprous whore. But there were no names foul enough to express her hatred or to exorcise her humiliation. Or to summarize adequately Olivier's sin, which was simply that he had not loved her. How dare he *not* love her? She was Sybille d'Astarac, he only a court-scum bastard. He should have worshiped her. Instead he had insulted her and fled. It made no sense. She spent those Sundays wishing him dead. But on Monday mornings she begged God to let him live, that she might have her revenge one day.

On a mild Monday, after Lady's Day, Pons rode back from Fanjeaux and Sybille played at being a wife, but neither of them felt happy about the reunion and Pons told her he would be leaving again soon.

"Oh really?" she said, wishing to sound interested.

"I shall begin my probation at Montréal seminary," he said. "Yes, I'm finally setting myself on the path to a full Christian life. Pray God I be judged worthy."

Startled out of her inattention, she laughed and said loudly, "Well, this is wonderful news. So now I'm to be a goodman's widow."

"Sybille," Pons said frowning, "I've spoken of this to you many times. Surely it isn't a surprise."

Yes, but she had not listened. His preaching was a possibility not to be taken seriously. More loudly she said, "All the same, you are deserting us. There will be no man here to—"

"Olivier."

"We will be a house of women with no man to protect us." Another weak, irresponsible man who thought only of himself, she said to herself. To Pons she said, "If you must know, the knight left me right after Christmas. Now you are running away."

Pons sighed. "He may return."

"No."

"You will find another."

"No." The only man she desired was Olivier; that was her shame.

On the morning of his departure for Montréal, Pons wept and made foolish speeches and told her he would always love her. She averted her eyes, unconvinced.

"But with my soul alone," Pons said and blew his nose. "No more with my body."

"Of course," she answered because she could think of nothing else to say. When had he loved her with his body? She wondered how he could have forgotten, and after they had exchanged the kiss of peace and the gate closed on him, she stood in the yard and cursed softly. A stableboy rolled up his eyes, horror-struck.

In May, after Pons had been gone two months, Simon de Montfort destroyed the city's red walls and filled in the moats. The old count disappeared over the Pyrenees. De Montfort rode into Toulouse with the French king's son, who was visiting Languedoc on what he advertised as a pilgrimage. Sybille and Fabrisse watched the cavalcade from the steps of Saint-Sernin. Prince Louis swiveled sunny smiles from side to side, as if he were riding in the streets of Paris, and he went home with half the jawbone of St. Vincent as a souvenir. Simon de Montfort immediately moved into the Château Narbonnais.

French soldiers patrolled the Garonne. They could be seen among the crowds on Rue Méjane, mopping their foreheads and buying cheese and summer fruit. All the fat merchants joked bitterly about having to study French now, and by the following summer some did learn to speak a few words; mostly they doubled and trebled their prices for De Montfort's men. That year, when the French lived in the count's château and the troubadours played elsewhere, Sybille resigned herself to solitude for the rest of her life. All the women in the world have a man, she told herself self-pityingly. Only I am alone and loveless. But as time went by, she thought less frequently of the husband who had just as good as divorced her to serve the heretic god.

Once, however, after Lammas Day, Pons and his traveling companion, a former baker from Casses, appeared suddenly in the hall. Sybille did not recognize him. Traveling preachers no longer wore blue robes—it was too dangerous—and the pair were dressed like weavers. They stayed only a single day and night. Sybille slept badly because she expected De Montfort's men to crash through the gate at any moment. In the morning she struggled to conceal her agitation from Pons.

"Lady," he smiled at her, "I understand your fears. But there's no cause for worry, I assure you."

"You're mad to risk one day in this city," Sybille told him. "If De Montfort—"

"He's got his hands full with the young count at Beaucaire." Pons swatted a mosquito singing in his beard. "As you know, this war will be over by Michaelmas."

"Eat meat," she said sharply. "Your skin gives you away." His white face would be spotted at some town gate and they would seize him without asking questions. Sybille did not want to think beyond that.

"Lady, young Raymond has been making a fool of De Montfort all summer. He can't even beat a youth of nineteen these days. Take my word for it, the end is clearly at hand."

Sybille made a sour squawk in her throat. Ever since April, when the old count and his son sailed into Marseille harbor, the whole south had been going insane with hope. It was true the French had suffered one defeat after another, that the old count had returned to Spain for more men to liberate Toulouse. But who could say what might happen in the meantime? She shook her head at Pons. "You take chances like this, you'll be burned by Michaelmas." From an upstairs window came a sudden crash of something breaking; Sybille wheeled and raced for the staircase.

Douce was stretched on her bed clutching her cittern. The shutters had not yet been opened, and the room was dark and unbearably warm. A servingwoman stooped near the bed, carefully collecting fragments of china between her fingertips and transferring them to a tray. She looked annoyed.

"Madam," she said to Sybille without looking up, "Na Douce is being naughty today."

Sybille pushed open the shutters. Light streaked over the broken crockery and a mess of gravy and meat. Slightly to the right, near a chest, she noticed a pile of feces. The servant was watching her. Sybille turned to the bed. "Mama," she called softly, "you must remember to use the chamber pot."

Behind her, the servant grunted, "Save your breath."

Douce smiled a sweet smile. "I'm thirsty."

"Mama," Sybille sighed, "please eat something. You can't live on water."

"Yes, daughter."

"If Cook sends up another tray, will you eat?"

"Yes, daughter."

Sybille knew she would not. It took hours of coaxing to get a few morsels of bread into Douce. And then, sometimes, she retched it up. She wanted only water or ale, vast amounts of it.

Fabrisse stood in the doorway, looking in. "God's good morning, Mama." She yawned noisily.

Douce did not answer. Thrusting aside the cittern, she got up and began to pace between the bed and the window. She detoured around the excrement, which she eyed with scorn.

When Douce's back was turned, Fabrisse asked, her voice low, "What happened?"

Sybille shrugged. Was she blind? The servant finished cleaning the floor and then limped to the bed, where she started tugging off the sheets. The soggy pile fell to the floor. Fabrisse said, "If she drank less water—"

"She can't help herself," Sybille said and toed the sheets into the passage.

"I'm going to read to her— Mama, let's read a story." From the folds of her gown she brought out the gospels. "Mama, slow down—" Douce paused, glanced at the Bible, and began pacing again, faster. The servant went out and closed the door.

Sybille said, "Leave her alone. You're making her jittery."

"The word of God can't harm her," Fabrisse said. She jigged to the window, trying to block her mother's path. "Lady Mother, sit down. I want to pray with you. Would you prefer St. John or St. Luke?"

"No," Douce whispered over her shoulder. "The pope would be angry with me."

"He won't care—he's dead." Fabrisse smiled at her mother. "I told you Innocent is dead. Remember?"

"Really?" Douce crossed herself, then reached for the cittern. She raked a thumb over the strings. "I'm sorry. I must pray for his soul."

Fabrisse laughed. "Soul? He was the Devil." Sybille flashed her a warning, but Fabrisse ignored it. "You don't want to pray for Satan, do you?"

"Leave off!" Sybille hissed at her sister. Still holding the cittern, Douce tumbled on the mattress and squirmed both knees level with her breasts. She lay curled, her beautiful eyes wide open. Sybille knelt on the edge of the bed, watching her. Fabrisse sat in the window seat, Holy Scriptures on her knees. Silent, they waited for Douce to move or speak. In the passage through the closed door came the sound of footsteps and water sloshing—Carenza or the old servant mopping the floors. After some five or six minutes had passed, Sybille said, "Pons was ordained very quickly, wouldn't you say?"

"So many of our people have been burned," Fabrisse said quickly. "Sister, why are you so cruel? Let me go to the seminary. I can do nothing for Mama."

"You promised to stay." She was annoyed to hear Fabrisse bringing up the subject again. It had been settled.

"I understand your not wanting to be alone. But can't you put yourself in my place?"

"No," Sybille said, trying to keep her patience. She peered at her mother to see if she was listening. Douce's cheek nuzzled the wood of the cittern. Her bones curved like water lilies. But she did not move. "No," she repeated to Fabrisse. She crossed the window and faced her, stubborn.

"Mama has found a refuge in her madness," Fabrisse murmured. "She has left the world. That is all I'm asking for myself. To leave and serve my faith."

Forgetful of Douce, Sybille leaned over Fabrisse, choking with anger. "Who isn't looking for a refuge? Everyone wants to escape. So it's death or suicide. Or a convent."

Fabrisse sat quietly, squinting at her.

"It is only I"—she strained to keep her voice down—"I who can't manage to find an escape for myself."

"Sybille," Fabrisse said softly, "that knight was your escape."

Rearing back in surprise, she strode to the bed. She stooped over her mother, gazing at the waxen throat, the untidy hair finer than silk. She ached to shake Douce and force her to dress. I need you to be my lady mother, she cried silently, because the knight did not love me, and she sweated with pain, remembering. She bent to kiss Douce's cheek, then turned to Fabrisse. "Well put," she said stiffly and went out.

When she clambered down the stairs into the yard, she saw Pons coming toward her. Without thinking, she suddenly fell down in a heap on the second step from the bottom. I feel as old as earth, she thought, and the sun has been up only a few hours.

Pons said to her solemnly, "When there is chaos in the world, there is also chaos in the soul."

Sybille grunted. "But what is one to do about that?"

"Accept reality," he answered promptly. "Stand fast. Don't run."

"Sermons," Sybille quavered at him, angry. "Don't talk to me about reality. My mama once loved and laughed. That was reality. Before the war she peed in the chamber pot and then in her new toilet. But that was another reality, before the war." Her head pitched to her knees and she burst into stored-up tears. "I loathe this life."

Above her head, she heard Pons say, "This is a mad world. But that's irrelevant. What's important is seeing life for what it is."

She did not want to listen and sobbed, "Everyone is alone, separate, off on some private journey of their own. No one gives a damn about anyone else." His big hands touched her back. "Before the war, people loved other people."

His arms went around her legs and she felt herself being swung into space. "Shhh," he crooned, as if he were soothing a bawling baby. Nose and mouth streaming uncontrollably, she crushed her face into his chest until his tunic smeared with wetness. He carried her through the sunshine toward the olive tree at the shadowy end of the yard, rocking her and murmuring about history.

History meant nothing to her. Eventually she groaned, "All I ever wanted of you—I wanted you to love me like my father loved my mother. He took care of her, he would not—" She was going to say "leave her," but she stopped. Suddenly it struck her that William had chosen not to return from Muret. Ah, Papa, were you thinking of Mama while you waited for the scarlet crosses? She started to cry again, this time softly as if her insides had rusted away and dissolved.

Pons murmured, "In another life we will be lovers, you and I. It was not destined in this one, Sybille."

Her head jerked up. A ragged patch of sky above Saint-Sernin's belltower blurred from cream to lemon. Is it my fate, she thought, to have no husband, no babes?

Pons set her down on the cobbles and said carefully, "This is not an age, I think, when men and women can love each other. Not in our land, not in this lifetime."

Swaying, she wiped her nose on her sleeve. There would be no other lifetimes. And suppose there were, what good did that do her now? "Ah, my dear friend," she said aloud, "those are hard words. Perhaps I should get myself a little dog to love." She tried to smile, but felt her voice wavering.

Pons said tenderly, "No, only one kind of love is appropriate now. Love God, serve Him." He fluffed her hair away from her cheek.

"Mayhap," she said uneasily, because she did not know how to go about loving God. And, she wondered, did she care to learn? She hid her face in the hill of his shoulder and sealed shut her eyes. "Pons, are you there?"

"I'm here," he said. His arms coiled around her.

She breathed in the coolness of the cobbles under the olive tree, then the warm, soapy smell of Pons's beard. After a while she said, "I must go inside." But she stayed still in his arms, all her wounds at rest.

Chapter Nine

Just after sunup the advance guard of Simon de Montfort's army rode through the Narbonne gate, cut off the hands of a baker who refused them bread, and let it be made known on behalf of the city's "legitimate" suzerain that he was approaching the wall-less city and that he intended to reward its treachery by destroying Toulouse to its foundations. If the burghers imagined this an empty threat, they would soon learn otherwise. By noon the consuls, terrified, had sped a delegation to De Montfort swearing loyalty, but he would not listen. The following day, the Wednesday before the fall quarterday, his troops stormed into the city and began setting afire Saint-Remesy, St. Stephen's square, and Joux-Aigues, three of the city's main quarters.

When people in these areas saw what the French were doing, they hurried to throw up barricades in the squares, hoping to block the enemy's advance. All that night they dragged barrels and beams to strengthen the barricades while somehow managing to hold off the French knights.

The Cerdan gate to the faubourg had been barred, so for the present De Montfort's troops remained some distance from Rue St. Bernard. Still, the street prepared to defend its mansions.

"Get my lord father's swords," Sybille said to Florent. "And sharpen every hatchet you can lay hands on. We shall plant a blade in some bastard's belly before they get us."

Florent grinned. "May God hear you."

After the house had been searched from tower to cellar and the makeshift weapons lined up in rows in the yard, Sybille went down to have a look. Fabrisse jogged at her heels, sullen. She said, "I hope you're not expecting my help. Who is going to use these things?"

"Guess."

"My faith forbids me to shed blood. Christ said—"

Sybille bit back a nasty reply. "Very sensible, sister," she snorted. She leaned forward to peer at the axes and kitchen cleavers, the fish-hooks and pestles. "You're going to stand around and wait to be slaughtered."

"What?" Fabrisse's voice fluttered.

Sybille started toward a crossbow. It was an antique all right, but Florent had cleaned it and amazingly found a handful of rusty arrows. She said, "Our great-grandfather fired this. Would you care to try it?"

"No. I'm going upstairs to pray." Fabrisse went to the steps and started up, mauve wimple bellying in the afternoon breeze. A yellow sun loomed over the belltower of Saint-Sernin, unreeling amber flames along the edges of the kitchen knives. Sybille lifted her head. In the distance plumes of brown smoke were billowing toward the faubourg like clouds of weary locusts. Otherwise the day seemed like any other, and it was hard to believe that beyond the Saracen Wall, Joux-Aigues was ablaze. She could not make up her mind what to do about the crossbow. Finally she called to the stableboy and told him to practice firing arrows at the rear wall of the stable.

The sun cooled. Twilight came. Later Sybille slipped up to the roof. A blanched orange glow leaped in the sky above the city. Every-thing was quiet, unreal. Beyond the Saracen Wall there were burned-out houses and people who had slept in their beds last night but would not this night. Toulousans had died today, Catholics and Good Christians alike, and for what? When matins sounded Sybille went down to bed. For a moment, in the soundless dark, she began to shiver with terror. What would she do if the French got into the faubourg? If they broke down her gate? She could not imagine herself bashing some crusader's skull, no matter how much she wanted to. She would be killed first.

"Damn Pons!" she cursed aloud in the darkness. Damn William, damn Pierre and Mathieu, for getting themselves killed and leaving us here alone. Damn all of them to hell forever and ever. Careless, thoughtless creatures, thinking of nobody but themselves. Damn Olivier de Ferrand. She drifted off before saying her prayers.

Simon de Montfort grouped his soldiers on Rue Droit. Knights, horses, stone-guns, arrows hurtled furiously toward the Cerdan gate.

So deafening was the first wave of the attack that the cobblestones in Saint-Sernin square seemed to move and the tremors could be felt even in Rue St. Bernard. Down in the Astarac courtyard, Florent marshaled the stableboys into a little army and shouted commands with a military zeal worthy of Charlemagne. Cook was busy boiling kettles of oil. Sybille watched all this from the top of the yard stairs. Fabrisse darted up behind her.

"Sister," she panted. "Come upstairs. Hurry, Mama wants you."

"Not now. Get someone to mind her. Or you do it. You're not doing anything."

"You don't understand. Sybille, she's dressing. God has made a miracle. I mean, her mind is clear. She—"

Sybille whirled to face Fabrisse. "Clear?" she repeated in disbelief. Her ears were full of Florent's yelling.

"Come and see," Fabrisse shouted. "I tell you there's been a miracle. She says God told her to get dressed."

Sybille squeezed past, sprinted to the second floor, and found Douce standing at the foot of the bed, where she was trying to button the sleeves of a silk gown. She glanced up at her daughter and shook her head in disgust. Sybille gaped at the lengths of apricot silk hanging on the emaciated body and could not utter a word.

"Why is Carenza never here when I need her?" Douce demanded. "That girl deserves a thrashing. I cannot wear this!"

Sybille forced her lips into a cautious smile. "Did you sleep well, Mama?" she mumured at last.

Douce pointed to the bed, piled with rumpled gowns. "Worthless. Utterly unfit to be seen in. Someone has ruined every gown I own." She fussed at the skirt of the apricot silk in helpless rage. "This is criminal. There was a lace hem on this and now—see—it's been ripped off, hasn't it? Yes."

"Mama." She took a step forward and stopped. Behind her back she heard Fabrisse cough softly.

"Someone has dared to enter my chamber without my permission," Douce said, her face harsh with anger. "Some unknown person has destroyed my property and I mean to find out who. And make no mistake, I will report this crime to the count's court and prosecute the case myself." Her voice rose.

"Please, Mama."

"I must go to the draper's at once." She pursed her lips. "But the problem is I have nothing to wear. Must I ride naked to Rue de la Pourpointerie? Apparently so."

Fabrisse shoved around Sybille, limped to the window seat, and slowly sank down, all the time keeping her eyes on their mother. When Sybille glanced at her sister, she saw Fabrisse smiling and sniffing insipidly, as if she had a front-row seat at the resurrection of Lazarus. Sybille wanted to walk over and smack her. Douce said sharply to Fabrisse, "Please, daughter. That sniveling is putting my teeth on edge."

"I'm sorry, Mama."

"I asked you before—what is the matter?"

"Nothing." Fabrisse wiped her nose on her sleeve. "I'm fine."

"For heaven's sake, if you can't tell me what's troubling you, then have the courtesy to retire to your chamber. Hear me?"

"I hear."

"Also," Douce grunted, "change your gown." She needled a scornful glance at Fabrisse's tattered bliaut. "I've seen better-dressed beggars, child." Fabrisse nodded, not moving.

Without warning, an explosion rocked the casement. From down in the yard came a chorus of screeches. Sybille thought she recognized Cook's roar. She ran to the window and peered down into Rue St. Bernard. The street was deserted, save for a dog barking. The French must have broken through the Cerdan gate, she thought. Her breath began to burn in her chest. She heard Douce say loudly, "What in God's name was that?"

"Thunder," Fabrisse mumbled.

Sybille pulled in her head and turned to Fabrisse, who blinked and looked away. In the distance people were shouting. A moment later there was a second crash, less noisy. Douce sat down hard on the bed, atop the discarded gowns.

Sybille breathed deeply. "My lady mother," she said, "the people in the faubourg have barricaded the Cerdan gate to keep out the French." She spoke in a slow, careful voice. "What you hear is De Montfort's stone-guns."

"The French?" Douce said, startled. "In Toulouse?"

"Yes, Mama. There has been bad fighting beyond the Saracen Wall since yesterday."

"Jesus in heaven!" Douce exclaimed. "What is the count doing?"

"He's—away."

Douce shook her head. Although the babble in the yard had ceased, echoes still vibrated through the room. She snatched a comb from among the pillows and began to swipe silently at her hair. Abruptly she burst out, "What a disgrace!" Raymond, she complained, did not have his head on straight. All his life he had been too busy with his women, that was his trouble. He was a good man but flighty. And now see what disasters his poor management had brought them. Sybille agreed. Had the consuls met? Douce asked. What did Pons de Capdenier and Pierre Embry the Elder have to say about all this? Sybille scratched her nose and said she did not know. She inched toward the door, anxious to go down to the yard and find out if the French had penetrated the faubourg.

Douce said, "A knave should be sent to the De Perellas. We must find out if they're safe."

"That's impossible," Sybille said. "The gate is barred." She shot a fretful look at her sister. When she went out, Fabrisse was saying to Douce, "Tomorrow, Mama. It's too dangerous today."

If we're still alive tomorrow, Sybille thought. Florent had no news. He believed the attack had failed, but there was no way to be sure. All afternoon the ground rattled. Sybille paced between the well and the olive tree. Once, still clad in the apricot silk, Douce appeared at the top of the yard stairs and waved gaily.

The hammering of the stones against the Cerdan gate went on until daylight began to slacken. Then there came silence more terrifying than the noise.

"Na Sybille," Florent said. "No one has eaten all day. Are we to have no supper?"

Ears cocked at every sound, the household sat on the cobbles in the yard gobbling cheese and yesterday's bread and cold herring. Sybille had bottles of Canary wine brought up from the cellar. Under the olive tree, Douce sat on the bench and ate and sipped wine; she smiled graciously and spoke a few words to each servant, as might some noble lady just returned from a long pilgrimage. After Saint-Sernin sounded compline, when the only sound in the yard was the breeze gnawing the olive branches, the lady of Astarac played her cittern and sang the old songs she had loved in her childhood: Jaufré Rudel, Marcabru, Cercamon.

Afterward, still cradling the cittern, she tottered across the yard on Fabrisse's arm. At the foot of the stairs, she turned to Sybille, who wound her arms softly around Douce's neck like a foundling restored.

"Mama," she whispered, "I love you so much—forever."

Douce put a hand on Sybille's hair and said cheerfully, "Come, don't let despair consume you. I know God will look after us. And when He raises up the sun tomorrow, we will all feel strong and rejoice in life." Her face was radiant, beautiful to see. "Good night, my lamb." Fabrisse took her upstairs.

The vigil went on. Not until almost matins did a crier round the corner of Saint-Sernin and come weaving down Rue St. Bernard. "Praise God!" he bellowed. One by one, gates creaked open and people rushed into the middle of the street. Sybille waited with Brune Maurand and her daughter, Eglantine. De Montfort had retreated, run back to the château.

"What of it?" Sybille said, to no one in particular. "He can return tomorrow." Stupid with exhaustion, she went up to bed.

Next morning, soon after the first blush of light, the Maurand gatekeeper found the broken body of Douce d'Astarac sprawled in Rue St. Bernard, below her open chamber window. A yard off, its strings spiraled into a blizzard of uncorked wires, lay her shattered cittern.

The rain came down. Rain had fallen yesterday, the day she had killed herself, and it was still falling. Good, Sybille thought. I could not bear the sun. Mama hated rain; she would not have enjoyed these past two days. It is no great tragedy she missed them. But what will I do when the rain stops?

In the library her mother's body, embalmed, hands cupping a crucifix, waited for burial. She would be laid to rest in the Saint-Sernin burial ground, a feat Sybille had managed for a suicide by means of a sizable donation to the abbot. Even so, no entombment was possible until the fighting ended.

The next few days, while rain drummed on the casements, Sybille found herself making circuits of Douce's chamber. The prie-dieu waited. Gowns slumped from the wall hooks. The crystal goblets glowed. Every object remained just where it had sat last week. No, she raged silently. These things have no right to exist when she does not.

From the bed she studied the marble floor. Despite repeated

scrubbings, Carenza had not been able to remove the stains. They seemed to be embedded in the marble. Excrement and urine is all she left, Sybille thought, pathetic reminders of illness and deterioration. What a joke this living is, when all you leave of yourself is shit.

She lay on her back across the bed. Fabrisse padded in. She stood at the foot of the bed, her expression placid. Finally she said, "There is nothing to keep me here now. You know that."

"Sister," Sybille said, "I did not invite you to come in. I want to be alone."

Fabrisse glanced at the prie-dieu. "Bishop Folquet is arranging a truce. Everyone who fought against De Montfort will be pardoned."

"Who says?"

"I heard. As soon as Mama is buried, I'm leaving." Sybille turned her face away, furious. "Sister, I have my own life."

The weather turned cold. At City Hall Simon de Montfort met with the consuls to sign a truce, and in Joux-Aigues Sybille and the Astarac banker attended to Douce's will with its donations to various churches and hospitals. The following morning Douce's little cortege stumbled down Rue St. Bernard toward the Saint-Sernin cemetery, and she was put in the ground and covered with earth. Fabrisse wept. Sybille did not. That evening after vespers, Fabrisse departed for the heretic convent in Fanjeaux. Sybille went up to her chamber and closed the door.

Over the weekend when the truce was to take effect, Simon de Montfort arrested the wealthiest burghers, then he seized their property and expelled them from the city. Raymond de Perella and Pierre Maurand were among those force-marched through the Narbonne gate by jeering French soldiers. All the bankers, the best knights, the most distinguished consuls, were insulted like leprous vermin and forced to march away at the double. Once De Montfort had rid himself of these people, he published an edict throughout the region, calling upon everyone capable of wielding a pick and shovel to come to Toulouse and destroy it.

"He's crazy," Sybille told Florent. "He wants us to destroy our own city? He'd have to kill us first."

Two days later, Florent announced Simon de Montfort was in the yard. When he came into the hall, Sybille was standing by the hearth, one hand fisted behind her back. Without speaking, he bowed, removed his cloak, and settled himself in a chair by the fire. Sybille did not move. Carenza poured white wine, and the Frenchman raised the goblet and took a sip daintily.

He said, "The fig tree putteth forth her green figs—"

"What?" Sybille blurted out. Then she recognized the verse from the Song of Solomon.

"—and the vines with the tender grapes give a good smell. Arise, my love, my fair one, and come away."

Before she could reply, he was staring off into the hearth and talking about a journey he once had taken to Champagne as a child. On a hot afternoon he had crawled over the black, spongy ground and lay down in a vineyard with the ripe fruit over his head and the cool light meshing him among green leaves. And when his mother called him, he was quiet and did not answer for a very long while because he was so happy under the vines.

"I still remember that day very clearly," he said, more to himself than to Sybille.

Sybille waited, suspicious. He had not come there to reminisce about his childhood.

"My sainted mother cried and said I was a naughty boy." He bobbed his chin at the goblet. "This is from the Astarac vineyard?"

"Yes, my lord." Legs weak, Sybille scanned the clean-shaven face, the cleft chin, the sandy hair crinkled with silver. He was taller than she had imagined, and in the glow of the flames his eyes were grave. This man's madness does not show, she thought. His mind appears rational.

Minutes passed. Their eyes met. De Montfort went on sipping the wine. He said several years earlier Lady Alice had transplanted a Bordeaux vine with moderate success; she had the patience for that sort of thing. Sybille scratched her nose. Carenza refilled his goblet. He went on about the growing of grapes and after a while he apologized for coming unannounced and hoped he was not inconveniencing Na Sybille, and she said he was not. It was a lot of fancy words.

Finally Sybille said, "After all, my lord, you are the count of Toulouse." She could hear her words floating between them in the air and felt amazed she could have uttered them.

De Montfort gazed at her over the rim of the goblet. He corrected her. "I am a knight of Jesus Christ. Your lord father is—deceased. According to my information."

"Yes. Deceased."

"Pierre d'Astarac," he grunted. "What do you know of his where-abouts?"

She raised both shoulders and let them drop. "Dead."

"Officially?"

Sybille smoothed her voice calm. "No—there is no record. But my brother has not been seen since Muret."

"All right. Never mind." De Montfort raised his head. "What of your lord husband? Pons de Villeneuve I believe is his name."

Alarmed, Sybille's head began to buzz. Suddenly she understood. He was interested only in the males. It was her house and money he wanted, but first he had to prove a male in her family had participated in the rebellion. She made her expression sorrowful. "My lord, you are bringing up painful matters."

De Montfort glanced away.

She bowed her head, mind straining for a persuasive lie. At last she said, "I've not seen my husband for more than a year. He left me for a woman in the Lauraguais." Quickly she looked up to see if he believed her. No doubt he heard this sort of lie a dozen times a day. He had risen and was placing his goblet on the trestle.

"Mark me, lady," he said. "Your husband must be a great fool." He bowed, deeply and gracefully, and turned to go down the hall. Sybille went behind him, sweat trickling from her armpits into the bliaut. He was finished with her; he was the fool, not she. At the entrance he turned, ducked his head over her hand, and brushed his lips soft against the flesh. He murmured, "I've heard it said your lady mother is one of the great beauties of Toulouse. Please convey my respects."

She started. "My mother," she gasped, "is dead. A week ago Tuesday. I—" Involuntarily her mouth quivered. She pressed her lips tight. Then she began to weep and jerked her body toward the wall. She could not make herself stop.

He said nothing and then he said, "Lady, the dead are fortunate. It is the living who deserve our pity."

After the clatter of hoofbeats had died away and the yard was empty, Sybille walked stiffly down the passage to the kitchen and ordered Cook to smash the goblet De Montfort had used.

Sybille strolled up Rue Méjane with her market basket. Along the street, on both sides, new construction was going up, and the hammering and banging sliced into the gray morning air. The previous autumn many of the shops had been destroyed by the French during the big demolition. But now, a year later, the rubble had been cleared at last and merchants were hanging out newly painted signs. Sybille counted four fishmongers.

At the corner of Rue des Nonnes, she stopped outside a butcher's stall. Leaning over a tray of giblets, she considered buying a pig's stomach to stuff with ground pork, filberts, and ginger. Her mouth began to water. Carenza would make a mess of it, she knew, but she had a taste for something toothsome for a change. When she learned the price of the stomach, she abandoned the idea reluctantly. Again she called to the butcher and pointed at a pile of spongy pink globules. "What's that?"

"Deer testicles," he told her. "Excellent in a sweet-and-sour sauce."

Sybille shook her head. Her purse did not hold enough for delicacies.

The butcher came out, wiping his hands on his tunic. "I have some nice whale liver."

A hand grasped Sybille's elbow from behind. She pulled free, startled. When she turned, a friar was smiling at her. "Na Sybille," he said amiably.

For a moment she stared at him and said nothing. Then she barked, "What?"

He cleared his throat. "Aren't you the daughter of William d'Astarac? You are, aren't you?"

"What of it?"

"Tidings, most esteemed lady." His curls brushed the collar of his white robe with its short black cape. The young man looked like a choirboy, slightly overripe. "It's Daniel Marty. I mean, Friar Daniel. Now I serve God with the Blessed Brother Dominic."

She stared at him blankly. She was acquainted with no Preaching Friar.

"My father was the armorer on Rue—En William's armorer. Remember?"

"Oh," Sybille said. She nodded politely at Daniel. "How does your lord father?"

"Dead." He crossed himself, a bit pompously, Sybille thought. "Heart," he added.

"I'm sorry." She turned away, thinking of gizzards. Two, maybe three pounds of gizzards would be cheap and make a decent-sized pie. If she remembered rightly, they had a good supply of acorns. Yes, a gizzard and acorn pie was what they would have tonight. Behind her back the friar was saying, "Gracious lady, are you still living on Rue St. Bernard?"

What business is it of his? she thought. He began fawning over her family, making statements and asking nonsense questions.

The noble lord and lady of Astarac were dead—he swore they were now sitting on the right hand of God's throne.

She hoped so.

How many babes did Na Sybille have?

None.

Forgive him, he had forgotten her lord husband had become a goodman. Why, he had heard Pons preach once at Peyrepertuse. His delivery had been impressive. Dramatic, if she knew what he meant.

She shrugged.

After she paid for the gizzards, she started up Rue Méjane, and Daniel trotted along at her side. He did not stop jabbering about Brother Dominic, whom he lauded as a saint. His familiar manner irritated Sybille, and she wondered how she could shake him off. Ahead, above the church, the sky was darkening. A drop of rain splashed her nose. At last they reached Saint-Sernin square, where she said an abrupt farewell and raced toward Rue St. Bernard without looking back.

By the time she neared her gate, the rain was falling steadily and her cloak was sodden. Florent came out to meet her.

"Is Dolosa better?" she asked him. The mare was the only mount left in the stable; if she sickened and died, Sybille feared she would have to walk for the rest of her life.

"Some, lady. What did you buy? It's been a week since we ate meat."

Sybille did not answer. She went in through the yard door to the kitchen and swung her basket to the trestle. Carenza was nowhere to be seen. She lifted out the provisions—white aubergines, salt, goat cheese, olives—and lined them up. She wished there were someone to talk to, though had there been she did not know what she would have said. Her lady mother had always told her she talked too much; everyone complained of her garrulousness. Now sometimes a whole day would pass without her uttering a single word. It occurred to her she might have been more friendly to the armorer's son. He had meant no harm. What is the matter with me? she wondered. I can't manage a simple conversation. Perhaps it is enough that I can still write. She went to her father's library and seated herself at the table.

Most days she was itching to start, but this afternoon she had no appetite for work. She glanced down at the unfinished song, which she was trying to compose in *trobar braus*. The harsh style suited her mood lately. On her tongue she shaped rhymes with spiky prongs—*ucs, usca, utz*. She completed the stanza, went back to the beginning, and read the whole thing again, then thrust aside the page critically. Mood, she reminded herself, is the most important factor. The more wretched my state of mind, the easier it is to do *trobar braus*. Apparently I am not sufficiently morose today.

All the long, wet afternoon she sorted through the songs she had written since Lammas, a pile of several dozen. Some were fairly decent, in her opinion; the bad ones and the stupid ones she laughed at and put aside for lighting candles. There was a *tenso*, in which two women were listing the lies told them by their lovers, each trying to top the other. That one was truly stupid but hilarious, so she saved it.

Hungry, she went to the kitchen and sat down at the trestle. The pie was almost done, and eventually Carenza brought it to the table and went to call Florent. While they ate, everyone was careful to say nothing about the blackened crust and underdone gizzards, but Sybille made a mental note never to request a pie again. Carenza should stick to stews and roasts.

"I wasn't raised to be a cook," Carenza bleated defensively.

"Was Florent? Was I?" Sybille chewed hard. "We must manage as best we can, the three of us. Isn't that right, Florent?"

The gatekeeper took a long swallow of wine. "Suppose you were to sell your gold-coin collar."

She had sold it already, but she asked, "For what?"

"A girl—to cook."

Sybille's temper inched up. "We have trouble feeding three mouths. You want a fourth?"

"If only Master Pons were here," Carenza fretted. "When there is no master in the house—men know how to get money. There are ways."

"Really?" Sybille said coldly. Fuming, she pretended to eat. "Half the houses in the city have no master now. And even those who do aren't able to collect the revenues from their farms. So it has nothing to do with Master Pons's being gone or my being a woman."

Florent cut another slice of pie and brought it dripping to his plate. "Lady, if you were to visit another banker, you could borrow—"

She cut him off angrily. "I have. I've borrowed and sold and begged and mortgaged. I can't make miracles." It was useless talking to them. Each evening at supper they had the same tiresome arguments about money. But they simply could not understand what she said. It was inconceivable to them that a wealthy family could be impoverished.

Florent said, "The gateman at the Maurands told me—"

"I don't care what he told you," Sybille said sourly. "Whatever it was, it's a lie. Brune Maurand is no better off than we." She dipped a morsel of scorched crust into the gravy. Her voice swung up. "I'm tired of being persecuted by you two. I do the best I can. If it doesn't suit you, take service elsewhere."

Carenza and Florent bent their necks over their plates, displeased. After a minute, Carenza looked up and piped, "Yes, but Na Douce's ruby ring would bring thirty silver marks. Why don't you—?"

"God's teeth, leave me alone!" she roared. Nobody spoke. She screeched, "I'm going to hang myself. Then you'll go begging your bread. Then you'll know what trouble is!"

The kitchen, despite the fire, remained damp. The cool weather had come too soon, Sybille thought. Another autumn racing toward another winter. How many of these shifts would she have to see before she died? No season pleased her. Midsummer had been too hot and too dry. No rain had fallen after St. John's Day, which had been good for the vines, but then the wells had gone dangerously low. Carenza began to clear away the platters. Then Florent carefully picked out the gizzards from the pie shell and transferred them to a bowl. Sybille looked at Carenza. "Boil them with wine and ginger—we can have them tomorrow." Florent told Sybille the old count was on his way to Toulouse. He was bringing with him the counts of Foix and Comminges, and all the exiled seigneurs of the city and those from Albi and the Quercy districts, and all the *faidit* knights who had been hiding in the forests or living in Spain. They would be liberated. The cobbler on Rue Matabiau had told him. Sybille laughed.

"Don't you believe it, madam?"

"No. Do you?"

He said he guessed not.

She laughed again, picked up a candle, and went out. She walked back through the hall, but when she got to the library she stopped with her hand on the door. On impulse, she turned and climbed the stairs to the upper floor.

She pushed the door to Douce's chamber and went inside, standing hesitantly in the shadows a moment before she lit the standing candle. She rarely came there, no one did. Soon after Douce died they closed off the upper floor and used only the first floor. Sybille had continued to take her meals in the great hall. But even that did not last long. They did not have enough wood to make fires in both the hall and the kitchen.

Sybille stared at the bed, ghostly in its white dust cover, then she began to move slowly around the room. She ran her fingers over the dusty prie-dieu. If things get any worse, she thought, we might have to abandon the ground floor, perhaps move into the cellar. The idea was absurd and it wasn't. A year ago, who would have dreamed the necessity for abandoning the upper floors?

She pulled the prie-dieu away from the wall. Kneeling, she groped for the loose tile, tugged with her nails, and removed it finally. From the hole she brought up a silk bag, untied it, and clanked Douce's remaining jewelry into her lap. Useless to take inventory, she thought. I know exactly what is left—a half-dozen ear pendants, the scarab necklace, two sheet-gold bracelets. She fingered Douce's gold bangle with the duck's head, a gift from William on the birth of Pierre. It was Roman, Sybille recalled, and dated back to perhaps the second century after Christ. That was what Douce had once told her. If that were really so, it might be truly valuable. Sybille sighed loudly. Much good it would do her now, because who had the money to buy it? Abruptly she collected the jewelry and stuffed it back in the hiding place.

The air in the room was stale and stuffy, and the dust was tickling her nose. She pushed open a casement, letting in a wave of moist air. As she turned, a chest caught her eye and she went over to lift the lid. Inside, wrapped in red silk, was her mother's broken cittern. Hastily she dropped the lid and backed off toward the window, telling herself she had forgotten where she had hidden it. Tomorrow, the thirteenth day of September, would be her natal day, and Saturday would mark one year since her lady mother had died. Now the memory of Douce no longer caused her pain. At Christmas last year, she realized that sometimes a whole day would go by without her once thinking of her mother.

She rubbed her face against the dusty curtains, sneezed, and felt exhausted. She no longer missed Douce. Nor Pons nor Fabrisse. She still felt the absence of Corba, who finally had gone to Montségur with her daughters. Corba had been her friend, the only person to whom she could talk about Olivier.

A chill breeze swathed the nape of her neck, and she told herself she should close the casement and go to bed, even if she could not fall asleep. Emptiness enveloped her body like a tight skin. It also camped inside her chest. Each day she struggled to fill up the void. She ate, slept, wrote verse, talked to Carenza and Florent, went to the market, but never could she entirely fill that empty space.

Dragging herself up, she turned to close the casement. To her surprise, a thick fog had cloaked the window, like magic. She knelt on the window seat and leaned over the sill. She saw nothing, not the street or the torch on the Maurand gate. "God's eyes," she said aloud, "look at that. You can't see a foot." She closed the window and went down to bed.

During the night, armored in fog, the count of Toulouse's army forded the Garonne near the Bazacle mill and entered the city by the postern gate. It was not yet daylight when Florent brought Sybille the news. She sat up and burst into tears. Naked, she rolled from the bed and pulled on her clothes. Florent blubbered, "Under the very noses of the bastards. Lady, under their noses! Our blessed count—"

Sybille heard nothing. Limbs weightless as air, her whole body pulled as by a wind, she raced into Rue St. Bernard and began running. The sky was still misty and colored light gray. In Saint-Sernin square Sybille joined the crowds streaming toward the river. There were men half dressed in only their breeches, and women with neither shawls nor shoes. Knights and ladies, varlets and scullions, young and old, they were running toward Saint-Pierre de Cuisines, half insane with excitement and love. In the steamy light Sybille looked up and saw the count's banners billowing down Rue Palmade. *Dieu! Tolosa!,* she cried under her breath, and the wind swirled around her ears.

At the corner of Rue St. Julien, she stopped and climbed on a grocer's barrel and waited. She could see the mounted knights filing slowly down the middle of the street, then the old count, and behind him the gallant young Raymond. In the muddy gutters people were tumbling to their knees and kissing the old count's feet and the hem of his tunic and his outstretched fingers, as if he had risen from the grave. They were all shouting at once, and the count laughed with tears streaming from his eyes and he yelled, "Holy Mary, give me back the city of my forebears! Better to die here than roam the world in shame!" Behind the counts, as far down the street as the eye could take in, rode the knights and vassals of Toulouse. Once people realized their fathers and husbands, their uncles and sons and brothers, had come home too, they burst out bawling again, and even if every bell in the faubourg had begun ringing at once nobody would have heard, so great was the uproar.

From atop the barrel Sybille stared and stared at the marching men until her eyes grew swollen. Then she saw Olivier de Ferrand. She stood stock-still, as if she had hardened into stone. When he had passed from view, she leaped to the cobbles and could not stop her limbs from trembling. *Domna sancta Maria,* she thought. It could not have been him. It was only some trick of my eyes. She jostled her way back toward Rue St. Bernard, dazed.

And so, Lord God be praised, the lawful seigneur of Toulouse came home, but there was no feasting or dancing. At City Hall, barely an hour later, the old count wasted no time issuing orders for the rebuilding of the demolished ramparts. The entire population of the city, from the oldest man to the youngest girl, from the most noble lady to the lowliest maidservant, was to bring pick or shovel and report for work. Not tomorrow. Not the next day. That very morning. By noon the sun had come out, and Sybille joined a team of women digging in the marshy ground near the Montoulieu gate. Bernadette Piquier, the banker's wife, had been elected captain.

Nearby, men and women were hammering together barricades of stakes and beams and throwing up wooden barbicans. These improvised fortifications looked like a good wind might blow them down. But they were not as flimsy as they seemed, because the following week when Simon de Montfort rushed back to the city, he was greeted by such a hailstorm of arrows that his cavalry fell back in a hurry and his youngest son was wounded. The Toulousans counterattacked and the French were forced to retreat beyond the Count's Meadow.

"Does the Lord help us or does He not?" crowed the banker's wife. "Look at those cowardly fellows—they aren't worth two poges." This Bernadette was a woman of about forty, dark-eyed, pink-cheeked, plump as a well-fed nightingale, with a tongue almost as sweet.

It was a warm fall. Every morning, as if she had been doing it all her life, Sybille rode to the Montoulieu gate and reported for work with Bernadette and the other women, turning over the soil and hauling it away. The hard physical labor made her feel alive and healthy. All the women talked about having new energy and sleeping like babes at night. Sybille had never seen human beings work so hard. The old city wall, destroyed by the French two years earlier, was being rebuilt by round-the-clock shifts.

The days were full and short. Sybille had no time to wonder about Olivier, no time to think at all. It seemed as if she had only arrived at the gate when suddenly the sun was waning and it was time to go home.

Officially Toulouse was under siege. In fact this was not so, because the French did not have enough troops to surround the city. De Montfort still held the château, and his army camped on the southern outskirts of the city, between the château and the Montoulieu gate. But so far this so-called siege was not inconveniencing anyone; the northern and western gates remained open for supplies and reinforcements, and barges from Bordeaux were still tying up along the Garonne. Everyone was busy and cocky, and the women of Bernadette's brigade told each other the French would be gone by Advent. Even Sybille found herself planning ahead and thinking she might go to Astarac at Christmas to collect her rents.

So when the crusaders charged the Montoulieu gate in the second week of October, it was a surprise to many. At dawn the French broke through the outer barricades crying, *"Montjoie St. Denis!"* and *"Holy Sepulcher!"* By the time Sybille got there, the moat already was littered with corpses, men were rushing the wall with scaling ladders, and the terrible shouting hurt her ears. She was set to work handing bolts to a crossbowman.

Once, midmorning, she worked up the courage to peek down into the moat. At first glance it gave the impression of a garden budding and flowering with red and white lilies, and she had to remind herself those splashes of pretty color were flesh and blood and brains. Shrinking back, she clapped her hand over her mouth.

The crossbowman, a Blagnac peasant named Folco, winked at her. "We are supplying new souls for hell and paradise," he said cheerfully. "Sinners or redeemed, we do not ask questions."

Sybille told him that was not funny. She stared at her feet.

Folco rested his hand comfortably on her shoulder. "Lady, you'll get used to it."

"Think so?"

He grinned at her and reached for his crossbow. "I don't think. Except to duck when I hear something coming."

A half hour before vespers, the French sounded retreat. Giddy, Sybille sank down on her haunches, thinking she had blanked out fear all day and was surprised at that. Folco complained about the crossbow and said his ambition was to become a gunner—it was a more sophisticated weapon. Bernadette was calling the women and ordering them to line up at the archers' slits and look down into the lists until she released them. Obediently, Sybille turned and watched in silence.

Below the gate was open. Mounted knights were herding out the French prisoners, about three dozen of them roped together. They were staggering with their heads down. Most of them were barefoot or dressed only in breeches and shirts. The butchering began. Sybille held herself still.

Afterward, the bodies were dismembered and the chunks of overred meat tidily stacked into carts, which then rolled back inside the gate.

The banker's wife climbed on a barrel. "Sisters," she called. The women swung around, green-faced every one, and gathered around her. Folco stood to one side, smiling and nodding his head approvingly. "Those heads—tomorrow they will be thrown back to the French." She pointed to a stone-gun. "Think of them as—missiles. Go home, sleep well."

Bernadette smiled at them. "Return at prime and bring rags to cover your noses. I promise you will need them."

Sybille went down to saddle Dolosa. She could feel bile spurting in her throat. The low sun lay in orange stripes along the cobbles and rippled down the sides of the houses. Dusk was coming earlier now. By the time she reached Saint-Romain, the sun had gone and she was shivering. Torches and bonfires were being lighted. Outside a wine shop, a clump of students were jangling nervous *eleisons* on gongs and fifes. Sybille, relaxing, maneuvered the mare slowly. She thought, One of these days I should start going to mass again, for Mama's sake. A knight wheeled his stallion sideways and rammed Dolosa's side. "Watch out, you son of a bitch!" she yelled at him.

He reined around, not a bit apologetic. "Watch yourself, booby," he snapped.

She brushed back the hair from her ears. "Olivier?"

For a minute he stared unsmiling over his stallion's head. Then he said, "Hello there, Sybille."

"Can't you even manage a smile?" she asked.

Olivier made a face. "Oh, Sybille," he drawled reproachfully, as if she had just held a dagger to his heart and demanded his purse.

Angry, she kicked her mare into a trot and clattered a few steps away from him. He called her name, and she slowed and watched him following her from the corner of her eye. When she had crossed through the Cerdan gate into the faubourg, he moved up even with her. He did not speak, and she wondered if he meant to follow her home.

He said mildly, "What's the matter with you? You're not speaking to me."

God's eyes!, she exploded under her breath. This knight has not changed—he is still a perfect ass. I will be quit of him before I reach my gate. "Neither have you said a word to me," she replied in a voice pretending pleasantness. Then, without turning her head, she growled, "I've not seen you these past three years, my lord. Where have you been hiding?"

"Away."

She swiveled her head. He was slouched in his saddle, studying her. He needed a haircut, she noticed. She leaned forward and made the corner into Rue St. Bernard. At her gate she reined in, wondering what would happen now. The gate stood open, and she walked Dolosa into the yard and dismounted. Olivier's horse followed. Abruptly she said, "Do you want to stay for supper?"

"Perhaps." He shrugged.

Heads bent over the bowls, they ate without looking up. Nobody spoke. At last Florent said, "Na Sybille, you must have some exciting tales for us. We heard the gate was nearly overrun."

"Oh, things got hot," she replied. "Make no mistake, we were in the thick of it." She did not want to mention the slaughtered prisoners. "I was—I am assisting a bowman. Tomorrow he may be transferred to a gun, so I'll be—" Olivier's eyes on her face were making her nervous.

He said, "You're working at Montoulieu?"

"Yes. Platform Five."

He gave a bland laugh. "Very interesting. Me too. I'm at Platform One."

She could think of nothing to say to that. Eyes lowered, she reached for the wine again. These past weeks she had not seen him, though it would have been a miracle if she had. Hundreds were defending Montoulieu. All of a sudden it struck her that Olivier may have been one of the executioners this evening; she had been too high up to glimpse their faces. She was afraid to ask him, and so she said it was a small world, wasn't it. Olivier turned to Florent and began recalling the toughness of the French foot soldiers and how some of them were no more than mere lads, who should have been home with their mothers. To see those poor children coming across the killing ground, being obliged to slay them, made a man want to go mad. God, he cried, would never forgive Rome for the sin of using child crusaders. Florent agreed.

Entranced, Sybille stared at the knight's face. His cheeks were grimy, his chin stubbled, but she had never seen a sweeter mouth. The gentle eyes, now purple, now bluish, flickered with held-back tears. To see his face you would have thought he had come directly from the right hand of God's golden throne. Oh *amics,* she thought, oh my friend, my joy of joy, oh Olivier, may you never come to harm, never perish, may your sweet soul be blessed forever. She looked into her empty bowl, looked away.

Carenza cleared the trestle and began washing up. The two men began to talk about fortifications. For something to do, Sybille got up to stand by the storeroom door. After a while she sat down again with her hands in her lap. Olivier paid no attention to her. When compline rang, the servants went quietly off.

Olivier looked at her appraisingly and said, "Well, lady." He got up and came around the trestle to sit next to her. Her body was very tense now. Without warning, he toppled toward her and dropped his head heavily into her lap. She lifted her hand and placed only the tips of her fingers on the curls. Then quickly she drew back.

He straightened. "Would you like to be seduced?" he said in a breathless voice.

"What do you mean seduced? You want to sleep here?"

"What do you want?"

"I want you to," she admitted.

"It would be dangerous." He laughed hoarsely.

"For whom?" she said, trying not to look dangerous.

"Me. Listen, for you too. Don't fool yourself."

"I'm not." She was.

They both got up. Grabbing a candle, she happily steered him through the dark hall. Their footsteps bounced on the marble tiles. "Carry me," she said to him. "I want you to carry me."

"Don't be silly," he said.

"Come on."

"That's not a sensible way to behave."

She was going to pester him, but she could see he was being difficult and she stopped.

In her room she set the candle on her writing table and faced him. He walked past her and started to pull off his shirt. When she saw he was making no move to kiss her, she turned away and began to plait her hair. She did not look at him. Behind her, she heard the bed creak. She blew out the candle, slipped out of her clothes, and crawled in beside him, careful not to touch him. He was breathing in that funny, jerky way, as if he had run upstairs. She jostled her soles against the tops of both his bare feet, cool as chilled peaches. Only then did he lock his arms around her waist.

She kissed him on the mouth. He did the things she liked, but passively, almost as if he were maneuvering the steps of a vaguely remembered dance. There was no passion there; still, she wanted his body so much she did not care. She wondered when he would get hard, and finally she wondered if he ever would. Then she stopped wondering and slid down.

"Why are you doing that?" he asked.

"I want to."

Resting her cheek against his thigh, she enclosed him like a womb. After a long while he went with a wail of pure terror, as if she had hit him. She squirmed up to the pillow and lay down next to him on her back. Her mouth tasted salty. It is I who have the strength, she whispered to herself. I have the power to hurt him if I want to. In the darkness she heard him say, "What did you get out of all that?"

She told him, not a thing. That was not entirely true, but it was too late at night to start defining her pleasure. He sighed noisily and advised her she was a fool.

Before cockcrow she wriggled out of sleep to find him above her. Keeping her eyes closed, she enjoyed herself without making a sound. If he knew she were awake, he might stop. Certainly he would stop. Or he would spoil it somehow.

Olivier left the house without breaking his fast, and Sybille washed her hair and ate ravenously of bread and Brie before riding to the gate. All morning long she sang lustily as she passed bolts to Folco. He complained about the slowness of his weapon and how he could fire no more than two shots a minute. Besides, his arm ached from winding back the cord. They got up speed when Sybille took over the loading of the bow, and Folco had only to aim and fire. After a midmorning sortie, the fighting slackened and the French began dragging up bundles of fagots to level the moat, but the bowmen picked them off in short order.

Folco went off to see the gate commander about switching to a stone-gun. While Sybille was waiting, Olivier clambered up and thrust a ribbon into her hand. In all her life she had never felt so happy. "Blue—oh, I love pale blue! It's so pretty." She smiled at him. "Where did you get it?"

Olivier shifted away as if she had not spoken. He looked down into the moat below. "It needs to be deepened," he said. "Then they won't be able to sap or bring up their cats. Let's make it hard for the fuckers."

Folco came back with a gun and a skin of wine. Sybille leaned against the sun-warmed wall and fingered and fingered the blue ribbon. It was exactly the color of sky on a summer afternoon. Olivier helped Folco set up the stone-gun; they talked about firepower and effectiveness at three hundred yards. Sybille swigged the warm wine and handed it to Folco. Olivier tapped at the gun and said, "They won't be back today, mark me."

"They won't?" Folco said, disappointed. He wanted to try out the new gun.

Sybille wondered if Olivier would be coming back to Rue St. Bernard in the evening, but she did not want to ask. When he was leaving the platform, he hugged her from behind and squeezed his mouth tight against her shoulder. Until that moment she had not realized how much she had missed him these past few years. At sundown on her way home, she bought Damascus plums and cone sugar. She instructed Carenza to stew them into a confection, then she changed into a clean gown, tied back her hair with the ribbon, and waited.

In spite of the siege, people were happy that winter and had a good time. They knew what they were fighting for. The crusaders, weary of fighting with no gain, grew less certain now. The pope's legate reproached Simon de Montfort for his lack of ardor. The French occupied St. Cyprien on the left bank and tried to get into the city by the bridges, but fortunately the Garonne flooded and they had to retreat.

At Easter Folco was killed, and Sybille took over the stone-gun. She knew about war now, about cats and mantelets and all the siege equipment for ramming walls, but most of all about killing. For luck, and because it comforted her, she tied Olivier's blue ribbon on the gun. The banker's wife got a young woman to help her load, the daughter of a Jewish money changer. Sybille put Rachel to work mixing pitch with sulfur and naphtha, because when the stone supply ran low she substituted small kegs full of Greek fire. She became fond of the gun, thought of it as a comrade, and named it Bel Vezer, although it was hardly "beautiful to see." Somebody told her it had been built by a carpenter from the neighborhood of Saint-Sernin, which she took as a good omen.

She alternately loved and hated Olivier, while she waited for the birth of his love. It refused to be born. It did not occur to her they could go on like this year after year. Finally, inevitably, he would have to love her.

Regularly each week, sometimes once, sometimes more, he climbed up to her gun in the late afternoon and accompanied her home. Never could she predict in advance whether she would be seeing the good, sweet Olivier, or the botched and botching Olivier. There was a great difference. Once, riding back to the faubourg, he pointed to a crucifix outside Saint-Romain and chortled, "Recognize that fellow up there?"

She replied stiffly, "It is you who are crucifying me," and failed to comment on his blasphemy. She crossed herself.

His favored method of torturing her, which only became so because he could see how much pain it caused, was to encourage her to sleep with somebody else. Hardly a week passed that he did not inquire in a provocative tone, "Found a lover yet?"

It was his way of constantly reminding her of his indifference. When she refused the bait, he went further and told her she had never swept him off his feet, not even at the start. He was still seeking some idyllic woman, a true soul mate, who would be a vehicle for his salvation. Sybille was not she.

"You await some phantom," she said to him. "You want me to bed another man. That's what you always say."

"Yes," Olivier answered. "Doesn't that make sense?"

"Not to me! Forgive me, I don't feel like it."

"You ought to, you know. Listen to me."

Oh, she hated him. "If you don't want me, why do you keep coming around? Tell me, will you please."

"Habit," he answered, and she laughed rather loudly, disbelieving.

Sybille grew angrier at the knight for humiliating her by his refusal to love her, and at herself for hoping he would change. She no longer bothered to censor her bitterness. In June when De Montfort mounted a new assault with his summer crusaders, she spent twelve hours a day at her gun. The French, desperate, built an immense tower, which they began to wheel up close to the wall. The men and women on the wall laughed; the Frenchmen high atop the cat laughed back, uneasy. For a moment they stared at each other, while both sides tried to think of suitable taunts. The gate commander, confident, shouted, "Take your time, pope's asslickers! Your Madam Cat will never trap our rats." The men on the cat began to flay the wall with arrows.

Before the day ended, the Toulousans had so badly damaged the tower that the French were forced to withdraw it for repairs. The next morning the cat was patched and ready, but the crusaders did not have a chance to use it because the Toulousans stormed their camp. A messenger brought the news to Simon de Montfort, who was on his knees hearing mass at the château. He did not lift his head. After communion he rushed to the field outside the Montoulieu gate.

It was a hot morning and no breeze blew coolness from the river. Standing at her gun, looking beyond the moat to the graveyard without sarcophagi, Sybille recognized Guy de Montfort. Simon's brother was supervising a siege-engine crew. The sun laid its fingers on her eyes and on the French shields and made her squint. To her right, a volley of arrows popped through the light toward the siege engine. Sybille unscrewed the windlass and Rachel fisted a rock into the lowered sling.

Rachel said, "There's Guy de Montfort in the blue shirt."

Sybille shielded her eyes and stared at the blue patch. The men around the engine were ignoring the arrows, as if they were gnats. She hoisted the sling into launch position and moved her fingers over the blue ribbon for luck.

"Na Sybille," Rachel called. "Why don't you aim for Guy?" She moved around behind the gun.

"Yes—yes. No, wait. He's been hit. I can't see. Rachel, who's that man running toward Guy?"

"Which man?"

Guy de Montfort shuffled forward a step. He was glancing up at the wall now, annoyed, and trying to pull the arrow from his thigh. The next moment he was hidden from Sybille's view by a mass of soldiers.

I could have killed him, Sybille thought. I should not have waited. If I had fired, he'd be dead now. Across the rutted ground hurried the man Sybille had glimpsed a moment earlier. His mouth was opening and closing, and he jerked his right arm clumsily above his head. Sybille craned her neck.

"Lady," Rachel shouted. "It's time to stop soon. I have some wine and bread for us."

"Bring them over, Na Rachel. My stomach is empty." Sybille smiled and slid her eyes over the running figure, then examined the man once more to make certain. It is Simon de Montfort, she thought excitedly. Don't ask me how but I know it is he, the great beast. Blank-eyed, she released the gun's trigger and jumped clear. She followed the flight of the stone, noiseless, on its way to entering human flesh. She stood very still. A pounding began in her left temple.

Later when Sybille would try to remember whether the rock had struck Simon full in the face, she could not. She only knew his head had smashed to pieces like a rotting pumpkin, could only remember the rain of bone and brain against Guy de Montfort's blue shirt.

The headless body toppled into the hot dust and sprawled there, one leg twitching. At last it stilled. Guy de Montfort turned aside to vomit.

Empty, Sybille sank down and put the side of her cheek against the base of the gun. Her eyes burned, and when she closed them she saw orange sparks behind her lids. Somewhere above her head she could hear women's voices, high and hysterical, silvering the morning air. They seemed very happy. They were yelling that Sybille had slain the beast. But Sybille could not move and looked straight ahead. She was thinking of Douce, dead, and of rain blowing down from the sky and De Montfort sitting by the fire in her father's chair. The little French boy had not listened to his mother's calls; he had nestled himself, insignificant, under the green vines.

Chapter Ten

After Michaelmas, when the crusaders had gone home, she wrote a song about the death of Simon de Montfort. First, as practice, she made some verse about unhappy love, but the subject bored her and she switched to the war. All during the last week of September she relaxed, allowing the ballad almost to compose itself. To be writing again after more than a year filled her with joy.

By New Year, after the accompaniment had been done by a good jongleur from Lastours and the ballad performed at the old count's Christmas court, it was almost impossible to attend a banquet, or for that matter even to walk through a square, without hearing someone humming the song, so popular had it grown. Sybille herself thought the whole thing ironic. Fine verse she had sweated out had been ignored—this nursery song had become a national anthem. It was crazy, but no crazier than life in Languedoc since De Montfort's death. After ten years of war, people viewed its sudden end as a miracle. Feverish with relief, they drank too much, threw away their money on the most frivolous items imaginable, behaved as if they had lost all reason. Nobody cared about sanity, and nobody questioned their not caring. All Sybille knew was, everybody wanted to sing, and what they wanted to sing was her ballad. Olivier said the secret of her success was the song's simplicity, although he did not intend the remark as a compliment. With greasy hands, he sat at the kitchen trestle and packed his mouth with fried aubergines. He wore a new red shirt; already it was ripped at the neck. He glanced over at her, grinning, and piped in a high voice:

Montfort
Es mort
Es mort
Es mort!
Viva Tolosa!

Sybille cut another slice of plum cake. She watched Olivier wiping his hands against his sleeve. She said, "You like to disparage my work, don't you? You think I'm a mediocre poet."

"Sybille, a toothless babe can grasp the idea—no, listen, it's true."

"Maybe. I don't know any babies."

"Even the feebleminded understand it. What more do you want?" He grinned again, amused.

She could see he was in a good mood and she smiled back. "The more I want, sweet heart, is for you to be nice to me."

He looked surprised and said mildly, "I am nice to you—you're not nice to me." He got up and removed the dirty bowls and began washing them. Since poor Carenza had run off with a one-armed soldier, Sybille insisted Olivier help with supper and wash up on those nights he visited. "I'm not your servant," she had told him defiantly, and he had offered no protest. He was scouring the pots with ashes. Her eyes raked the beautiful blond curls, low on his neck. She called to his back, "We need more wood for the fire."

"*You* need it," he corrected. "There is no 'we.' I don't live here."

The kitchen was growing chilly. Sybille put her hands among the folds of her skirt. She thought of Carenza and her infantry soldier, who had lost his arm at Muret. Perhaps Carenza was fortunate, after all. These days there were few men left to marry, with or without all their limbs. Suddenly she was downcast.

"This is the time to buy weapons," Olivier was saying. "Swords are down to eighty sous. God, that's something I never thought to see."

"What is the sense of buying arms now? The killing is over."

"Because they'll be back. Don't fool yourself."

She gave a jagged laugh. "God, you're mad. Don't you ever expect anything good to happen?"

"Not very often."

Sybille tried not to think of the long days stretching ahead. Her father's house, once among the finest in Toulouse, had fallen into a sorry-looking ruin, and the fact that this was also true for many of the city's mansions did not lessen her grief. She should give up this place; she could not go on forever like a lone mouse scrabbling around an abandoned barn. Often Corba had urged her to live with them in town or at Montségur. But the idea of accepting hospitality in another's household depressed her. She was, God knew, a woman of property. Astarac belonged to her, although she could not imagine spending even one night in that somber heap. But there was Cantal, her grandmother's castle at Fanjeaux. It was a possibility. As a child she had been happy there. She could round up the villeins, still get in a winter crop of wheat if she hurried. It was a perfectly sensible plan.

But how could she go to Fanjeaux? She would have to leave Olivier.

The next morning it was freezing and a pale winter sun crusted the cobbles in the yard. Shivering in her old fur cloak, Sybille walked out to the stable to feed the mounts. When she returned to the kitchen, Olivier was at the table eating almonds and cheese. She began to talk about Na Beatritz and the fief at Fanjeaux, reminding him that he had always dreamed of owning land and a house. She would give Cantal to him. They could go there together and work the land and live simply, as country people do.

Olivier said he needed none of her charity; the young count had talked of giving him an estate in the Agenais. He and Sybille were not husband and wife, anyhow. She meant nothing to him. Sybille fingered the hem of her sleeve. By the time he had finished rejecting the idea, he was booming and breathless, red-faced as a pomegranate.

She waited for him to catch his breath, and then she said, "Try some of that soft cheese. It's seasoned with coriander."

Several times in the following weeks she again brought up the notion, hoping to sway Olivier. The young count may have made promises—he made them to many of his followers—but everyone knew he was slow to make good. Indeed, it might take years. In the meantime she and Olivier could live a decent life. Olivier, stubborn, would not budge. Their living together at Fanjeaux, he told her, would be too dangerous. For him.

"What are you saying?" Sybille asked. "That it would seem like being wed and that frightens you?"

Olivier reddened. "Not frightens," he denied quickly. "Makes me nervous. You're a clever woman. But I understand your motives. Once you get your hooks into me, I'll not get free again."

"And you're so weak I could enslave you as easily as all that? You seem to be giving me a lot of credit suddenly."

Olivier frowned at her. "I say it would be dangerous."

For a moment she said nothing. Obviously he wished to resist even the most tenuous sort of alignment with her. She should have known she was wasting her breath.

Everything she wanted he held back, like a miser hunkering over his sacks of deniers; she wished she understood why. After that, resigned, Sybille forgot about Fanjeaux, because during Lent the pope began preaching a new crusade, and it became clear that peace would not hold. De Montfort's son, Amaury, urged the king of France to send an army into Languedoc. The end of it was that, unbelievable as it seemed to the exhausted southerners, the war was starting up again only a few short months after the victory celebrations. It seemed a sort of plague that God, or the Devil, persisted in sending them. Why they could not say.

The French king sent his son, the same pious Prince Louis Sybille and Fabrisse had once watched from the steps of Saint-Sernin, and with the prince marched six hundred knights and ten thousand archers. In the first days of May, just when the almond trees were starting to flower on the hillsides, the force joined Amaury de Montfort's troops outside Marmande and captured the town as if its walls had been made of butter. All the townsfolk were butchered, some five thousand it was said. Sybille did not wish to think of this atrocity.

Olivier did, and came to her kitchen to report each new bit of information in particulars that made her stomach jerk. "Babes in arms had their bellies stove in or their limbs hacked off."

"Why are you telling me this? To make me go mad?"

"So you have more to hate." He twisted his thumb ring as if to wrench it off.

"I have enough."

"No," he told her. "Livers and hearts looked like they had been ground into mash. You know who commanded the Marmande garrison, who surrendered the town in exchange for his own life? Your father's nephew—Centulle of Astarac. He looks after his own ass, doesn't he?"

"I'm not responsible for my kin."

"No one else escaped. Not a single soul."

Finally Sybille said Marmande was Béziers all over again. Olivier disagreed. The Béziers massacre had been an accident; this one had been executed in cold blood, to terrorize. He leaned toward her. "And when they come to our city," he said quietly, like a gypsy murmuring over her cards, "they will be eager to lay hands on the woman who killed Simon de Montfort. Who not only slew him but made rhymes about his headless body. I would imagine anyway. Hearts and livers."

She tried not to listen. "Mother of Jesus," she cried, trembling. "Stop it!" She walked away, telling herself he was exaggerating, though she knew he was not. She went out into the yard and pulled weeds in her herb bed for an hour, and then she knelt unmoving among the thyme for another hour and stared at the dirt under her fingernails. It could not happen—they could not slaughter every person in Languedoc. More to the point, they could not kill Sybille d'Astarac. Then she warned herself they could.

From the corner of her eye she watched Olivier come out the kitchen door, draw up water from the well, and carry it into the stable. His expression looked unworried, even strangely cheerful. When he came out again, he pulled off his shirt and flung it behind the water trough. He walked toward her, rubbing nervous fingers over his chest. Sybille turned to stare up at him.

Olivier said she could not remain in Toulouse. Not now.

"You don't know they are coming here."

"You should go to Fanjeaux." He scratched his chin.

"I don't want to."

"We will depart tomorrow," Olivier told her. "Before daybreak."

When she heard the "we," she fell silent and bowed her head. After supper she made a bundle of her quills and parchment, her least shabby gowns, and Douce's remaining jewelry. The next morning, in the coolness before sunup, they trotted out the Narbonne gate and headed south. Along the road, in the mist-flushed fields, men and women were weeding the vines and tender green stalks of corn. Children stood screaming on rocks and unleashed their slingshots at the crows. If it were not for the jagged chestnut stumps, the charred slopes on which once had stood fine châteaux, Sybille might have imagined herself a child again, setting out on the family's summer visit to Na Beatritz. Had she traveled this road twelve summers or thirteen?

They all blurred into one. Once she recognized every castle keep and watchtower. Now many of those landmarks had bled away into the dimness of the limestone gorges, with castles and whole villages gulped back into the clumps of woodland.

Down the road Sybille could see the village of Oratoire and its black-stone abbey, angry as a thundercloud. But when they drew near, she noticed quite a few of the houses had been burned and gutted and no effort made to rebuild. The crusaders had done their work well. She glanced over at Olivier, who had said nothing the past hour except to remark he disliked her russet gown, the one she had had made for her father's burial. He was keeping his eyes forward on the road, and when she called to him, he turned and gave a listless smile.

"I remember this place," she said.

He mumbled something but she did not catch the words.

"Olivier, let's stop for water."

In the square he walked his stallion over to the well and slumped to the ground. Sybille followed. They dipped up water. Squatting in the mud near the well were two small boys forming excrement pies. Sybille glanced around in all directions but saw no one. She said to the oldest of the children, "Where is your mama?" She put on a smile.

He glanced up, eyed her without interest, shrugged, and lowered his gaze. Quickly she said to Olivier, "There used to be an inn over there that made the most marvelous sausages."

"Was there?" he said crossly.

Clearly he found the sound of her voice annoying. Rebuffed, she strolled around the square to stretch her legs while Olivier watered the mounts, and hoped his bad temper would not be contagious. She had not asked him to make this journey. Why was he being difficult? Heaps of wreckage marked the spot where the inn had been. She stooped to pick up a kettle scaly with rust, then threw it down into the weeds. Sausages, partridges with morels, even violet-tinted marzipan that clung to the roof of her mouth. Her stomach began to growl. When she went back to the well, Olivier was complaining. The water tasted brackish, he felt tired, probably it would rain before nightfall.

He is determined to make this as unpleasant as possible, Sybille thought. I ought not to allow his melancholy to affect me. She tugged at his sleeve and said very cautiously, "There has been much suffering in this district, my lord."

He shrank back. "In every district," he corrected with a scornful shake of the head. "What did you expect?"

"Yes," she said, raising her voice. "But this is the first I've seen it with my own eyes. I apologize for my ignorance. I had no way of knowing, now did I? It is hardly fair of you to be so irritable with me. If you don't want to take me to Fanjeaux, then leave and I'll go on alone."

Olivier warned her that the great castle of Fanjeaux had been occupied by the French and was partially destroyed. Possibly her grandmother's castle was no longer even there.

"Why didn't you tell me this before?"

"I didn't want to alarm you."

She laughed limply. "I'm alarmed now."

"Do you want to go back?"

"No."

He said they could reach Montferrand by dusk. "We're wasting time arguing like this."

As they left Oratoire, the sound of the terce bells rose from behind the abbey walls. The pale bowl of the sky brightened to lemon and then to bright orange. Olivier's warning had shaken her. She listened to her mare's hooves smiting the sun-baked road. Ten yards ahead Olivier jogged along as if they were strangers. After a while she called to his back, "Friend! Olivier!"

He reined in a little but did not turn his head. "Your grandmother was a heretic, wasn't she?"

She trotted up even and twitched a withering smile. "Everybody in those parts is a heretic. What of it?" She was determined not to allow him to scare her.

"You're a dangerous person to associate with, aren't you? Between your verse and all those heretic kin of yours—"

"Then keep other company," she barked, and Olivier laughed. Sybille spurred Dolosa into a gallop and left him behind.

The following day the noon heat lay scorching on the ash-gray stones of the castle walls. Beatritz d'Astarac had been dead six years, but Sybille saw Cantal had been inhabited since then. Here and there in the circular ward lay hauberks and shields whose red crosses were now obscured by rust. Piles of rubbish breathed the smell of decay across the hot cobbles where Sybille and Fabrisse and their brothers had once played blindman's tag.

"Good luck," Olivier said. "They've left the walls and roof. It doesn't even look like they tried to burn it. Considerate of them."

She let the mare's reins drop and walked toward the well. The air was heavy with the droning of flies. A sweet, rotten stench hummed toward her, and she stopped, open hand groping for her nostrils. "What's that?" she whispered to Olivier. "That funny smell?"

"Wait," he said and brushed by her. She saw him lean over the mossy parapet and jam his head into the well. A moment later, he straightened, squinting.

"Is there water in it?" she asked, nervous. "We can't live here without water."

"We'll have to carry water from the stream." He was standing with his back to her, but she noticed he was crossing himself.

"Olivier—"

Olivier stepped back. "You'd better go inside," he said briskly. "I'll come up in a few minutes."

"All right." A rat scuttled past the hem of her gown. "I— Olivier, what's in there?"

He laughed hoarsely. "Not what. Who."

Sybille turned at once and scrambled up the ramp with a feeling of foreboding. She glanced up at the stone tympanum arching over the doorway. In relief an armored Mathieu de Cantal, Na Beatritz's grandfather, was slaying a snarling lion, a warning to his enemies. She pushed open the door.

Stomach knotted, she advanced into the shadows of the vaulted hall and cast her eyes at the wreckage. They must have used the benches and cupboards and fire screens for kindling. Automatically her eyes sought Na Beatritz's high carved chair with its wooden canopy and the footstool covered in red silk. They were not there. The only piece of furniture was a trestle, huddled against the south wall.

The sight of the damage was so painful she could not move for a while. Abruptly she swung around and hurried outside. She sat up on the ramp and tipped back her head. A bird pirouetted overhead in the blue sky. Olivier climbed toward her.

"What do you think, Olivier? Can we stay here?"

He lifted surprised eyes. "Certainly. We are lucky, I say. How many vassals attached to this fief?"

Sybille shrugged. "A dozen. Maybe more. I don't remember."

"We will need help," he said smoothly. She reached out and drew him down against her knees. When she slid her hand down the collar of his shirt to stroke his bare shoulders, he murmured, "God's eyes, don't you think of anything but lying together?"

She said quietly into his ear, "Make me go."

His face rested against the inside of her thigh. Through the wool she felt his breath, hot and moist. "What is it you want, lady?" he whispered.

She closed her eyes and pressed herself against him. Smiling, she said, "Make me—I told you."

"Tell me again," he said. "Louder."

"Don't tease me." She reached around to strum his genitals through his breeches. Stiffening, he heaved a sigh. She said, "I want the same thing you want."

"I want nothing," he said in a muffled voice.

She laughed softly and tongued a curl with her lips. His hair was gossamer-fine, as if he had been born last week. His mother must have had hair like this.

"How badly do you want it?" he asked.

"Badly," she admitted.

"Here?"

Opening her eyes, she laughed again. "I know a place in the orchard."

He sat up and gave her a look through slitted lids. "I feel tired. It's time for a nap."

They went down into the yard, crossed the drawbridge, and ran down the slope into the apple orchard. Brilliant sunlight fell through the branches; the clover carpeting the earth was flecked with gold. Olivier stretched out carefully on his back. Sybille kicked off her slippers, then flung herself on top of him, face downward, hips thrust forward.

"Don't be so rough," he complained.

Slowly she felt for his feet with her toes. She saw he had closed his eyes already and turned aside his head, shutting her out. The old hurts wobbled in the back of her mind.

She twisted off him into the grass and flopped on her back, struggling for control, and clasped her hands over her eyes. Suddenly a coolness needled her stomach, and she was surprised to realize he had slid his hand up her skirt. She called, under her breath, "Olivier—"

No answer. He was swinging himself up, and then he bent over her. Above the wrinkled bunches of fabric she watched him slowly lower his mouth to her center. She gazed at the golden curls a minute longer before shutting her eyes. All around her the green leaves of the apple trees were blurring; the birds hushed themselves; the wind bowed like a courtier and withdrew. Head thrown back, Sybille splayed her palms over the clover and ground the tips of her fingers into the sod beneath. The earth tremored with little sighs, moans rising and sinking like the faint tickling of a moth's gossamer wings, tiny noises she had never heard and could not identify. All these sounds were like raindroplets streaming in her ears. After a long while, she thought, "That is me!" and smiled.

At once the sounds vanished and she half sat up, struggling with shame. "Don't," she cried out to Olivier.

He raised up to stare at her. "Why not?" he said. "Isn't that nice?"

"Yes. It's nice."

"I want to make you happy," Olivier said. Then, more insistent, "This is what you want—you said so."

Now he was sitting crosslegged between her thighs, observing her, fingers moving excitedly. His whole face seemed transformed, youthful and sweet as a boy's. He looked happy, heaven knows why. You can't fool me, Sybille thought numbly. You were unreal when we came down here; you are unreal now. Where is the real Olivier? Perhaps there is no such person. And yet the fluttering of his fingertips on her moist flesh was real enough. She sank back, telling herself this was another of his tricks, a prelude to humiliation. At that moment she let out a yell. Sitting up, she seized his head between her hands, stroking, kissing the corners of his mouth and the curls swirling over his forehead. They began to stare into each other's wide eyes, shaky.

"Sybille?"

"Yes, Olivier?" She watched him tuck his lower lip between his teeth. The gesture pleased her. "I am here," she said and tugged off his shirt. As God made us all, she thought, I know this strange man belongs to me, no matter what he may say to the contrary. I know it and he knows it.

"You deserve better than me," Olivier said.

That was true. But we do not always desire what we deserve. Sybille kept silent, wondering what he would do next.

He did nothing, only went on smiling into her eyes. She took off all the clothing that stood between them, rolled him on his back, and knelt above him, all-powerful. She waited for a gust of protests but none came. Below her, Olivier closed his eyes. His hair was perfumed by clover and apple blossoms, and his breath was coming out in little gasps. She was mastering him, controlling him as deliberately as she would tame a colt, and she gloried in it. Perhaps he would not notice.

Olivier clasped his hands around her waist. She continued to watch his face. Once, later, his lids opened for a second and he blurted out, "Sybille, I'm yours," and quickly closed them.

The unexpected words stunned Sybille. She wished she knew what they meant. Probably nothing, she warned herself. It was only the involuntary cry of a man surrendering to his pleasure. She could have been any woman in Christendom.

A moment later he lay soft and spent, his mouth curved down peacefully. She lifted her face toward the branches of the trees. Many summers ago when she was a very young child, barely walking, this orchard had been a meadow where Pierre and Mathieu played guilles, and Douce sat on the side cheering one son, then the other. But when Na Beatritz planted the apple trees, the boys had to shift their ball games to the rocky stretch of land north of the castle, and they complained about the inconvenience for years after that. Remembering now, it seemed unimaginable to Sybille that those spindly trees had grown and endured and her brothers were gone.

The afternoon wore on. Sybille and Olivier slept heavily in the cool of the shadows. When they woke, the air was chilly and their stomachs felt painfully empty. They dressed quickly.

"You look rested," Sybille said. "What shall we do now?"

"Rested," Olivier grunted. He sounded irritable. "The whole afternoon is wasted. I must ride into town. There is much to be done."

He started up the slope toward the moat and Sybille stumbled after him. Clouds hung like white lace over the dark tower. The portcullis was up and the gate open. As they came into the ward, she saw two men in ragged jerkins squatting on their hams, and when they caught sight of her and Olivier they rose, faces set in hostile expressions.

Sybille thought she recognized the elder of the two. He was Pays, a villein who held a few acres of Astarac land and who owed service to her grandmother; he had cleaned the moat and supplied the castle with firewood. His companion, squirrel-faced, she did not know. Sybille had never seen human beings so disgustingly filthy. "Greetings," she called and started toward them.

The men looked past her to Olivier and she paused. Pays said intensely, "My lord, you are trespassing."

"Dog," Olivier spat. "Kneel to the lady or I'll break your bones." Reluctantly they sank to the cobbles. From beneath his fringe of hair the younger one gave Sybille a stare bristling with fright.

Pays croaked, "This is private property."

"A pity you animals weren't so particular about the last trespasser here," Olivier shouted, hot.

They scrambled up. Pays came closer. He said Cantal belonged to Beatritz d'Astarac; his mistress did not tolerate poachers or trespassers.

"Potato face," Olivier said, "your mistress is dead."

But Pays insisted she was not; she left a month ago on a pilgrimage to Compostela.

Sybille circled around to stand beside Olivier. "My lord, this is a silly dispute. They mean no harm. Let me talk to them." She turned to Pays, smiling, and spoke slowly, with obvious patience. "Good people, your loyalty is very fine. But I know Na Beatritz is dead. I'm Sybille, her granddaughter."

The villeins exchanged swift glances.

"Stupid," the younger one said to Pays.

"Bah, what of it?" Pays answered. Hangdog, they stared down at the cobbles.

Sybille said, "It's very simple. We have traveled many leagues. From Toulouse. I intend to live here with En Olivier, this knight who has consented to be my protector. We require your labor to make the castle habitable again. Do you understand, Pays?"

He received the information without enthusiasm. "At least you aren't French," he muttered at last.

Olivier roared, "This son of a bitch lacks respect for his betters."

Sybille stared at Pays and repeated patiently, "Have you understood what I said?"

"Oh yes, good lady."

"You're sure."

"Yes, I think so, lady."

Olivier turned away in disgust. Over his shoulder, he groaned to her, "Ah, woe is me! It will take a year to right this place with fools like these."

Sybille examined Pay's face. "Answer me this. Who ransacked the keep?"

His lips spread into a scornful smile. "Why, the crusaders of course."

"When?"

Pays shrugged.

Olivier met Sybille's eyes and crossed over to Pays. "The bodies in the well. Who are they, old pig?"

Sybille crossed herself. The villein looked around absently and scratched his tangled beard. Sybille demanded, "Speak."

"I don't know," he said quickly. "Our enemy are devils. They did evil things."

"Mother of the Savior," Olivier burst out, impatient. "I wasn't born yesterday. No French have been in this district since last autumn. Those corpses are recent. They stink."

"If you don't believe him," Pay's companion piped, "we will have to go home."

Sybille felt weariness scaling her back and shoulders. She thought of the evening ahead, with nowhere to sleep, nothing to eat. She wished she were home in Rue St. Bernard. Coming here had been a mistake. She sighed to Olivier, "Let them go. What difference does it make whose corpses those are?"

Olivier said he wanted to know. There was a long silence, and then Pays said a Breton, one of Simon de Montfort's knights, had settled in the castle. With a local woman, a sinful slut.

"He married someone from the district?" Sybille asked.

"Not married—only a leman. One of the Tavernier girls. But they had a babe."

Sybille felt a chill shiver her spine. She could not decide which was more horrifying: the idea of someone becoming a crusader's leman or the thought of the bodies clogging the well. She asked how long they had been dead.

"Easter. Maybe."

"Who killed them?" She meant who had polluted the well and destroyed the keep.

Pays said he did not know. Olivier laughed. Sybille cleared her throat.

After a moment she asked tautly, "The babe too?" Her teeth were chattering.

Both peasants shrugged in unison. "When loathsome beasts couple," Pays said, "their get belongs to Satan. It is no sin to slay them."

I have not the strength for this, Sybille thought. She walked blindly to Olivier and squeezed his elbow. "Let's go into town." He nodded. "We can sleep at the inn. The well—tomorrow is time enough."

His eyes roved the ward, shifted abruptly upward to the keep. "It will take a dozen villeins to straighten this mess. And supplies must be gotten."

Sybille said she wanted to buy seeds to plant a vegetable garden.

"And you must find a servant to stay here with you, Sybille."

She watched the peasants bow and walk rapidly toward the gate. The sky was turning deep red. She gulped a deep breath, assuring herself he would not leave her here alone. "We don't need servants," she said hastily.

Sagging his head to one side, he drawled, indignant, "Sybille. You know I must return to Toulouse."

She was on the verge of crying. "Stay," she pleaded and put a hand on his sleeve.

He pushed her away. She had been dreaming if she imagined for one instant he would remain with her. Never had he made such a promise. She knew that. And so on.

Sybille was not listening. She mounted her mare and huddled hollow in the saddle, as if she were already alone.

They stayed five days in Fanjeaux at the Rose of Sharon Inn, buying provisions at the market and tracking down villeins who held land from the Astaracs and owed service, unperformed these past few years but owed nonetheless. Olivier worked hard to get the castle repaired and a new well dug, and he rode out to Cantal each morning and spent the day supervising the men. Returning at dusk, he and Sybille ate and drank before the inn's hearth, and Sybille talked restlessly of the soups she planned to make—dried peas and bacon, watercress, cheese. All the best soups were spiced with marjoram and sweet basil, so she needed to have an herb garden.

"Yesterday I heard frogs in the moat," said Olivier. "What about fried frogs' legs?"

"That sounds good, and a snail bed would be nice. I have a taste for snails." And then, remembering he would not be with her, she bit her lips.

Though she knew in advance it would do no good, she went to

the church and said a short prayer, asking heaven to make Olivier stay. On her knees, she thought, I'll bet God is not available to grant miracles right now. He's taking the day off to visit His banker in Avignon. No, He has gone on pilgrimage to Rocamadour and won't be back until Michaelmas. She went on like that for a quarter hour until her manic hilarity dissolved into bitterness. Then she went out into the market and purchased pickled olives and a crock of fancy strawberry jelly, extravagances she could not afford, before returning to the inn to join Olivier.

On the road back to the castle, the tips of the cypresses lunged at a bleak white sky. Sybille and Olivier bent their foreheads into the wind. Abruptly Olivier slowed his horse to a jog and yelled, "I found your grandmother's chair—it was in Pays's hut."

She turned her head, surprised and pleased.

"The footstool is still missing. No doubt it will turn up eventually."

"No doubt," she echoed. She prepared herself and then she said carefully, "My lord, when are you going?"

"Going?" Uncomfortable, he began to squirm in the saddle but she kept silent. "I have no idea. When I'm no longer needed, I suppose."

"When will that be?" she persisted.

"Why, how do I know? Soon, soon." His features took on a playful smirk. "Well, Sybille. I can see you are eager to be rid of me."

"Just asking," she replied, smiling in her grief. "I must plan—"

Cutting her off, he said, "Your trouble is you ask too much, too often."

"A defect of mine." Surely not, she thought. I have become, somehow, a person who dares ask only for a few crumbs now and then. It is you, my misbegotten knight, who is unable to give anything. What you regard as an emperor's ransom I could stuff in my left eye. And still have space for a fistful of motes. She wished she could laugh at her misery. When Olivier goes, oh Lord, please send me a faithful knight and a basket of cheese pasties. She smiled and spurred her mount forward.

Gradually she accepted the idea of Olivier's leaving. A week passed. Each morning she scrambled out of bed before the sun was up, making lists in her head of the jobs to be done. Alongside the neighboring castles in the district, those belonging to the Durforts and the

Tonneins, Na Beatritz's tower was decidedly small. There were three stories. The kitchen was on the ward level, and it was dark and cramped and lacked an air of being a place in which to sit around and talk. The whole second floor was taken up by the hall with its central fireplace and raised dais and the tapestries Na Beatritz had inherited from her godmother. As a child, Sybille had always known where to find her grandmother, and she would patter up to the canopied armchair near the hearth and rest her head on the silk footstool next to Na Beatritz's feet. Above the hall was another floor of sleeping chambers crowded with a profusion of featherbeds separated only by curtains, and there was always a feeling that everyone in the castle was sleeping in one big bed. Sybille liked this when she was a child, it made her feel safe. Later on, when she wanted to daydream, she longed passionately to sleep by herself. But of course such a wish was out of the question in a country castle.

Sybille knew restoring Cantal to its former condition would be hopeless; she lacked the money, for one thing. Instead, she just concentrated on making the castle livable. Inside she attacked first the hall, kitchen, and sleeping chamber, and then she planted a garden alongside the curtain wall, near the gatehouse. Olivier managed to requisition a cow and half a dozen chickens, and now in the ward there was a continual squawking and mooing, which Sybille found difficult to get used to. She spent one whole day scouring sooty tiles in the kitchen and found they were red. Next to the servants' quarters, she cleaned out a storeroom and discovered it had once been a chapel. The stained-glass panes had been boarded over, and the altar stone and two sarcophagi, encased in decades of grime, were hidden under piles of kegs and blackened kitchen utensils. Among the mice and the spiders, leaning on a broom, she tried to imagine who lay there and when they had lived in the castle.

The desecrated chapel angered Olivier, and for several days he went around cursing the heretics, her grandmother included, and saying he did not blame the crusaders who burned Good Christians. She cursed back and refused to speak to him, but started again when she realized soon she would have no one to talk to. Olivier harangued her. "Get a servant girl," he said and leaned back on his stool. "Better yet, some farm boy with a thick prick." He howled with laughter. She went upstairs to bed and, in her head, composed a fast rhyme about a woman who bashes in her husband's head with a lance.

Pays came to the gate with news that there was some sort of excitement in town, and Olivier rode off to find out what was going on. He did not return that night, and Sybille snuggled sleepless in one corner of the big featherbed. She fell asleep toward prime and woke at noon when she heard voices in the ward. She threw on a shift and plunged down to the hall without stopping to unplait her hair.

From the arrow loop overlooking the ward she could see Olivier talking to a local knight, Bernard Oth. Olivier was just sliding out of his saddle, and from the angle of his head she knew something was wrong.

"I know it's cut off," he roared and flung down the reins. "It's bad enough I left—but not being able to go back!" The knight replied, but his answer was too low for Sybille to catch. Olivier paid no attention. "How can we take another siege—?"

Bernard Oth's face was expressionless. He leaned down, put his hand on Olivier's shoulder, and said something. Sybille moved away from the slit and went to the trestle. From a loaf of stale bread she cut slices and poured from a jar of wine. She ate standing.

The door crashed and Olivier pounded into the hall.

"What happened?" Sybille said calmly.

He dropped on a bench and began pulling off a boot. "Don't just stand there. Get meat. I haven't eaten since yesterday."

But clearly he had been drinking. As she walked by him toward the kitchen stairwell, she smelled sour wine. His breath and clothing reeked of it. Down in the kitchen she grabbed a smoked ham she had been saving and a round of cheese and came back up to the hall.

With both hands he snatched the ham and began gnawing hunks off the bone. "This tastes like shit," he said in a mean voice. She gave him a napkin, on which he blew his nose.

Sybille looked at the napkin, then into Olivier's blue-purple eyes. "I'm waiting to hear what happened," she said. "Let's have it."

"You'll be happy to know the French are besieging Toulouse." She drew in her breath. "The young count is shut up in there with only a thousand knights. He had the relics of St. Exupère exposed in the crypt at Saint-Sernin."

Sybille saw his eyes were filling with tears. "That does not make me happy," she said, half lying.

"There's no way to get into the city now," he wailed. "No way." The tears began rolling down his cheeks.

"Why are you crying?"

"I'm not."

"It's not my fault," she said. But it was, for he was not thinking of the besieged Toulousans but of himself, trapped at Fanjeaux with her. "Please stop crying. When the siege is over, you can go home." She stroked his hair.

"Get away," he whimpered.

It was August. After no rain the whole month of July, it poured for five straight days, and now the sky was still low with ashy clouds.

"Let's go into town," Sybille said to Olivier.

"Let's do that," he said, but did not get up.

An hour later she said, "I'm leaving without you," and he rose reluctantly and even put on a clean shirt.

They had fallen into the habit of taking a weekly ride into Fanjeaux so they could pick up supplies on market day but partly to break the monotony. Olivier, silent and depressed, would spend whole days lying in bed. Sybille knew his silence was not entirely deliberate, but still it had a side effect of punishing her. She longed to talk to someone.

They rode below the Durforts' castle and reached the fork that led to Fanjeaux. After sidelong glances at Olivier's clamped lips, Sybille called, "What's the matter?"

"Nothing."

"Talk to me then."

Olivier avoided her eyes. "People begin conversations by talking themselves," he said brusquely. "They don't order others to talk to them."

"Come on." She smiled and edged the mare closer. "Cheer up. You look like you've swallowed a toad. Look at that mountain. See those pretty oaks. The world isn't such a bad place."

"That's your side of it," he said. He added quickly, "The world is a rotten place. Even a booby can see that."

She gave in then and kept her mouth shut. Her stomach was feeling queasy again. Two weeks earlier, she had been sickish in the mornings and once she had even vomited. Briefly she had wondered if perhaps she had conceived. Then the nausea disappeared and she forgot about it. Now it was back, a persistent sourish taste in her mouth and throat. She gripped the reins tighter. "I feel sick," she announced.

Olivier said he was sorry, where did it hurt?

"My stomach."

"Go get a cup of spiced wine at the inn," he suggested.

"That's what I'll do, yes."

When they had reined up their mounts in the square, Olivier got into a conversation with Isarn-Bernard, a burgher with whom he had become friendly. Sybille waited a minute, then sidled away and went straight to the apothecary. The woman was alone in her shop, mixing herbs with a large pestle and mortar.

"Something for a nervous stomach," Sybille said. She felt on the verge of vomiting. "Ginger and clove perhaps."

"You look unwell," the apothecary agreed quickly. She put down the pestle and mortar, reached for a bowl, and ducked it under Sybille's chin. When Sybille tried to bring something up, nothing came but a thin, colorless fizz. After a minute or two, she raised her head and wiped her mouth. She stared at the shelves lined with labeled jars and boxes: antimony, henbane, garlic, gum arabic.

She swallowed and said, "How about castorea? Isn't that good for the stomach?"

The apothecary was studying her professionally. "Had this before lately?"

"A few weeks back," Sybille admitted. "But I drank water instead of wine at meals and it went away." Vomiting must have helped. She felt better now.

"When did you last pass blood?" the woman inquired.

"I don't know," said Sybille, after a pause. "Before St. John's Day—or was it around Rogation. It was warm—I don't remember."

The apothecary sat down again on her stool and picked up the mortar. "You've gotten yourself with a babe," she announced.

"Oh no," Sybille said mildly. "That's impossible."

"That's what they all say." She smiled. "Have you been lying with a man?"

"I—"

A man came into the shop and asked for camphor. Slightly dizzy, Sybille swiveled toward the wall and examined a jar labeled cassia fistula. When the customer left, she swung around and said to the apothecary, "Are you sure?"

The woman did not answer directly. She said impassively, "If you want to kill the seed, I have ergot."

Sybille twined her fingers together, shaken. "Maybe it's only some bad pork I ate."

The woman gave a shrug of dismissal. "Have it your way." She poured a white powder into the mortar and began grinding. Sybille went outside. A cart rumbled by. Walking slowly behind it, she retraced her steps to the marketplace and told herself she could not be pregnant. Ever since she had first lain with Olivier, she had used Hecate's magic poultice. Never had his seed reached her womb. But now? Her mind raced wildly in circles. Had Hecate withdrawn her protection? Perhaps the magic wore off eventually and the midwife had neglected to warn her. Then she remembered the afternoon in the apple orchard, the day they had arrived at Cantal. Blessed Mary, help me, she moaned. Olivier will never forgive me.

When she got to the square, she searched the crowd. Olivier was not there. Twenty yards away, a man was shouting, but the noisy cluster of people around him drowned out his words. Their excited voices burst staccato into the colorless air and glided away. "Fucking lie—" a woman rumbled. War news, Sybille thought, and turned away. She felt exposed, as if the expression on her face already betrayed her flat belly.

The church bell was striking sext, deafening the square. She stopped at a stall where a woman was selling twice-baked bread and bought two of the crispy flat wafers, which settled her stomach temporarily. Then she went on, around the treeless square, as slowly as she could. Suddenly she caught sight of Olivier swaggering toward her.

"Hello there," he called out. "Isarn-Bernard says Prince Louis has raised the siege and left Toulouse."

"Wishful thinking."

He stopped and stood, legs apart, hitching up his breeches. "That's what I say. He's supposed to have left his siege engines behind too."

She half turned to peer over her shoulder to see how others were reacting. Using a hand-hewn board, five or six knights were calmly dicing outside the carpenter's shop. "It can't be true, can it?" she asked Olivier.

"No. Did you get the wine?"

"Yes," she lied. If the prince gave up, she thought, he must have a brain no bigger than a parsley leaf.

Olivier said, "How much money do you have? I want to buy sausages."

She frowned. "That butcher is crooked. Last time he—"

"Want to hear a joke?" He slid his arm around her shoulder. "Bertrand the Booby asks the butcher for a discount because he's been a loyal customer seven years. And the butcher says, 'Seven years! And you're still alive?'" Sybille stared ahead, face blank. She felt dizzy. "You're not laughing," Olivier complained.

She shrugged. "I've heard it before. Olivier, I want to go home."

"We just got here," he protested. "You dragged me here and now you want to leave without buying anything. You should have—"

"I'm sick," she said quietly and started toward the horses without looking around. Behind her, he was saying, "Give me a couple of poges for a sausage, all right? Then we'll go."

She nodded and fumbled at her belt. To make up for his disappointment, she gave him three deniers. He touched her hair. While he was gone, she leaned against the mare's neck and slapped at the flies. She wished God would give her a sign. Then she thought it would make no difference what Olivier thought of the babe. Once the siege was raised, he would join the young count and she would be completely alone. A child might be company for her. But she had no great wish to bear a bastard. A woman's life is difficult, she groaned, too difficult. The truth was, she feared childbed. Perplexed, she kept swatting flies, which helped pass the minutes.

Olivier came back with the sausages. The smell of the pork and the grease made Sybille's stomach lurch. She patted Dolosa's neck, as if to reassure the mare. Olivier put out a hand to help her into the saddle. "How do you feel?" he asked.

"I told you, I'm sick." She nudged the mare forward.

"You know, it's possible Prince Louis might leave soon," he said. "But Amaury de Montfort isn't going anywhere. Isarn-Bernard says if Louis does pull out, we're going to go raiding. Get back Laurac from Hugh d'Lacy."

She let him chatter about Isarn-Bernard and the latest rumor until they got to the Durforts' estate, and from there it was only a short distance to Cantal. He fell silent, then said, "I saved a sausage for you. But I guess you don't feel like it now."

"No. You have it."

He reached over, took her hand, and nestled it in his palm, as protective as Holy Mary. The gesture made tears come to her eyes, and she turned, full of childish gratitude, and cried, "Oh, Olivier. You're so sweet." These days it took very little to make her happy.

He replied promptly, "No, I'm not," but he did not release her hand.

When they rode into the ward, he lifted her out of the saddle and carried her up to bed. All gentleness, he stretched her out, removed her slippers, and brought a cool cloth for her temples. She slept, happier than she had felt in months. When she woke, he was lying next to her in bed, whistling. Outside, against the shutters, rain began to tap lightly in the summer night.

Sybille rested her face in the slope of his neck and listened to the water on the shutters.

"Sybille," Olivier said, "you always want to couple. You don't understand it's good to lie quietly like this. A man and a woman were made to just lie together with their bodies touching."

She said mildly, "I like this too." She looked at him in the candlelight and saw his eyes were closed and his face was shining.

In a rush, he said, "Sybille, you're so good to me. You're so lovely. You take good care of me."

She did not answer, only lay there savoring the words, turning them slowly in her head and extracting the juice and rolling it, unbelievably delicious, over her tongue so that the sensation would not consume itself too quickly.

"The only thing wrong with you," he went on, "is that the mama bird and the papa bird fed you too many worms."

She stirred uneasily against the soft flesh of his neck. "What does that mean—too many worms?"

"Oh," he breathed, "you wouldn't understand."

"Wait a bit, my lord. If I wouldn't understand, why did you make that remark?" She fought down a surge of the old familiar anger. "I know my lord father loved me too much, gave me too much, but what of it? And if I once was petted and spoiled, surely that is no longer so."

"That's true," he said, conciliatory. "You're no different than women from other noble families. I only meant you want too much from people and you tire them out. You tire them out greatly."

Sybille could not bear to quarrel now, so she said, "I see. And you? You never demand too much, Olivier?"

He grazed his fingers along the tops of her buttocks. "Oh, I do. Everyone does. Listen, I think I should just rest here a while with you."

He cupped his body into all her slopes and valleys, as if he were fitting together the pieces of a puzzle, and she said to herself, How content he is tonight, content and sweet. She remembered the first days and weeks of their being together, the wild happiness before she realized he was capable of hurting her. He had loved her. Or at the very least was beginning to love her and she was beginning to love him, and then she wrote *Ieu Sui* to tell him about it. Why did his love change to abuse when he read the verse? She never should have shown it to him. Unknowingly, she had made a terrible mistake, never to be undone, and now there was no chance of his ever loving her again. It did not seem fair, although she thought there was very little in living that was fair. The rain had thinned to a hiss, and she suddenly blurted out loudly, "Olivier, I'm going to have a babe." It came out like a gust of wind accompanying the rain.

Silence.

At last he said, "Why?"

"I don't know."

"Is that why you've been sick?"

"Yes. I suppose." Raising up on her elbows, she squinted into the darkness to see how much anxiety showed in his face, for his voice was utterly calm, which unnerved her. He began to ask questions, and she answered them as best she could, with long pauses. At first he seemed no more than politely interested, as if he were requesting details about how some confection is prepared, and he nodded from time to time as she spoke. When she could think of nothing more to say, she dropped her head to his shoulder. After five or six minutes he said, "So it is the will of God—"

"Do you think that is true?" she asked, startled.

"Must be. It was no desire of mine."

"Nor of mine," she added.

He rolled on his side and kissed her ear, then his fingertips tightened around her waist. "I'm going to be a father," he sighed happily, and not until that moment did she realize he was not displeased about her pregnancy. He was not glad, to be sure, but he was not displeased either. She heard him chortle, "A son—I'm going to have a son." And when she whispered it might be female, he said, "No, it will be a son, because I'll ask God to make me one."

"Silly! Do you think you can order what you want?"

"Oh yes." He hugged her clumsily.

She fumbled around in the dark, searching for her fears and found them missing. Hiding, she thought, run away for a little while but they will be back tomorrow. After Olivier goes, my belly will start to bloat up and it will end in pain. But another living creature will be here, and he will be called Olivier d'Astarac, and he will be sweet as his father might have been, and yes, he will love me as his father cannot. Once she had him, a new life would begin for her, she knew that. She clasped together her fingers and asked God to set the seed well and deliver her of a healthy boy because she would not be able to bear another loss. Then she lay still in Olivier's arms and slept.

In the gray light of dawn, she heard the birds cooing outside the shutters and felt for Olivier among the tumbled sheets, but he was not there. After a few minutes, he came up the stairs with a cup of wine, which he set down on the chest. He was wearing a fresh shirt.

She squinted at him, eyes half shut, and for a moment they regarded each other in silence. Without warning he leaped onto the bed and crouched over her on his hands and knees, feet tucked up under his buttocks. She lifted her face, amused. "You look like a little frog sitting there," she murmured sleepily, "all ready to jump."

He grinned like a small, mischievous boy. "A big frog," he beamed, puffed up, "I'm a big frog."

"As you wish, my lord. A splendid big frog."

"Begetting a son is big frog work," he said solemnly.

She blinked her eyes wide, drinking in the angles of his cheekbones and the wine-blue richness of his eyes.

"Do me a favor, lady."

"Yes. What do you desire?"

"Pull up your shift."

"All right. Why?"

"I'd like to thump you."

Afterward, his whole body covering her like another skin, she reminded herself he did not love her.

By Monday the news of Prince Louis's abrupt departure had been confirmed, and talk of this startling development dominated every conversation. Many people insisted his going must have resulted from some secret agreement between the prince and the young count, because otherwise the whole thing was utterly inexplicable. Olivier believed Prince Louis wanted Toulouse for himself and was not in the least eager to conquer the city, only to hand it over to Amaury de Montfort. But no one knew the truth.

Olivier lingered until the fall quarterday, getting wheat and rye ground at the Durforts' mill and stacking the sacks of flour in the storeroom. He bought Sybille a chess set. As the days passed and the leaves tumbled to the forest floor, Sybille began to hope he would not go after all, but the Wednesday after Michaelmas he loaded his arms, hooked his shield to the saddle, and started off for Toulouse with Bernard Oth.

Allhallows passed. Looking at herself naked, Sybille noticed her belly beginning to swell, and by the start of Advent she felt as big as a cathedral. The baby kicked, especially in the early evenings.

For many weeks she had no word at all from Olivier. At first she rode into Fanjeaux every week to pick up news of the young count's whereabouts. He and his knights were said to be in the Agenais district, plowing triumphantly from castle to castle and driving out the French barons who had been given land by Simon de Montfort. By this time all of these usurpers had settled down comfortably on somebody's stolen fief, frequently with some lord's stolen wife, and were still claiming they had a right to them and acting as innocent as spring water. The young count was in a hurry to send these scamps back to France—or to hell, he did not care which—and restore the domains to their lawful seigneurs.

The French suffered defeat after defeat. The next thing Sybille heard was that the count's army was up in the Quercy district, and then, after Martinmas, suddenly they were nearby, attacking the fortress of Montréal, where the infamous Alain de Roucy was holed up. When the fortress was captured and De Roucy taken prisoner and beheaded, all the best families in the district held banquets and the guests stayed drunk for a week and coupled like rats in straw.

At least this was the gossip Sybille heard. She herself waited at home with some vague hope that Olivier would come to see her, for Montréal was less than two leagues away. A dozen times a day she climbed awkwardly to the turret to watch the road. She stood there gazing down over the barren treetops. A haze of gray light painted the swampy bowl of the moat. The road sloping into the forest lay empty before her eyes. Olivier must be close enough to send a message, maybe to see her.

It was not possible he would ignore her.

It was possible; it was what he was doing.

Her legs and thighs tingled, and her back began to ache from so many trips up and down the staircase. She went back down to the hall to cry.

All that autumn she tried to find a maid. Sybille had some vague idea of getting a daughter of a petty nobleman, someone who might share her life as a companion, not a servant. More than anything else, she longed for an intelligent person with whom she could converse.

In the end she arranged for two peasant children, a brother and sister, who were slow-witted but industrious. She spoke to them only when necessary. During those months she wrote constantly, using the supply of parchment she had found tucked away at the bottom of a chest. She talked aloud to herself and to the baby growing in her womb, and occasionally she visited her neighbors or ventured into town for diversion. The fear of loneliness had penetrated very deep, but now it began to lose some of its terrors. She went to bed before compline and slept until terce, a full twelve hours or more, and never remembered a single dream. One cold, gray day, as she was making a shirt for the baby, she heard women's voices in the ward, and the boy tore up to the hall saying two goodwomen were here. She waddled to the arrow slit, looked down into the shaded yard, and watched the pair in their hooded heretic gowns. They were huddled together, just inside the portcullis.

"Roger," she said, "those ladies look cold and tired. Have Rousse fetch soup and wine, and then tell them I would like to pay my respects."

The boy hesitated. He said, "Lady, will you come down?"

"No. I shall receive them here." She waved him off.

She put away her sewing and went to stand near the fire, walking heavily on swollen legs and wanting to drop into the canopy chair. She forced herself to remain standing, for she must give the ritual adoration.

Poor women, she thought. They must have walked many leagues and they lost their way, to end up on this deserted road. But then I too have lost my way, to wind up on this deserted road. In a way the difference between us is not so great. Except they have a mission and I have none. She stared emptily into the flames.

The goodwomen padded in. While they still were at the far end of the hall, Sybille began giving the customary three bows before they approached. She rose up at last, puffing. Before she could greet them, she heard a faintly familiar voice.

"Well, well, sister—"

"What?" Sybille stammered. "What did you say?"

"I said sister. It's Fabrisse. Have you forgotten me?"

Sybille's heart thudded against her ribs. She stared closely at the woman's features, which did not resemble her sister's. The face was waxy-white, lined as a dried fig. She came up to Sybille and gave her the kiss of peace, and Sybille flinched involuntarily. Her eyes moved to the other goodwoman, who was watching all this and smiling placidly.

"And you are her companion," Sybille managed to say, "and you preach together and you know she is Fabrisse d'Astarac. I beg your forgiveness for my discourtesy but—"

"Perhaps," Fabrisse broke in, "I have changed a little bit."

Sybille shook her head. She was shocked beyond speech. "No, not so much," she lied. She was looking at the other woman, unable to gaze directly at her sister. She went on, "I mean, your voice is the same, sister." The last statement was true. The woman was, in fact, Fabrisse. Fabrisse as she should have appeared as an old woman. She is only five years my elder, Sybille thought, she is only thirty. What has she done to herself? Sybille's hands were trembling. "Forgive me—"

The servant girl came up from the kitchen with wine and cups. As Sybille was pouring the wine, she remembered preachers often disdained wine, drank only water. But the goodwomen said nothing. The one who called herself Raymonde drank and smiled at Sybille at the same time. The flesh under her eyes was brown and puffy.

Twisting her neck, Fabrisse gazed around the hall. "Ah," she sighed pompously to Raymonde, "this place was once a truly lovely château. Tiny but elegant. Now it is pitiful to see." She glanced over at Sybille.

"I know," Sybille whispered, struggling to overcome her discomfort. She loved her sister, even though they had never really gotten along well. She began to talk hurriedly, describing the condition in which she had found the castle and her attempts to repair it.

Fabrisse listened. When Sybille paused, she said, "Yes, they told us in town you were living here. At the alewife's they said your sister and her lord husband are out there and your lady sister is pregnant. But I knew perfectly well you have no husband and I was curious." She added sharply, "Where's the man?" and gawked around as if he might be hiding in the hall.

"I'm alone," breathed Sybille. Obviously Fabrisse's association with the one true faith had not made her kinder; she spoke as sarcastically as ever, although Sybille noticed she was almost tender to Raymonde.

Fabrisse laughed and winked at her companion. "But earlier, sister. Certainly there must have been a man here before." She had yet to look directly at Sybille's stomach.

Sybille crossed her arms over her stomach. "Yes," she said quietly. "I came here with Olivier de Ferrand. He's the father of my babe. But he left to fight with the young count. It's quite simple, you see."

Fabrisse frowned at her and said, "Oh yes, Olivier," and then nothing more. Rousse brought up bread and bowls of barley soup. Raymonde and Fabrisse got to their feet and clasped their hands and turned their faces up to the rafters. Sybille slowly hoisted herself up and bowed her head.

There was silence. The minutes began to pass. Endless silence, time enough to say thirty or forty paternosters. Dear God, this is absurd, thought Sybille, who was desperate to get off her feet. The soup must be quite cold by now.

At last she heard Raymonde's voice: *"Benedicite, Kyrie Eleison, Christie Eleison, Kyrie Eleison."*

No sooner was that finished, Fabrisse chimed in: "God Who blessed the five loaves and the two fishes in the wilderness for His disciples, bless this table and the things on it." She made the sign of the cross. "In the Name of the Father, Son, and Holy Spirit." They sat. The hall was hushed, with only the crackling of the fire and the watery sounds of the cold soup. Sybille asked the women where they had traveled, how long had they been together? had they suffered persecution? and so on.

Raymonde, smile still fixed, did most of the answering. She seemed completely unaware of the tension between the sisters, or if she did notice, chose to ignore it. As she spoke, she continued to smile, even laughed now and then. Her manner of speaking seemed slow and artificial, as if she were measuring every word before it left from her tongue. They finished the soup.

Fabrisse said she could not remember having seen that tapestry before. She pointed to the far wall.

"It used to hang beside Na Beatritz's bed," Sybille said. "She liked the little white unicorn."

"Really, I never saw it before," Fabrisse insisted, and her companion smiled sympathetically.

Suddenly wild, Sybille decided to risk being discourteous and she blurted out, "Fabrisse, sister. Let's not speak of tapestries. How are you? Tell me, has life been hard for you? Please, sister, talk to me—"

Fabrisse shot a look at Raymonde, then leaned toward Sybille. "My dear, I have been talking to you. You were not paying attention. I wonder why you speak of life being difficult. Life only affects our bodies, bodies that will be destroyed like cobwebs, because they are the work of the Devil."

"Sleeping outdoors in winter is easy? Abstaining from love and meat and—" She broke off. In the ward, Rousse's voice rose, calling her brother to his dinner, then there was silence again. Sybille held her cup tightly.

"As I've told you," Fabrisse intoned, "we lead the true Christian life. Did Christ complain of the hardness of His life? He knew this world belongs to Satan. It is carnal, corrupt—"

"Friend," Raymonde interrupted, "we have little time left."

"Soon," Fabrisse replied. "Only in the spiritual world can my sister find the goodness she seeks. But she does not understand that because she's an undeveloped soul. Perhaps when she has experienced several more incarnations it will become clear."

Sybille, furious, clenched her fingers to restrain her temper. Ordinarily she could listen to heretics discuss their beliefs without fuming; theirs was simply another view of existence and should be respected. But now, hearing her sister's jibes, she despised their secretiveness, their smug condescension toward any person who did not believe as they did. It was they who lacked toleration and courtesy. They were not, she raged to herself, nice people, which was odd because they made such a fetish out of being little replicas of our Lord Jesus.

"We must go," Fabrisse announced, looking away.

"Go?"

"We have business in Prouille."

"But you can sleep here tonight, can't you?" Sybille did not really want them to stay, but neither could she bear to part from her sister after this cold reunion. The goodwomen got to their feet, lifted their heads for another prayer, then headed for the door. In a daze Sybille trailed after them. She noticed the back of her sister's gown was stained with blood. "Fabrisse?" she called.

"Yes, sister," Fabrisse grunted.

"I wanted to ask you, have you had word of Pons?"

Fabrisse did not stop to turn her head but continued out the door and started down the ramp. Wind snarled through the gaps in the curtain wall. Sybille heard her say, "I saw him at Easter. At Montségur."

"Yes." Sybille raised her voice. "But how is he?"

Raymonde said, "It was hot in there, wasn't it?"

"He's in good health?" Sybille cried helplessly. "What did he say to you? Did he ask about me?" Fabrisse and Raymonde were hurrying toward the gate, as if Sybille did not exist. "Fabrisse!"

She stopped and smiled. "I just told you. Pons belongs to the true church. He saves souls, he touches neither meat nor women. What more is there to say?"

Everything, Sybille thought. You have told me nothing. She nodded, bowed her head for a moment, then raised her eyes to Fabrisse. "Farewell, sister," she murmured, "God be with you."

"The true god is always with me, little sister."

The two women stared hard into each other's faces. Sybille smoothed her gown over her stomach. She very nearly said she was sorry but stopped herself. *Mea culpa. Mea culpa, mea maxima culpa.* Old habits. Fabrisse looked quickly away, took the smiling Raymonde's arm, and they disappeared over the drawbridge.

Spring came early. Gorse and broom painted the hillsides yellow. The fields were swathed blue with scillas, and crocuses bloomed madly along the edge of the moat. Sybille went to visit the neighborhood midwife and told her she would send Roger for her when the pains began. Each morning she woke expecting to feel her belly tingling. Now she wished only to get the thing over with; she wanted to hold in her arms this small person she had been making all these months, because she had come to think of him as a long, long poem, special and important. Without warning, Olivier came back; he hung up his arms on the wall of the hall and talked to Pays about the ploughing and oversaw the planting, so Sybille realized he was ready to settle down. His behavior was agreeable, even sweet. Life is good, Sybille thought happily. Or at least it is good for the time being.

In the first days of Lent, she gave birth to a large, healthy girl child. Sybille named her Nova, because her coming marked the beginning of a new life for all of them. Besides, she liked the sound of the simple name. *No-va.* She liked rolling it over her tongue. The next week she and Olivier took the baby into Fanjeaux to be christened at the church, and when they returned that night they drank plum wine by the fire, and she tried talking to him about the future, a subject to which her mind turned constantly.

"Are you going to be content here, my lord?" she asked hesitantly. "Or will you get restless and run off?"

"How can I answer that?" he said, frowning. "Who can say what will happen a year from now, or even next month? Amaury is still burning heretics and the Church isn't finished with us either. That is certain."

When she looked away morosely and stared into the fire, he said in a quiet voice, "Lady, I know you want a promise from me." But given the uncertainty of all their lives now, any promise he might make would be worthless. He was only telling her the truth, and he hoped she would think about it.

Leaning over, she wound her arms about his shoulders. "There is always a chance the Church will leave us in peace," she told him and kissed his hair.

"Peace?" He laughed. "I can't remember what peace feels like. I can't even imagine it. Peace is not in store for us in this life."

"You sound like a heretic," she said with a smile. "They think life is a tour through hell with the Devil as guide."

"Those assholes," he growled. "What do they know?"

She got up and went to the basket where Nova lay sleeping. Soon the baby would be waking, hungry for her breast. She bent to touch her nose on the tuft of light blond hair sprouting from Nova's skull. My daughter, she said under her breath, my joy. Over her shoulder she said to Olivier, "Live and be happy. Is it foolish to try and be happy while we can?"

"That makes sense," he agreed.

In bed later, with Nova snuggled between them in the pitch dark, Olivier reached over to touch Sybille's face. "Lady," he whispered, "I'm not like my father. I intend to care for you and the babe as best I can."

Her eyes filled with tears. "Olivier."

He patted her cheek. "Shhh. You'll wake Baby."

Comforted, she said a prayer telling God no matter what hardships lay ahead she would never forget His kingdom and His creatures were good.

Chapter Eleven

Count Raymond of Toulouse, the old count, died of a fever. In his final hours he sent to Saint-Sernin, begging for the Last Sacraments. The priests refused, saying he was an excommunicate and should know better than to make such a request. His son brought the coffin to the Hospital of St. John, where Raymond had wished to be buried, but the monks refused to admit it. So the young count left the coffin in the garden, just outside the cemetery gate, where weeds sprang up around it and monkish rats nibbled delicately on the bones.

In the early summer of the year Nova was three, Olivier was called to join the young count, as people still called him, in Carcassonne, and Sybille and Nova accompanied him. The young count had made a queer truce with Amaury de Montfort, and now Amaury had invited him to be his guest in Carcassonne, French headquarters and the place his father was buried. Raymond, for his part, had no objection to being feted by Simon de Montfort's son; in fact, he often said he liked Amaury and surely it was apparent Amaury was as sick of this war as he was. No fool, the young count nonetheless took care to arrive in Carcassonne with as many of his vassals as he could round up. So Olivier de Ferrand was summoned to the side of his overlord and childhood playmate, and Sybille insisted upon going with him. After four monotonous years in the country, the prospect of traveling anywhere, especially to Carcassonne, seemed exciting.

The Villeneuve mansion, which Sybille had fled in her shift fourteen years earlier, was now the residence of a French knight, one of the two or three dozen among Amaury's entourage. The house still looked elegant and well kept, and when Sybille led Nova up to the gate, the child would not believe her mother once had lived in such a grand dwelling. Glancing down at her patched and faded gown, Sybille could think of no words to convince her. They crossed Rue Château and made their way through the crowds of wives and the shopkeepers whose wares overflowed into the street.

Every morning she and Nova prayed at Saint-Nazaire, then spent the rest of the day touring the city. For the first few hours, the little girl would run ahead of Sybille, but later, as she became fretful in the summer heat, her legs tired, and Sybille had to carry her. They went up one street and down the next, in the late afternoon always winding up in Rue Château at the Villeneuve gate. It seemed to Sybille all she had to do was pull the bell and she could walk through the open gate, where Pons would be waiting for her. But Pons was not there, only two soldiers dicing near the stable and piles of rubbish studded with flies.

"Pons de Villeneuve," she said under her breath, as if speaking his name would make the soldiers disappear. Had the war not come, she would be mistress here. And Pons? Perhaps he would not be a preacher. She tried to think precisely what she would say to Pons, should ever she meet him again, and what he would say if he could see Nova. She peered down at the child, who was hanging on the side of her skirt.

"Hungry," Nova whimpered.

"My soul, child! Didn't I buy you figs a little while ago? And didn't you spit them out?"

Nova stretched up her neck. Tendrils of flattened hair curled whitish against her cheeks. "Carry me," she said.

Sybille plucked her up and bounced her on her hip.

"I love you too much," Nova said gravely.

She smiled into her blue eyes. *"So* much," she laughed. "Not too much."

Sybille carried Nova back to the house in Rue Porte d'Aude, where the young count and his knights were billeted. Amaury de Montfort had sent over a sheep and many tuns of Gascony wine, and the smell of crackling fat rushed at her nose as she entered the courtyard. Overhead the color of the sky was slowly thickening to a deep blue. Torches flared along the walls, and the sounds of the city merged with the drunken laughter of the men gathered around the roasting meat. Sicart Marjevols came swinging across the cobbles toward Sybille with his vielle slung over his shoulder. He winked at her. "Na

Sybille," he called, "name it—I'll play it." Then he added quickly, "Any song but *Montfort es mort,* I mean."

"*Once in the Auvergne, past Limousin.*" She smiled. "No, wait. Do you know *Now we are come to the cold time?*"

"I think so," the knight said. "I see you're an admirer of Azalais de Porcairages."

She nodded emphatically. "A fine *trobairitz,*" she said, shifting Nova to her left hip. The child tipped back her head.

"Mama, sing *Montfort es mort, es mort* . . ."

Sybille frowned. "Not now," she said to her. "It would be discourteous. Do you understand?"

"Now," the child said stubbornly.

"Be still," she hissed.

"Now!"

A crowd was beginning to gather around Sicart Marjevols. "I think it's time for you to be abed," said Sybille and started to make her way toward the steps.

When Sybille returned to the yard, someone was uncorking another tun of wine and a red stream snaked between the paving stones, wetting the soles of Sybille's slippers. She swerved around the spit and got herself a chunk of roast lamb, and moved away from the heat of the logs to a bench by the shadowy wall. Sicart Marjevols was playing William the Troubadour's song about nothing, and two knights were dancing in the firelight with women Sybille had never seen before, not their wives. She filled her mouth with the lamb and chewed slowly, to make it last. She had not had good meat for a long time. When she finished, still hungry, she went back hoping for a second piece. A bagpipe player had joined Sicart, and more people were dancing. Sybille thought the bagpipe player should stick to fighting; he was no musician.

At the spit she asked the carver for a slice not too charred and took it hot in her hand. Pink juice dribbled down between her fingers. She thanked the carver and added cheerfully, "Save some for the young count, hear me."

He shook his head. "Master won't care, lady," he said. "He's at the château. Dining with the De Montfort lad." He wiped grease from his long knife.

"It's a pity," she mumbled without thinking. He gave her a quizzical glance, and she said, "I remember attending banquets at the château when Raymond-Roger Trencavel was viscount here. I mean, isn't it a pity?" She turned away quickly and looked idly at the dancers, not really watching, just observing the jerking movements of their arms and legs. Suddenly, she noticed Olivier among them and stiffened. He was dancing with the daughter of a knight from Puylaurens, a pug-nosed damsel about fourteen, but his eyes were closed and he swayed, as indifferent to her as a sleepwalker at midnight.

Jealous, Sybille moved away, changed her mind, turned again to watch Olivier and the girl. It was an hour until compline. The night breeze fluttered the fleur-de-lis banners hanging on the gatehouse. Sybille remembered the family who had owned the house before the war. It had belonged to a heretic who once had been provost of the city. Or was it mayor? He had been rich; his daughter married a wealthy Italian banker who handled the Trencavel investments in Lombardy. She thought of Nova upstairs, sleeping on the floor of that family's bedchamber and of the Frenchmen who now slept in the Villeneuve beds with their ivory headpieces and knobs of red gold. The music dragged on. The girl with Olivier had long legs and a tiny waist. It had been a tiring day and it was not yet compline.

She waited until the dancers stopped spinning, caught Olivier's eyes, and gestured broadly. As she watched, he bent his mouth to the girl's ear; she giggled. He came over to Sybille, eyes filmy with reluctance.

"Hello there, my lord," she said cheerfully, struggling to sieve the sourness from her voice. "I see you're enjoying yourself."

"I *was* enjoying myself," he said listlessly.

She asked him if he felt tired. He did not feel tired.

"Go to bed if you're sleepy," he told her.

"Come with me," she begged.

He avoided her eyes. "The count is with Amaury. I have to wait up for him. He's offering to divorce his wife and marry Amaury's sister."

Sybille's eyes rounded with disgust, thinking of Sancia of Aragon. An hour earlier, passing the door of her chamber, she had heard her singing to the little princess, Jeanne. Unknown to the infanta of Aragon, her lord husband was down the street, bargaining away her position and title. "Pah, he's despicable!" she murmured in a shaking voice.

"I think he's heroic," Olivier said pompously. Sybille snorted contemptuously. "He's a prince."

"That's nice," she said, looking away.

"A good prince still makes sacrifices, even in this booby age. He moves heaven and earth for the welfare of his people."

Only when it suits his own desires, Sybille thought. She liked the young count because he had a beautiful face and could charm the good angels down from the gates of heaven. But she did not really trust him. He was a womanizer, like his father. That whole family had never been known for its respectful treatment of women. Use and discard.

"I'm going to bed," Sybille announced. She began threading her way through the crowd, moving toward the steps. The place reeked of wine fumes and sour breaths. There was yelling near the gate. A knight on the watchtower suddenly screeched, "On guard! On guard!" Without turning, Sybille began to ascend the staircase. She had no idea what was going on and did not care. All this racket must have woken Nova, she thought.

A woman screamed a long, drawn-out scream that sent waves of terror through the air. Sybille twisted around. Two horsemen rocked through the gate, and the crowd opened a path for them. One of the men was clothed in a greenish robe edged with gold brocade that picked up sparks from the torches. Behind him rode a man lashed to his stallion, fettered in chains from neck to feet. His head had fallen forward on his chest, as if the weight of the chains were choking the breath out of him. He looked half dead. This was the young count.

Sybille stared down amazed. The woman's voice went on screaming. Amaury de Montfort reined in his mount in the center of the yard, near the reddish-gray embers of the fire. "Greetings, friends," he said, smiling down at the flushed faces. "The son of the noble Simon de Montfort—viscount of Carcassonne, count of Leicester, uh, knight of Christ—salutes you."

The skin all over Sybille's body broke into sweat. With one arm she groped for the wall to steady herself. He's going to kill us, she thought. I must be dreaming.

"Why so glum?" Amaury said. "Aren't you enjoying my hospitality? Come on, good people. I've been obliged to arrest your liege lord, but your lives are in no immediate danger, I promise you." The young count, neck still slumped, was silent.

A voice shrill with hatred called out, "You farty little whore.

You're just a lackey of the pope!" Amaury's head shot up. In all directions the crowd began lunging and thrashing, this way and that, like a pack of horses trying to bolt but unable to see a gate. In fact, there was no escape because Amaury's soldiers had fanned out, blocking the gate. The mass of twitching bodies began to cower and push.

"Oh, don't run away," Amaury cried. He put on a false smile, full of affected good humor. "The palace dungeons aren't so bad. I've seen them myself and I tell you their reputation is greatly overrated." He glanced around the yard to see what kind of reception his words were having; he looked excited. "How many heretics here? Any sodomists? Fornicators? Yes or no? Never mind, we won't burn you until tomorrow. Have another cup of wine, friends."

Sybille could not get enough air into her lungs. A woman scrambled past her on the stairs, keening. I must go inside, she thought. My daughter is in there, she will be afraid. But her feet were frozen to the steps.

Amaury frowned. He turned toward the count, who was now staring up, eyes bulging. "Wait a minute," Amaury bellowed. "What shall I do with this rotten wood?"

Sybille saw that the young count's cheeks were slick with blood. The French must have flogged him. Below a child began to squeal. Amaury de Montfort beckoned to a soldier behind him.

"Quickly," he ordered. "Unbind this dog." Three men dragged Raymond from his horse, steadied him on the cobbles; they started to pull off the chains. Amaury watched, impassive. The young count, free, stumbled and fell. Suddenly Amaury gave a high yell and fell over the count in a hug, and the two men rolled together on the cobbles. Sybille did not know the exact moment she first heard laughter, but suddenly people were laughing and everyone heard it, and then she realized it was coming from Amaury and Raymond. They rolled again, then pushed themselves to their feet, shaking wildly with laughter.

"It's a joke," Raymond gasped for breath. "Only a joke—" He flung his arms around Amaury. "Ha ha!"

The Frenchman laughed with wide-open mouth. He swiped at Raymond's stained cheeks. Arm in arm, they strolled to the wine barrel, howling all the way. Someone handed them cups. Sybille saw them smiling and embracing, playful as monkeys. They were having a good time.

Sybille's legs were weak. She fled inside, up to the third floor, where Nova slept with her mouth drooling against the pillow. Lying down beside the child, she cursed the sons of Simon de Montfort and Raymond of Toulouse. They had wanted to amuse themselves. What did they care if they frightened people half to death? Was talk of burning heretics a joking matter?

"Bastards—stupid, primitive bastards," she breathed against Nova's hair. "How they loved making fools of us." She tightened herself against the child's body until Nova began to squirm. It was sweltering, and the air in the windowless chamber was stale and smelled of urine. Sybille stripped to her shift and lay down on the pallet next to Nova's. A faint sound of music sluiced into her ears and then it was quiet again. She sprawled there in the dark longing to have Olivier beside her, until eventually she realized he was not coming. Turning on her side, she shut her eyes and slept.

When they had been in Carcassonne two weeks, and the novelty of drinking and feasting had begun to pall, Raymond and Amaury announced they would hold a formal peace conference at Saint-Flour, some three days' journey north of Carcassonne. The two of them were eating meals together and Raymond often slept at the château, in Amaury's chamber it was said. All of the young count's followers sang his praises. They passed cups around and congratulated him on how well he had handled the French boy and said they expected the Saint-Flour meeting to result in a real peace treaty.

"Why Saint-Flour?" Sybille asked Olivier. "They can talk here."

Olivier spat noisily on his boot and rubbed with the hem of his shirt. He said, "That is Amaury's idea. We're not disposed to argue, so long as he agrees to treat with us. The place isn't important."

Sybille glanced around the hall. Two kitchen girls plucking capons, a woman holding a mirror, dabbing wormwood juice on her blemishes, several squires quarreling over dice in the corner. She asked, "How long is all this going to take?"

"I have no idea," Olivier said cheerfully.

"I can't go with you," she said dully. "The vines need to be pruned. I'm worried about—"

Nova came up, a piece of loaf sugar stuck to the palm of one hand. "Pony ride," she said to her father. "You promised yesterday and now it's today."

Olivier looked up. "You're going home." He smiled. "You and your mama will be leaving today."

"Good," Nova said and stuffed the sugar into her mouth.

"I never touched a Frenchwoman," Olivier said. "Think whatever you like, I don't care."

He sounded angry. He was angry from the minute he rode into the yard that afternoon. They sat at the trestle and Sybille sent Roger for wine. It is clear he is not happy to be home, she thought in anger. Roger brought the wine and poured, sloppily. Sybille waited until he was out of earshot before she spoke to Olivier again.

"You are so cold," she said coolly. "These past two months I've not seen you."

"Not my fault."

"Very well. But now you're back, you're cold."

Olivier said, "I've been in the saddle since dawn. I'm tired." His face was hard, dark.

"Olivier."

He sighed irritably. Lifting his cup, he drained it in one gulp.

He looked ten pounds heavier and just as handsome as ever, but tired and downcast. In this mood she would get nowhere by being hard. She forced her voice gentle and whispered, "Olivier, I've missed you." She stretched her arm across the trestle.

He put down his cup and reached for the wrist. "Is the child well?"

"Yes. Every day she asks when you're coming home."

He nodded, releasing her. "Has the corn been ground yet?"

"Last week. Olivier, tell me about the king."

"Oh. He's dead, didn't you hear? He was dead before we got to Sens, but nobody, alas, thought to inform us."

Sybille straightened her back. "And Prince Louis, didn't he come?"

"Too busy with his coronation. He sent Amaury ten thousand silver marks." He raised his head, face expressionless.

Then the war would go on. She hunched over one elbow, then she squinted at Olivier and shook her head, not knowing what to say. "Ten thousand," she repeated.

"Mouse piss in the ocean. He owes his men thirty thousand in back wages." Olivier got up stiffly and walked to the hearth. "He'll pull out of Carcassonne by Christmas, mark me."

Sybille looked at his back, startled. "Olivier, why would he do that?"

"He's broke, I told you. And his credit is no good either. He tried to borrow money." Olivier turned to her, laughing. "You know what he wanted to put up as collateral? I'll bet you can't guess. Narbonne, Minerve, Carcassonne—"

She gasped. "But he doesn't own Carcassonne!"

"Certainly he does." Olivier cleared his throat. "The pope gave it to him. Fortunately the bankers in France have a little sense. Nobody was willing to advance him a sou." He walked to the circular staircase and started up to the bedchamber. Sybille, rubbing her nose, followed. Olivier toppled on the bed without pulling off his muddy boots.

"Olivier, Amaury may have no money. All the same he's not going to give up . . ." Her voice trailed off.

He closed his eyes. "Take off my boots," he said, yawning. "He agrees to go home if he can keep Carcassonne and leave garrisons in five or six other places. Raymond swore he wouldn't lay a hand on Amaury's property."

She tugged off his boots and placed them alongside the chest to clean in the morning. "Do you mind if I lie down?" she asked.

"Suit yourself. It's your bed."

She stretched out next to him, wrapping one leg over his thigh. He turned his face away into the pillow. She thought, I will believe all this about Amaury's leaving when it happens.

He twisted toward her, smiling with closed eyes. "When Amaury has crossed the Rhone, the young count'll grab Carcassonne and give it back to that little snot-nose Trencavel, I guess."

Pressing her face against his shoulder, she told him if that were the case, she could not imagine why he was so gloomy, and he said he was not gloomy, he was dead tired, and why did she keep pestering him? Hearing Nova's voice below, she got up and went down to the hall.

"Where have you been, missy?"

"I found a snake."

"Stay away from them. Your lord father has come home."

Nova made a leap for the staircase. When Sybille caught her fat bottom and pulled her back, she began to shriek and kick.

"Shhh. He's sleeping now."

Nova said, tearful, "Did he bring me something? I was a good girl."

"Nova," she said softly, "the war is going to be over soon. Listen, my sweet lark, things will be different, you'll see. I'm going to buy you marzipan and ribbons for your hair. Lots and lots of pretty ribbons. Won't you like that?"

"Yes, Lady Mother," Nova said, pleased.

It was strange. The war seemed to end again. Fifteen years after the Béziers massacre, they got back their independence and their old seigneurs, or at least the sons, for the fathers were dead. It was strange because people thought they could revert to their old lives and a lot of them tried. Troubadours wrote new *cansos* bewailing grief-stricken lovers and cold-hearted ladies. Barons held the old kinds of banquets, same gold plates but less on them. Wives in the bazaars bought egg-white lotions promising perfectly white complexions. They lived from memory.

After the nerve-racking years, the days passed one on the tail of the next, devoid of calamities and near-calamities. It astonished Sybille that she and Olivier managed to lead ordinary lives; they worked hard at tending their estate, they hunted in winter and swam through the summer heat, and they taught Nova to read and write good Latin and do counting. Now and then they visited their neighbors and on holy days went into town.

In the evenings, after Olivier and Nova had gone to bed, Sybille sat before the hearth placidly with parchment and quill on her knees. She felt like an empty shell, lacking that tension she knew was required to write a *canso* but not knowing how to find it. It seemed to her the only times that she had experienced true inspiration were immediately after periods of immense upheaval, and now that nothing was happening in her life fine verse would be, alas, impossible. She stared into the firelight. Lord, Lord, she thought, how dull I've grown! Dull and old, dying one day at a time, for she already had passed thirty.

Above in the sleeping chamber, she heard the impatient growl in Olivier's voice. He called, "Sybille—Sybille, aren't you coming up, Sybille?"

She whispered to herself, "Old. I'm old and getting older." She did not mention getting lonelier, but there was that too. Without thinking, she pressed her fingers into her ears.

In the year of our Lord, 1225, it was easy to ignore events taking place in other parts of the world, if one lived in the forests of Fanjeaux. Sybille knew the pope had excommunicated the young count and that Amaury de Montfort had sold his southern titles to the king of France, but she, like nearly everyone else, made the error of missing the importance of all this. King Louis was now overlord of Languedoc, with the Church's blessing, and all he need do to annex another province was come down and collect it. It was a pleasant position to be in, for a king.

So the following year, on the tenth of June, the royal army pulled up outside Avignon. The consuls sent an envoy insisting they were the king's obedient servants, more from courtesy than sincerity. But when Louis requested admission to the city, they flatly, but courteously, refused. Louis, hot to avenge this insult to Christ's army, vowed he would not budge until he had taken Avignon. He ordered the siege engines set up.

Olivier went into Fanjeaux to borrow seventy-five sous. He wanted a new blade for his sword and a saddle with a high-backed cantle. He got the loan but had to promise the wheat from the north field. He came back talking eagerly of writing a letter to King Louis.

"What!" Sybille cried. She was furious about the wheat. God knew, the harvest would be meager enough without giving half away. "Have you gone crazy? When did you dream this up?" She turned her back on him.

"Address the letter," he said, "to the noble Louis Capet, king of France, and so forth, blah-blah, however is proper." Sybille did not move. " 'Greetings. We are zealous to place ourselves beneath the shadow of your wings and' "—he paused dramatically—" 'and under your wise dominion.' "

She threw him a withering look, as if he were a befuddled schoolboy. "Are you out of your mind? He hasn't come near Fanjeaux and already you want to surrender. You're a lunatic, but I never took you for a coward."

"Hold your tongue!" he shouted, face suddenly scarlet. "You know nothing about this." He took a menacing step toward her, knocking over the silk footstool. "Bernard Oth has written to Louis—"

"That heretic," she snorted. "That yellow dog. He's worried about going to prison. Or to the fire. But we're not heretics."

Olivier sprawled in the canopy chair. "Bernard Oth," he said softly, "has come back to the faith."

She did not believe it. There hadn't been a Catholic in that family for generations. Bernard Oth's grandmother had been a preacher when Sybille was a small child; she remembered the old lady visiting Na Beatritz in this very hall.

Olivier said, "He's pledged military aid against Louis's enemies."

"Oh, enemies," Sybille retorted. "Meaning the young count. Meaning heretics. In other words, he's switched sides."

Olivier screwed up his face. "Come on, Sybille. It's just temporary. He doesn't mean it. Listen, it takes brains to outwit those bastards, can't you see that."

She walked away, staring up at the white unicorn pirouetting in the tapestry. Finally she called, "My lord, let me ask you a question." She paused. "Has the young count sent a letter of submission?" She turned to look at him.

Olivier averted his eyes. At last he murmured, "No."

"Ha! Nor will he."

Olivier shrugged.

"Nor will I." She thrust her chin into the air. "Olivier, if you insist, I will gladly write the letter for you. But don't include my name. Not mine." She strode quickly toward the kitchen stairwell, her skirt swelling behind her. She heard him call mockingly, "Queen Sybille—mother of her country!"

He did not refer to the letter again and two weeks later left for Toulouse to join the young count's guerrilla army, which was raiding the rear of Louis's camp.

She awoke shivering after matins. The candle had guttered. She kept her eyes open for an instant, then closed them quickly. From beyond the curtain Nova called, "Mama, someone is yelling on the other side of the moat."

"I don't hear anything."

"Mama—"

"It's the wind. Go back to sleep." She burrowed her nose under the pillow.

The floorboards creaked. Sybille was fully awake now and annoyed. Nova suddenly slid under the coverlet. "Lady Mother," she squealed, "someone is down there. It's King Louis. He's going to kill us."

"It's the wind," Sybille repeated, not convincingly. She cocked her ears, straining hard to hear the sound Nova had heard. Silence. She waited. There was a faint staccato noise. She held her breath. It happened again. Perspiration began to form on her upper lip. "It's only a broken shutter," she said as coolly as possible. "But I'll go down and get Roger up."

"It's King Louis," Nova whispered.

"Stay here." She tucked the coverlet around Nova's ears and pressed her lips against her hair. Breasts sticky with sweat, she dressed quickly. In the dark Nova was panting. "Stay here," Sybille said again and groped her way down the staircase.

In the room off the kitchen where Roger and Rousse slept, she lit a candle. "Roger—"

The flame leaped. The boy was cowering on his pallet. "I'm frightened," he wheezed. "I have no sword—"

She wheeled and walked out the kitchen door into the ward. A patch of moonlight struck the dark shape of the gate tower and bounced off the iron bars of the portcullis. There was no mistake now. Someone was shouting, trying to get in. Panicky, she shuffled closer to the gate. "Hello there? Hello there?" she heard a voice roar. Relief cracked down her spine. Laughing maniacally, she began to crank up the portcullis.

A moment later the hooves of Olivier's stallion were clattering on the cobblestones, and Sybille hurtled against the stirrup. He reached down to seize her waist and dragged her up across his thighs, with her skirt flying. The mount was circling the ward, trampling baskets of apples. Full of joy, face pressed tight against his chest, she clung to him with both arms. "Sybille," she heard him moan. "Sybille, Sybille—" He whispered her name over and over, holding her so tight she tasted wool on her tongue.

But a minute after that, he was growling, "Idiot. Don't you know better than to raise the portcullis without finding out who it is? *Sancta Maria!*"

"Oh," Sybille gasped helplessly. "My lord, you are—outrageous."

He followed her up to the hall, both hands gripping her waist. "I'd like to eat you alive," he murmured. She laughed.

She lit the fire and went down for wine and bread.

Olivier was full of energy. "I've not had a decent meal since Martinmas," he said. She stood to one side, watching him.

Olivier drained his cup and set it on the floor. "He's dead," he cried out abruptly. "The king died last Friday."

"Killed!" she exclaimed.

He bent forward over the cup. "No, some sickness. Flux of the bowels, a fever, who knows. They sewed him up in an oxhide and took him home."

She put food on a plate. When Olivier reached for the bread, she noticed the little finger on his right hand was missing, the stump nestled comfortably against the knuckle of his fourth finger. She sat staring down, stared, and gave a tiny cry, appalled.

His eyes followed her gaze. "It's nothing to weep about," he said too loudly. She pretended to look away. "Listen," he said, "I could have lost something more important than that finger." He laughed bitterly.

His finger is gone, she moaned to herself. Part of his body is gone. She swallowed and said to him, "Yes, that's true." She almost asked him how it had happened but thought better of it.

Olivier was eating olives, sucking off the pulp and spitting the pits into the fire. She glanced furtively at his hand. For five minutes both of them were silent, then Sybille said, "The little prince is only—what? Eleven, twelve? So we are safe for a while." She said it without conviction.

"That depends on Queen Blanche." He stood up and stretched. His shirt was filthy, his hair dark with oil and dirt. She would have to delouse him tomorrow. "They say she's tricky."

"Oh, Olivier. She can't bring an army down here. She's a woman." She paused. "Besides, she and the young count are cousins."

He sniffed.

"And one of her forebears," Sybille added, "was William the Troubadour."

He sniffed again, rubbing his chin. "And that automatically makes her sane? No, she's a lunatic like the rest of them. How did the vines do this year?"

"All right."

"Rye?"

"Poorly," she answered and hugged her arms around her waist. "I have a pig that needs salting." She was afraid to tell him it was the only one.

He crossed to her, leaned over, and kissed her mouth. His lips were soft as butter, she had forgotten how ripe and soft. His hand went under her breast, and they sank down next to the hearth.

***

In the morning, when the cock had crowed three times and she was asleep beneath the furs in their big bed, he drew her hips to him again. She pulled away.

"What's the matter?" he crooned into her ear.

"This is sinful."

"Well," Olivier said, "not a very great sin."

She giggled. "Put yourself between my thighs."

"By all means."

On the other side of the curtain she could hear Nova tramping around. She was talking to her caged bird. Sybille said, "Move about there a little." She breathed a sigh of pleasure, her body softening, and pressed her fingers against his shoulder.

A month later she was vomiting and her breasts were sore. She told Olivier she was pregnant.

"What can I do?" Olivier asked. "They will slay me before I have a chance to raise my sword."

Sybille dragged her bulging body back to the turret window and stared down so she could see the rows of standing corn and the soldiers moving toward them with scythes. Clutching his arm, she said, "It's a mistake, they're only trying to frighten us. Wait a minute. Look, they're unarmed. How can they harm us?"

"God's balls, Sybille!" He gave her a look as if to say she had lost her wits.

"Maybe we should go down and speak to them. If we tell them we're Catholics, they might leave us alone."

The sun was just crawling up on the heels of the fading sickle moon, and the dusty air felt warm already. It would be another broiling day. Sybille would be glad when the hot days were finished and the babe born at last. She had not suffered backaches with Nova as she did with this one. Olivier leaned out, trying to see something, and cursed under his breath.

"Watch out—they'll see you. What are they doing?"

"There! All around the field! Archers!" He jerked in his head.

Startled, Sybille shoved her face around his shoulder. Now she noticed several armed soldiers standing alert with their bows. Her eyes shifted to the men carrying the scythes. They were moving into the rows now; they began whizzing the scythes from side to side, as me-

242

chanical as a parade of wooden marionettes. The half-grown stalks slithered silently to the ground. She gasped, "Olivier, how can we live without corn? We'll starve! Starve!"

"Fucking maniacs!" he shouted out the window.

"Don't!" Her hands groped for his mouth. "Shhh. Do you want them to hear you?"

He butted her away. "Blanche's pimps!" he yelled. "You pimp for that *con* in Paris! Whoresons!"

Sybille took a step backward. "Stop it," she commanded.

He stopped and shrank back a little. "Ah, that bitch is clever. She isn't going to waste a whole army on us. She sends just enough men to make war on corn. And then when we've starved to death, she'll come down and pick up what's left and say it was God's will."

Sybille stood staring at the back of his head. "Why can't they leave us be?" she asked him, frantic. "We're Catholics. What do they want from us?"

"I can't stand this," he said without turning his head. "Go down for wine. I need a drink."

She needed one too. But she did not move. Together they stood in the window and watched the sun rise as the soldiers pumped their arms. Once Olivier said, "So this is how a woman makes war."

Sunlight winked on the steel edges of the scythes. Around the soldiers' feet the corn lay flat at last. Without resting, they tramped briskly through the stalks toward the wall at the edge of the field, past the honeysuckle hedges, past the marsh. When they reached the vineyard, they stopped and threw down the scythes.

"There go the vines," Olivier warned.

One of the soldiers stooped and came up with both hands full of roots and green leaves. He tossed them aside, careless. Sybille went down for the wine.

Everywhere she went that summer people were talking of food. When she rode to Fanjeaux at Lammas to buy henbane oil for Nova's earaches, the alewife gave her a recipe for soup made from chestnuts and roots. Sybille thanked Gaillarde, laughing to herself in disbelief, but it was clear she was completely serious. There were French soldiers in Gaillarde's tavern. Sybille had never seen that before. They walked back and forth drinking double beer. She hurried away.

On her way home she felt her stomach cramping and had to slow

Dolosa to a walk, although the pain was still barely noticeable. At supper she had no appetite and went up to bed. Olivier rode to Durfort to find the midwife. By compline, it was over. The child was a male, tiny and scrawny. His skin was a sickly yellowish gray. He did not howl, as Nova had done, only lay wearily at her side, as if he had found the passage into life too exhausting to comment upon. Sybille gave him the name William.

By the end of the following week, she realized he was dying and wept over him as he made weak attempts to nurse. Olivier, frightened, refused to come near him, but went to the witch woman in Prouille for an angelica amulet to prevent the Devil from taking hold of William. He sent the amulet upstairs with Rousse, along with instructions to tie it under the baby's left armpit. Sybille, hoping for a miracle, obeyed.

Toward noon a goodman came to the gate. Olivier was away hunting pigeons, and Roger escorted him up to the hall. Without introducing himself, the goodman went straight to the cradle, peered at William's filmy eyes, and advised Sybille to stop giving him the breast, for his physical body would certainly die before many days had passed. Better Sybille should liberate his divine spirit.

"God will decide the day of his death," she told him. "Not I."

"Lady," he said firmly, "the *endura* isn't painful. Once the *consolamentum* is given—" He smiled at her.

She shrugged.

"The babe's spirit is a part of God, you see. A shining spark from the divine fire."

She studied his robe, which was shredding at the shoulders. Wishing to be courteous, she did not argue with him.

"If you release him," the preacher said, "the soul will return to its source."

She finally said, "Stop talking to me like this. You know we're Catholics."

If William were hereticated, the goodman said, his soul would fly to heaven. Sybille sent him away, but he returned twice that day, until Olivier was forced to chase him off with his sword. "Stop harassing us, you devil!" he shouted at him. William died in the night.

The week after William died, Sybille saw French soldiers from the turret window, watched them trotting in twos and threes in the direction of Fanjeaux or Montréal. On Thursday when Olivier came back from a horse fair in Montréal, he brought news of heretics having been caught and beaten by drunken soldiers who also threatened to tie them up on a fiery stake.

"They beat goodmen?" she asked him.

"Ordinary believers."

"But why?"

"Do you think drunks take time to distinguish."

Her skin prickled. "Even De Montfort never burned a believer. It was only the preachers he was after."

"Yes."

"You think this is important," she said. "Is it a sign we're in for trouble—the heretics, I mean?"

He stood silent a minute and rubbed his nose. "Pierre Isarn was burned at Caunes," he said.

Oh God, I wish he'd kept this from me, she thought. If they can burn a sweet old man like the bishop of Carcassonne, they can burn anyone. She asked dully, "When did this happen?"

"Last month. And there have been others as well, mark me. Do I think this is an omen? Yes, I do. Let's not delude ourselves."

In the late afternoon there were local people walking along the road toward Durfort. Some well-known heretic deacon was preaching that night in the village, and Rousse and Roger asked permission to go. Such sermons were great events to the Good Christians, who would walk leagues to hear an important preacher, and Sybille gave them the evening off. Shortly before matins Nova went to bed and Sybille sat in the hall reading Augustine to Olivier, who would not pick up a book but did not mind listening. Dogs barked and snarled on the far side of the moat.

"Nova's ear is better?" he interrupted.

"Yes. No complaints."

He said, "Lots of commotion out there tonight." He cocked his head. "The goodman must have had a big crowd."

"Obviously. You'll have to lower the bridge for Roger." Sybille yawned. "I'm going to bed." Whether or not she waited for him, he would not want to couple.

"Fine. Go." He looked up, indifferent.

Taking a candle, she swung up the staircase and settled on a chest to cut her fingernails. Somewhere below, voices clattered dimly but she paid no attention. There was a running sound in the ward. Roger and Rousse must be back; Olivier must be asking about the sermon. Rousse's head suddenly darted between the curtains—her mouth was working frantically.

"Lady," she panted. "Master wants you."

"What?" Sybille groaned. "I'm abed, tell him."

"Please, hurry up. Lady, there's trouble." Her voice quivered.

Sybille bit her lip. "Very well," she sighed. The curtains closed. She went down the stairs, paused halfway, and stopped dead because she could not believe what she saw. Pons, in his blue robe, was seated in her canopy chair sipping water. "No, no, my friend," he was saying calmly to Olivier. "I know too well what the consequences may be for you. The true God will look after me." He handed the cup to Olivier. Jerking himself up with his pilgrim's staff, he held on to the chair with one hand before hobbling a few steps. His gown hung limply with sweat.

"I can escort you to Mazerolles," Olivier said.

"I need no guard."

"Begging your pardon, how can you walk on that ankle?"

"Rest assured, I can reach the forest path and shelter under a tree. I know these parts well, my friend."

"But they'll be hunting for you."

"Don't concern yourself about me, please. I've grown skilled at eluding pursuers." Pons smiled, not a bit agitated.

Sybille, halfway down the stairs, stopped and squinted. Then she continued down and went over to her husband. "Greetings, my lord," she heard herself say.

Pons faced her, smiling. "Dearest friend."

She greeted him with the three ritual bows, and then said hurriedly, "Pons, is it really you? Yes, it is. Well, I thought never to see you again. But here you are and—"

Behind Pons, Olivier was fidgeting with his girdle. "I fear En Pons is in danger," he said. "Soldiers were chasing him earlier."

Pons was staring around the hall. "Yes, I remember this hall well." He tottered toward the unicorn tapestry, pointing with his staff. "This is different. Charlemagne hung here. What happened to it?"

She came up to him. "Vandalized."

"Pity."

Olivier cleared his throat. "Yes, as I was saying, they may still be looking for you." He was beginning to look uncomfortable because

Pons went on smiling and gazing leisurely around the hall, as if he were paying a social call.

Finally Pons turned to him. "My dear friend, I'll be on my way in a minute." He paused. "If I might ask a favor—a little something to take with me. Bread, fish if you have it."

"Yes, yes," Sybille hurried to say. "I'll get it." She was almost to the kitchen stairs when there came the sound of horsemen galloping hard on the road. Sybille stopped.

Olivier wiped his palms against his shirt. They waited, watching each other's faces and listening intently.

"Who is it?" Sybille whispered.

The clatter of hoofbeats drew closer, stopped, and then men began to shout and slam swords on the gate. She glanced at Olivier. He did not look at her or at Pons. "God's pardon," he said formally, "but I must go down now. Best hide yourself, En Pons." Pons nodded and Olivier started down the hall.

She ran after him. "Olivier! Where?"

He said, "In the storeroom. In the sarcophagus."

"But he'll suffocate!"

"Better to suffocate than burn."

That night a party of eight Frenchmen searched the castle, going from floor to floor in a tentative way, as if they were guilty of trespassing, which of course they were. The knight apparently in command, one with a reddish beard, was courteous and bowed deeply to Sybille. When she told him their young daughter was abed and would be frightened to be awakened by soldiers, he smiled sympathetically, begged her pardon, in French, and told her to go get the child. Nova did not want to wake up and had to be carried down by Olivier. He laid her by the hearth on cushions.

When the search party had peered into every corner, they returned to the hall and stood against the wall, nudging each other. Sybille sat tightly in her canopy chair; Olivier stood near the hearth. He said to the commander, "Sire, as you can see, we are hiding no fugitive. What crime has this person committed?"

The commander did not answer for a while. Finally he said, "The heretic Pons of Carcassonne. He carries plague."

The muscles in her jaw tightened. She said hastily, "We aren't heretics here. We don't keep company with he.etics."

He glanced at her face, then turned to Olivier. "Tell me this," he said. "How long have you lived in this district?"

"Eight years."

The Frenchman went on asking questions:

Were the Durforts heretic believers?

Olivier, after a moment's hesitation, said he did not know. One heard rumors, but he knew nothing for a fact. He avoided Sybille's eyes when he said it.

Did Aude de Tonnein adore a heretic preacher in the square at Fanjeaux?

Olivier had never seen her do such a thing.

Did Bernard Oth have a sister who was a preacher?

Olivier, pale, denied it.

This is awful, Sybille thought, they want us to betray our neighbors. What business is it of their's—this is not their country.

An hour went by. The hall was overheated. Cold sweat dripped down Sybille's back.

More questions:

Had Olivier ever seen Count Raymond adore a heretic preacher?

For God's sake, Sybille cried to herself. What will be asked next?

Didn't the young count send for a goodman when he was pissing blood last year?

It was nearly lauds when the soldiers departed. Olivier rushed downstairs to drag Pons's fainting body from the coffin.

It rained mist for four days. Then the sun came out and the woods began to turn umber and russet. Pons stayed at Cantal until the Nativity of the Virgin while his ankle mended. He hobbled about with a cheerful look, saying the true God would drive the French from Languedoc and they must all be patient in the meantime. Once when Sybille referred offhandedly to Job and the ordeals God had sent him, Pons mildly corrected her, insisting the god of the Old Testament was not the true God but the Devil. Surely she knew that.

She swallowed. "Well, yes. Your faith believes that. My lord, I was not thinking when I spoke. No offense."

Mornings and evenings he could be found in the far corner of the hall, on his knees, a dark patch against the whitewashed wall. For an hour or more at a time, he did not seem to move; in fact he appeared to be asleep or daydreaming. One morning Sybille went up to him. Curious, she asked if he had been praying. He said, No, he was meditating.

"Oh? On what?"

He doubted she would understand.

She said possibly she might understand, that she was not stupid.

"I could try but it would be a waste of time."

"You can't explain?"

"My friend, we don't speak the same language," he said in a voice edged with sweetness. In his waxy-white face the eyes were closed as a padlocked gate.

"I see," Sybille said, hurt. She walked away. Downstairs in the kitchen, she wondered why they no longer spoke the same language. Obviously he was referring to the different faiths, but she guessed it was something more. From the day of his arrival, he had treated her with unfailing respect, calling her his friend, which was precisely how he treated everyone in the castle. None of the others, however, was his wife. He seemed detached, from others, from himself. He had no word of intimacy for her, and she noticed he avoided touching her, even accidentally. On the other hand, he did not reproach her for her pseudo-marriage or for the existence of Nova, both of which he seemed to accept fully. She then realized that Pons made her feel uncomfortable.

With most of the olive trees destroyed by the French, they had to squeeze walnuts or have no oil for the coming winter. Olivier spent every day in the forest collecting acorns, walnuts, and chestnuts. It was humble work but he bore it without complaint. He was solicitous of Pons, calling him "friend" and "brother," as chummy as if Sybille had never been Pons's wife.

But the one who loved Pons and fetched for him and ran to his side in the sunny ward while the wind whirled heaps of orange leaves at his feet was Nova. When Pons saw her scampering toward him, he would hold out his arms. From his girdle he brought out a book, not the gospels, which he carried inside his robe, but a small, thin volume of crudely done woodcuts.

Sybille came out the kitchen door and crossed to the well. With the leaves drifting over the wall, the bucket was littered with twigs and leaves, and she carefully picked them out. She lowered the bucket, watching Nova and Pons from the corner of her eye. Life has turned out queerly, she thought. If the war had not come, that could have been his own daughter sitting on his lap. There would be blue ribbons in her hair.

Nova sat on his knees, excited. She said, "Show me the fool again. See, he's going to step off the cliff and hurt himself. He's so stupid."

Pons laughed. "Not really stupid. He's just ignorant, as all of us are and we—"

"I'm not ignorant," Nova protested immediately.

"Let me finish, my friend. We all have divine spirits but they're imprisoned in these bodies. We are ignorant—ignorant of our divinity."

Nova, without a word, turned the pages until she came to a beautiful woman seated in a garden lush as paradise. She wore a crown of stars and held a scepter in one hand. Nova pointed. "There! That's Queen Blanche, isn't it?"

"Might be. Might not be. She is any empress. The material world is her domain and she—"

But Nova was busy turning the pages. "Ah! Pope Gregory," she exclaimed. "My lord, it's the pope, isn't it?"

Pons put his face close to her hair. "It's a pope, that's right. He helps to rule this world, along with the empress and emperor. Crowned vipers, all of them. Cronies of Satan, lambs in demeanor, wolves in their rapacity."

Nova straightened her back, surprised. "He doesn't look like a wolf," she protested.

He shook his head. "I know he doesn't," he told her. "Surfaces can't be trusted, child. Sweet Nova. You're so pretty. But if you weren't pretty"—he stroked her braid—"if you had a crooked nose and a big ugly wart on your chin, I would still love you."

"A wart!" she tittered. "Oooh-no."

"The true God loves your soul," he said firmly, "not your body. Besides, you weren't always a pretty little damsel, were you? You've had many bodies. Many lives in many bodies."

Nova frowned. "That isn't what Mama says. After we die, our bodies rise from the dead."

"Here. Let's go on, shall we?" He flipped the pages slowly, describing each picture.

"Stop!" she shrieked. "Oh, my lord. That's you." She bent over a picture of a hooded man walking along a dark, lonely road with a lantern. "Your picture is here. You're leaving your cave at Peyrepertuse."

"Shhh. We must not speak of the place I live. It's our secret."

"But how did you—?"

Pons laughed. "It is not I, my sweet friend. Not only I. It's the seeker on his journey."

"But where is he going?" Nova persisted.

"Traveling the road that leads him out of his prison."

"I see no bars."

"This world is a prison with invisible bars," he murmured. "The seeker—it is you, Nova—the seeker is climbing up a stony path. Up and up. Until she merges again with the true God."

"But En Pons, I'm not a preacher. How could that be me?" She looked up, spied Sybille, and waved. "Mama, come here."

Sybille went to stand beside them. She stared at the picture.

"Mama, doesn't this man look like En Pons? Tell him. He says it's me."

Rousse came into the ward with a jar of slops. Pons smiled up at Sybille and winked. At last she said, "I know nothing of these matters. But if En Pons says it's you, well—perhaps that is true."

"I think it's him," Nova said and turned the page.

The young count went up to Meaux in Champagne to talk peace with his cousin Blanche because his people could endure no more hardship. In the first days of his arrival he was welcomed by a great conclave of archbishops, bishops, and abbots and feted lavishly by the count of Champagne, but then, having trapped him, they treated him as a repentant criminal and hauled him to Paris. Where they shut him up in a tower of the Louvre. From Easter to Michaelmas, Olivier and Sybille went into town every Saturday to get news of his release.

The terms of the Meaux treaty, which Blanche forced her kinsman to sign, was common knowledge. Heralds read it in the main square. At Isarn-Bernard's house in Fanjeaux, the men and women sat around the trestle and drank strong cider, and they talked thoughtfully. They spoke of hope, but more often of hopelessness, and sometimes they talked about what they once had believed. For a long time they had been talking about life as it used to be; now they realized life might never be the way it used to be. By now they were confused about what was causing their miseries. Twenty years ago, when they were hardly more than children, they had liked to believe it was Pope

Innocent, and when he died the war would be over. Then it was Simon de Montfort, but he was dead too. And still it had not ended. The war had taken on a life of its own, until it seemed it didn't matter who had begun it or that a million people had died; it would just go on and on, with no end in sight, forever.

Sybille sat at the end of the trestle by the fire wth Isarn-Bernard's wife; Condors. It was a bleak afternoon despite the candles Condors had lit. At the far end, the men played tables, and there was the sharp noise of the dice bouncing on the board over and over again and the jingle of coins. A servant girl went around refilling their cups. Downstairs in the kitchen, someone was frying fish and burning it badly, the smell of hot oil thick in the air of the hall.

"Listen," Olivier said to Isarn-Bernard. "The end will come when every Frenchman in our land is slain. Don't you agree, friend?"

"Fucking right," said Isarn-Bernard, nose like a ripe strawberry. "Yes, I think that's true."

Sybille sat with her hands in her lap. She did not believe it. She knew it meant killing every man and woman in France, every Dominican and Franciscan friar in Languedoc, every Catholic priest and bishop in Europe. They would have to kill the pope in Rome and his legates all over the world, and that could never be done. It was silly. She smiled wearily at Condors.

Condors sighed. "They shouldn't have beaten the count in his shirt and breeches. That was despicable."

Sybille said, "It's more despicable, forcing him to marry his only child to Blanche's son."

"How old is she, little Princess Jeanne?"

"Nine. About Nova's age." Sybille shrugged. "I saw her once at Carcassonne with her mother."

"Anyway, Jeanne can't marry the queen's son. They're cousins."

"Do you think that will stop them!" Sybille exclaimed. "They'll get a dispensation." She made a face. "The pope would give them a dispensation if they were brother and sister."

Condors laughed. "You know," she said, "Jeanne may be the sole heiress to Toulouse now. But the countess could have more children."

Olivier looked up from the board. "She's barren," he said.

Sybille said, "No—she's not. She had the princess."

"She's still barren," he insisted, smug as a priest.

Sybille stared back, feeling savage. "Maybe the count never lies with her." She went on, "Lots of wives don't conceive. They're fertile.

But they're wed to sleeping pricks." Olivier reddened and turned away.

Condors let out a peal of laughter, and Sybille laughed with her. Isarn-Bernard pretended he wasn't listening.

The men stopped their game. A church bell began to peal nones. Olivier pushed aside the board and dice. He raked all the poges into his lap. The servant girl came in with another pitcher of cider and set it in the center of the trestle, but no one reached for it.

Isarn-Bernard said scornfully that the marriage of Princess Jeanne to Blanche's son Alphonse was irrelevant, typical female foggy thinking. What was bad about the treaty were the indemnities they would have to pay, the thousands of marks to keep a royal garrison at the Château Narbonnais and to be found a theological university in Toulouse and to pay for Roman churches damaged during the war. He went on wearily listing monies owed to the French.

"No, my friend," Olivier interrupted. It was not the money, because how could they pay Blanche twenty thousand marks they didn't have. He paused. In his opinion, worse was the promise to tear down the walls of Toulouse and give the count's palace to Blanche. He had spent his youth there and he hated the idea of the French living there. His lips squeezed into a thin line. And even worse was the promise to dismantle so many of their fortresses. What would become of Fanjeaux when its ramparts were torn down and the stone-guns taken away? What would become of them?

Isarn-Bernard groaned, morose.

Sybille, listening without speaking, thought, Yes, all that is true and bad. It would be foolish to deny it. She cleared her throat. "The Church has taken back the young count, at least they pretend to. I imagine they had a good reason for deciding to forgive him."

Olivier said the reason was obvious, for God's sake. Blanche, the pious bitch, could not treat with an excommunicate.

"Perhaps I'm wrong," she went on, "perhaps the Church isn't expecting Raymond to persecute heretics, to arrest and burn them. But I suspect that's what they want him to do. Correct me if I'm wrong."

Isarn-Bernard could not remember any provision in the treaty that spoke of burning Good Christians. "The count would not have agreed. He wouldn't kill his own subjects. Forget that idea."

She said she supposed he was right, and Olivier said it was time they went home.

They sat in silence.

Chapter Twelve

They were going to sit out the apocalypse.

They were going to lie hidden at Cantal until someone, the king of Aragon or Emperor Frederick or perhaps even God, rescued the country.

In a dozen years, complaining first of bad harvests, then of no harvests, they moved from mere hard times to starvation. There was no other name for it, Sybille thought. Among the villeins on her land there were two kinds, the quiet and the very quiet. The quiet ate pottages of dead leaves without complaining; the very quiet snatched up men and women and children on the road to Laurac, and dined on the flesh of human and horse in their wattle huts, and sometimes they salted the meat and sold it in the marketplaces at Fanjeaux or Montréal. She did not have to wonder who ate human meat, because their faces showed color and their stomachs did not bloat out like pigs' bladders, and she warned Nova never to cross the bridge without Olivier or Roger at her side.

The girl's body was rounding, and her chest sprouted little breasts as hard as sour apples. Sybille taught her to play the lute. Every evening after supper Nova sat barefoot in the hall and practiced her songs, while Sybille did her mending and Olivier dozed. The child had no gift for music. She obediently strummed out the tunes, to please her mother, and afterward snuggled her face against Sybille's side, silently pleading for praise. When Sybille obliged she laughed happily and babbled, "I love you, Mama, I love you." For her father she had only the coolest of smiles; she observed his moods and bad temper with indifference. But when he teased her, trying to break down her polite disdain, she lashed back at him until the sounds of their quarreling drove Sybille to the stable.

Aude de Tonnein brought news from town, news of Preaching Friars from Toulouse here to ask questions of people. This meant nothing to Sybille; she had nothing to tell the Dominicans. Aude said they must go into town and take an oath to fight heresy, and Nova must go too. Every girl child over the age of twelve was obliged to swear. It was a new law. "Let them grow pimples on their snouts," Sybille said, and Aude agreed. Sybille did not go.

Easter came, with nightingales shrieking in the chestnut trees, and Sybille sowed watercress seeds in her kitchen garden and waited for them to sprout. Olivier worked in the field north of the castle. Once, after the village priest had ridden by on his mule, Olivier came into the ward at midday and told Sybille they should go to Fanjeaux and see the Preaching Friars; the priest had insisted, although when Olivier had asked why, he could not give a good reason.

All through the next week they were busy with the weeding and hoeing, but the following week they said they guessed it had to be done, and they rode to town.

The friars had set up an office in the cloister behind the church. From the corridor, where people had been asked to wait, Sybille could see an expanse of green grass. At the far end of the cloister, a long table and chairs had been placed under a colonnade, and two white-robed friars sat behind the table while a clerk moved his pen over a sheet of parchment. A woman in a lavender wimple was standing before the table, her shoulders lifting into an impatient shrug from time to time. Sybille noticed the woman had not been allowed to sit, even though there were stools. The clerk brought a Bible and the woman placed her hand on it. She stood there another quarter of an hour before they dismissed her. She crossed the cloister, head up. When she neared, Sybille could not help putting out her hand.

"What do they want?" she whispered.

"Nothing. Loyalty to the superior faith."

"Thank you," Sybille said.

"Not at all."

It was late morning when their turn came. Sybille and Olivier crossed the cloister, with Nova trailing behind on long, coltish legs. The friars looked young and well fed; their cheeks had color and their fingernails were immaculate. Their similar expressions, grave, slightly smug, made it difficult at first to tell them apart. Actually, there was a difference—the one on Sybille's left was chewing carob, raking his front teeth down the pods and discarding them in a neat pile on the table. The other one wore a short beard. The friars, whispering, did not look up immediately. When finally they did, neither one introduced himself.

The clerk fumbled for a clean sheet of parchment and pulled his pen from a jar. The bearded Dominican asked their names, ages, and place of residence, and the clerk wrote down Olivier's answers in a neat, tiny script. The friars did not waste parchment.

These preliminaries over, the other friar announced that every male over fourteen and every female over twelve was being requested to abjure heresy and swear loyalty to the Holy Roman Church. Conversely, he said, they would be interested in the names of all individuals disloyal to the Church. Heretics, he meant. Sybille nodded, thinking that if she were to give the names of every heretic in the district, she would be standing there until next Christmas.

The friar with the beard asked Nova if she had made her communion at Easter. She had. Good. She must also make it at Pentecost and Christmas. He turned to Olivier. "As head of household, you are obliged to attend mass on Sundays and feast days," he said. "Or pay a fine of twelve deniers. Of course in case of serious illness—" He waved his hand. Abruptly he changed the subject. "Any heretics living on your land?" he asked briskly.

"No," Olivier lied, equally briskly.

The clerk wrote "no" and looked up, pen poised.

The friar went on, as if reading from a book, "Whosoever is convicted of allowing a heretic to live on his domain shall lose said domain, and himself be handed over to civil authorities for justice." He paused to clear his throat. "If any heretics are found on your land, you will be held liable and—"

"But," Olivier broke in, "what if I know nothing about it?"

"No matter," replied his partner. "You're still responsible. Any house in which a heretic is found will be burned and the property on which the house stands will be forfeit."

Olivier's face darkened. "It seems unfair—" Sybille nudged him silent. The friars continued talking, taking turns with the explanations of the new regulations. The one eating carob looked up. He said any person might hunt heretics on the Cantal fief and that Olivier and Sybille were obliged to render assistance. His flat voice flowed on, but Sybille, stunned, had stopped listening.

The clerk rose, came around the table, and presented the Bible to Olivier. After they all had sworn the oaths, the clerk said they must renew their oaths in two years' time.

Nova, restless, was shuffling her feet against the stone floor. She leaned toward Sybille's ear. "Mama," she whispered, "let's go." Sybille pressed her arm in warning. The clerk tipped back his head, glaring at Nova.

"Now," said the bearded friar. "Give us the names of heretics you know. Speak slowly and enunciate, so we can get the spellings correct. Please begin." He fixed his attention on Olivier's face.

"I assure you, this is information I don't have."

"You know of none?"

"Not really."

Both friars smiled. "Come, come, En Olivier. How long have you been in this district?"

Sybille glanced at Olivier from the corner of her eye. His face was taut, his lips clamped. She said smoothly, "My lords, he is a citizen of Toulouse. It is I who grew up in this district."

Olivier blinked at her. He said something under his breath. In unison the friars twisted their necks toward her.

"My family is Catholic and we do not mix with the others." The first friar frowned. "But there are certain families who *reputedly* follow the other faith. I can't swear to the accuracy of the rumors. It is merely what I've always heard." She shifted to her right leg, wondering if she could get away with it.

They seemed to be waiting. She said, "Bernard Oth is one, yes. And Prades Benet is another. Oh, and En Aimery of Montréal and his sister. What was her name?" Her hands were sweating. So far she had named three dead persons and Bernard Oth, who was a self-confessed heretic, now returned to the Church. None of them would be hurt by being named.

She had stopped, and the friars were studying her face. One of them asked, "So few?"

"Perhaps several others but—"

"Who?"

"—but I can't recall right now."

"Should you happen to remember," the bearded friar said, smiling, "will you return and tell us?"

Sybille smiled back. "Certainly."

"I'm hungry," Nova said.

With his hand he waved a salute of dismissal. "Eat, child. Go. God be with you."

They turned and began to walk toward the grass. Behind her, Sybille heard the bearded friar call out softly, "Na Sybille." She turned back. "Na Sybille, was your paternal grandmother a Beatritz d'Astarac?" She nodded. "Beatritz d'Astarac née Cantal has been named by more than a hundred witnesses as a heretic believer." He smiled, showing a row of gleaming teeth. "But mayhap they are mistaken. You did say your family has never strayed from the superior faith, didn't you?"

She forced herself to meet his eyes. "They are mistaken," she said coldly. She turned and walked slowly to the edge of the stone pavement and then across the grassy close.

Outside in the street, she toppled against the granite wall of the church. "They know," she whispered to Olivier. "How do they know?"

His face glistened with sweat. "How?" he snorted. "Do you think you were the only one clever enough to name the dead?"

"This is—outrageous," she spat. "Olivier, what are they going to do with the names?"

Olivier laughed. "Those boobies. It gives them something to do all day, doesn't it? At night they lie about sucking each other's cocks."

"Papa!" Nova squealed. "Papa, that's not nice."

"It's true," he muttered. "Perverts. Dominic's dogs. Let's get out of here."

In single file they maneuvered through the narrow streets toward the square, where they had left their mounts. The bells of the church began to peal sext. Sybille could not get out of her mind the image of the Dominican asking about Na Beatritz. "Oh my God, my God," she moaned over her shoulder to Olivier. He nudged her forward, not replying. Suddenly, behind him, Nova screamed, "Ho! Bastard, come back here!" Sybille swung around.

A small boy, perhaps five or six, was scrambling away, slipping on the cobblestones. Nova raced after him and clawed at his filthy sleeve, but he wriggled free and fell to his knees. He thrust something into his mouth and began to gnaw. Nova grabbed for it. In an instant he was on his feet and gone, disappearing into the crowds of shoppers.

"Little prick!" Nova shouted, out of breath. "Mama, he stole my comb!"

"Forget it," Olivier said and took her arm. "You'll never find him."

"He grabbed it right out of my girdle. I'll kill him!"

"Shhh, shhh," Olivier said to her. "You can carve another. Let's move along, get through this mob." Sybille pushed forward, walking fast. Nova slipped in next to her.

"Stupid little bastard," she sputtered. "He thought it was something to eat. He was actually eating it. Did you see?"

"I saw," Sybille murmured. His theft had not even gained him something edible.

The next week when Olivier went to Fanjeaux again, he learned the Preaching Friars had a list of people they were going to try posthumously. Sybille was in the ward hanging up wet laundry when he returned. She straightened and watched a grinning Olivier vault from his saddle. The afternoon was sultry with moisture in the air. The smell of lye soap clung to her fingers and arms, and she sneezed.

"Why are you smiling like that?"

He laughed and caught the bay by its bridle. "Those two friars we saw—they're dead. Dominic's dogs are asking questions in hell now."

"Dead?" she said blankly.

He was leading the horse into the stable. "You heard me," he called over his shoulder. "They should have been more careful where they walked after dark."

The sun was hot on Sybille's back. She let a wet shirt fall to the slippery cobbles and went after him into the stable. "Killing monks is a sin," she said, her eyes big. "Even if they are wicked. Who did it?"

Olivier shrugged. He unbuckled the bay's girth straps, and the horse rolled back its head, snorting. Olivier picked up a bucket and went out to the well, and when he came back he said, "Someone inspired by God. To slit the throats of those boobies."

"It's a bad business—"

"God's will be done. Why should we cry?" He let the bay drink. "The bodies were found in a well."

"What happens now?" she asked.

"Nothing," he said. "You want something to happen?" Pushing past, he strode outside to the well again, and she followed slowly. He crouched over the parapet, splashed water on his head, paused, then cupped his hands and drank in gulps. Then he stood there with his neck bent, peering down into the well. He turned and stared steadily at her face.

"Your mother," he said, "is being tried by the Preaching Friars."

"Your jokes don't amuse me," she said sharply.

"If you'd listen—"

"Make jokes about your filthy friends! Don't insult my lady mother." She edged toward him, burning.

As she watched, he sat on the parapet and swung one leg back and forth slowly. Neither of them spoke. Olivier yawned. She continued to watch his face, but he did not go on. He was shaking his wet hair, spattering drops of water on the cobbles.

She leaned against the hot stones of the well. "What is it you were saying?" she whispered.

"Yesterday, maybe the day before—the count's herald read the list."

"Tried for what?" she cried.

"For what?" he repeated sarcastically. He jerked his neck toward Na Beatritz's tower. "For *her* sins maybe, who knows. Isarn-Bernard says your mother's name was on the list."

"He's crazy," she snapped. "He heard wrong."

"Suit yourself. I thought you would want to know."

Nova was signaling her from the kitchen doorway. The wrinkled bliaut she wore made her look childish and shorter. "Why is my tooth aching again?" she called.

Sybille dragged closer. "I don't know," she said.

"You're my mother," Nova flared. "Why don't you make it stop hurting?"

Sybille shouted back, "I'm not God!" A humming sound swam in her ears. Douce's name could not be on any list of heretics or heretic sympathizers; her mother had been a true believer in the Roman Church. Nova, who had been staring at her, backed away and slammed into the kitchen. Sybille went back to Olivier. "It's not possible, is it?"

"Suit yourself."

She slapped at a hornet. "Do you believe it?" she asked in a muffled voice.

"I don't know." He got to his feet and stretched. "Isarn-Bernard says a lot of names were read. A hundred, maybe more. All wealthy folk. Land. Houses. Vineyards. They condemn the owners, then they take the property."

Sybille said nothing. Then: "But my mother is dead."

"You aren't." He rocked back on his heels.

She thought, this must be the outer limit of irrationality. The Church is indicting dead Catholics who can't defend themselves and taking their heirs' property. The Church already has more money than God and the Devil combined. "What do you think?" she said to Olivier.

He shook his head.

"Should I go to Toulouse and try to do something?"

"Can't hurt."

Sybille nodded. She craned her neck up toward the sun. It was past nones. "The coverlets won't dry today," she said.

"I'm sorry," he said kindly.

Not that week or the next but the one following, they left the Durforts' bailiff in charge of the fields, gave Rousse and Roger instructions for guarding the tower, and set off for Toulouse. Sybille rode Dolosa, and Nova went pillion on the bay with Olivier. They spent the night at L'Espinet, and early next morning approached the Narbonne gate and joined the lines of carts, workmen, and knights waiting to enter the city.

"Oh, woe is me!" moaned Olivier. "With this traffic, it will take us an hour to reach the faubourg."

Nova, nervous, had been pestering them the entire trip, and now she started again. "But how do you know the house is still there? And where will I live if it's not?"

"In a nunnery," Sybille snapped, and she glanced away in exasperation. They passed through the gate into the Rue d'Alfaro and then got stalled behind a butcher's wagon. The smell of the bloody carcasses snicked at her nostrils. She put her hand over her nose. Trying not to breathe, Sybille swerved Dolosa around the butcher's wagon and wedged her between a litter and a mare, whose foal trotted at her heels. At the next corner she reined in, to wait for Olivier. Fourteen years had passed since she had ridden away to the safety of Cantal, and now she could only stare in amazement. She said to Olivier, "Everything looks different and strange. Did you ever see that farrier's shop before?"

"No. It's new." He hunched his shoulders. "Let's go up Rue Droit and see if there's less traffic."

"If the house is positively not habitable, we can go across the street to Brune Maurand's. Or to the Baconias', they'll take us in."

Single file, they beat a path up Rue Droit and rode through the Cerdan gate. It was midmorning before they rounded Saint-Sernin and entered Rue St. Bernard, past the Baconias' house, the Bonnets', the Maurands'. When they reined in at the Astarac gate, their faces were very sober and Olivier said, "Well, it could have been burned or razed."

The gate had been ripped from its hinges and taken away, but the house was standing. Sybille stood in her stirrups and stared into the deserted courtyard. The wooden staircase leading up to the hall was gone, as was the olive tree. It is sad, Sybille thought, when people are forced to steal their neighbors' gates because they have no wood for their hearths. Surely they would not have robbed William d'Astarac's carved oak gate for any other reason, surely they meant no disrespect. She bumped Dolosa into the yard and looked around. Behind her, Olivier's bay pawed at the cobbles, his shoes clicking, clicking, like the beating of a heart.

"It isn't what I expected," Nova said miserably.

"I think," her father said, "it isn't what any of us expected. It's not important. After all, we won't be here long."

They tethered the horses in the yard and went in through the kitchen. Sybille took hold of Nova's hand, and they fumbled their way up to the great hall. It smelled of mildew and dampness. Like travelers adventuring in a foreign land, they tramped all over the house and gawked and squinted without saying much. Once Sybille remarked, "There used to be a rose window up there, remember, Olivier?" but there was really nothing to say. When they returned to the kitchen, Olivier cleared his throat and said perhaps it would be best to camp down there. They could easily make a fire in the hearth and sleep and eat around it.

Sybille nodded, still dazed. "Yes. That's what I was thinking." In the corner near the storeroom, a mouse scampered confidently through the forests of dust. Nova shook a fist at the creature.

In the afternoon Sybille crossed to the Maurand mansion and rang the gate bell. The porter unbarred the gate and stuck his head out. "Is that Sybille d'Astarac! God's chin, I think it is. Hold on, lady."

When she was inside, the man said he was very happy to see her, but he did not know if Na Brune could receive her. She might be sleeping.

"At this hour!" Sybille exclaimed. "What's wrong with her?"

"Your pardon, my lady. But Madam is an invalid."

"I didn't know. And N' Eglantine. Is she here?"

"Wed," answered the porter, startled. "Wed to En Peytavi. Ten years now."

Sybille boomed out a laugh. "Peytavi Borsier?"

"Oh yes." He blinked. "That's right."

She laughed again. Mathieu's friend, forever egging him on to some mischief. So he had married little horse-faced Eglantine.

She sat under a pear tree while the porter went upstairs. The sun was slicking the water in the fountain an orangy color. She kept looking up and down the courtyard, comparing it with her own across the way. Overhead in the tree a nightingale trilled. After quite a long time, the porter came back and took her inside and up to Na Brune's chamber on the second floor.

It was a small, stuffy room with an immense featherbed and shutters bolted tight against the sunlight. A single candle stump smoldered. A tiny woman with stringy white hair sat propped against the pillows; the bedclothes were crumpled around her neck. When Sybille approached, she began to whimper softly. "Is it you, child? God, God, it's you. Come closer, my eyes are bad."

Unnerved, Sybille went up to the bed and kissed her on the cheek courteously. The porter had been telling the truth; she appeared to be extremely ill and nearly blind.

"I should get dressed," Brune said, "but what's the use? I can't walk. Why are you so upset, child? We all get old and die. Cheer up, I'm going to come back as a man in my next life."

Sybille was sweating profusely. Next to the bed was a chest cluttered with pots of herb mixtures. She pushed them aside and sat down on the edge. "There's no gate on our house," she blurted out.

Brune squinted at her through bleared eyes. "No, of course not. The gate has been gone for years. My advice is to put up a new gate."

"I'm only staying a few days. It's not worth it. I'm going right back to Fanjeaux."

Tufts of feathers sprouted from Brune's pillows, gusted into the air, flapped lazily to the floor, and drifted to the corners of the chamber. "That's where your grandmother lived, isn't it? I visited her one winter on my way to Narbonne. It was when she was thinking of wedding that baron from Termes. Remember him?"

Sybille blinked. "No," she stammered. "I didn't know—"

"You don't remember En—wait a minute, I'll get it. En Giraud, that's right."

This was news to Sybille. "Tell me, why didn't she marry him?"

"Why?" Brune said sharply. "Fanatical Catholic. That was before the terrible trouble began. But Na Beatritz was too smart to hitch herself to a Roman. She was too smart. So she told him no man who worshiped Satan would ever get into her bed and sent him back to Termes." She was rubbing her eyes.

Sybille looked around at the plain bare walls. Once there had been tapestries and curtains of Genoese silk, white and gold curtains. Douce had always admired them. She sat silent awhile, her stomach cramping at the thought of her mother. Brune leaned over the side of the bed and hawked into a bucket. Head on the pillow again, she began boasting about the males in her family—her husband, Pierre, her sons, Pierre and Raymond the One-eyed. Her nephew, Aldric, was a consul; her son-in-law, Peytavi, was an important officer in the church. Did Sybille know?

Sybille said she did not; she got little news in the country.

The woman grunted. Sybille fell silent again.

"Do you know Galvan Seguier?" Sybille shook her head. "My husband's brother-in-law, he's a Waldensian. Condemned and burned by Friar Daniel. On the steps of Saint-Romain."

She must be raving, Sybille thought. It could not possibly be true.

Brune puckered her mouth into a grin. "Daniel was stoned. People tried to throw him in the river, but he got loose. I wish I could have seen it."

Sybille did not comment. She was thinking of her mother and the indictment, not about Galvan Seguier. She could not even grasp what Brune was talking about. It was too fantastic.

"Can't you talk, Na Sybille?" the old woman was muttering. "You were always making a commotion. Tongue loose at both ends, your mother always said."

Sybille stood. "I've quieted down," she said stiffly. She was unbearably thirsty but did not want to ask for a drink. Earlier she had considered telling Brune about Douce's indictment. But what was the point of agitating the old woman? She bowed and started toward the door.

Behind her back, Brune Maurand was saying, "The lord bishop is coming later. Bishop Bertrand. He talks." She raised her voice. "Come back another day. When you have something to say. Careful going down. The steps are loose."

Hitching up her skirt, Sybille ran down to the hall and out into the courtyard. The porter was asleep, his face froglike. The gate was ajar. She stepped sideways into the street.

"Mama!" Nova called out from the Astarac yard.

She went over.

Olivier went to the Dominican friary near the Narbonne gate, to make inquiries about the case of Douce d'Astarac. The line of citizens waiting to see one of the friars, or even a clerk, stretched down Rue de la Hâche and around the corner into Rue des Moulins. On the cobbles sat men and women with their families. Women gave the breast to infants and changed napkins as calmly as if they had been at home. Dinners were pulled from baskets and consumed, and bones and crusts were discarded absentmindedly.

Practically none of these people had received a summons from the Preaching Friars; they had come because the previous Sunday their parish priests had announced a fortnight's grace period for all who wished to come forward voluntarily and confess their errors. Those who neglected to present themselves within the allotted period would be liable to prosecution and prison. Olivier had heard of this new procedure, but he was astonished so many Catholics believed themselves guilty of heretical thinking and, moreover, that they were standing in line all day to confess their faults.

He shoved in at the head of the line and gave the porter a sou. "Your wife must come in person," the lay friar told him. "She should speak to Friar Pierre Seila or Friar William Arnald. Tell her to expect to wait. It usually takes three or four days. You can see for yourself—there's a mob here." He clawed in his ear with his thumb. "We're supposed to get some Friars Minor to help but nobody's come yet. What was that? No, what does she need with a lawyer?"

Impatiently Sybille pulled the last fig from her girdle, bit down hard, and swallowed without tasting. It must be close to vespers, she thought wearily. In an hour the porter would be closing the gate. Another wasted day, the fourth this week. She craned her neck. Ten, no eleven, people ahead of her. She popped the rest of the fig in her mouth.

His wineskin flat, the knight standing ahead of her hiccuped and said, "I have to pee again—save my place," and weaved up the street. What annoyed Sybille was the lack of respect these friars had for people. Who did they think they were, treating people like animals? Corralling them there from sunup to sundown, obliging them to urinate in public like dogs? She propped her shoulders against the monastery wall.

A man came zigzagging up the street, stopping every two or three feet and twitching his fist frantically. "Ladies and gentlemen! Good citizens, listen to me! I'm no heretic. I have a wife. Her name is Juliana. Some of you may know her. I am a man who fucks his wife twice a week."

"Lucky you!" someone in the line shouted. "That's more than I get."

"Wait! Wait!" he cried. "I eat meat. I tell lies. Ask anybody who knows me."

A woman yelled, "Ho! Braggart! Who cares!"

"Don't laugh. I cheat! I curse! My good friends, you've heard me swear. I take the name of the Lord in vain!" His eyes were popping. "I'M A GOOD CATHOLIC!"

The whole line started to applaud. Sybille burst into laughter.

The porter took a step toward the man. "Really, Jean Tisseyre, are you back? Didn't I tell you never to show your face again? You'd better tend to your anvil and furnace or there'll be more than gold melting." He grinned. "Crackle, crackle—you'll roast nicely."

Sybille recognized his name. He was a goldsmith who owned a fancy shop in Rue Palmade and was known for his skill in bas-relief.

"Liar, you liar!" the goldsmith screamed wildly. "You'll never burn me. You can try, but you'll never burn me. I'm not a heretic! I'm a good Catholic!" He continued babbling until the porter chased him down Rue de la Hâche.

After this excitement the crowd seemed content to settle down and wait in silence. The tipsy knight who had gone to relieve himself came back and stepped into the line in front of Sybille. He was sober. "What do these half-wits want?" he groaned without looking at her. "I'll gladly pay them a fine, but why do I have to stand here for days to do it?"

The vespers bell pealed. Quickly the line began to disperse, and Sybille went home.

Three days later, Olivier had an audience with his old friend Count Raymond, who listened sympathetically—even sorrowfully, Olivier thought, because there were tears in his eyes—and then promised to look into the matter immediately. He did add that he was powerless to interfere in matters of heresy, but this was different: The Astaracs were one of the most noble families in Toulouse and Raymond himself had known Na Douce to be the most devout of Catholic ladies. Surely this was an unjust accusation.

A week passed. Sybille worried about the fields of rye and legumes ripening at Cantal. Every day Olivier rode to the count's house, dawdling and lounging about with Raymond's retinue and drinking too much wine.

"This isn't a feast, you know!" Sybille cried, losing patience. "What about my lady mother? Did he talk to the friars?"

"It looks bad," Olivier finally said. "They claim she gave charity banquets to raise money for the heretic church."

Sybille, hearing this slander, had trouble speaking. At last she said, "For the relief of refugees after Béziers and Carcassonne, yes. Not for the heretic church. She didn't think to ask people their faith. Are the friars against helping the poor?"

But Olivier, as confused as she, had no answer to that question. He continued to spend his days hanging around the count's house, but he no longer bothered to bring up the subject of Douce d'Astarac. In all fairness to Olivier, it would have done no good if he had. So that was why the following Thursday Sybille and Nova saw a corpse labeled "Douce d'Astarac" being dragged on a hurdle down Rue Méjane, right down the middle of the thoroughfare between the stalls hung with ropes of garlic, where piles of snow-white onions and purple-black aubergines calmly overflowed their baskets.

It was midmorning, and the street was crowded with women marketing. Sybille's basket was filled with potatoes and green peppers. Suddenly a bell tinkled. Farther up the street the air began shuddering with screams, then came a public crier reciting the names of the dead. "Citizens!" he intoned. "Whoso does like, will suffer a like fate! *"Qui atal fara, atal pendra!"* The crier looked fairly composed, considering the hideous cavalcade bumping along behind him.

People began scrambling into the shops, shrieking and wailing.

Or they huddled silently against the produce tables. Sybille dropped her basket. She did not move. When the first hurdle loomed into view, she yanked Nova's head against her chest and gripped it there. The hurdles were being pulled by men who had tied rags around their faces, just like masks in a pantomime. Signboards, roped to the hurdles, proclaimed the skeleton of Raymonda, wife of Bertrand de Roaix. There came a jumbled heap of bones, once Geraud Peyrier according to the sign. And there was a fairly recent carcass, still oozing maggots and worms—Pierre Em—Sybille missed the rest of the name. The entire street had become a charnel house.

"Shame! Shame on you!" a woman cried out in a hoarse voice.

"Madam," one of the masked men answered, "Get a glimpse of Hades! Follow me. I'll get you a front-row seat!" He plodded forward.

Some of the corpses had not been carefully strapped to the hurdles. Bumping over the cobbles, a skull or a legbone covered with black flies would tumble off and roll away.

A woman standing beside Sybille turned. "Where are they taking them?" Without waiting for an answer, she murmured, "To the Count's Meadow, I guess. Horrible. Heartless demons." She turned away.

Sybille stared and stared, unable to look away; Nova was curled around her body. When the hurdle marked "Douce d'Astarac" moved into view, she gasped. On it sprawled the rotting carcass of a thing that could not have been dead more than a few months. Sybille looked at the skull. Part had been eaten away; from the rest sprouted black hair. The gravediggers, in a rush, had taken the wrong corpse. Or mislabeled it. Sybille swayed, then she began to laugh. More hurdles passed by, skeleton after skeleton, and by now the street was packed with dogs, their tongues threshing the air, necks thrust forward to snatch an unexpected feast. Sybille clutched her daughter to her breast.

Minute followed minute, and then the street was empty again and no more hurdles came, and she knew it had ended. Nova's head reared up slowly, and she stood erect, hair plastered over her forehead. She said to Sybille, "You promised to buy me an orange."

There was nothing else to do. So Sybille bought her daughter an orange. They walked home with the sun in their eyes, Nova squirting the juice into her mouth, as if it were any other day.

* * *

She had seen the bodies. She had stood outside the grocer's, read the signboards, watched without vomiting or weeping. She should not have looked. Now, too late, she knew she should have buried her eyes, because the images circled in her mind until she felt she would go mad. In her imagination she watched the masked beasts shoveling the flesh and bones onto the fire, saw their arms swinging in arcs, heard the flames hissing.

In the mornings she sat on a bench in the yard, her face tipped up to the sun. At midday, when the heat was unbearable, her eyes would begin to swim, and she would go into the kitchen and lie on her pallet, teeth chattering, her hair awry, her mouth fixed in an anxious smile.

"Rest now, Mama," Nova said. "I love you more than anything in the world. Do you want some water? Do you have a headache?"

There was nothing Sybille desired. She shook a white louse from her coverlet and tried to pray. It was the first time she had approached God since returning to the city. *Confiteor Deo Omnipotenti,* she said silently. O Eternal Father, most kind friend, prince of all creation, king without end, how much greater was Your suffering than mine.

But she could not keep from thinking of her mother. Let me say this to You, my Lord, and may You correct me if I'm wrong. How could it be possible, Lord, that You permitted this terrible thing to be done to my lady mother? Are You so sleepy that You took no heed of her plight? Help me to understand why You and all the blessed saints remained silent while they tossed her bones onto the pyre. Our Father which art in the heavens, how is it that You did not protest? Do not suppose I am asking lightly—I implore You for a serious answer. *In nomine patris et filii et spiritus sancti. Amen.*

Lying on her back, she felt no better for having posed these questions to God, and she felt still worse when she realized He was refusing her even the smallest whisper of a reply. From her pallet she watched Nova clumsily chopping onions for soup and wiping her eyes on her wrist. Olivier came home from the count's, late as usual, and they ate before the hearth, and Nova washed the bowls. When everything had been put away, and Nova asleep, she and Olivier talked about the city and fear, and then, inevitably, about returning to Fanjeaux. Olivier urged their return. Sybille, weak, pleaded for delay. Next week, she told him. Or as soon as she felt strong again, unable to name a date.

After a few days passed, he brought up the subject again. "We're going to lose the harvest. What will we eat this winter?"

"What news at the count's? Is he going to arrest those devils? You're his friend. Tell me what he plans to do."

"I don't know. Stop changing the subject."

Sybille ignored him. "Can't he put a stop to this insanity? Somebody must."

"Yes, of course," Olivier agreed. "It's a disgrace. Jean Tisseyre's been burned. They arrested him for disturbing the peace and packed him off to Alleman's. He—"

The imbecile goldsmith from Rue Palmade, the man who cursed and enjoyed his wife twice a week. Sybille broke in, "You said burned. Not jailed. Why did they burn him, for God's sake?"

"I'm telling you," Olivier said stolidly. "They put him in a cell with some goodmen who'd just been captured by the bailiff of Lavaur. By next morning he converted."

"Overnight?" Sybille laughed. It was absurd. And yet why not? If you were going to bolt the Church of Rome, you might have to do it between dusk and dawn. Do it quick before God wakes up. She turned her head away.

Olivier continued, "And when they burned the goodmen, Jean Tisseyre asked to share their fate. You should have seen the riots at the meadow. People are just crazy for patriots."

She gaped at him. "Did you go? Did you? Olivier, why don't you answer me?"

"When did I say I was there?"

"Just a second ago. You said—"

Olivier swore he had not been present, had no appetite for watching people die in torment. "It's the truth," he insisted. "No appetite."

"Good," she said. She half-disbelieved him.

The quarterday came and went before they knew it. Father Sicard from Saint-Sernin and two knights wanted to search the house for concealed heretics, but Sybille, boiling, cursed them until they slunk away down the street. Slowly she found herself thinking less of Douce. While talking every day about going home, they nonetheless continued to linger. The young count took Olivier and a dozen other knights to Comminges to consult with its count, and afterward he composed a letter to Pope Gregory, complaining that the Holy See's

Inquisitors were provoking great disturbances among his people. The excesses of the friars, he warned, were stirring up people against the Church. Was this what His Holiness desired? If the Inquisitors' zeal went uncurbed, he could not answer for the safety of Friar William Arnald and the rest.

Friar Pierre Seila and Friar William Arnald went out of Toulouse, to make an expedition into the Quercy district. The countryside was magnificent, and the cool, dry autumn made touring especially pleasant. In the fields the wheat was being cut. At Cahors the friars successfully conducted posthumous trials, and dug up and burned corpses. They moved on to Moissac. Two hundred and ten citizens were found guilty of heresy and condemned to the stake, but four escaped to the Belleperche monastery, where the monks gave them asylum and disguised them as lay brothers. The Benedictines at Belleperche did not approve of the Dominicans; they criticized their methods as being excessively high-handed.

Olivier was in no rush to return. With the count's nephew, Raymond d'Alfaro, he went to Avignonet for a hunt and lingered there until the rains began on Allhallows. Sybille began to worry. For many weeks she and Nova worked at stripping all the wood paneling off the walls of her father's library. They hacked the once-exquisite oak into small pieces for firewood and stacked them in the passageway beyond the kitchen. On the Monday after the feast of All Saints, the tardy Olivier clomped into the yard on a new Spanish horse. Nova raced out and stroked the mount's flanks with both hands. Olivier dismounted, handed the reins to his daughter, and sauntered toward Sybille through a blanket of dead leaves, smiling serenely as if he were the lord of all creation. She noticed he was wearing a fur-lined cloak.

"Hello there, lady," he called. "How have you been?"

"Well, well," she said sarcastically. "I see life has been treating you well." She ran piercing eyes over the cloak.

"I see your tongue still cuts," he replied. He pulled the cloak around his ears. "I won this at Gaja. Dicing. Never a kind word for me, is there?"

He's infuriating, she thought. So is his cloak with the fancy fur. She gave him an angry smile. "Kind words you want, do you? Need I remind you that you've left us here to starve these past six weeks—"

"Five."

"—while you pleasured yourself with your fat-bellied friends."

"You're making me wish I was still with them." His voice was sulky, like that of a naughty runaway boy who supposes everyone will be pleased to see him again.

"Go back then," she erupted. "I won't care. Irresponsible asshole."

He stepped toward her. "Lady, please. That is no way to talk in front of the child. Please don't."

She shook her head wearily. "Oh yes. Now you want to protect her. What about the last six weeks? Who was protecting her then?"

"You fared well enough, you and Nova." He caught her arm.

"Through no doing of yours, that is certain." She stared past him at Nova, who was watering the mount. Olivier bent to kiss her cheek. She sighed, "My lord—"

"Come on, fetch me some wine. I could do with a drink." He towed her into the kitchen. Sybille brought a cup and poured wine. He wriggled free of the fur cloak, folded it carefully, and laid it on the bench. She looked at his face, browned from the wind, and then into the large blue eyes. She sighed again.

He paced restlessly around the kitchen, drinking, while she put the morning's leftovers to heat on the fire. Olivier said cautiously, "Well, lady. Aren't you going to speak to me?"

She had nothing to say. One day had been little different from the next. "What do you want to know? I missed you."

"That's to be expected," he said. "I missed you."

"Yes," she said, hoping it was true. "They burned a Waldensian from Rue Cogossac. Otherwise, no change here. People are still getting summonses. Lots of penances given out. I think they must be waiting until Seila and Arnald get back from Quercy."

"The pope's promised relief," Olivier said. "He's appointed a Franciscan to help with the interrogations. Stephen de Saint-Thibéry."

"Jesus have mercy!" she exclaimed in alarm. "The Minorites are just as bloodthirsty as the Dominicans."

At the trestle, Olivier began stuffing his mouth with cod. "This needs more basil," he said. "There's a bad situation up in Albi. The minute somebody is arrested, people rush to steal the door of his house."

She blinked at him. "Why?"

"Why. Because it's bye-bye, obviously. They figure he's never coming back." He laughed.

A wind began to blow in the yard and icy air drifted in the half-open door. Crossing to close it, Sybille called to ask Nova if she wanted food, but she was interested only in the horse. She shut the door, came back to sit down opposite Olivier, and gazed down at her hands. "Let's go home."

"All right."

"When?"

"Advent." He yawned. "Christmas at the latest, I promise."

"Yes." She sighed, "Ah, it's probably no better there. But I've no love left in my heart for this city. I wanted Nova to grow up here like a lady instead of some loutish country girl. But what is so wonderful about this?" She spat a bitter laugh. "Here we are, three rats in our hole. This is no life for the child. At Cantal, at least the air is clean."

Olivier mopped the bowl with a crust of bread and pushed it aside. From his girdle he pulled a comb painted with tiny red and white flowers. "Here's a little gift for you," he mumbled. He started to lay it next to the bowl, but she caught his hand, smiling. In the light of the fire, the comb sparkled like a precious relic. She turned it over and over.

"You're so sweet," she whispered, on the edge of tears.

"No, I'm not," he said quickly.

Afterward, discomfited by the gift of the comb, his mood turned irritable. Why was there no hook on which to hang his cloak? Had she sent a message to the bailiff of Durfort to find out how much their rye and corn had fetched? What a mess she had made of their affairs! "Let me be!" she cried thickly, her wounds reopened. She stalked away.

"There she goes!" he shouted. "Running away on her stumpy little legs."

She ran out to the stable and dropped into the hay, next to Nova, trembling so badly her teeth chattered. Why did she love him? He was now forty-one, and he was losing his beauty. He had grown slightly paunchy around the middle, and on the crown of his head there was a bald spot the size of a sou. Her love for him had lasted a long time, despite his abuse. His lack of love for her had also lasted a long time. An immense sadness settled in her chest.

Nova was combing the stallion's mane and talking to him like a younger brother. She looked over at her mother. "I love him, don't you? What is Papa doing? Why are you sitting there?"

"Resting and thinking. Why?"

"Aren't we going over to Na Brune's today?"

"That's right, sweet heart. I'd forgotten."

Nova said flippantly, "Maybe the old bitch has died. Then we won't have to go."

"What a thing to say," Sybille said sharply. "That's not kind."

Nova laid her face against the stallion's. He pulled away, flicking his ears. "I don't care," she muttered, all defiance. "I don't like her. God, she stinks."

"What of it? She's dying."

"She's always yapping about her rich heretic friends. And about dying—so she can be hereticated by Bishop Bertrand."

That is true, Sybille thought. Without comment, she got up and went out into the muddy yard. She trudged to the kitchen door and opened it and peered in. Olivier, on his pallet, was snoring. She closed the door again and hurried across the street to the Maurand house.

At dusk, when she returned, Olivier was sitting cross-legged on the pallet in his breeches and seemed more cheerful. He had taken off his shirt and sent Nova to wash it. He watched uneasily as Sybille pulled off her boots.

"Is the old lady dead?" he asked in a mild voice.

"Not yet. High fever. Bishop Bertrand is giving her the *consolamentum* tomorrow." She pulled off her gown and stockings and hung them near the fire. They reeked of Brune's vile lovage decoctions.

"Bah!" Olivier said. "The bishop won't come. It's too dangerous. He'll send a goodman."

Sybille started to braid her hair. "He'll be there, don't worry. Peytavi fixed it."

Nova laughed. "She's leaving a thousand livres to the church. He'll come."

"Yes, yes." Olivier grinned at her. "Oh, you're right."

Sybille smiled but said nothing. Her head ached slightly. She put on a clean gown and began peeling garlic. Olivier told Nova about an acrobat he had seen in Gaja, who had swallowed knives and had a trick dog who danced through hoops.

Next morning the bishop of Toulouse, washing his hands after mass, was preparing to enter the Dominican refectory for a dinner of baked mussels when he learned that Peytavi Borsier's mother-in-law was about to be hereticated in Rue St. Bernard. That was all Raymond du Fauga needed to hear, and he hurried to the Maurand house.

The gate was ajar and the yard deserted because minutes earlier Peytavi and his assistant, Bernard de Drémil, had ridden in to visit the dying Brune. The two men had gone first to the kitchen for drink and food. The servants too were gathered in the kitchen, before Master Pierre and his sons returned from the city. Bishop Raymond and the half-dozen friars accompanying him, all young and enthusiastic, burst into Na Brune's bedchamber. Her maid quickly called out, "Look, my lady, the lord bishop is here to see you," but Brune was far past recognition of so subtle a warning. The bishop seated himself next to the bed. At once he began talking about contempt for the world and all earthly things, and since she had been awaiting Bishop Bertrand and since Bishop Raymond's remarks reflected heretic beliefs, she responded without hesitation. "No, my lord, I have no concern for this miserable life." Her lips rounded with pleasure.

"There are two gods. One is good and benign and the creator of invisible and incorruptible things. The other is malign and evil—the creator of the visible and transitory."

"Yes."

"Christ and the Blessed Virgin and the Blessed John the Evangelist all came down from heaven—they were not of this flesh."

"Of course not."

Bishop Raymond raised his hand before Na Brune's face. "Do you see this hand?" He spoke in a quiet, almost tender, voice.

"No, my lord. My eyes are done for."

"I am holding up my left hand. If you can't observe it, imagine it. When I am dead, will this flesh rise again?"

"I hope," Brune whispered, "any person who believes that will die of gout."

Lowering his hand, the bishop whacked it against the post of the bed. "This flesh won't rise again except as a wooden post," he said, and she agreed. "The great beast of Rome—"

"Beg pardon, my lord. What's that you say?"

"I said the great whoremaster in Rome and all his henchmen will wither away within twenty years. All those Preaching Friars are murderers. Do you believe what I have just said?"

She did.

He raised his voice. "You must not say anything but what you believe firmly in your heart."

"My lord," Brune replied hoarsely, "what I say is what I believe! I am committed to the true church of Jesus Christ!"

Then Bishop Raymond bounded to his feet and thrust a boiled-looking red face close to Brune's. "That's enough!" he flared up triumphantly. "What you've just confessed is the faith of the heretics. Do you know those heresies are condemned?"

Brune, her breath coming in small gasps, clutched at the coverlet in confusion.

Behind the bishop, the friars bounced on the balls of their feet and inched closer. "I am the bishop of Toulouse," cried the bishop, "and I preach the superior faith. Woman, renounce Satan!"

"Pierre." Brune called weakly for her absent husband. "What is this beast doing here?"

Getting heated up, Raymond du Fauga advised her to recant before it was too late, but Brune did not respond. When he urged her to accept the beliefs of the Roman Church, she considered this carefully and said, "Never."

The bishop had not yet broken his fast for the day, and his stomach was rumbling. At last he said, "In the name of Jesus Christ and the Blessed Dominic, I condemn you as an obdurate heretic." He turned to the friars gathered around the bed. "Let us take her to the Count's Meadow and burn her forthwith."

One of the men was a puffy-eyed friar named William Pelhisson, who had secret ambitions to be a writer. He had been taking mental notes of this exchange. Properly surprised, he exclaimed, "My lord, are you serious?"

"Oh, I am, I am. I'm taking her to be burned at once. Forthwith!"

The maid blubbered, "But look, she can't walk."

"Nonsense. What has that got to do with it? We can have her carried on her bed."

Hysterical, the maid fell to her knees. "My lord, have mercy," she moaned. "She'll be dead by sundown. Let her die in peace. Please."

Friar William whispered to Friar Nicholas, "This business will not take long. If we hurry, we'll still be there in time for dinner."

"That's what I was thinking," said Friar Nicholas.

* * *

Six Preaching Friars and the lord bishop of Toulouse, carrying a bed down Rue St. Bernard, attracted attention, and every resident of the street, Sybille among them, rushed out to see what was going on. They skittered along behind the cortege, asking respectful questions cautiously.

The day was clear and frosty. A brisk wind humming in from the east made the bishop's robes belly out behind him. His legs, jerking behind Na Brune's featherbed, had a peculiar jiggling gait that made Sybille think of a jester who mimics a person desperate to urinate. The young friars, puffing, the bed perched on their shoulders as if on stilts, contributed to the impression of viewing a comic play on All Fools' Day. The only wrong notes in all this were the expressions of the people bordering the streets. Horror-struck, they gaped with fish mouths warped wide open.

Isn't anybody going to do something? Sybille wondered. There are hundreds, even thousands, of us and only seven of them. Has nobody the courage to seize these devils and slit their throats? If these are men of God, they do not appear so, and surely He will forgive us a thousand times over for slaying them.

Ahead the bed lurched against a sky of white and mottled blue. The sun glittered on the stained-glass windows of the Hospital of St. John and cut into the ramparts of the Château Narbonnais. Along the sides of the streets, frozen like stone gargoyles, people shielded their eyes with their hands and stared and held their breaths. Not once did Brune Maurand, tucked into her bed, make a single cry.

Sybille ran behind the bishop as one pulled along by a rope. When the procession reached the Count's Meadow, the friars lowered the bed to the brownish grass, and the bishop sent one of them to the château to fetch an executioner. Sybille crept closer to the bed with its vair coverlet, its mounded pillows, its linen sheets edged in creamy lace. It looked unoccupied; Brune's unconscious body had vanished among the bed clothing, as if she had risen between the faubourg and the meadow and walked away.

The friar returned with the executioner. Both men, out of breath, had been running with their arms full of straw bundles, which they dumped on a patch of blackened earth between two old oaks, next to a thick iron post. The executioner walked quickly to the bishop, stood with his arms folded, listening, then crossed to the featherbed and lifted out Na Brune. The body was limp, and for a minute Sybille imagined, prayed, she was already dead. With a good deal of difficulty, the executioner propped Brune against the post and fastened her there with ropes around her ankles, knees, groin, and waist, and then under her arms. When she was tightly bound, he wound a chain around her neck. Then the bishop called him over and pointed out that Brune was facing east, which was not fitting for a heretic, and the executioner had to unloosen all the ropes and the chain, shift her to the west, and replace them. He was swearing. Fanned around the meadow in a wide semicircle, groups of people stood in rows and gazed calmly at these activities, their eyes beyond pity.

The executioner began piling straw around Brune, up to her chin, until only her head was visible. One of the friars, who had been collecting twigs under the oaks, now carried them over to the stake with both hands and gingerly strewed them on top of the straw. For three or four minutes, nothing happened. Raymond du Fauga and the friars were talking together. Then the bishop turned and jigged over to the stake. He did not look at Brune. His eyes were on the featherbed as he said loudly, "I, bishop of Toulouse, have carefully weighed the sins of Brune Maurand and judge her to be a heretic. And I condemn her and her memory to be burned in detestation of so heinous an offense and—" He broke off, realizing he had forgotten something, and held out his cross. He added in a voice suddenly friendly, "Brune Maurand, do you persist in your errors?"

Brune's head did not move. Her eyes were shut. With a gesture of impatience, the bishop clapped his hands and the executioner strode up to light the straw. He flexed his fingers before fumbling with the flint. Slowly the fire caught and started to nibble at the straw, but a minute or two after that the straw turned brown and roared up in a sheet of flame. Brune's head jerked up. "Pierre!" she screamed. Then: *"Why are they doing this to me!"*

From the onlookers to the south of the oaks, a voice rang out, "Take her down!" Then there was silence again in the crowd.

"Pierre! I'm so cold!"

Sybille did not look at Brune. She listened to the noise coming from the fire, and she thought angrily, Oh, for God's sake, stop. Why doesn't she stop that screaming? There was no pity in her heart, only rage at Na Brune for making the hideous sound that tormented her ears. She glanced at Bishop Raymond. His face was streaked with sweat. With his forefinger, he signaled the friars that it was time to leave, and all of them started across the field in the direction of the Narbonne gate. They did not stop to look back at Brune. Their white robes with the swinging black capes made them look like a covey of half-bleached ravens. The spectators turned their heads to watch the friars go.

Brune was still alive in the fire, and she still screamed, although she could not be seen behind the river of orange flames. Beside the pyre, the executioner stood watch, his face bland.

Plumes of greasy black smoke were rising into the air. Sybille coughed and dug her heels into the ground. She held her hand tight over her nose and mouth, so her lungs felt ready to burst, but the smell penetrated just the same. It has a queer odor, she thought. It is strange and unappetizing, unlike the smell of meat roasting, and then she thought, I wonder when she will die. I pray it will be soon.

Warm sunlight was flooding the field. Despite the warmth of the fire and the sun, Sybille suddenly shivered. Go home, she told herself. Do you believe it is possible to understand this?

The screaming stopped.

Sybille stood up straight. The wind began to rise. A few ashes drifted down on her shoulders and hands. Burning grease crouched in the air. She thought she could taste hair, teeth, nails, skin in her mouth. A man standing beside her was blowing his nose in his sleeve. She turned sideways to look at him. He crossed himself. His hair was dusted with ashes, like a fine layer of crumbs. Choking, Sybille stared at the sooty gray flakes disappearing into his hair and scalp. How were these ashes any different from those in her hearth? They were not so dissimilar, she told herself. But she did not believe it. A tree trunk had never lived, laughed, wept. Wood had no immortal soul. She looked down at the skin of her own hands and brought them close to her face, inspecting one of the bristly ashes. It held within itself a woman's life, her dreams, prayers, songs. Brune Maurand still lives in this ash, she thought.

Midday. High sky. Pools of golden light. The hour for taking in nourishment so the body may survive. The hour of life.

The witnesses remained there a long time before they slowly began to disperse. The ashes went on falling like silence.

At home, Sybille's gown smelled of grease. After dinner, she washed it.

* * *

One of the Preaching Friars delivered a summons to Olivier, and although Olivier insisted he was not a resident of the city, the man shoved it into his hand and darted up Rue St. Bernard. Olivier complained to the count, swearing he had nothing to confess, and if he did he was perfectly capable of appearing voluntarily. Raymond advised him to go, all the better since he had a clear conscience. "I wish I could help you, my friend," he said, "but I can't even help myself, you know that." Resigned, Olivier rode back to Rue St. Bernard and asked Sybille to wash his best shirt.

"This seems to be a routine summons," he told her. "I can't see why the Inquisition should have any special reason for calling me, or why they would keep me long. Anyway, there's no sense worrying. You and Nova start to pack. When I get back, we'll start for home."

"I have nothing to pack," Sybille said.

On Monday Olivier attended mass at Saint-Sernin, then rode into the city. The summons, signed by Friar Daniel Marty, requested his presence at Garrigues' Garden, the Dominican commune just the other side of the Saracen Wall. All that morning, nerves fluttering, Sybille wrote to pass the time. In the afternoon she read the verse aloud to Nova, but the girl rubbed her eyes and squirmed with boredom. In recent years, to Sybille's dismay, Nova exhibited almost total indifference to her poetry. It was, she would remark cuttingly, boring. So now Sybille put away the parchment and stared at the kitchen wall. It occurred to her that everything that was happening was destined to be. Perhaps, if the other faith was right and all of them had lived before, they were being punished for unspeakable crimes committed in a former existence. That was what some people were saying, because explaining it as a punishment for the sins of this life led nowhere. Sybille did not believe she had lived before. On the other hand, she could not believe any of them deserved to have their lives twisted this way. So, in the end, there were no answers at all. And because life took on colors of absurdity, so did everything about her, and she would not have been surprised to look up at the sky one morning and find a moon instead of a sun.

When each day had slipped away, she and Nova put their pallets side by side and slept with their feet touching. In the middle of every night, Sybille would be awakened by the sound of some crazy person screaming. The faubourg had always been peaceful at night, but now it belonged to the insane. Sometimes the noise came from the direction of Saint-Sernin, sometimes you could hear it from the city. It might come from anywhere, because there was always someone going mad.

Sybille lay awake in the dark. O Eternal Father, may Your Majesty be pleased to grant me the return of Olivier, for I love him above all men. As mean as he is, he's all I've got. You can see that. *Sed libera nos a malo. Amen.* The kitchen smelled like stale grease. Trying not to wake Nova, she pulled the coverlet over her head and whimpered very softly.

They were out when Olivier returned on Thursday. She and Nova had not yet come back from the candler's on Rue Gotine, and Olivier lit a fire in the hearth and began to heat wine for himself. When Sybille lifted the latch a half hour later, he was hunched at the trestle, scowling.

"Where the devil have you been?" he grumbled. "If this is the kind of welcome I get, I could have stayed with the friars." He looked exhausted.

That whole day and far into the night they talked about the interrogation. Olivier insisted he had been well treated, more courteously than he had imagined possible. He had held a low opinion of the Preaching Friars, but perhaps their cruelty had been exaggerated because Friar Daniel had been very polite. Of course, Olivier allowed, Daniel had been tough when it came to asking questions, but not necessarily from any desire to harass the innocent. Rather, he seemed to have a passionate hatred for heresy. At least that was Olivier's impression.

Skeptical, Sybille cried, "But what about the questions?"

"What about them?"

"What did he ask? Did he want names?"

"He was very curious about the count. Wanted to know if I'd ever seen him adoring a goodman, that sort of thing."

"For the love of God," she groaned, "do you think they suspect Raymond of heresy? All right, never mind. What did he ask about you?"

Olivier laughed. "I played the village idiot. He mentioned about a hundred names to me. Mostly heretics but not all. I kept saying I knew nothing about their beliefs." He began mimicking his answers to the Inquisitor. " 'Reverend Father,' " he drawled, " 'to be perfectly truthful, I've heard En Giraud sympathizes with the heretics, but the old fool is always careful to say nothing in my presence. Heavens, I would be the first to tell you if he had.' Nobody ever did anything in my presence." He had a proud grin on his lips.

"In other words," she said, "you pretended to be a bumpkin and he believed you. In other words, you walked out scot-free. Is that how it ended?"

Olivier began to look uncomfortable. "The friar was very disappointed he had to send me a summons. He felt I should have come of my own volition. And—" He stopped, sucking in his breath.

She tensed. He was hiding something.

"—he seemed to have all the facts about one of my sundry sins. So he slapped me with a fine of fifty livres tournois. I said, 'Dear friar, thanks, but where would I get fifty livres?' So then he suggested a pilgrimage to Compostela and I said—"

"My lord," said Sybille very slowly, "what sin are you referring to?"

"God help me!" His tone altered. "Are you going to jump on me too? It's nothing important. A woman I once knew, a declared heretic. I attended a sermon with her."

"Is that all?" she asked, excessively sweet. The Church held his going to the sermon a sin, but she was eager to ferret out his other sins. "Did you lie with her?"

"Of course not! She's the lady wife of Otho de Montbrun. Are you accusing me of violating the honor and purity of a noble lady whose lord husband happens to be a friend of mine? May I die of gout if I—"

That meant she had been his leman. It had not occurred to her that Olivier might actually have been unfaithful, except with some peasant girl or laundress, certainly not with a noblewoman. When had this liaison taken place? she wondered. Had he treated the lady wife of Otho de Montbrun badly? No doubt. Oh, how she longed to punish the false bastard, to stuff him into a sack and throw him into the Garonne! It would be marvelous to imagine. She had to force herself to speak to him. "So how did you explain your fucking this noble lady to the friar?"

"What is this?" he said angrily. "An investigation by the Holy Office? I refuse to answer your questions. I don't like the tone of your voice." He stamped to the door and slammed out into the dark, cold yard. Ears cocked, she could hear him banging the stable door and the stallion whinnying. After a few minutes she got up and collected the cups and crawled into her pallet. As her body sank into sleep, she realized they had not kissed since his return.

They had no chance to talk the next day because he went off to the count's—to boast, Sybille supposed, about his cleverness in having foiled the Inquisitor. When he returned at twilight, she was grating cheese for a soup. She said, "Let's go tomorrow. Our business here is finished."

"We can't," he said. "Not tomorrow." He sounded nervous.

"Why not?"

"Friar Daniel wants to see you."

"Indeed!" She wheeled to face him. "You said nothing of this yesterday. Why does he want me? I have nothing to tell him!"

"Yes, well. He asked many questions about you. It seems he once knew you. He esteems you highly."

"He must be crazy!" she protested. "I'm acquainted with no Preaching Friar. What silliness. And you believed him?"

Olivier shrugged. "I had no reason to disbelieve him. In any case, I promised you would call on him. There will be no summons. He said it's just a formality. Then we can leave."

The candles in their wooden holders flung up tall purple shadows against the storeroom door. She stared at him, seething with anger and suspicion. "I don't believe," she said after a long while, "you could have made such a promise. Was this a condition for your release?"

His mouth hung open. "Holy Mary, what are you saying? We shared a cup of wine before I left." Olivier was shaking his head in amazement. "He didn't insist you come in. I assure you, it was a request, that's all. You're under no obligation to go."

"In that case—"

"But I gave my word." This was said almost tearfully. "Don't you see, I did give my word, didn't I?"

She nodded, though she was cursing him under her breath. Was it her fault he had promised? She could easily guess what the friar wanted of her. "It's been years since I've seen Fabrisse. Or Pons."

"That's right," he said with great assurance. "That's what you tell him. You have nothing to hide."

She folded her arms over her chest. "You had no right to make that promise."

He sighed uneasily. "I guess not. But lady, it didn't seem extraordinary at the time." He said he had been eager to get home and see her—he had not been thinking clearly. He sat at the trestle and filled a cup with wine.

So, Sybille thought, your interrogation was not so pleasant as you pretend.

Suddenly the door opened, letting in the smell of pure, cold air mingled with fumes of burning oil from the street's cooking fires. The candle flickered. Nova jolted in, cheeks crimson. The girl was spending more time away from the house; she complained of boredom and feeling cooped up. Recently she had become acquainted with a girl of her own age who lived in a lane off Rue Pouzonville, and now her chief pleasure was in visiting this Cortesia. She came home only when the sun was going down. "I need two deniers," she announced to her father. She went to the hearth and rubbed her hands together.

"Two deniers," he repeated without interest. "What for?"

"Combs," she said, coming up to him. "Blue combs for my hair." She hitched up her skirt and sank down opposite him.

Olivier, lifting his cup, did not respond.

"I'd love to have combs like Cortesia's," Nova went on.

He put down the cup. "Maybe in Fanjeaux. Next year." He glanced at Sybille. "This wine is terrible, lady. But I suppose you could find nothing better."

May your prick grow scabs, Sybille fumed. She carried the steaming kettle to the trestle and set it before him.

"Papa."

"What is it now?" he said as he dipped soup into their bowls. He did not say a blessing. It was something they had stopped doing since coming back to Toulouse.

Nova said, "When are we going?"

"Going where?"

"Home," she said. "You said we're—"

"Monday, Tuesday. As soon as your mother talks to the friar."

Nova did not appear to be listening, but a moment later she dropped her spoon and burst into tears. "They'll put my lady mama in prison! They'll burn her up!"

Sybille leaned over and took the girl in her arms. "Oh, baby," she said softly, "that's not so. You shouldn't—I'm going to have a chat with Friar Daniel. There's nothing to fear."

The girl clutched at her. "Don't go," she cried over and over.

Finally Olivier said in a loud voice, "You heard your mother. Drink your soup before it gets cold."

Chapter Thirteen

Garrigues' Garden was a fifteen-minute walk from Rue St. Bernard. The property lay along either side of the Saracen Wall dividing the faubourg from the city. For a generation it had belonged to the Garrigue brothers, but after their deaths it had been acquired by Pons de Capdenier the Younger, who had made a gift of it to the Preaching Friars. This was one of the many pieces of real estate they had received from philanthropic Catholics in Toulouse.

Visitors who had been summoned by the friars entered through a chased-filigree gate and cut through a grove of lime and wild-cherry trees, and in the summer, when the branches were twined with greenery and the linnets ruffled the stillness with their singing, it was an enclave of innocence and coolness in contrast to the traffic shuttling outside in the sweltering streets. Now the leafless branches over Sybille's head rose starkly against the winter sky, the birds were silent, and the air sighed of dead leaves. In her childhood she had known the garden like the back of her hand. With her brothers and their boisterous friends, she had played games of blindman's buff and prisoner's base in the ruined tower and devoured green strawberries and apples.

Remembering, tears began to wriggle in her nose. She shook herself and hurried up the path, only then noticing that the tower had been rebuilt. Some of the original masonry had been retained, but most of it was new. If she was not mistaken, it was taller, more forbidding, and the loopholes were so narrow they barely permitted the passage of an arrow. Scattered through the garden were small stone houses such as one might find in a village. Certainly the place did not look like a religious settlement—there was no cloister, no chapter house or church. When she approached the largest of the houses, a guard shuffled forward, motioning her to a door at the side. He said helpfully, "Right through there. You're in the right place."

"I see it. Thank you. Pardon me, but what have they done to the tower? It looks different."

"I should say so. They've added about fifty feet to its height. Thickened the walls too. They say it could withstand an army of Saracens."

"Saracens!" She laughed. "What would they be doing in Toulouse?"

"Never can tell," he said.

She pulled the door handle and found herself in a reception hall where some half-dozen people were waiting, hushed, on benches. At her entrance they all looked up, examined her with varying degrees of interest, then lowered their eyes again. Sybille stood hesitantly, then one of the women pointed to a bald man sitting under the window and whispered, "You're after him." Her tone was brusque. "Don't try to cheat on your turn."

"What a big rush you're in!" the man said sarcastically. "I'd gladly let her go ahead of me."

At this the rest glanced at each other and smiled. Sybille sat down next to the bald man and folded her hands in her lap. Five minutes passed. Nobody spoke or coughed or sneezed. Now and then someone would flick an eye toward the closed door at the far end of the chamber. Finally Sybille leaned close to the bald man. "How long have you been waiting?" she whispered.

"Too long." He yawned. "God, how that devil loves to drag these things out!"

The man opposite fluttered. "Shut up, you jackass. The walls have ears. Any sensible person knows that."

"I am a sensible person, thank you."

After this exchange, everyone settled down again. Sybille looked around the room to see if she recognized anyone. She counted seven people. Five men of middle age, well dressed. Merchants perhaps. The large woman who had spoken to her when she first came in was obviously from the poor class; her gown was faded and mud-stained. In the corner, near the door to the audience chamber, sat a young woman, pretty, with a round, serious face and dark brown plaits threaded with red ribbons. She had on a well-cut gown and scarlet leather boots that laced elegantly up the sides of her calves. Sybille eyed them admiringly.

More time passed. An hour, two hours. Sybille began to lose

track. The stillness held them like prisoners. The large woman took an apple from her sleeve, took one bite, and quickly put it back. Nobody was moving about. It was almost as if they feared the very shifting of their limbs would place them in some terrible danger. It is strange, Sybille thought. In all this time nobody has come out of the friar's chamber. At this rate, I may have to return tomorrow. She was annoyed by the slowness, the pulsing silence, the absence of a guard or clerk to whom she might give her name or ask if it was worth her while to hang about all day.

It was getting warm in the room, and she removed her cloak and folded it over her lap. The door opened. A friar put out his head and one hand and motioned to one of the men. He jumped up at once and followed the friar. Saint-Romain began tolling sext.

Sybille's chin kept slumping down on her chest. She would make an effort to jerk it up, then a minute later her eyelids would droop, her neck muscles unhinge, and the chin again would heave against the base of her throat. She wanted desperately to go home and take a nap.

Suddenly there was a loud noise, and her ears snapped open. "Who the hell do they think they are!" cried the pretty woman wearing the red boots. "I'm not going to wait here another minute. It's time we all went home!"

Everyone stared in astonishment. Immediately the bald man tried to wave her silent.

She ignored him. "Are you going to let them get away with this?" she said loudly. "Why has nobody come out that door? They go in but they don't come out. What do they do with them? I won't let them put me in a dungeon!" Her voice rose.

The large woman bent her head to the man next to her. The man at the end of the bench whispered, "Lady, please," but the more he tried to restrain her the louder she got.

Then she began to unfurl shriek after shriek. "What have they got in that tower out there? Dungeons. Torture chambers. Why are they tormenting us? Why do they want us to betray our friends?" She looked around at their faces and howled, "What are you fools gaping at? Whoever believes these criminals do God's work must be deluded. These curs have never heard of God. They serve the underworld. They crave blood!"

The door of Friar Daniel's chamber banged open, and a clerk's head appeared. His eyes bulged. "What is it?" he demanded.

The woman did not appear to notice him. "I DON'T CARE ABOUT THE HERETICS! They can burn them all if they like. But why are they arresting Catholics? Why are people who've attended mass all their lives rotting in prison? Why are they being burned? Answer me that!" Her cheeks were blood red. "When will we fight back?"

The clerk stepped into the reception hall. Behind him strutted two guards, who hurled themselves at the woman. Grabbing her arms, they swooped her off the bench. Her face went on howling, endless and harsh. There was a grandeur about the noise, like an earsplitting gust of trumpets before a battle. Sybille wanted to shout, "Yes, yes, Lady Whoeveryouare! You speak the truth. *Are we a land of dead sheep?*"

Instead, she clutched her cloak and said nothing. She glanced around. On the benches everyone pretended not to hear. The guards dragged the woman down the middle of the hall, toward the outer door. As she spun by, Sybille looked closely. She had very glossy, dark brown hair and in her braids the kind of watered-silk ribbons that you could buy before the war. The friar ran to open the door for the guards. They hustled her out, and the friar quickly closed the door after them and returned to the audience chamber and shut the door.

Sybille could still hear the woman, but her screeching grew fainter. They were taking her to the tower, she knew. She did not want to think about what would happen to her. Finally the screams dwindled and the room was quiet again.

The large woman disappeared into the friar's chamber. As the afternoon wore on, the door kept opening and closing, and the reception hall slowly emptied, until Sybille was the only one left and outside the afternoon light crawled over the horizon. She waited, muscles strung out taut. The door opened.

"Greetings, dear lady. Greetings. Delighted to see you. Pardon me a thousand times for the long, long delay. Please have a seat. No, take this stool, it's cushioned. You must be exhausted, am I right?" Friar Daniel Marty took her cloak and held it out to the clerk, who hooked it on the back of the door.

The Inquisitor had light-colored curls that had not been recently cut, and they tumbled casually from his tonsure down over his ears.

Everything about him was clean: his deep-blue eyes, his fresh complexion, the white robe, laundered and unwrinkled, the gold and black cross shining on his chest. Sybille inspected him carefully. For good reason she had imagined someone lethal, but this man glowed, so that he looked as if he had been newly minted that morning by God Himself. He sat down behind a long table, which was bare except for a blazing candelabrum. In the corner, by the embered hearth, the clerk slumped on a high stool behind a writing stand.

Sybille was struck by the brightness of her surroundings. The walls were white, the papers on the clerk's desk, the friars' robes, even the polished tiles beneath her feet were a holy white. She was soothed, and when she looked up at Daniel Marty and found him smiling into her eyes, she was reassured even further. He did not frighten her. Without waiting for him to speak first, she felt encouraged to plunge ahead, her voice cool and businesslike. "I'm Sybille d'Astarac. I don't believe we have ever met—probably you are mistaking me for someone else."

He shook his head. "No, this goes back quite a few years. I'm the son of Barthélemy Marty. You visited the armory with your father and—"

Marty was a common name, but when he mentioned the armory, memories began to uncoil in her mind. No great flood of recollections. No sudden revelation. She simply remembered watching her father and the other men as they haggled over prices of swords and spurs, and she was unsure which of Barthélemy Marty's apprentices had been his own son.

"—and we got to know each other. To tell the honest truth, I was very taken with you."

He spoke as a person accustomed to living in close proximity to others, with a frankness and seductive ease of manner that assumed no barriers could possibly exist between people. Sybille could not decide whether she found his familiarity comforting or wildly, and offensively, inappropriate. She forced a polite smile.

"You were so—how can I describe you? Nice. Friendly and talkative. You stood out." He gave her a look that was almost tender. "You loved to joke and laugh. Don't you remember?"

"Perhaps," Sybille said to him. "I'm told I was a high-spirited child," and they looked at each other and smiled.

Daniel laughed throatily.

"So we are acquainted. Excuse me. My bad memory. A pleasure seeing you again after so many years."

He laughed again.

"What's so funny?"

"Nothing. Oh, I was just thinking—the way people's lives cross and cross again."

She crossed her legs, trying to get comfortable on the footstool, then folded her hands calmly in her lap.

"I understand you live in Fanjeaux now."

"Fifteen years last June," she said. She sat up very straight.

"Have you been visiting Toulouse long?"

"Only a few months."

"Holiday?"

"Family business," she said cautiously. She didn't dare mention her mother's indictment and burning, although she would not have been surprised had he known of it.

"Is it true you've become a *trobairitz* of some note?"

"If you mean do I still compose verse, no. I farm my fief and take care of my daughter—that occupies all my time." She glanced at the clerk, almost having forgotten his presence. He was sitting with his head bowed. He looked half asleep.

"Lady," Daniel was saying, "there are a few questions I was hoping to ask you. That's why I'm so grateful you took the time to come here and visit me."

She decided to set him straight at once. "I have nothing to tell you, Friar Daniel," she announced briskly. "In April I spoke to the Preaching Friars in Fanjeaux. My daughter and her father and I all took the oath, and we spent several hours testifying about local heretics. We had no real information to contribute. We are Catholics, and we always have been and always will be." It was time she got home. Nova and Olivier would be wanting their suppers.

Daniel turned to the clerk, who handed him a stack of papers. He placed them on the table but did not glance at them. "My very good lady," he said very slowly. "As I'm sure you know . . . the mechanism of memory is truly remarkable. The banal floats on the surface, while the momentous sinks below. We believe an event has been lost—erased. But heavens, just look what happened a minute ago." He grinned. "You were utterly convinced you didn't know me. But within minutes, the fact of it is you *did* remember! Isn't that amazing?"

She watched him fold his arms and rest them on the papers. "I guess so," she admitted. "But that doesn't mean I hang about with heretics. If that's what you think, you've got it all wrong." The appearance of the papers worried her. She added fiercely, "I swear, I'm not even acquainted with any."

He lifted his eyebrows. "Not acquainted with any, you say?" he asked amiably. "That's odd. I am."

Sybille looked at him warily.

"Come, come, Na Sybille. This whole land has suckled heresy with its mothers' milk." His voice was almost playful.

Hesitating, she said, "I only meant that none of my friends are heretics. Of course I've known some, I—" She searched his face to see if he were setting a snare for her, but in his expression she detected only sincerity.

Without warning, he murmured, "Let me ask you a question. Wasn't your closest friend a woman named De Perella?" So smoothly did he drop the question on the table between them that she almost missed it.

She sat silent, a little disconcerted by his abruptness. Then she parried, "I haven't seen Corba in years."

"But you aren't denying she was once an intimate?" His smile was helpful.

From the tail of her eye, she noticed the clerk picking up his pen and dipping it into the inkstand. At once her concentration scattered. She wanted desperately to deny knowing Corba, and for a second considered actually doing it. He would not believe her. She thrust out her chin and sniffed. "My dear friar," she answered haughtily, "how could I deny it? I was not raised to be a liar or a hypocrite or to do my friends the discourtesy of denying I know them. I—" She went on babbling and giving Daniel an eloquent dissertation defining the morals and manners of the upper class. Finally he interrupted.

"I know, I know," he murmured. "Lady, believe me, I understand the meaning of honor. I never suggested you would behave otherwise." He leaned forward, frowning slightly. "But I see a small problem arising here. Let me explain something to you. I have to leave soon and you seem to be a bit confused about why we are here together. Now this is extremely important."

When he paused to clear his throat, she said irritably, "Don't you think I'm listening? I've heard every word you've said." Her eyes flicked to the clerk who, to her astonishment, seemed to be writing down the words she had just uttered in a ledger. He paused, apparently waiting, and looked up. She glared at the clerk. "Wait a minute," she said to Daniel. "What is he doing?"

"Friar Luke?"

"Whatever his name is. Is he recording this?"

"That's right," Daniel said to her. "Don't worry. It's customary."

Precisely. It was customary to record interrogations of suspects. But she was not a suspect. Before she could point this out to Daniel, he was already hurrying on.

"As I was saying, there's a serious point you're missing. As you can see for yourself, I have no wish to put you in an uncomfortable position. You may have heard a lot of gossip about the Order of the Blessed Dominic. Don't believe it. We aren't bad people. On the contrary"—he smiled reassuringly at her—"we are the jongleurs of God. He regards us so highly—forgive my lack of humility—that He has chosen us for this important mission." He rambled on, using words like "pestilence" and "infection" and "extermination," and he quoted the Savior as saying if thy right eye offend thee, pluck it out. He seemed to regard his work as a kind of plucking operation, as if Languedoc were a scabby sheep.

Through all of this, Sybille wished he would be less long-winded. She noticed it had gotten dark outside. Early morning was the last time she had eaten, and her stomach was making creaky noises. The next time Daniel stopped for breath, she said politely, "Obviously you're a man of strong convictions—"

His voice overrode hers. He said he was waging a war on God's behalf—he expected to win. *God* expected to win. Now then, she must please pardon him, but he hoped they might consider the case of the De Perellas. They had been excommunicated, of course. Summoned to appear before the Inquisition the previous year. Fled the city. Now thought to be residing in the Ariège, at the castle of Montségur. He said they had donated Montségur to the inferior faith for a headquarters. Was Sybille aware of that fact? She said she thought so.

She was conscious of Daniel scrutinizing her face. When he told her Corba and Raymond had been condemned *in absentia,* she tried to show no reaction and repeated the word "condemned" in a matter-of-fact tone.

"Sentenced to be burned," he emphasized.

"Without a trial?" Sybille then asked.

He answered quickly, "When I see a soul capable of salvation, I do it and I rejoice. But I also know what to do with obdurate heretics, criminals unsuited to rehabilitation." He lifted both palms helplessly to the ceiling and threw back his head. He asked her when she had last seen Corba.

"Years ago. Do you think I remember?" She did not wait for the reply but asked him what he wanted from her. Clearly he had a complete dossier on the De Perellas. What more could she add?

"Names, places, dates," Daniel said.

In his chair he twisted his head toward Friar Luke—his eyes caught the candlelight, twinkling bluish. He inquired about his appointments for the next day, then nodded briefly as the list of names was read to him. He rubbed his thumb over his lower lip, as if he were hesitating about something. When his face swiveled back to Sybille, she decided it was time to make her departure and stood up. Through petaled lashes, Daniel smiled at her with his eyes.

She smiled back. You'll get nothing from me, she thought. "I really would like to help you," Sybille told him, "but it's late and whenever I'm tired, I can't think straight. Perhaps another time." By daybreak she knew she would be on the road to Fanjeaux.

"Exactly my thoughts," Daniel said. "Which is why I would like you to shelter here tonight as our guest. You can have a good rest and we can get to work again first thing in the morning."

Sybille protested vehemently. "That's impossible. What about my child? I have her supper to make. She'll be worried if I don't return. What is this—an arrest?"

He denied it. Nevertheless, he would be grateful if she stayed. It would be more convenient for both of them.

"Am I a prisoner?"

"Of course not."

She shifted nervously from one foot to the other. "And yet you won't allow me to leave. Of what are you accusing me?"

"Nothing. Heavens! I can understand a child being frightened if her mother isn't there to tuck her in." He seemed to be coaxing Sybille, worried that she might refuse. "Dear lady, let's send a courier to tell her not to worry, because there are reasons why I'd like you to stay. That's about all I'm free to tell you, but you may be sure God has His reasons. And I have every sympathy for your responsibilities to your child."

"Friar Daniel!" She sensed her voice skittering into a shout, stopped, then continued in a lower tone. "What do you want from me?"

"I've already explained it to you," Daniel patiently said.

He had not. Hadn't she come there of her own free will? She had received no citation from the friars. Then why was he keeping her a prisoner? Frustrated, she tapped her foot on the tiles. "I'm sorry, Reverend Friar. You explained nothing. At least nothing I can comprehend. Please repeat."

Daniel said he apologized. He would try to present it as simply as he could. He wanted her to reawaken her memories and tell him everything. That was all.

"Memories of what?" she asked angrily. She scratched her wrist nervously. "Of who?"

"Pons de Villeneuve, deacon in the"—he bent his head, took a quick look at the papers on the table, looked up at her—"Albigeois, according to my latest reports. And your lawful husband, as I needn't remind you." He smiled wryly.

Hearing Pons's name made her start in dismay. Surely they didn't imagine she would testify against her husband. She said hastily, "Him I know nothing about. He abandoned me. It's been twenty years now."

"Nineteen," Daniel said. He began calling names across to her: Fabrisse d'Astarac, Douce d'Astarac, Andrew Fauré, Beatritz de Cantal, Raymond Gros, Jordan de Villeneuve, Pierre-Roger de Mirepoix, Bernard Oth ... He went on naming people, looking directly into her eyes and talking in a tone so pleasant, so savoring, he might have been presenting a guest list for a banquet.

Once she tried to break in, but he raised his hand and talked over her voice. The shower of names drowned her ears. Many of them belonged to the dead. Others she had not thought of in years. Some she recognized as important heretics because she had heard Pons speak of them. Suddenly it struck her that Friar Daniel was not reading the names from his papers. At the start he had glanced down for a second but had not lowered his eyes again. Now she was really panicky. She wondered, Why would he go to the trouble of memorizing all those names? She inched closer to the table and tried to see how long the list was. But the sleeves of Daniel's robe covered the sheet. He stopped talking, took a breath, then said distinctly, "And William de Ferrand."

"William who?" she gasped, her face white.

Daniel smiled sorrowfully. "I deliberately put that one last. Believe me, lady, I regret having to mention your son at all. I know what pain it must cause you."

Sybille staggered. To keep herself from falling, she sank back on the stool, her breath pounding in her chest. Her son had lived only eleven days. That he might be guilty of heresy was incomprehensible. She looked up at Daniel. He had pushed to his feet and was handing the stack of papers to the clerk, calling him "Brother" and advising him to rub his aching wrist with camphor.

He was going to keep her there tonight. Because God wished it, he said. But it was not possible that the voice of God could emerge from that mouth. Daniel, smiling like a nightingale in a cage, said she looked exhausted; he thought they had accomplished enough for one day. He jerked his head toward Friar Luke, who made for an inner door. She could hear him calling out in the passageway beyond. She glanced at Daniel, who was still caressing her with his smile.

When Friar Luke returned, a guard accompanied him and Daniel nodded. Clearly this was a dismissal. Slowly Sybille boosted herself to her feet. Sweat drenched the back of her gown.

"Until tomorrow," Daniel said cheerfully. "Get a good night's rest. Wake refreshed." He was smiling at her. "Your daughter will be notified. That's a promise."

The guard was waiting. As she went toward him she heard Daniel murmur, "Lady, put your mind at rest. Don't worry." She did not look back.

They went down a short passageway, cut through a common room full of benches and chairs, then suddenly they were outside under the cold moon. The guard, walking rapidly, did not look back to see if she were following. I could run away from that fool, she thought. Shivering, she flung her cloak over her shoulders. For a minute or two, she thought they were going toward the tower, and her heart beat as if it would hammer open her rib cage. Then she realized they were heading away from it, ducking under the low-boughed trees and walking deeper into the garden. Through the branches ahead she could see a low, black, oblong shape and torches. Closer, she distinguished a two-story building, but the top was hidden by trees.

The guard handed her over to a tall, unsmiling friar, who muttered something under his breath but did not answer when Sybille told him she was hungry. He picked up a torch and motioned to her. Key ring clinking, he led her down a narrow central passage lined with closed doors. She strained her ears but no voices or movements broke the silence. She called to the friar, "Am I the only guest in this hostel?" but he pretended not to hear. At the end of the passage he stopped and fumbled with his keys.

The tiny room, in the light of the torch, was almost devoid of furnishings: crucifix, thin mattress, bucket for the necessities of nature—a chamber for the discomfort of a monk or a prisoner. There was no pillow or coverlet to keep off the cold. The window bars reflected the torch flames.

The friar was backing out the door hastily. Terror wound through her like a thread woven into a tapestry. She scrambled to stop him before he could leave. She asked when she would get supper and was told food could be found on the floor, near the window. It was waiting for her.

"I need a candle," Sybille complained. "I can't eat in the dark. How can I see what I'm eating?"

The friar shrugged.

Could he bring her a cup of wine and a coverlet? Because she caught colds when chilled. He slammed the door.

Alone in the room she cried, "Come back here!" but he did not. Sybille heard his footsteps hurrying down the passageway. When the sound had guttered, she banged her fists against the door, calling him "cur" and "shit nose," until she had exhausted her stock of names.

She stood motionless, letting her eyes adjust to the pitch dark, then began to feel her way toward the window. When she felt a half-loaf of bread and a gourd of water, she drank but could not bring herself to eat even though her stomach was empty. The water rushing down her throat calmed her.

She was deathly tired. Stumbling to the mattress, Sybille slowly rolled out on her stomach and told herself the friar must have made a mistake. In a few minutes he would return and apologize. She was Sybille d'Astarac. But he did not return.

Her thoughts floundered in confused circles. Friar Daniel had repeatedly urged her not to worry. Now she was sealed up in a cold, dark room. If he had lied to her about being a prisoner, he may not have sent a message to Nova and Olivier. What would they think when she failed to return? Thinking of Olivier—would he come to

Garrigues' Garden seeking her tonight?—Sybille pulled the cloak around her ears and listened to the wind whirling along the branches of the apple trees. She waited for her weariness to lift, intending to piece everything together before she slept. It was important to stay awake now, to rehearse what she would say to Daniel in the morning.

In the dark it was hard to keep her eyes open. She forced herself to think: How much, or little, will he accept in exchange for my release? Why should I tell him anything? He can't detain me indefinitely. It is illegal. Is it illegal? If I cooperate, will he release me? What does cooperation really mean? He can't force me to talk. Unless he can. Suddenly the fatigue overtook her and she was asleep.

Endlessly she paced the room, determined to unravel the mystery of what she was doing there.

Eight paces to the window.

Turn.

Eight paces to the door.

Every assumption she once held about human nature suddenly seemed invalid. Suppose, she told herself, Daniel Marty was what he appeared to be—actually was God's servant whose sole motive was to deliver souls, untarnished, to the gates of paradise. She thought he was, in some distorted way she could not define, sincere. But at the same time she felt certain he was a madman living in some foreign country with its own laws and ethics. Or she was the mad one, because she and he spoke the same language but the words had utterly different meanings.

She went to the window for the hundredth time. The afternoon was passing. Through the bars she could see trees, a few brittle shrubs, a deserted dovecote, its occupants having had the wisdom to seek more congenial climes. There was not a living creature in sight. She watched as the shadows began to trellis the dovecote.

She would show him she was his superior. To assume an attitude of cooperation and meekness but to incriminate no one, to admit to recalling certain events in general but not in detail: This was her plan. She would enact an innocent or, if need be, a witless fool. If he condemned her to bread and water, she would feed herself from the empty platter of defiance.

But neither bread nor water appeared that day.

Outside the window, the shadows turned lavender, then dark purple and black.

Friar Luke held out the Bible. "Swear to tell the truth regarding all you know of the inferior faith."

She could feel her stomach begin to cramp again. "I don't know what you may ask me. Perhaps I can't answer your questions."

"I think you can," Daniel told her. He spoke as if she were a backward child. "I'm interested in your associations with ordained heretics, male or female. Have you ever received the kiss of peace from a preacher? Eaten bread they blessed? Adored them with the three-bow ritual? Were you ever present at a heretication?"

He waited. It was silent in the room, save for the logs crackling in the fireplace.

"I have nothing to say. You have no right to ask me these things. Need I remind you I received no citation but came here only to please my—En Olivier."

"I am aware of that." Daniel began leafing through the papers on the table, but he did no more than touch them briefly. "But I feel it is my duty to tell you—more than two hundred witnesses, give or take a dozen, mentioned your name before this tribunal as a woman who has been on familiar terms with heretics all her life." He stopped to let that statement sink in. When Sybille simply went on staring at him, he bit his lip and said very gravely, "Lady, among those two hundred there are—how many?—probably fifty who swear you are a secret heretic. I beg you to treat your presence here as a matter of the utmost seriousness."

Inwardly she felt some part of herself collapse. He had tricked Olivier, had tricked both of them from the very start into betraying her. She swallowed hard, struggling to hold on to her composure.

"You are upset," Daniel was saying.

"I am ill," she replied. "My stomach is empty and you give me no food."

"I will."

"When?"

"I have no desire to starve you. But you refuse to cooperate." He glanced at Friar Luke for confirmation. "What else can I do?"

On the stool Sybille felt herself growing faint. She thrust out her chin at Daniel. "Why are you tormenting me?" she cried.

"Tormenting you?" He faced her fiercely. "I want your con-

fession. Do you think I enjoy seeing you hungry? You are tormenting me!"

Trembling, she stared down at her hands. "I tell you I have nothing to confess."

He waited two or three minutes before answering so that she
began to think the interview had ended. She folded her arms over her
aching belly. When she was lulled into expecting nothing more, he
threw her a glance so passionate, so nakedly violent in its intensity,
that she flinched. "I want Pons de Villeneuve," he said softly. "I want
to know where his lair is, what he looks like. He is skilled in his disguises and hiding places but he can be taken. You—you are the one
who will help me burn him."

She averted her eyes, repelled. So she must buy her release at the
expense of Pons's life. "How can I tell you anything?" she gasped. "I
haven't seen him, I—"

"Be truthful," Daniel chided. He stroked his relic bag. "Remember, I know things about you that you yourself have forgotten. But
you will remember by and by. Within you, sweet lady, lies locked an
emperor's treasure-house."

Sybille said, "You're mistaken. If I were to meet my lord husband
on the street, I wouldn't recognize him. Nor do I know where he
lives." Some cave, she thought. Near Peyrepertuse. "Don't you understand? It is not in my power to give you what you want."

Daniel gestured to the clerk. "Take her away."

With both hands she pushed herself to her feet and tottered
forward, dizzy. In her mouth she could taste her rage, smell her
breath, putrefying and foul. She stared coldly at Daniel. Her lips
opened, and from some shadowy depths within herself came a cry:
"Give me water that I may drink and rinse my mouth. Give me a
comb, at least." It was not a plea but a command.

There was the faintest of smiles on Daniel's lips. "You will always look ravishing to me."

She continued to stare. "I have no wish to become a stinking
piece of shit like you."

"Ah, lady," he murmured. "You and I—we are the same. You
will see."

That afternoon she did something she had not done since arriv-
ing at Garrigues' Garden. She prayed. "Almighty Father, Blessed
Mary, can You hear me in this place? Tell me what to do! Show me

how to keep from going mad. Are You there, are You there? HELP ME!"

Toward sundown she heard the door being unlocked. A guard entered and crossed over to pick up the slop bucket. He carried it into the hall. On the mattress Sybille did not move. She heard him emptying it into another container, got a whiff of the stench before he brought it back. She sprawled there, staring at his lumpish body shuttling back and forth. He went out a second time and returned with water, a small chunk of cheese, and black bread, which he placed on the floor.

"Where is the comb?" Her voice rang out sharply in the small room. "I asked for a comb."

His eyes, blank, turned on her.

"A comb. You heard me."

He shrugged his shoulders as he got to his feet.

"Stupid bastard. Don't you know what a comb is? Get me a comb!"

The guard said nothing. He dragged to the door without looking back. The lock turned. "Fuck yourself!" Sybille shouted and lunged for the cheese. She devoured it like a ravenous animal, felt it hit the pit of her stomach and at once begin to erupt. She crawled to the bucket and vomited. Stupid, she moaned aloud. Oh, you've wasted it. Then she knelt on the mattress and divided the bread into two halves. One she put aside in case they gave her nothing tomorrow; the other she crumbled into bites the size of peas and put them on her tongue, one by one, measuring two or three minutes between swallows.

Darkness came. She drank a little of the water and felt better. What day is it? she wondered. She had left Rue St. Bernard on Saturday morning. This was the third night she had lain here. Was this only Monday evening? It did not seem possible. Footsteps came down the passageway, went back a few minutes later. When the sound was gone, she put her head down on the mattress and thought of Nova and began to cry.

In the middle of the night she woke and could not understand what she was doing alone in this strange room. Then she remembered and could not fall back to sleep. Rain beat at the window. She thought of Nova alone and began to cry again. Our Father Which Art in Heaven, what kind of God are You? Your silence is incomprehensible. What harm have I ever done to anybody? What harm have the heretics done? Hallowed be Thy Name, but I beg of You, tell me what You want from me. To save myself I must acquiesce to evil. Answer me this: Must I, must I? Without waiting for an answer, she lay down and fell asleep again.

In the morning the rain was still falling. She stood by the window, gazing out into the watery garden that had known the cooing of pigeons and the singsong of children's games and the sweet blossoms of trees that ripened their fruit in peace. All that day Daniel did not send for her. She sat on the mattress, and the stone walls rose up around her. What were they doing in Rue St. Bernard? She supposed Olivier by now had gone to the count. She had been here four days; surely that was sufficient time for Raymond to achieve the release of a noblewoman like Sybille d'Astarac.

She went to the window again. She was homesick. It was the first time she had been separated from Nova. She wanted Olivier's arms about her. It is wonderful, she thought, to sleep in the arms of a man.

Then she thought of Daniel with his pretty eyes, his sorrowful smile, behind the big table shining with polish. In his armchair he sat in holy robes and fingered his relic bag of old bones and laved her with the smiles of a lover. But he was not as intelligent as he imagined. She had noticed something. Whenever he brought up some question to which he badly wanted an answer, he gave himself away by saying, "Let me ask you a question." She was determined to deny him the answers he craved. He could starve her to death, but she would give him nothing. To think that she could injure him filled her with joy, and she felt as reckless as if she had drunk a pitcher of unwatered wine.

They did not bring her food. That evening she ate the rest of the coarse bread, gritty on her tongue. She lay down to sleep, and when the sun came up the next morning she was surprised to see a tray inside the door and to realize she had slept so deeply. There was a pitcher of water, about a half-pound of bread with a small piece of cheese, and a bowl, now cold, of what she guessed was cabbage soup. Standing, she rinsed her mouth, combed her hair with her fingers, and filled her stomach. Then she settled down on the mattress.

The sunshine glittered on the branches of the trees. When she had been sitting there perhaps an hour, a key turned in the lock and the tall friar put in his head. He jerked his head once. She got her cloak and followed him down the passageway and outside. The air was cold, but the sun fell gently warm on the crown of her head.

Just beyond the doorway by a pear tree, Daniel stood holding a dog. When he saw her, he stooped to put the animal on the ground and walked over to her. His eyes smiling, he asked, "Are you well today, lady?"

"Yes," she said irritably. "You have not given me a comb."

"But you have not been kind to me," he said with sadness.

When the dog rubbed an ear against her leg, she bent to touch its fur. The feel of the silky white hair made her want to cry, and she jerked her fingers away.

"Don't worry, lady," Daniel said. "Pet him all you want. He likes it."

Then he turned, and they began walking down a gravel path and out through the garden. The dog raced in circles between the trees, attacking twigs and chasing squirrels. Observing his energy made Sybille feel sluggish. After walking only a few yards, she began to tire, as if her leg muscles had snapped.

"Don't you think he's precious?" asked Daniel.

"I guess so." He was fluffy white, with a long, curly coat and a stubby tail that seemed in perpetual motion.

Daniel bent for a stick. "Arnaud!" he called. "Here, boy. Get it, Arnaud!" He tossed the stick high into the air. "He's just a pup. I wish I knew his age. Can you tell?"

"No."

"It isn't as if I chose him. He chose me. He belonged to someone's estate—forfeited when that person went to prison. Alas, I didn't have a chance to inquire about the dog's age." Arnaud flew like an arrow across the brown grass. Sybille looked up at the sky with a bitter smile on her lips. In some dungeon a man rotted while the proceeds of his house went to the French treasury and his pet to the arms of the Inquisitor. Daniel whistled for the dog. They skirted a gray house and started up a sloping field in the direction of the tower. Sybille could see its dark bulk ahead.

"Do you think I can mate him soon?" asked Daniel.

"I don't know," said Sybille. "Where are you taking me?"

"Don't worry," he replied. His voice became honey-sweet. "I thought you might enjoy a short walk. The sun's nice and warm. Not like December." He whistled again, and when Arnaud dashed up, Daniel scooped him into his arms and held him belly up, like a baby.

She turned to him, remembering the shields and hauberks and uncouth men in his father's armory. She said, "If you want me to speak, you must behave like a gentleman."

He nodded at once, his mouth pouting a submissive grin. "But if you're unreasonable—"

"Give me a comb."

"You're among monks. Not in a lady's bedchamber."

She repeated, "Get it. Then we'll see what happens." He nodded hesitantly. "You can always take it away."

He said, "That's true. I'll think about it."

"I thought you liked me." She fawned at him through her lashes. "If you really like me, you won't hurt me."

"Lady! Didn't I tell you not to worry? I would never hurt you."

She looked away, fighting for the strength to endure this deadly game until they reached the prison house. Daniel did not speak. The dog was asleep, and he held it cautiously, apparently fearful of disturbing its rest. They turned and walked slowly back through the park, not talking, like a lord and lady out for a stroll. Once they passed a group of novices, who nodded and smiled at them.

At the entrance to the house, under the eyes of the jailer friar, Daniel bowed deeply to her. Suddenly he said in a thick voice, "You're mine."

"The comb."

"Even if there is no comb, you're still mine." Their eyes interlaced. He bent close to her face. "My dear lady, God sent you—I have prayed, you can't know. God gave you to me."

When she backed away hastily, she saw his eyes were burning with the fever of possession, as if he longed to suck her, cell by cell, into his own being. She turned and went toward the jailer.

Sybille was escorted to the Inquisition chamber each morning to sit on the cushioned stool and confess her sins to God's representative. The previous week she had been given a comb and a handful of wood ashes, even though her water ration remained the same and she dared not squander it on cleanliness. It was enough that she had the means again to feel human, and she rose at dawn to torment the knots from her hair and twist it into braids. The sight of the two neat plaits falling in dignity over the bodice of her grimy gown seemed to give her strength to parry Daniel's questions, to keep him from undermining her walls as if she were a fortress under siege, and to hold out until help came from the count.

Friar Daniel had grown obsessed with Sybille, to the extent that his first thoughts upon waking were of her face—he had foolishly confessed this to her one day. After saying the morning office and breaking his fast, he would hurry straight to his chamber, where Sybille waited on the stool. They sat some six feet apart. Very gently, with Arnaud dozing on his lap, Daniel probed deeper and deeper into Sybille's recollections of the forty years she had lived. No bit of trivia was rejected as banal, or irrelevant, or even too shockingly carnal. He pushed her backward in time, halted for a while, then urged her forward a week, a month, a year. Innocent questions about the vanished world of her youth. Innocent answers: She reeled off entertaining vignettes, long-forgotten conversations, weather reports, descriptions of gowns, costs of tournaments, intimate details of domestic brawls, and stale extramarital liaisons better never exhumed, but she saw Daniel could not conceal his delight. Encyclopedias of deflowerings and rapes, aristocratic impotence and late menarches and unwanted pregnancies whose fruits were passed off as legitimate little louts to betrayed husbands. Daniel laughed, fingered the relic bag with its fingernail parings of the Blessed Dominic. She rambled on, keeping carefully to the path of innocence, praying she would not slip and make some disastrous admission, until Friar Luke moaned and complained of his aching wrist.

Suddenly Daniel would make a barely perceptible movement of his hands. "Now let me ask you a question, Na Sybille. Once more, describe Pons the last time you two met."

"I don't remember."

"Blue robes or black?"

She frowned. "He was not yet ordained, I've told you. He probably wore a shirt and breeches. And a cloak because it was winter."

He looked faintly annoyed. "I know you've seen him in recent years. I know it! He was in the diocese of Fanjeaux before the treaty of Meaux and then again the year afterward. He—"

"I didn't see him."

He riffled nervous fingers through his hair and regained his control. Each stared into the other's eyes, determined. Daniel was silent. Then he let out a long sigh and spoke. "As I've told you many times, violence is abhorrent to my nature. There have been a few occasions when I've been forced to use persuasion for the salvation of a person's soul, but it always sickened me and gave me dreadful nightmares." Sybille nodded sympathetically. "I don't enjoy using force. I'm a humane person but—but I must get God what He wants."

She said quickly, "I understand perfectly."

"It doesn't seem so." There was sullenness in his voice, as if he thought she were deliberately wronging him.

Bending forward a little, she said, "My dear friar, do you think I enjoy dining on the shit you throw to me like a dog? Do you imagine I laugh and frolic alone at night in my cell, delighted to be parted from my child?" Eyes flashing bitterness, she paused. "My husband walked away from me—he left me with no protection, no money. No servants. I lived alone in that house and anybody could have forced my gate and murdered me!"

Tears gushed into her eyes. Daniel turned away.

"Do you really believe I would refuse you your—paltry bits of information if I knew them? That I wouldn't exchange them for my freedom so fast you'd drop off your chair? DO YOU THINK I'M CRAZY?" She broke off, blowing her nose on her sleeve.

His only reply was a sigh. He sagged his head low to smooth his mouth against the top of Arnaud's head. Sybille saw that his shoulders drooped. He looks exhausted, she thought. He must be longing for a nap or a cup of wine. Or for another suspect who, terror-stricken, will betray his friends and kin in an hour. She went on wiping her nose and thinking those thoughts when Daniel lifted his head and said quietly, "You have no idea how weary I am."

She gave an involuntary hiss of surprise.

"Na Sybille, nobody knows. It is killing to do this work of the Lord's. To sit here day after day and listen to the wicked mock the Almighty. Nothing surprises me anymore. No lie, no blasphemy. I've heard it all."

Sybille sat dumbfounded. He was actually pleading for her sympathy. Worse, she was horrified to realize she did pity him, yearned in some side chamber of her heart to alleviate his misery. It was not pathetic bluffing, for his face was grooved with fatigue and profound discouragement.

He looked down at Arnaud. "You should sit here, in my place. Then you would understand. I want to tell you something. There are whole days when I don't hear a word. Sometimes when I'm especially tired, I dream of laying down this burden, of spending my days in some peaceful cloister. I've seen enough of life. God and the Blessed Dominic know I deserve rest." His gaze stayed on the animal, whose white fur blurred into the white wool of the monastic robe.

They sat there without speaking for a long time. There was a kind of agreement in that silence, almost a fusion of minds, as if they both knew they had reached a stalemate incapable of resolution.

Daniel stroked his fingers over Arnaud's nose, then looked up at Sybille expectantly.

"I cannot—" She did not need to complete the sentence.

He lifted the dog into his arms and stood, then looked into her face with an expression of either pity or sorrow. "This tribunal," he said, "is having you transferred to very strict confinement in the tower. There you may do penance for your sins and learn whatever lessons God chooses to teach you." He took a step toward the door. "We shall not meet again." Leaving her there with Friar Luke, Daniel went out with Arnaud and closed the door.

Chapter Fourteen

Toulouse, red rose of the south, huddled frozen in the December wind. Saint-Sernin, Saint-Romain, Saint-Etienne, La Dalbade, and Notre Dame de la Daurade creaked out their cold Christmas psalms and rumbled fanfares of bells endlessly. Deer, beaver, bears, herons, and peacocks hung in the stalls, above the butchers in their bloody tunics. Inside the taverns along Rue Droit, men in fur cloaks raised henaps of hot spiced wine while they whispered rebellion, and the jongleurs wailed the adulterous lyrics of William the Troubadour. And behind the dark ramparts of the Château Narbonnais, the men of France caroused on the wines of the Midi through the night.

In the pitch dark Sybille arranged her cloak on the cold earth and sat upright with her hands folded tensely in her lap. It was not until three or four hours had passed that she began to understand. They were going to keep her in there. Then she put her hands to her temples and unleashed scream after furious scream.

There was no answer. She sat awake until she could no longer bear her thoughts, slumped over, and blurred into sleep, woke confused a few hours later with strange pains in all her joints. She could not tell if it was morning. It was still dark in the cell except for the shaft of pearly gray light that penetrated the loophole.

She sat up shivering, pushed her hands against the stones, then got to her feet and tested her legs. The cell was an oblong cage some six steps in length and maybe two steps across, dark and airless and made from a slit in the wall of the tower. In a coffin like this, she thought, I have barely room to stretch full length. Cold gray walls two arms thick, an iron ring riveted into the wall, a shredded pile of straw in one corner. In the bare earth: a hole thick with excrement. There was no bucket.

She lay down again and buried her head in the cloak, wishing she had never woken. A moment later, something soft padded against her leg and she sprang up, howling as if the executioner had grabbed her. Chest tight with fear, she slumped against the wall—when hadn't there been rats in prison?—and willed her heart not to burst her ribs. She peered down. Where had he gone? Where had he come from? The loophole? The sewage hole? He could come and go as he pleased. She could not. She heard him shuffling and squeaking in the straw, but it was impossible to see.

Terror hung in the darkness. She drew a long, trembling breath. "Dogs," she cried aloud.

I would never hurt you, Na Sybille.

"Coward." It was the worst insult she knew. "COWARD! FLESH-EATING COWARD!"

But, lady, we are alike, the two of us. Didn't I tell you that?

"I'll get out of here and I'll kill you. God help you, because I'll break your skull and grind your brains under my heel."

Lady, have you forgotten? We shall not meet again.

We shall, she thought. Just then the bolt began to grate back. There was a rapid crunching movement, a cascade of yellow light, and a hand deftly poked a jug and a hunk of bread through the crack, then the glow was gone. Sybille shouted hoarsely, "Wait! Wait! I want to talk to you!" She had not even caught a glimpse of the man.

The food sat waiting. Clutching the jug, she gulped down the water in one long draft. She was sure to be thirsty later, but she did not care. She wanted it now. She sat down and held the bread over her lap, afraid of losing a crumb. She pinched off a granule, chewed it carefully, licked her tongue around her lips. When a sliver only the size of her thumbnail was left, she thought better of her haste and tucked it into her cloak for later.

The hours drummed on, how many she could not measure. It seemed just as dark as when she had woken. Both knees drawn up to her waist, she rolled on her side and sobbed violently until exhaustion flushed through her limbs and she felt drunk.

The second day was worse. She could no longer escape so easily into sleep. Crying and thinking were all she could do. The cold was bone-numbing, the silence cut only by the scrabbling of the rat and the sound Sybille made as she frantically smashed the bodies of fat lice between her nails. That morning there had been bread but no water. She had yelled and cursed but the jailer did not come back. All that day she was nauseated. The next morning she was ready, and when she heard the bolt being strained back, she stuck her foot in the widening crack.

"Give me water!" The inside of her mouth was shriveled so dry she could barely work her tongue. It was dark in the passageway. He was in shadow behind the torch, and she could hear only his voice baying at her.

"You didn't put your empty jug by the door."

"Jug?"

"No empty jug, no water."

"Nobody told me." She tried to peer into the darkness, but he threw in the bread and pulled the door shut. "Fuck yourself, pig," she said.

She dropped on the cloak, flailing her fists weakly. After a while she got up and went to squat over the hole. I can't bear this, she thought, then crawled back on the cloak, smelling her own stink. She felt drained from the small movements it had taken to urinate. Suddenly she heard the door being unbolted again, and she pitched her body forward and flung out clawing hands. "Wait!" she said.

He silently thrust a jug at her and started to draw back.

"Don't go!" she cried. "Please—when are they going to let me out?"

He did not answer.

"Speak to me. Please." No answer, but she could hear him breathing. "Speak. Come on, I know you can speak—I heard you." She didn't care if she could see him. All she wanted was to hear the sound of his voice. "Please."

She could hear him hesitating. Finally, he muttered, "Lady, I'm not allowed to talk to you." But his tone was polite, almost respectful, and she felt tears trickling out of her eyes.

The door crashed shut, the light was gone, and then she heard nothing. She sat in the dark, taking one sip, then another, as if each was the last she would ever taste.

"Pons, my friend," she said aloud, "I'm doing this for your sake."

She finished the last of the water, tasting it still in her mouth. But, she wondered, what did you ever do for me? Love me? Give me children? A home like other women? No, you left me for a doltish god who teaches that touching my skin is wicked. You hypothesized divine sparks held captive in casings of flesh and blood. This god of yours, he frowns upon everything I hold precious. This is not his world. And it is for him—and you—that I sit here. With what do I feed myself now? He feeds on these sparks of his own divinity; you feed on infinite fields of righteousness; I feed on pain and degradation.

Once, in what she guessed was the afternoon, she decided men were to blame for all the sorrows of her life. Pons had not cherished her. So she fell in love with a cripple like Olivier de Ferrand. Who also had not loved her, who had betrayed her by delivering her into the hands of Daniel. Who hungered for burned flesh. The three of them together had buried her here.

Her hands and feet were numb with cold. She tucked her feet under the hem of her gown and wished she had her heavy cloak, the one with the fur hood in the chest at Cantal. I should have brought it to Toulouse, even though it was summer. But she had not brought it, just as she had not judged Daniel correctly. Indeed, she had wildly misread the man, and it was foolish now to blame herself for what she had not done or not seen.

Suddenly, in spite of all her admonitions and determinedly sensible advice, she felt herself giving way to despair and nausea again. She gazed blindly at the four walls of the cell and saw nothing, not even death, which she might have welcomed, because death at least would be something. Here there was nothing.

Excuse me, Na Sybille. That is a lie. You have something. Well, don't you?

Nothing.

Let me ask you a question. Haven't I provided you with rats and vermin? Also the Lord's creatures, I must remind you.

Silence.

Not only that. You have human company.

Where?

You have yourself.

Myself! My gown's soiled, my limbs are rotting, my flesh stinks—

Come, come. Isn't all that beside the point? It is your soul that stinks.

You have the manners of a villein.

Possibly. But we are talking about your self, that is to say, your immortal soul.

You know nothing of me or my soul.

There! You've misjudged me again!

I do not believe—

Precisely. You do not believe. You do not believe in God's love. Pause. *Do you, Na Sybille?*

I don't know.

Do you believe in the teachings of the Holy Catholic Church?

I don't know.

How can you not know and still claim your soul is without sin?

God cannot be trusted.

Not trusted! Indeed.

A god worthy of praise would not let these things happen.

You are aware, dear lady, that that is a heretic belief.

Yes, but I am not a heretic.

What then?

I can't tell you.

Try.

God is—asleep.

Asleep.

Yes. Sometimes I think He does not even exist.

Sometimes. You are not certain.

No. I only know He must be irresponsible.

And so your soul will face Him with, shall we say, reproach.

No.

What then?

Rage.

I believe you have proved my point. Have you anything more to add?

Nothing.

She had no sense of time. Perhaps a week passed. Or only a few days. Obviously the days dawned and ended, but this particular phenomenon no longer interested her. At the outset she should have devised some system to mark the passage of time, scratches on the wall maybe, but what good would that do? It was too dark to see them. So she did not think about it. Instead, she thought of Nova and Olivier. Had they returned to Fanjeaux? It would be much too dangerous to remain in Rue St. Bernard, and soon they would be running out of money. Pray God they had left the city. Nova had the same information about Pons as Sybille. Eventually Daniel might realize it and send for the girl. If Olivier was wise, he would foresee this and flee. But then Olivier was not wise.

"His stupidity exiled me here," she whispered out loud. He pledged his precious word of honor to a peasant who knows nothing of honor, and now I suffer and he is free. Well, that is over. I must forget I loved him. She tried to think of other things.

With the creatures of the dark, she crouched under her cloak, day after day. Sometimes she was aware of herself under there, clawing at the remorseless lice, congealed in the foulness of her sweat and excrement and secretions and menstrual blood, and she said to herself: You are repulsive. You are not human. Being human means you do not sit in a cage wallowing in your own dung and piss, with matted hair and fingernails like talons. Being human means you own your own body and you, my dear, do not. You are like an infant, with no lady mother to care for you; no one cares. And twisted sideways there, noticing herself, she felt mortally sick and thought, What am I now? I have disappeared from this lost world and the world goes on, and my loss will matter only to Nova and someday not even to her. Nova will think of me as extinct. She saw herself, proud Sybille d'Astarac, on the day they would take her out of there, a skeleton cast in rotting flesh, and she did not like to think of anyone she knew seeing her.

He would see her, of course. To him, she would always be ravishing. You are doing this to me, she thought. My body, in all its exquisite hideousness, will excite you surely. Ah, Arnaud! He would never cage you in here with your filth. You, my adorable one, sleep next to him in his bed. You are a dog, I am only a woman. She opened her eyes, seeing a fluted shadow along the loophole, smelling her rancid hair, and she was suddenly afraid of becoming mad, like her mother. She was thinking, Perhaps I am mad already and don't know it. Exactly when does a person know she is mad? My lady mother did not. Giddy, she settled her head on the earth and shut her eyes again, not thinking of ageless Douce or Nova or of anyone except herself.

When the door opened, she was half-asleep. She paid no attention. Then the jailer's torch swept briefly over her legs, and she flinched from the jagged glare. Light was not something she desired.

She did not want to see, feel, think, smell, talk, hear. The desire to taste is also gone, she thought. Not entirely. But almost.

"Lady." He was standing in the doorway.

There was nothing she wanted to say to him.

"You did not eat your bread ration."

What of it?

"Are you ill?"

"Go away," she said to him. "I'm already half-dead."

At this, he turned on his heel and was gone.

A morning came finally when her head was clear and she found herself reaching eagerly for the bread. So she knew it was not over yet.

"If you're hoping to walk out of here, lady," she said with a laugh, "you must have the brains of a flea."

She felt very hungry and thirsty. While she was chewing the bread, the rat advanced boldly up to her left knee and crouched there. She could see his eyes glittering. It looked as though he were begging to share her dinner, and she calmly shook her head at him. "There is not enough for both of us," she said. "Go find another trestle, my friend." With an almost sullen jerk, he skittered away into the straw.

She finished the bread and slowly sipped the water and waited to see if the nausea would return and her stomach begin to cramp again. There were a few mild spasms, but she was used to them by now. Getting up and stretching her body, she put her weight on both feet and then stepped unsteadily to the loophole. For nearly an hour she urged herself back and forth, unknotting her muscles until she felt very tired and knew she should stop.

Sitting, she rolled herself in her cloak and listened for the rat. He was asleep or hiding. Or perhaps he is calling on a more philanthropic prisoner, she thought. I wish you luck, friend. By the color outside the loophole she knew it had been daylight only a short time and there were plenty of hours remaining until she would feel sleepy again. Realizing this, she felt panic gushing furiously in her chest. Calm yourself, lady, she warned. But the fear took its time departing. Then she sat there waiting for the rustling of the rat. Silence. Soon she was thinking of Nova, and of a song she had written for her daughter on her fifth natal day. She sang it through to herself once, then twice. A moment passed and then she began humming silently again, this time an uneven little tune. She paused again, pricked her ears. What is that? she wondered. Certainly nothing I've heard before. Well now, lady. Is something happening here? She tried it again, thinking the tune was too mournful. She fumbled for words but caught nothing. You call yourself a *trobairitz,* she thought bitterly. Even in this place you have trouble putting one well-rhymed word next to another, find pain in the act of composition. Life, she spat, is too painful to live.

But creation begins when you least expect it, and she found herself repeating the phrase aloud: "Life is too painful to live." She approached it, tried to retreat to a theme that held more cheer, more love, for sweet Jesus' sake, more hope. She was afraid to continue. Waiting, she picked three lice from her hair. Then she continued.

An hour later she had the first stanza of a *sirventes,* seven raw lines, but she knew for the first time she had a chance of surviving. Maybe. Something in her snapped, and she flung herself face downward on the ground and sobbed and sobbed with more happiness than she could remember feeling in years. For a long time she went on sniffling, mouth mewling against the cloak like a little girl, legs drawn up under her skirt. In that position she tried the *sirventes* again and changed *companhier* to *bon amics,* then *bon amics* to *bels dous amics.*

She listened frowning as she sang it twice more in her head. Not dazzling, she decided. In fact, rather dreadful, but it would suffice for now. Go on to the next stanza, she told herself. You can always come back, and hours later she did.

She went on composing verse in her mind like a soldier scales a wall, afraid to push forward but more afraid to fall back to the ground. When she stopped she felt terror. She went back to work. As the days slipped by, the body whose disintegration she had observed with such loathing grew less real, less demanding, and for long hours she was able to escape it altogether. It became like an outworn hair shirt she could put on and off at will. She existed now in some province of her mind only occasionally visited before, when she had been entirely absorbed in her writing. She lived in her verse and to the rest she was indifferent.

One day, as she was doing the fine tuning on a *tenso* between a woman like herself and a knight like Olivier, she heard voices outside her door, but they barely impinged on her mind. Then, without warning, the door crashed open, and she threw up both hands to shield her eyes from the torchlight.

"Sybille d'Astarac?" a man said.

Yes, she thought, but I need a word to rhyme with "knight." The voice came at her again, closer, insistent. "Sybille d'Astarac?" It was not the jailer. This was a voice she had never heard. He was saying that Sybille d'Astarac had been summoned by the Holy Tribunal for further questioning and must state if she was in fact the prisoner just named. She opened her mouth and said in a voice she could barely hear, "I am Sybille—" but got no further. She went on sitting there until hands gripped her shoulders and she felt herself being dragged out the door, into the dark tunnel of the passage. When she strained to lift her head, nothing happened and so she lay with her head down and did not try again. The hands went around her body, lifting her from the ground, and her head fell back slightly. A man was carrying her, bellowing she must keep her eyes closed, but she had no interest in anything except the smell of his tunic and beard, so sharp and clean it stung the inside of her nose. "Don't open them until I get you a blindfold!" he warned.

If they had left me another day, she thought, I could have finished the *tenso*. Perhaps I still can do it. The man was still talking about her eyes, how she would ruin them unless she kept them shut. If my eyes are ruined, she thought angrily, it will not be something I do to myself. It will be their fault. She started to speak but it was too difficult, and she let herself be spun along in the stranger's arms. Finally he laid her on the ground, and she stayed there, gasping, listening to the jailers laughing and talking very loudly.

"ASK HER IF SHE HAS ANYTHING TO SAY!" "HOLY JESUS! THIS ONE STINKS LIKE THE DEVIL'S OWN TURDS!" "THE HAIR HAS TO GO!" "GET HER TO TALK FIRST!" She listened to them talking about her, as if she were a dog who could not comprehend human language.

After a while she heard the voice of the man who had come for her. "Sybille d'Astarac, can you hear me?"

Stop yelling, she thought. With effort, she gave a small twitch of the head.

He said, "Do you have a statement to make?"

Statement, she laughed to herself. This fool can't be serious.

Several minutes passed, during which he repeated the question twice again.

At last her lips widened into a kind of a smile. She whispered, "Yes."

He waited.

"This place . . . could use"—she forced open her eyelids—"a new cook." Her eyes exploded in showers of yellow sparks as she plunged unconscious.

"Let me ask you a question." Daniel, holding Arnaud on his lap, looked exactly as he had the last time. The only differences Sybille noticed were that his hair was shorter and the relic bag was greased with finger marks.

For mid-January, the day was balmy, gray-skied. They had led her slowly down the slope and across the garden to the Inquisitor's chambers. The wind gusted among the sodden leaves and pulled at the skirt of the new linen gown hanging from her shoulders like a shroud for a giant. The short walk had taken all her strength and left her breathing hard.

She was not listening to Daniel's question. "I do not know," she croaked.

"So your earlier statements about having no contact with Pons de Villeneuve were incorrect."

"I do not know."

Daniel swiveled his head, threw an intense look at Friar Luke. He turned back to Sybille, fingers working furiously at the relic bag. "What you mean is you're willing to sacrifice your life for his."

She sat there awhile, dazed by the clean, bright room. "I do not know." She did know. She had no intention of becoming a martyr for the heretic cause. Far from it: She had resolved to say anything, even the truth, to prevent it. But in these first hours with Daniel, she was using all her energy to keep herself from toppling off the stool.

Daniel cleared his throat and scrutinized her over Arnaud's ears. "Na Sybille, this is terrible. Can't you give me your attention?" He lowered the dog to the tiles.

She bowed her head, suddenly on the edge of tears.

"You last had contact with him—when?"

She shrugged. "Before this pestilence of yours began."

"Impudent remarks like that," he murmured coldly, "do you no good. And I think the sooner you realize it the better." He shuffled his papers. "I'll be frank, lady. You have shamelessly defiled God and His Church. Your crimes—the lies with which you have polluted this holy place over the past seven weeks—are too disgusting to contemplate. In my experience as an inquisitor, there is sufficient cause to bind you by the chains of excommunication as a knowing defender of heretics." Daniel then turned to the clerk behind the writing desk and requested his accounts ledger.

Ignoring Sybille, he spread the book on the table and began to read entries aloud. "For large wood, fifty-five sous six deniers. For vine branches and straw, twenty-three sous and nine deniers. For four stakes, ten sous nine deniers." Sybille swallowed and looked away.

Daniel went on, his eyes smoldering with the mixed incense of ecstasy and sadism. "For ropes to tie the prisoners, four sous seven deniers. For the executioner, eighty sous." He looked up and snapped at Friar Luke, "Eighty! That's too much."

Friar Luke shrugged. "For four persons—"

"In all, I make that eight livres fourteen sous seven deniers. A little more than two livres apiece." An annoyed frown pulled his mouth to one side.

Friar Luke agreed the cost of burning a few heretics at a time was high.

"And inefficient," Daniel moaned. "It's a pity we can't dispose of large numbers at once." He turned back to the ledger, scratching his nose thoughtfully.

"We might save them up," Friar Luke offered, "and do a big batch. Like De Montfort at Lavaur. Four hundred, wasn't it?"

Daniel said that was not what he had in mind. "I was thinking of something enormous. Like a thousand."

"Oh, that's impossible," said the other friar.

Daniel closed the ledger, fingered its black-leather binding, and stared at Sybille. After a minute he said in a calm, almost weary voice, "The time is flying. We must continue."

The stratagems she had devised the past three days had slipped away after she had been ushered into the room. Her mind was choked with fatigue. And there was something else: Among the jailers she had been able to retain her sense of invisibility, even to pretend that the locks shorn above her ears were unreal. But when Daniel had entered with the dog at his heels, suddenly she had felt exposed and saw herself with his eyes, plucked, emaciated, ugly. She raised a tear-stained face to him. "I am not used to being despised," she whispered, as if that summed up everything that had happened to her since she had come to Garrigues' Garden.

Daniel said very rapidly, "Yes, I know. Then have pity on God. For He, too, is not used to being despised."

She looked at the logs in the hearth. They were pouring heat into the little room, and the unaccustomed warmth was making sweat run down her back. She groped for the places where the braids once had been. She was still not used to their absence. Behind the table Arnaud opened his mouth and yawned slowly. She said weakly, "He came to Cantal eight years ago, uninvited." Friar Luke's pen began to scratch furiously.

"Why?"

"Soldiers were after him." She could see the triumph rising in Daniel's eyes.

"You fed him. Gave him a bed."

"I had no choice. He was injured. His ankle, I think."

"Giving shelter to a heretic—"

"Was not against the law then." She threw him a challenging look. He nodded reluctantly. "Once he was healed, he left. That is all."

"Lady, lady, that is just the start." He glanced at Friar Luke before giving her a reproachful smile. "How long did he stay?"

"I don't remember."

"A week, two weeks?"

"I cannot recall."

Daniel leaped to his feet, so that poor Arnaud let out a surprised yelp. He set him on the tiles, and the dog waddled to the hearth and flopped on his belly. "You must have had many conversations with him."

"No," she grunted, thinking that was the truth. Whatever Pons had said had no meaning for her and so she had not listened.

"It's inconceivable he would not have talked with you. Admit it!" His voice rattled with excitement. "I beg you, what did he say about the previous ten years? Where is his refuge? What city? What forest? What cave? Don't lie to me." He stared at her mouth, waiting for the answers to drop out, temples sweating. He was almost panting.

She studied his face. Was there loss of control there? What could she do with that? "How you do wear yourself out—trying to get answers that don't exist." She smiled.

"Oh, they exist all right."

"Not in me." She laughed quietly. "He never mentioned his secret hiding place. And do you know why, Friar Daniel? It's very simple. He did not trust me."

By the hearth, alongside Arnaud, Daniel collapsed abruptly on his knees, bent his head to pray with knuckles clenched white over the relic bag. A log fell with a hissing thud. Friar Luke came down off his stool and went out. Alone with Daniel, Sybille stood up and went to the side window. She could see his lips moving, heard him once whisper tautly, "Mercy, Father-God. Mercy on this sinful woman," but she gave a loud sniff of contempt and did not care if he heard. A friar ran by the window. It was drizzling and he had his hood up.

Before she noticed, Daniel was on his feet, pacing and speaking to her in a low voice. After her death, he said, she would join the damned and suffer in flames throughout eternity while worms gnawed at her skull. The Blessed Dominic himself had just transmitted this prophecy to Daniel as he had knelt there praying. Daniel waited for this to soak in. Despite herself, Sybille's knees began to tremble and she looked away. The fervency in his voice, his absolute conviction that God had spoken to him through Dominic de Guzmán, welled through the room, terrified her and made her falter. Blindly she swayed to the stool and seated herself. She stared at Daniel, who was sitting behind the table again. He said, "Give me the truth. God ordains it."

For a moment she did not move, then turned her face to the ground. Which god is he talking about? she wondered. Pons's god? Dominic's barbarous god? The pope's? Perhaps Douce's god, whom she had known and loved as a small girl. Was there no upper limit to the number of gods, good and evil, waiting to suck up one's substance? At last she looked into Daniel's waiting eyes, blue as a Lammas Day sky. "I have nothing to say," she repeated for the fiftieth time that morning.

A long silence followed during which Friar Luke carried in a tray with three bowls of pea soup and a loaf of warm bread, and passed them around. They began to eat. Arnaud came over beside her and propped himself on his haunches, ransacking her bowl with his eyes, making smacking sounds with his tongue. They ate in silence, occasionally broken by the sloshing of the hot soup. Abruptly Daniel bent toward her. "Let me ask you a question, Na Sybille." He picked up a chunk of bread and turned it over in his hand.

She looked up. There was a knifelike edge to his voice that made her heart pulse faster and warned her to be careful. He was crumbling little bits of bread into his bowl.

"What would you do if I told you that in two hours you must burn?" he asked and searched her face.

She swallowed the soup in her mouth, licked her lips, took her time while she considered her reply very carefully. "I think," she began and then stopped, her heart kicking savagely. She waited ten seconds, then she plunged off the precipice, risking everything. "I think what I would do is finish this soup." She went on eating.

The bread between Daniel's fingers splashed into his bowl, spattering the front of his robe with a trail of faint green dots. Behind him, Friar Luke tittered. Daniel said, "The soup needs more salt, Brother Luke."

"I—I think you're right, Brother," Friar Luke stammered. "I'll speak to Cook."

Then, to Sybille's surprise, Daniel fell silent. He carried his half-full bowl to the hearth and whistled for Arnaud. While the dog ate, he knelt there all hunched up. There was something about the childish droop of the shoulders that moved her deeply because it made her think of Nova—not Nova in any pose she could recall seeing her, but how she must look now, aching for her lost mother. She kept her eyes on Daniel. Finally, very slowly, he straightened and faced her.

She waited for his fury but instead she heard a timid moan. He cried, "I know you're holding back. Don't ask me how, but I know." There was no anger in his face, only the watery anguish of Tantalus, moaning open-mouthed beneath the fruited tree. "You take pleasure in taunting me. And you mock God, whose will it is that your husband be apprehended."

"And burned," she added grimly. It came to her that some peculiar shift had taken place, as if they were two knights locked in single combat. But now, in some unexpected way, she had wrested—or been given—the advantage. Intoxication roared through her body, and she squeezed herself up tall on the stool. Forgotten was the shame of her hair, forgotten was Pons and his spark-greedy god, so intent was she on destroying the blond man who stood before her. She gazed into his eyes with a very small smile that reduced thirteen centuries of theological hairsplitting to a dialectical conflict between male and female. "You," she murmured, "are a little snot-nosed peasant." She heard him gasp. "When you open your mouth, it is not the voice of God I hear. It is you—the armorer's son, a mongrel so inferior, so insignificant, I would not waste my spittle on him."

"The living God will—"

Her look silenced him. "You dare to speak to me of God! It is the Devil—no, some force worse than the Devil—to whom you deliver up your offerings of human flesh and tears. It is you, you and your bestial Dominic, who are the fiends Christ revealed to St. John. It is you behind the fourth seal."

"Na Sybille!"

"It is you who sit the pale horse! You whose name is death! You who slay with sword and hunger and fire!"

He took a step backward toward the hearth, so the flames almost caught the skirt of his robe.

"When the stars of heaven fall to earth," she cried, "I will believe you have the right to judge me."

Without looking at her, he left the chamber. A second later Friar Luke swept after him. An icy draft from the passageway rustled the flames and made Arnaud sit up, sniffing.

She got to her feet and crossed to the hearth. The dog sniffed politely at the hem of her gown. She got down and gathered him into her lap and began to stroke his fur.

She was returned to the house where she first had been imprisoned, though to a different room. There was no further word from Daniel for six days. Then, late one afternoon, an innocent-faced friar who looked little older than Nova came to fetch her.

Beneath the lifeless trees, the earth was already frosting itself for the night. Sybille could see the beginning of a moon. "Do you know why I'm being summoned?" she asked the friar.

"I believe the charges are to be read."

"Charges?"

"Articles of accusation, lady. You're to sign them."

So she was expected to vomit up her guilt. She glanced over at him. "And if a person refuses?"

He was looking straight ahead. "They are handed over to the secular court for punishment."

Her eyes chiseled into the side of his face. She forced out a laugh and said, "And what counsel would you have for me, Reverend Friar?"

"I think," he said without turning, "you should sign."

She was quaking with the cold. They walked on in the gathering dusk.

* * *

She waited quietly on the stool. Hello there, my friend, she thought. This is the end of your song. Life is something you sing, a well-rhymed *canso* composed by some clever troubadour. Isn't it? But where is your singing now? To sing, one must be alive in this physical body. Any poor fool knows that.

You had a choice.

There was no choice.

You have always been a person of limited imagination. Haven't you?

At last the door opened and Daniel Marty strode in with his immaculate skirts swirling gracefully as lilies in the wind. Behind him marched the clerk and a friar she had never seen before. He had a wide, puffy face and a flabby skin that gave off a brownish-gray luster. He looked like a moldy squirrel. She rose, stole a glance at Daniel's face, but he avoided her eyes. Friar Luke hopped onto his stool and opened the ledger. The two Inquisitors seated themselves behind the table, motioned her down, and still the unknown friar did not identify himself. For a moment there was silence in the chamber, then Daniel murmured deferentially, "Brother William, shall we proceed?"

It is William Arnaud, Sybille thought. She knew of him. He was the maniac who had conducted the auto-da-fé at Moissac where more than two hundred had been burned. So Daniel had brought along a butcher for support. William Arnaud, his head bowed, said to her, "I trust you are Sybille d'Astarac."

"Yes."

He raised his eyes, studied her ten seconds, not more, and then jerked his head at Friar Luke. There is no blood in this one, Sybille thought. "Proceed," he said.

Luke leafed through some papers, cleared his throat, began. Sybille stared at the fire while he read the deposition:

"In the name of our Lord Jesus Christ, amen. In the year of our Lord, the eighteenth of January, 1235.

"We, Brother William Arnaud and Brother Daniel Marty of the Order of Friars Preachers, appointed as Inquisitors of heretical depravity in the city and diocese of Toulouse by apostolic authority, find that:

"Article one: Sybille d'Astarac [hereafter known as the accused] has been acquainted with Pons de Villeneuve, Fabrisse d'Astarac (Fauré), Beatriz de Cantal, Douce d'Astarac, Raymond and Corba de

Perella, and other heretics too numerous to list; has known these individuals to be heretics; and has been seen with them on divers occasions in the presence of witnesses.

"Article two: Accused did have familiar intercourse with heretics from the day of her birth, having had the misfortune to be born into a line polluted with the heretical poison.

"Article three: Accused did knowingly receive into her house countless persons condemned for depraved and heretical beliefs, as well as ordained ministers, deacons, and bishops of the heretical sect, and on divers occasions did praise their saintliness, their exemplary lives, and their faith and beliefs.

"Article four: Accused did hear said ordained heretics preach on divers occasions and believed them to be good men and women.

"Article five: Accused did shelter said ordained heretics.

"Article six: Accused did eat bread that had been blessed by them, saying 'God who blessed the five loaves and two fishes' and so forth.

"Article seven: Accused did frequently greet them and show reverence after the heretical fashion, that is, bending the knees, inclining and rising thrice, and saying each time, 'Benedicite.'

"Article eight: Accused was present at the heretication of William de Ferrand, accused's own son, done on the ninth of August, 1227, by Raymond Gros, then a preacher of heretical depravity.

"Article nine: Accused, despite her oath sworn upon the Holy Gospels that she would persecute all heretics, reveal their evil deeds, arrest them or cause them to be arrested, nevertheless persisted in giving them aid and comfort, as a dog gorged with rotten meat will return to its vomit.

"Article ten: Accused did assert, after swearing to maintain and preserve the Catholic Faith, that our Holy Father the Pope and the prelates of the Holy Church and the representatives of God resident in Toulouse for investigating heresy were miscreants; and she did speak out against our Catholic faith and all those who keep it; and she did rashly transgress against God and the Holy Church in the ways aforesaid.

"Article eleven: Accused has knowingly suppressed the truth about herself and others of the heretical sect."

Then the clerk lowered the paper and glanced at Friar William. There was silence. The eyes of both Inquisitors were on Sybille's face.

"Have you anything to say?" Friar William Arnaud asked.

"I am," she lied quietly, "a true and good Catholic."

He and Daniel put their heads together. Then, without turning, Friar William called to the clerk: "Article twelve: The accused has not appreciated our kindly and loving enlightenment. All the enumerated accusations the accused has admitted to be true." Then he commanded her to rise, to step forward and sign the deposition if she was able to write her name or, if not, to make her mark.

She did so. She was ordered to wait in the reception hall.

The young friar who had come for her was lounging next to the door. When she looked around, she was surprised to see the benches empty. She stood in the center of the room in an attitude halfway between flight and paralysis. The friar inclined his head toward one of the benches.

She shook her head. "I prefer to stand." Her legs were trembling so violently she knew she could not control them if she sat.

The friar coughed. "They are recobbling Rue Olm Sec." He meant the stretch along the Minorite Friars' houses.

"I didn't know that."

"It looks much better."

"The street has never been impressive." He knows they are going to burn me, she thought. "For architectural beauty, I've always preferred Rue du Taur."

He smiled prettily. "Of course, of course. I wouldn't disagree, lady."

There was a long silence. After a time, the young man sat down on the bench nearest the door. Arms folded around her waist, Sybille continued to stand. She continued to shake. Some fifteen minutes later the door to the Inquisitors' chamber opened and Friar Luke's white figure stood there motioning to her. She turned to enter and made her face show nothing. He pointed to a place on the tiles, next to the stool.

They had lit the candelabra, and the tapers sparked clouds of soft lemon light. She faced the Inquisitors to hear their verdict, as countless others had waited for the disposal of their lives these past two years. It was Friar William who read the sentence, burying his face deep in the paper. He must have close sight, Sybille thought.

"You have sinned grievously," he began and went on to describe her as a deceitful, pernicious, blaspheming, dissolute woman. "Nevertheless"—he paused to scratch his ear—"we, guided by divine mercy, recognize that your heart is touched with repentence—"

Not at all.

"—and you wish to return to the unity of the Church."

Astounded, she darted her eyes at Daniel, but he was studying his tidily folded hands.

"We, therefore, the Inquisitors abovementioned, after duly consulting the opinions of many worthy men, lay and religious alike, and having as our sole purpose the fulfillment of God's will, do declare and pronounce Sybille d'Astarac—"

My name is Sybille d'Astarac, yes, I'd almost forgotten. She tried to concentrate.

"—a repentant heretic and we direct you to do penance for your crimes against God and the Church. According to the prescription of canon law—"

They are going to release me.

"—we command you to betake yourself without delay to the decent and humane prison prepared for you in the city of Toulouse—"

No.

"—and we command you to remain there in perpetuity—"

No.

"—and to weep over your evil acts."

No. No. No.

"Furthermore," he went on, "we decree that the houses and the estate of Sybille d'Astarac, together with all their appurtenances, shall be razed to the ground utterly, and we hereby order their destruction; furthermore, we decree that the material stuff of the said houses shall be delivered to the flames, unless it seems profitable to us to employ the said materials for pious ends."

The friar yanked the paper from his face. With a gesture of impatience, he handed it to the clerk, who hastily finished: "Done at Toulouse, in the place called Garrigues' Garden, in the presence of William Arnaud and Daniel Marty of the Order of Preachers, and Luke of Albi, scribe for the Inquisition."

Perpetuity, she thought, a word meaning forever.

Life was over.

The rest was doing something she had always despised. Waiting.

The day began, as always, with the sound of bells. In the tower of the cathedral church of Saint-Etienne, ropes jerked, bells rocked, bronze hammered on bronze. On the buttresses the carven gargoyles quaked.

From the window of the women's prison where they had taken

her, Sybille could look up and see the roof of the apse with its stone angel, hands folded in prayer. The two-story building had once been a hospital for clergy and pilgrims, but more urgent needs had arisen, and now it housed those officially diagnosed as suffering from diseases of the soul. Saint-Etienne was said, by both inmates and jailers, to be a "good" prison, although with its present population of nearly two hundred, it was abominably overcrowded.

Each morning, kettles of soup were brought up and the women reheated them over braziers. Throughout the day they entertained themselves by singing, embroidering, gossiping, and fighting among themselves like small girls, and every night they lay down, elbow touching elbow, on thin straw mattresses. Visitors were occasionally permitted, as well as mail and food parcels, but the latter frequently found their way into the hands of the jailers and stayed there. On Sundays small groups were allowed to walk in the bishop's garden, but Sybille did not take advantage of this privilege until spring.

Most of the women, she quickly discovered, were burghers' wives and daughters awaiting sentencing. Too guilty to be released with a penance, not guilty enough for the fire, they were detained there, some for as long as six months, while the Holy Tribunal caught up on its paper work and decided what to do with them. Sybille felt nothing in common with them. None had had their hair cut off or had been subjected to strict confinement. Another difference: They had hopes of release. She had none. She refused to talk to them and sat rigid by the window all day, crying and staring at the stone angel. Hearing them chatter behind her, Sybille could hardly bear their silliness, their screeching conversations, which sounded bizarre and unreal.

The second week, a woman planted herself next to Sybille at the window. Her hands smelled of almonds. She kept talking loudly about her interrogation, which had taken place in the crypt of the cathedral, and about the cells down there until Sybille wanted to scream and push her into one of those dungeons. Her head, as usual, was pounding.

"Listen," the woman barked. Another woman came up with her sewing and gave Sybille a gap-toothed smile. "Here's something to make you laugh. Did you hear the one about the heretic condemned to the fire?"

Sybille kept her face turned away.

"Well, they caught Hot—his name was Hot—adoring a goodman and they threw both of them in prison. But Hot bribed the jailer and had one leg over the wall when the goodman grabbed his other leg. 'Come back! Come back now!' the goodman shouted.

" 'Why?' asked Hot.

" 'Why? Because they're ready to burn us!' "

Both women pounded each other's shoulders and howled until their eyes filled with tears. Sybille did not move a muscle in her face.

"Sourpuss," the first woman shouted. She poked Sybille in the ribs. Sybille slapped her away and burst into tears.

That night in the darkness, Sybille lay crying on her mattress and could not stifle the sounds of her weeping. The woman sleeping beside her finally propped herself up. "My friend," she said tentatively, "is there something I can do to help you?"

She wanted to answer but she could not.

"I think you should see Friar Nicholas. He's not like the rest of them. He really cares about us."

Sybille burst into bitter laughter.

The woman sighed and lay down. She did not speak again, even though Sybille went on wailing noisily.

Ah, lady, you are wrong about your Friar Nicholas. There is no pity for us in heaven or on earth.

All the rest of that winter, while Sybille grieved and flooded the mattress with her tears and watched her hair slowly lengthening toward her shoulders, the friars cut back on new prosecutions. They closed old cases with penances and sentences, they dug up corpses, and they debated what response, if any, to make to Count Raymond's most recent protest. During Lent they announced another grace period for voluntary confessions, and on Good Friday, the very last day, hundreds of Toulousans were lined up outside the friaries to inform against their neighbors. Not cheerfully. But if you didn't look out for your own skin, who would?

As a result of those confessions, the friars had a whole new batch of leads to follow up. Until then, in terms of numbers at least, the bulk of their investigations had involved merchants and artisans and the petty nobility. Now, however, they were able to focus on the city's best families. Throughout the summer William Arnaud and Daniel Marty prepared careful cases against a dozen prominent Toulousans, and on Michaelmas issued them summonses to appear before the tribunal. Eight of the twelve were consuls. Seriously threatened now, people realized the Preaching Friars were not only prosecuting heretics but were disposing of the aristocracy, who opposed the French. None of the consuls answered the summonses—only an idiot would walk into that trap. With the count's support, they demanded that the cases against them be dropped and that Arnaud and Marty leave the city. But the friars stubbornly refused. On the fifteenth of October, the consuls forcibly expelled them.

From Carcassonne, where Arnaud and Marty had now set up their tribunal in exile, a considerable number of citations came every day by courier. In the women's prison they heard that lay friars and priests were running around the city attempting to serve the summonses. This further enraged the consuls, who declared a boycott of the Order of Preaching Friars, but what this actually meant was unclear. Across the close in the episcopal palace, Bishop Raymond du Fauga took to his bed with a fever.

The next morning a mob of armed men gathered at the main gate of the close. A triple guard was put on the prison door to keep the women from bolting. The bishop's knights, swords drawn, stationed themselves under the trees. From high up in the tower of the cathedral, the bells began to clang terce.

All the women in the prison tried to crowd at the windows. After an hour had passed, they watched the men outside the gate force their way in and pour across the close toward the bishop's palace. Throughout the scuffle the women remained at their posts without saying much. Sybille, who had been shoved back from her usual place, could see nothing of what was taking place. She could hear shouting and swearing. From time to time, news was called back by those at the windows: Several canons were being roughed up; somebody was trying to smash the outdoor pulpit; men were battering the door of the palace. All of this came to nothing because the bishop's guard soon pushed the invaders back into Rue St. Etienne.

The invaders did not go home. They took up positions outside the cathedral steps and at each gate leading into the episcopal complex, and dug in for a siege. If the bishop and his dogs of Dominic wanted to remain inside the cloister, very well, they were welcome to stay. But they would have to go hungry.

The prison kitchen sent up half-rations the next morning. Bewildered, the women could not understand why the besiegers wanted to starve them as well. Don't take away our food, friends. We're the ones you want to save. Throw us bread over the wall. Bread, a few 'cheese pasties, a tun of good red wine. We're on your side, friends. Don't you care about us?

Before too many days had passed, the women realized the besiegers were not worrying about them. And if they did worry, there was nothing they could do about it, no way to send them rations. The bishop of Toulouse, annoyed and inconvenienced, went to Narbonne.

The following week the prisoners were getting about three ounces of stale bread each morning and a cup of water. The noise level inside had subsided considerably. As day after day moved by, some of the women fell ill, two died; mostly they wandered about sluggishly or lay on their mattresses, wilted and frightened. Lethargy gathered soundlessly over the once raucous rooms.

Hour after hour, Sybille gazed out at the shadowy cloister. In her head, she sat at her writing table in Rue St. Bernard, dressed up in a gold-embroidered gown, and she penned a short message to God: "Greetings. Sorry to disturb Your Majesty, but I really would like to bring something important to Your attention. Life in Your Saint-Etienne prison is terrible. Surely You can see we're suffering." She crossed out "suffering," inserted "dying." "If conditions don't improve, I really don't see how I can recommend Your Church to my friends. Fare You well. Sybille d'Astarac."

Not that she knew where to send the letter.

Chapter Fifteen

The knight came just after dawn, running across the frost-glazed grass of the cloister with a mace nuzzled in his fist. Sybille woke to hear wood splintering and the keening of women's voices. Not crying, not screaming, but more like the whimpering of frightened animals. She rose and went out to the common room. The knight stood there shouting, but she could make no sense of his words. When he spoke his teeth flashed white. He wore high leather boots, which had left muddy tracks on the tiles. His shiny black hair fell down over his forehead, and his cheeks were tinted as ruddy as a perfect apple. He looked unreal. The women crowded around him, blinking and stretching out stringy fingers. They touched his clean blue tunic. Under the wool lay solid tissue—muscles, fat, blood. They wanted to make sure he was not an apparition.

"Gone?" Sybille heard someone ask. There was no excitement.

"God's toes—why don't you believe me?" He raised his voice. "Since Friday."

Sybille pushed up close. She smoothed her fingers along his sleeve. "The friars left?" she asked.

"I wouldn't call it leaving." He grinned. "Thrown out is more like it. We chased them over Daurade bridge to St. Cyprien."

"All of them?" she persisted.

All. For a few days, five or six sick friars had been permitted to stay on, but now even they were gone.

"My lord," a voice called out. "Where did they go?"

He said, "How the hell should I know?"

"They'll be back," a woman behind Sybille mumbled.

The women went on gazing at him, then slowly they began to hobble away. They went back to their mattresses or sank down on the tiles in the common room, as if the knight had never come. Sybille edged over to the open doorway and watched a group of knights see-sawing like sailors across the cloister. They moved in and out of focus. She hesitated a moment, then put one foot over the threshold, strad-dling freedom. Half turning, she glanced back inside at the knight, then swiveled to stare at the men advancing toward her. She dragged the other foot over the doorway and stood there. The November morning was cold, bright, the white sky lathered with a few ragged clouds. From its great height, the hulk of the cathedral loomed steeply over the cloister, shutting out the sunlight and breathing reproach. She felt safe and protected in the cloister, and this sudden realization unnerved her for five seconds. She began moving very slowly across the porch and down the steps, as if she were going toward a lover she did not trust. She shivered. The wind pierced her thin gown, but she crept timidly forward. Ten yards ahead, one of the knights called out to her.

"Hello, lady! Where's your cloak? Can't you see it's cold, you silly girl?"

Sybille halted. She gaped at them, incredulous. They were smiling at her. All of them were good-looking young men.

The knight started up again: "Hie, lady! Get yourself a warm cloak. No sense in getting sick now you're free."

The others yelled at him, amused. "Give her yours, Jean. Where's your Christian charity, you cockroach?"

"Mine? I'll bloody well freeze." But a moment later he was throwing the long, black cloak around her shoulders, pulling the col-lar around her ears and pressing a handful of coins into her palm. She opened her mouth, but before she could thank him, they were lum-bering on, laughing, arms swinging at their sides. She twisted to stare; they did not look back.

At the cloister gate, her memory fled. There was Rue St. Etienne and the busy little square with its beggars. Directly opposite were the relic shops and a tavern. Men were going in and out, and she heard the clinking of cups and coins. But she had no idea in which direction lay the faubourg or even the Cerdan gate. She felt the urge to turn round and go back into the cloister. Finally she forced herself to step into the stream of traffic and thrash along aimlessly for a few minutes. The sun was flowing like honey now. At the next corner, she stopped and asked a passerby for directions to the Cerdan gate. She was so fatigued she longed to drop on the cold cobbles and stay there. Now it occurred to her it would be a waste of time going to Rue St. Bernard. What would she find there? Not Olivier or Nova, only piles of bricks and an empty space where the house once had stood. She trudged on.

For hours she did nothing but pad up one street and down another, limping in circles and letting herself be jostled by other human beings. She did not know what to do with herself. The streets hummed with people and hammering horses and carts. There were women in fur cloaks, hair slicked back with silver bands, women carrying in their arms blinking babies who opened mouths and showed her fat, toothless gums. The city was like a foreign country with outlandish clothing and strange behavior. She collapsed outside a baker's stall and examined the coins she had been clasping. Two deniers, three half-deniers, a couple of sticky poges. Full of reverence, she stared at them for perhaps twenty minutes before rising and buying a small loaf of bread. Then she came back and sat again, chewing the precious bread slowly and inspecting the people. There was a woman in a berry-red cloak, and Sybille watched her move her exquisite head, like a rose on a long stem. She was talking and laughing with a knight holding a palfrey by the bridle. How, Sybille wondered, would she have behaved in Garrigues' Garden? What would have become of all her laughter, her dignity, her juice?

Slowly the afternoon passed. The sun dipped down. She got to her feet and began to walk, even though she was dead tired. The streets were swamped now, everyone going home to have their suppers. She listened to people talking about the friars, who were living at Braqueville, their farm over on St. Cyprien. William Arnaud had excommunicated not only the city's consuls but the count himself. It was a pity. When Sybille reached the Cerdan gate, there was a snarl of carts and horses, and she had to wait nearly a quarter hour just to get into the faubourg.

She walked along Rue Méjane, past the hospital of St. Raymond, and into Saint-Sernin square. When she got to the church, she went inside and started down the center aisle toward the crossing. Looking up at the rows of pointed arches, she felt as if some force was clutching her, pulling her up, until she was spinning above the ground. And she began to cry softly. How many masses had she heard there, how many milky mornings had she sat with her hand in Douce's, squinting at the silver and gold crosses and the stained glass, feeling her childish certainties that God was there, in Saint-Sernin? If He was anywhere, He must be sealed in with the statue of St. Michael and the statue of St. Gabriel with his dewy stone lilies. And now she wept, because it was another lie. God had never been there.

A priest appeared on the high altar and began to light candles for vespers. Two men clacked up to the rail, knelt mechanically, and began to pray. Sybille sidled to a column and hid so she would not have to pretend. After the elevation of the Host, she propped her spine against the column and stretched out her legs on the paving stone. She sat quietly. *What am I going to do?* she asked. There was no answer. Then she approached the question from another angle: *How am I going to live and stay sane?* There was no answer to that either. The church was silent. She lay down next to the pillar in her new cloak and slept.

At prime the bells woke her. She struggled sleepily out into the howling cold air and made her way around the church into Rue St. Bernard. Yesterday's weakness seemed to have dissipated a little. At the very first gate, the house once owned by the Bonnets, she pulled the bell and, without giving her name, asked the porter what had happened to the family living in the Astarac mansion. He was holding a crust of bread soaked in some kind of gravy. "Which people?" he yawned.

"A man and a woman and their daughter. A maiden of about fifteen."

His forehead crinkled into a frown. At last he said, "Gone. Months ago."

"Where?"

"Away." He went on chewing.

"Away where?"

He looked annoyed. "Heavens, what a pest you are. Ringing the bell at dawn. Asking all sorts of questions—"

She said very firmly, "Please, I'm the girl's godmother. It is very important I find her. I would be grateful if you'd ask your mistress, or anyone at all, for news of these people."

He let her in. For perhaps ten minutes she fidgeted in the yard before he came back and said, "Now I was right. Na Gauzia says they're gone. The lady left first and then her husband, that was her second husband, he went away with the girl. As for where any of them went, how would she know? But perhaps—she says perhaps because she's only guessing—perhaps they went back where they came from."

Oh, what an idiot. "Yes—where is that?" she prompted hoarsely.

"Albi. Or maybe it was Comminges."

She barked, "That's not where they come from!"

"Well, lady," he said testily, "if you know so much, why are you asking me?"

Groaning, Sybille quickly stalked into Rue St. Bernard and stood there cursing him. God help her, finding a moron like that. You knew this would be futile, she berated herself. Deliberately she made herself look down the street toward the place her house had once stood, but she could see nothing. Several houses were in the way, and it was impossible, from that end of the street, to know what ruins lay behind the wall.

They had gone home. Where else? It was almost fifteen leagues to Fanjeaux. That isn't so far, she thought. Go back to the Cerdan gate, through the city to the Narbonne gate, then out among the unenclosed suburbs to the open highway. She would place one foot in front of the other, stopping to rest when she felt tired, each step taking her farther away from Garrigues' Garden. In no time she would be home.

She straightened her spine and started back toward Saint-Sernin, a free person.

She did not know why she was ringing the bell of Sainte Marthe's convent, except that darkness had fallen quickly and it was beginning to drizzle. This was the nearest dwelling and, like all religious communities, would not turn away a footsore traveler who needed shelter for the night.

The gate was opened by an unsmiling nun, who stared at her and then somewhat impolitely pointed to a ramshackle hut at the far end of the muddy yard. Sybille thanked her and began to walk toward it.

Behind her, she heard the portress call out, "Where are you coming from?"

"What does it matter, Sister?" Sybille said without stopping.

"Do you wish to see the prioress?"

She swung around then and gave her a startled look. She faltered, "I don't—there is no reason I must see her. I mean, it's not customary, is it?"

The nun shrugged. "These days one can't be too careful. We can't risk admitting some heretic, can we?"

Sybille stared at the ground. "No," she murmured. "You can't do that." The nun swung around on her heel and went back to the gate-house, and Sybille reeled on to the shack. A small fire was smoking in the center of the room, sending pearly smoke up to the hole in the thatched roof. She looked around. The only person there was an old woman curled up snoring under her cloak. Sybille squatted by the embers, regretting she had rung the bell. Had the portress sensed something unusual about her? It could be nothing more than routine suspicion. She was reasonably sure there was no cause for alarm. How could they distinguish her from that other woman across the room? She did not look like an escaped criminal. Sybille therefore had made herself comfortable and was hoping for soup and bread when the portress suddenly appeared in the doorway.

She beckoned with her shoulder, not looking at Sybille. "N'Es-clarmonde wants you." There was a grim expression around her mouth that made Sybille nervous. With an irritated sigh, she got up slowly and followed the woman into the yard. The rain was coming down in sheets now, with gusts of wind. Making an effort to sound casual, she asked, "Which order is this, Sister?"

"Minorite," she answered, but it was obvious she did not want to converse.

In silence they went into the cloister gate, along a covered walk-way, and into a low-ceilinged reception hall, damp and cold. The portress left. Sybille sat down on a bench, shivering. She was hungry and very tired. The journey had been excruciating, much more so than she had anticipated. Her legs were weak, and she had discovered she could cover less than one league a day, and that only by halting for frequent rests.

A half hour, perhaps longer, crept by. At last the inner door squeaked open, and N'Esclarmonde, a woman of fifty with a large, fleshy face and an aggressive chin, stood scrutinizing Sybille. She offered no greeting, merely nodded curtly, and motioned Sybille in-side, where she sat down in a straight-backed chair by the fire. There was only one chair. Sybille stood by the door, bracing herself on both feet.

Without preamble, the prioress embarked on an extensive dis-course, bemoaning the terrible times in which they lived. Sybille lis-tened indifferently, thinking the woman was stating the obvious in a melodramatic way that robbed her words of meaning, indeed made them sound trivial. She nevertheless slapped on a thoughtful expres-sion and from time to time bobbed her head. When the prioress ventured the opinion that God had deliberately sent these trials as a sort of purification, Sybille bowed her head. Unexpectedly changing the subject, the prioress said sternly, "What town are you coming from?"

Sybille looked up. She hesitated, but only for a second, then said, "Grisolles." Very emphatic. *Grisolles!*

"And your destination?"

"Narbonne."

"A long journey." She glanced down briefly at the paving stones. "You don't look up to it."

"I," Sybille stammered, "I am recovering from an illness."

"Are you?" She fixed Sybille with a stare that said, You had better be forthright with me if you want to avoid trouble.

Now Sybille stared back at her. She decided to play her most haughty self. "See here, lady," she growled. "This sort of interrogation is most discourteous. Forgive me for saying this, but it is also unpardonably unkind. As you can see for yourself, I'm unwell. Three weeks ago I buried my mother and now my only desire is to return to my husband and children." The prioress, bent forward in her chair, seemed eager to interrupt. "If I had expected this reception, I should have slept in the woods. I don't have the strength for it." Her voice trailed off. Lord Jesus, Sybille moaned to herself, what have I done? I've dug my own grave with this cold-blooded bitch.

The prioress sat squarely in her chair. "Let's get to the point. I've seen many undernourished travelers." Her eyes narrowed. "But I would not put you in that class."

"No?"

"No. You're all skin and bones. From the evidence of your"—she paused—"skeletal appearance, you could be an ordained heretic—"

"I told you I'm sick. I have nothing more to say."

"—or you've been in prison. Possibly you were released to do penance. In which case you are in violation because I see no yellow cross on your cloak. Or you fled."

She's smart, thought Sybille. So I resemble a skeleton.

"My intuition," the prioress was saying, "tells me the latter is true."

"Intuition is not fact." She has no way of proving anything, Sybille thought, but she watched the woman uneasily.

N'Esclarmonde's face loomed hard and white in the firelight. "I don't want trouble here," she said. "I have the feeling you bring trouble."

Sybille said she was wrong. "And I'll be delighted to leave at once. I'm not eager to accept hospitality from a place such as this."

"I'm sure you're not, but fortunately I have use for an extra pair of hands and—"

"I'm not an extra pair of hands. My family needs me."

The prioress was silent. Meanwhile Sybille had been backing toward the door. After a moment, N'Esclarmonde said, "Let's try to look at this matter in another light. You claim you're anxious to get home. If I should report you to the Holy Office, your homecoming would certainly be delayed. Of course, if you're telling me the truth, you'll be released. Eventually. But think what an inconvenience it would be. A great inconvenience."

It was madness to trust anyone these days. Before ringing the bell of a convent, she should have bedded down in some village with the beggars and whores. Now it was too late. She said angrily, "What exactly do you want of me, Lady Prioress?"

"There are works of piety to be done here."

"Such as?"

"Help in the harvest fields. Slaughtering."

The impulse to call her a leprous bitch twitched on the tip of Sybille's tongue. Instead, she raised her voice and asked, "At what wages?"

The prioress snorted in surprise. "With three meals a day, what more do you want?" She heaved herself to her feet and stood with her hands on her hips. "You expect wages!" She snorted again but with a kind of begrudging admiration for Sybille's audacity.

Sybille swallowed. Her decision had to be swift. Would accepting the bribe be an admission of guilt? Very likely the prioress pulled this trick with other travelers. Should she call her bluff? Doing that might send her to Daniel Marty in Carcassonne. She said, "Thirty days, no longer."

Smiling slightly, the prioress nodded and replied, "Very well. If that is all you can give to the Lord—"

"And three meals with a double portion of meat or fish." When N'Esclarmonde hesitated, Sybille added, "How can I work if I'm weak?"

The prioress promised to try.

But she did not keep her word because the next morning in the refectory, Sybille tried to scoop up a second helping of fish stew and the nun heading the table called her a wicked slut. "You can feast at your own trestle—we here are only poor ladies of the Lord."

Sybille shouted back in indignation, as if she were a child promised a sweet, promised but denied for no reason. "You poor ladies of the Lord have fuller bellies than most people. I don't notice you poor ladies suffering."

"I don't like your tone," said the nun.

"Too bad."

"Charity—"

"Not charity. I'm to do physical labor while you poor ladies sit on your asses praying all day." She suspected she was going too far but she didn't care.

The sister whitened. "I shall report this to N'Esclarmonde," she hissed.

"Please do," Sybille told her.

In the weeks she was detained at Sainte Marthe, Sybille managed to get her promised extra rations only five times. Nonetheless she reckoned that she was doing better than most people those days and the proof was that she began to regain a little of her weight. The farm belonging to Sainte Marthe was more prosperous than any she had seen between Toulouse and Montferrand. The reason was that the crusaders had never burned their crops and vines, and the Minorite Sisters had gone right on sowing and harvesting their fields as if there had been no war at all.

For five or six days in the middle of November, the subprioress sent her out to the woods behind the convent, where the acorns were ripe and the pigs were loosed to root and rove under the flame-colored oaks. With the swineherds who owed service to Sainte Marthe and their shaggy dogs, Sybille tossed sticks up into the branches and knocked down the acorns into the herds of snouting, squealing pigs. She felt happy to be out of doors under the clean sky, with the smell of dead leaves and even of the pigs in her nose. At dusk, as she trudged back up the slope to the convent, her skull felt whole and strong. At the end of the month, after the slaughter, she was brought indoors to help with the pickling, a job she liked a good deal less.

During the days, she had small contact with the nuns, but at night she would chat with them in the dormitory or latrine. After they had come back from compline once, she happened to mention the Dominicans had been expelled from Toulouse. To her surprise, they seemed astonished and insisted she must be lying.

"Doesn't anyone tell you what goes on in the world? The friars were driven out weeks ago. With the count's blessing. Yes, it's true. Ask your lady prioress."

They gathered around and goggled tear-pouched eyes in bewilderment. One of them piped, "But why? The brothers of the sainted Dominic labor in the Lord's vineyard. They've done miracles in our land."

Sybille snapped, "Burning innocent people is a miracle? Tell me, because I'd like to know."

A novice murmured, "May God punish the count and his followers."

"People are fettered in dungeons like dogs. People are burned without trials. Children are forced to inform on their parents. Who deserves the punishment? Not the count! Oh, go back to your beds. You're all so stupid." After matins she woke suddenly shaking from a dream in which Daniel Marty was pushing her into the tower dungeon. Her heart was pounding. She lay awake for an hour.

The following day, N'Esclarmonde summoned Sybille to her chamber after vespers and said she was releasing her from their agreement.

"But I have another five days," Sybille pointed out.

"I want you out of here."

Amen and alleluia, Sybille shouted to herself.

"You set a bad example for my flock."

"Oh?"

"A disturbing influence in this house of God."

Sybille was tempted to say N'Esclarmonde herself set a poor example for her flock when she entered church with her twelve hunting dogs. But she pruned that remark, discarded it, and finally said, "Keeping me here like some slave was wrong. You will have to settle up with God."

"You're not a Catholic," the prioress told her.

"How do you know?"

"It's easy to see."

"I'm not a believer in the two gods."

"I know you're not of the faith," N'Esclarmonde insisted.

Sybille went to the dormitory for her cloak and hurried down to the cold yard. It was dark now and she had eaten nothing since noon. In the refectory they would soon be serving hot meat and vegetables. She should have begged to stay the night and left after breakfast. When the portress saw her, she came gusting out of the gatehouse and rushed to unbar the gate. Sybille said, "Fare thee well, Sister. How far to the nearest village?"

In the torchlight the woman's face was as relieved as if she were ejecting a plague-carrier. "Not far. Half hour maybe." She shrugged. "Thank you."

The closing gate plunged out the light and cast her suddenly into the darkness. Staring at the road, Sybille felt as though she were standing naked on the rim of hell. She was filled with a hunger more intense than any physical desire she had ever known, would have given away her soul to believe as did those women nestled snug behind the walls. They trusted blindly because they had never known doubt, or were incapable of examining their own hearts, or because they had the courage to believe in God and His Church on this earth. His only Church.

She knew that God had veiled His light from her. From the very first day at Garrigues' Garden, He had spoken to her through Daniel Marty. He would not speak again.

She drifted up the moonless road.

Olivier and Nova had stayed at Cantal a very short time. The Dominicans had chased them out and nailed to the gate a sign saying the unholy castle had been condemned. Sybille went out to have a look because she did not believe Olivier would disappear without leaving behind some message for her. She broke in the postern gate, scoured the tower from cellar to turret, flicked dust from Nova's old nibbled doll, found a rusty lute string and the first draft of a poem she had later torn up. When she saw that all signs of her life there had been obliterated and she could shed no more tears, she went back to Fanjeaux.

"What more can I say?" Isarn-Bernard whispered. "They were out there until Easter. Maybe later. But I didn't see him after that."

A single candle stub sputtered on the floor of the cellar. Isarn-Bernard had sent his servants to bed, but every few minutes he sidled to the kitchen door, opened it a crack, and peered out cautiously. His back to Sybille, he mumbled.

She missed his words. "He said what?"

"I'm trying to remember. He talked about going to Mirepoix. Or was it Montségur?"

"Which?"

Half turning, he shook his head. "You know Olivier. He's always talking about one thing or another. He spoke of taking service with the count of Foix—"

"Jesus Lord God! Try to remember, can't you?"

Isarn-Bernard shifted around and bumped the door shut with his elbow. "Lower your voice. Do you want all of us to be arrested? God knows, I'm compromising my whole household by hiding you here."

She bit down angrily on her lip. "Turn me in then—I don't care." She was eating the cold remains of the family's supper—cabbage seasoned with oil—because Isarn-Bernard had not dared attract the cook's attention. Catching the terror in his eyes, she softened her tone. "So your servants are spies too?"

"Everyone is a spy. What's the use of pretending, Na Sybille? My daughter is a spy, my wife—yes, even I would betray you if I was faced with losing everything I own."

She regretted not seeing Condors; Isarn-Bernard had refused to tell her of Sybille's return because the fewer people who knew, the better. Sybille sighed. "Did Olivier tell you I was dead?"

Isarn-Bernard said, No, only that the Inquisition had taken her. He came over and crouched opposite on a sack of onions. "Lady, don't think you aren't welcome here—"

"I'll leave before sunup," Sybille said. "Perhaps the Durforts know something."

He shook his head. "They've flown."

"Where?" Their voices echoed softly in the hollow chamber.

"To the goddam mountains. The Durforts, the Tonneins, *faidits* all of them now."

Faidits, she repeated to herself. The best families in the district are now outlaws. What happened to their castles and vineyards and the gold plate for a hundred? She glanced at Isarn-Bernard's face in the flickering light of the candle, but the barking of a dog in the street jerked her eyes to the door. She gasped, then slumped back on the sacks. Oh God, she moaned silently, this is insane. Again she looked at Isarn-Bernard and opened her mouth to speak, but he was holding up his hand.

"There's something I've kept back," he said. "Lady, I didn't want to mention this but—may I be frank? There was a certain woman in Mirepoix." Isarn-Bernard stared into the corner, hesitating. "Someone Olivier used to visit frequently. It's possible she knows where they've gone."

Trembling, Sybille drew herself up with dignity. She waited twenty seconds. "You mean a concubine?" she asked calmly.

"Well," he hedged, "that's not for me to say. I mean, presumably. But who knows?"

"And her name?"

Isarn-Bernard was rubbing his nose. "You think I remember names? She's the sister of a knight he diced with, a fellow called Le Rouge. I never knew his real name."

Sybille sat silent on the sacks, listening to Isarn-Bernard and thinking Olivier had not waited long to replace her. On these pleasure trips to Mirepoix, had he left Nova behind at Cantal, or had he taken her along to this Le Rouge house while he fucked the woman? Isarn-Bernard went upstairs to get furs so she could make up a bed for herself.

When alone, she thought, I hope there are no bad dreams tonight. Why can't I sleep a whole night without wakening? These nightmares of the tower are cruel tricks played by my own mind. She sat and waited for Isarn-Bernard.

Abandoned manor houses, burned villages, slopes quiet and frozen under the winter sky, as if they had never blazed coppery with grain. At every turn in the road, the land screamed out its pain and the deserted castles rose up like couriers proclaiming history's forgotten battles. The weather was clear and by late morning the sun warm enough to throw off her cloak. Sybille found the walking calmed her. She strode along behind a cart loaded with somebody's household furnishings. They had left Orsans behind when she noticed a rider on a white stallion rein in sharply, then pull his mount to a halt.

She kept right on walking. He appeared to be waiting for her, and she wondered if perhaps she knew him, if he was some neighbor who had happened to recognize her. But drawing near, she saw she had never set eyes on him before. She was about to swerve around him when he called out, "God's pardon, are you going toward Mirepoix?"

She squinted. "Yes," she said. "What of it?"

He gave her a pretty smile. "I have room. You can ride if you wish." His cloak was hemmed with gray vair, and his polished boots and silver spurs gave him an appearance of prewar elegance you did not see every day.

"Well—" Sybille hesitated. He looked like a courteous man, but how could she be sure?

Immediately the knight said, "Don't be afraid. I mean you no harm, I assure you."

Still smiling, he edged the mount closer. She looked him straight in the face. He was past his first youth but younger than she, about thirty, she guessed, thin, lanky, with brown hair and a well-barbered beard. She thought happily, This is a piece of good luck. Why should I walk when I might ride? Making her voice indifferent, she said, "Very well." She was careful not to return his smile. "But I have no money to pay you."

"Lady." He grinned reproachfully. "You do me an injustice. Don't think I expect payment."

She tossed her walking stick over a hedge. He reached down to pull her up, spurred the stallion, and they galloped away, almost flying like the wind along the hard-packed earth. Suddenly she found herself smiling. About what she could not say. Waves of happiness lanced through her. Not relief from her terrors, not mere pleasure to feel the wind sifting across her face, but happiness of the kind she had once known long ago. "My name," he was yelling over his shoulder, "is Jacques de Lévis." He told Sybille his fief was at Camon-sur-l'Hers.

Her hands were clutched awkwardly at his waist, firm and narrow beneath his coat. De Lévis, she mused. A well-known surname in these parts. Highborn, rich heretics. She heard him ask, "What's yours?"

"Sybille," she said.

"Yes. Sybille what?" When he got no reply, he gave a laugh soft with bitterness. "Ah God, God, what has become of courtesy and friendship? Those accursed friars have destroyed every drop of trust. Now we must drink from a cup full of suspicion."

She thought, This man bears no love for the Preaching Friars, and she began to warm toward him. For that reason, and because he was good-looking and had a nice laugh, she laughed too. She let her fingers ease on his waist. I am forty-two next September, she thought. Old but not yet elderly. He has a good body. It was not carnality that had crept into her mind, but merely the pleasure felt by a woman of her age when a fine-looking younger man gives her his attention. She decided she liked him, and she reminded him Toulouse had expelled the friars. Perhaps this was an omen and every city would do likewise and the Inquisition would be suspended.

"Don't believe it," he said. After a moment he added that evil was a weed you might cut down but never destroy. "Its seeds lie dormant. Then it blooms again." It was obvious, wasn't it?

It was obvious also that he was a man fond of metaphors. He glanced back at her. Their eyes met, and then he turned forward again. She thought, But that was a stupid metaphor. I can do better. "Perhaps evil," she shouted into his ear, "is woven into the very fabric of our lives, but woven in some hidden design. Maybe it can never be eradicated. But don't you think we're obliged to fight evil just the same?" She smiled a challenge at the back of his head.

Under her hands she felt his body move into a shrug. Begging her pardon, but he disagreed. Life was terrible. Struggle was useless. There was no way around it. One might hope, but in the end hope would be crushed.

Sybille threw back her head, impatient at the knight's depressing attitude. Looking at life through his eyes, there was no possibility of happiness. And she thought angrily, What has he to complain about? He has fine clothes, he has not suffered imprisonment. But she squelched her irritation. "My lord," she fluttered, "evil clothes itself in many disguises. So long as we have the eyes to recognize it, we can fight." She raised her voice. "So there is always hope." She waited for his response with eagerness, relishing the excitement of this debate.

Jacques de Lévis was silent. Sybille had the feeling he disliked hearing her opinions unless they agreed with his. Now the sun was going behind a cloud. The wind funneled down the back of her neck. The pastures lay shadowy on either side of the road. At this rate they would reach Mirepoix before vespers. Maybe she could find that woman today. That concubine. That whore. When De Lévis next spoke, it was to ask her how she happened to be going to Mirepoix.

"I'm seeking the house of a knight called Le Rouge," she said. He looked around grinning, which made her add hastily, "I wish to see his sister. Do you know this family?"

"Who does not?" he said. They lived in Rue de l'Eglise. He did not question her further, for which she was thankful, but began talking about himself. He was a widower; his lady wife and his four precious blond sons, who had taken after their mother in coloring, had all been lost to a pox in less than two weeks. Now, alone, he could only weep and drink, and he confessed he drank too much. He seemed far away in grief, and Sybille hesitated, then finally reached up to pat his shoulder. That accounts for his gloomy words, she thought. The man was grieving. He too had known sorrow. She stroked his arm.

Late afternoon they entered the city through the north gate and jogged into the commercial quarter. The streets were thick with women in their white wimples and dogs and pigeons foraging for scraps. The aroma of roasting meat from the cookshops was making Sybille's mouth water. After a quarter hour, the knight reined up outside an inn and, without turning, invited her to do him the honor of supping with him.

Sybille's eyes widened in horrified amazement. "No lady would go into such a place with a man."

"God forbid!" he broke in. "I'm suggesting nothing improper."

She slipped to the cobbles. A groom came up and led away the knight's mount. They stood facing each other, Jacques with his mouth drooping. "I know," she said softly. "Forgive me." She started up the steps, with Jacques at her heels.

An hour later, in a little room on the solar floor, they sat eating awkwardly at a table. Directly below, the common room was crowded with customers yelling and laughing. Jacques refilled her cup and got up to jab at the fire. From the corner of her eye, she could see the curtained bed in the corner. He did not seem to notice, and he went on talking about Montségur. More than sermons were heard at the heretic fortress these days. It was now an arsenal with a vast store of arms. The heart of the resistance, he called it. Nervously, Sybille drained half the cup in a gulp and then felt her head give a little spin.

"Lady," Jacques said. He took the stool beside her. "I noticed something different about you the minute I saw you."

She swallowed, suddenly wary. Had she been careless?

"Do you know what you remind me of?" he said. She waited uneasily. He was smiling now. "A boy. A slender, beautiful youth."

Sybille laughed in relief. For all those women overweight and aging, here at last was a cure-all. Forget lotions, forget honey and vinegar. Spend a year with the Preaching Friars instead. Oh, this is too much, she thought. He thinks I'm young, boyish. "God's eyes," she burst out, "you're an idiot." She laughed again.

"Oh," he said gravely and drew back. "I meant no discourtesy. I like you."

"You don't know me," Sybille said. He glanced at her face but said nothing. Sybille reached for the wine, sipped, put the cup down. Below a cittern started up. People were beginning to sing.

> *Ai! Tolosa et Provensa!*
> *E la terra d'Argensa!*

Tears flickered in her eyes. She jumped to her feet and went to stand by the fire. Jacques remained seated. Then he rose and stepped toward her. Before she could stop him, he buried his outstretched fingers in the hair at the nape of her neck and scooped her soft against himself. Hunger to touch his bare skin tore through her. She lifted an open mouth, her whole body shamelessly pulsing, aching to consume itself.

His tongue touched the top of hers. "This is what you wish?" he murmured.

Sybille moaned. She fumbled her hands along both sides of his waist. The floor shivered with Sicart Marjevol's lament:

> *Ai! Bezers et Carcassey!*
> *Quo vos vi! quo vos vei!*

Jacques likened them to two water droplets rushing together, and said he wished they could flow out to sea. His fingertips were rubbing the hard tips of her breasts.

> Oh! Béziers and Carcassonne!
> I saw you then—I look on you today!

She heard him croon, "I like you, Na Sybille."

She shook her head. "I don't want you to like me," she said. She arched herself against him. He gave a bewildered laugh. "I want you to love me." She meant fusion, soul melded to soul, flesh to mossy-sheer flesh. No division, no loneliness, no tearing asunder when she wasn't looking.

"That can be arranged," he declared, sounding so certain of himself. He swung her up into his arms and went toward the bed.

> Oh! Toulouse and Provence!
> And the fair land of Argence!

* * *

When she woke, the other side of the bed was empty. She did not get up at once but lingered among the yellowy sheets, wondering if Jacques had gone to get them bread and ale. The minutes crawled by. Eventually she dressed and went downstairs, looking first into the common room and then going out to the courtyard. It was cold outside. A boy was watering a black mare. She went up to him and cleared her throat. "En Jacques de Lévis."

"Yes." He scratched his neck.

"Have you seen him today?"

"Yes, lady."

Impatient: "Well?"

"Why, he went home to see Na Helis."

"Who?" she croaked, looking sharply into his face.

"Na Helis de—his lady wife."

Her jaw popped open. She let out a howl of amazed laughter. Outside in the street, a fish vendor began to screech. "You mean," she called to the stableboy, "he went home to his lady wife and his four blond sons who take after their mother."

"Yes, lady," he said and went into the stable. Sybille laughed again. Oh God, I know You must be up there. You are still playing these wretched jokes on me. She swayed across the yard into the street, where she stood for a minute, peering both ways. Then she set off for the house of Le Rouge.

"Did you lie with Olivier?" she said through tight lips. "I must know."

Stéphanie Arsen crossed her hands in her lap. She was a sweet-faced, even prim, woman of perhaps forty-five who looked like she had a sensible head on her shoulders. After a pause, she said crisply, "Only once," and closed her mouth. A look passed between the two women. Sybille nodded, gratified in some perverse way. She thought, If their penises don't work properly with one woman they try another, just to make sure; if their penises do work, they try another. Just to make sure. It was extraordinary.

"Alas, I have no patience with that sort of thing." Stéphanie sounded almost apologetic.

"He was better in his youth," Sybille said stiffly, wanting to save face for herself. Sitting back on the stool, she looked around the room again. Gold crucifix, an empty birdcage, a battered lute. On a chest a mirror and a profusion of little pots—lotions, creams, face paints. Stéphanie was staring at her. Sybille dismissed Olivier with a jerk of her head. "I want my daughter back."

Stéphanie got up to pile more charcoal on the brazier, although the room was already overheated. Then she went to sit on the bed. "They were going to the mountains," she told Sybille. "Like everyone else."

"Pamiers? Foix? Where in the mountains?"

She shook her head impatiently. "Montségur, most likely."

There was a long silence. Sybille finished her wine without tasting it. She hesitated. "Then you think I should go to Montségur?"

"That is my advice."

She stared down at the blue tiles, wondering if this journey too would end in heartache. It was many, many leagues to the mountains. If she failed to find Nova at Montségur, where would she look then?

Toiling up the road from Lavelanet, she rounded a turn and suddenly glimpsed it through two pine boughs. Against the silvery blue sky the mountain swelled before her like a distant pillar of snow, blazing as if a colossal jeweler had carefully anointed it with crystals. Across its two humps soared the castle of Montségur with its white walls flashing in the winter sunlight. The stone face winked down at her. Each time she blinked it seemed to shift expression—now sharp and pointed, now curving magically, now engorged, ugly. There was something remote, even frightening, about it. Averting her eyes, she hurried on.

It was almost twilight when she came into Montségur village. The town was layered thickly with snow. Before the war it had been a community of some twenty stone houses crouched at the foot of the mountain. Now it resembled a pig's bladder bloated to the breaking point. The original houses shriveled among the hundreds of wood and daub cabins thrown up on the spur of the moment. Cookshops blew bubbles of smoke into the clear evening air. Along the clogged lanes spilled pilgrims, peddlers, shepherds, merchants with fat purses, knights decked out in mail surcoats and straddling expensive war horses. And youngsters. Sybille marveled at the great numbers of them. Along the road she had met others like them, bands of homeless, parentless youth roaming the countryside. Some of them were little better than gangs of thieves and whores. She could not blame them. How else were they to eat? But they made her uncomfortable because they made her think of Nova.

Light-headed from the mountain air, she pushed up to a dairy stall to inquire if there was a pilgrim's hostel in the town. On Rue Lantar, she learned, but it was always full—she should not waste her time going there. She went anyway and spent a restless night wedged between two snoring sisters from Chalabre.

For several days Sybille made a search for Nova and Olivier. But Montségur was a town of transients. No one seemed to know anyone's name, and asking proved futile. One afternoon, as she was passing through the artisans' quarter, she noticed a young woman walking a little way ahead. Something about the woman's gait, the puffs of pale hair blowing from the hood, made her look twice. But this person, carrying a basket, was not a child. Sybille watched her cross the street and enter a courtyard.

On impulse, she quickened her steps. The courtyard gate was open. Inside, the hooded woman stood arguing with a man in a cloak of rich burgundy wool. She let the basket drop to the hard-packed snow. Sybille hesitated, then she called out, "God's pardon, friends—" and her voice trailed off.

The man and woman paused to glance at Sybille. For a long while no one spoke. Then the woman stammered, "Mama?" She did not move. "Where did you come from, Mama?"

She was a half-realized woman, with Olivier's long legs and pale hair, but with a face still chiseled with the markings of childhood. Still, she hung back until Sybille realized something was wrong. For so many months she had envisioned her reunion with a tearful Nova, baby-grasping arms folded around her neck. But this Nova did not cry; she did not even smile. Suddenly tongue-tied, Sybille said, "The sister of Le Rouge told me you might be here, you and your lord father."

"He's not here."

"Since November I've been seeking you. I went to Cantal—" She stopped and moved her eyes to the man. He bowed, then strode across the yard and disappeared into the house. Between the opening and closing of the door, Sybille got a glimpse of a workroom and women sitting around a table. She turned to Nova. "That man is—"

"A wool merchant."

"Is he a heretic?"

"Everyone here is a heretic." Nova pressed her lips together.

The girl was as forbidding as a stone rampart. Sybille tried again. "Do you live here?"

"Live. Work. I'm one of his apprentices." Her eyes shifted away.

"Your father. Where is he?"

"He did his best. He brought me here and got me apprenticed to En Philippe. 'She's not afraid of hard work,' he told En Philippe. Well, I didn't care. I get a bed and my food every day, don't I?"

A dozen feet separated them. Sybille forced herself to cross them, to reach out and take Nova in her arms. The girl turned her head away. Her body under Sybille's hands was rigid. "My love," Sybille whispered against her hood. "I'm here now. I won't leave you again. We'll be happy now, you'll see."

Over her shoulder, Nova said, "You're dead. Why have you come back?"

Sybille lowered her arms and backed away. Nova was standing with her fists clenched at her sides; she did not look at Sybille. After a minute, she said stiffly, "Well, I must go sort wool now. I finish around vespers, if you want to come back then." She picked up the basket and skittered into the workshop without looking back.

Chapter Sixteen

That wet spring, Sybille sat sweating in her little house surrounded by Philippe Cervel's wool. It was supposed to be sorted into grades of fine, medium, and coarse, and then rinsed to remove the grease. She spread it to dry on boards near the hearth, and then picked out bits of debris and soil with a forceps or clipped them with a small shears. When the wool had been combed and carded, Nova would take it back to En Philippe and bring home another batch. The house was always steamy and smelled of lye and wet fleece.

At first Sybille had felt she was simply taking up her life where she had left it, but soon she realized it was a new life. She became a wage earner, and she lived in a peasant house. Her noble name had become superfluous, and if she did not work they would have to beg food and lodging. She began to think: Perhaps I'm fortunate. There is a small cloth industry here. One day I may learn the skills to be a fuller or dyer. This one-room house is no better than a swineherd's hut at Cantal, but I will make it our home. I suffer from nightmares, but now they come less frequently. This is a new life for me and Nova. It has got to be, because the old one has vanished without leaving a single footprint.

There was no sign of Olivier. Nova said he had sent money once from Queribus with a *faidit,* but the purse contained only a few deniers, and she was sure the knight had taken it, even though he claimed he had been robbed. The next time she saw her father, she told him not to send money again. But Sybille could not forgive his selling their daughter, like an unwanted urchin, to the first heretic merchant he met.

The day after Palm Sunday, Olivier came to the Cervel workshop, a Damascus sword at his belt, to visit his daughter. He was in a hurry;

the bailiff of Avignonet was expecting him. Nova sent him over to the house.

He did not exactly enter but stood spiked in the doorframe, split open by Sybille's rage. Face to face, they went at each other. He had not, he snarled, betrayed her. It was she who had abandoned him by refusing to tell Daniel Marty about Pons. What difference did it make? Sooner or later, Pons would burn. Sybille was a stupid, disloyal *con* who had thrown away their property for no reason and left him with a child to look after.

"Son of a strumpet and a monk!" Sybille hissed throatily. "May leprosy rot your balls."

Backing out, Olivier plunged into the rain and was gone. Cold rain danced slantwise through the open door. The whole exchange, from beginning to end, had taken place within the space of a dozen paternosters. After yearning for the sight of his face these endless months, she had glimpsed it finally through a thick curtain of anger, blind even to the color of his cloak.

That afternoon she was so angry she could do no work. She sat at the trestle, feeling her hatred with her toes, and let the fire go out.

At dusk Nova came home, her hair messy as usual. She had a sack tucked under her arm, a gift from her father, but she had not opened it. Sybille untied the sack and held up half a leg of lamb, as long as her hand. It did not appear maggoty. It was good meat, she decided, and fought the impulse to fling it into the rain simply because it had come from Olivier. There had been no meat in their house since her arrival at Montségur. Tonight, for once, her daughter would dine well. She relit the fire and hung the lamb on a hook to roast. Nova, silent, went behind the curtain to the sleeping corner and flopped onto her mattress. Aside from giving Sybille the meat, she did not mention her father; it was almost as if she had not seen him. After a while Sybille put her head through the curtain. She noticed the girl was shaking. "What's wrong?" she asked. "You haven't caught a chill, have you?"

"It's nothing." Her face was buried in the sheepskin. But she often did that when she returned from En Philippe's and supper was cooking, so Sybille dropped the curtain and went back to the hearth.

When the lamb was done, she generously carved several crisp-edged slices for each of them and put the platters on the trestle. Nova, silent, cheeks bloodless, seated herself slowly. Sybille began to eat. This is wonderful, she thought. Nova stared into her lap.

"Do you feel better?"

Nova grunted.

"Then eat," she urged. "Who knows when we shall have a feast like this again?"

Nova stared at the hearth, then at the baskets of fleece waiting to be sorted. The food stayed on her platter, untouched. She began to play with a spoon, tapping it nervously against the trestle top.

Three or four minutes passed.

Sybille, her mouth full of lamb, became increasingly agitated. She swallowed, wiped her hands. The pinkish slices still sat on Nova's plate. Nova did not speak. Sybille did not speak, but then she said loudly, "Why don't you eat? This isn't good enough for you? I'm sorry. Then go eat elsewhere."

As Sybille sat watching her daughter, she was not aware of the fury spurting in her chest. All she knew was that Nova seemed to be mocking her. "Do you know what they gave me in prison? Stale bread, water. I would have given my life for a meal like this."

Nova did not respond. There was a look in her eyes that enraged Sybille.

"Brat! Stop staring at me. Eat!"

Nova sprang up and seized her platter with both hands.

"Nova—"

With all her might, Nova hurled the dish at the shutters. The meat splattered, the wooden platter thudded to the ground and rolled away among the baskets of wool. Before Sybille could move, Nova opened her mouth and began to scream.

She ran to quiet the girl. The screaming terrified her. The walls were thin, and everyone on the lane would think the girl was being murdered. But Nova was not easy to hush. She went on filling the house with shriek after shriek, as though possessed by devils. Knocking over the bench, Sybille locked her hands on Nova's shoulders, but she wrenched free, swatted wildly with her fists, and stared at her mother with unseeing eyes. She would not stop screaming. Frantic now, Sybille dragged her, kicking, to her pallet and pushed her down. Then Nova stopped, but her breath was coming and going as if her lungs had been crushed. Sybille did not know what to do; she sat down next to her. "Nova, please. Nova, what is it? I won't make you eat the meat." There was no answer. After a while Sybille got up, filled a bowl with water, and carried it to the pallet.

"Here." She dampened her sleeve and dabbed it at the girl's face. She was sprawled sideways, chewing on her thumbnail. "Nova? Talk to me, baby."

Nova looked at her. An hour later, still crouched by the pallet, Sybille bent over her grimly. "You must tell me. I beg you—was it the meat?" Nova waited many minutes before replying and then it was only a nod. "What about it?"

"Nothing."

"Tell me."

It was nothing, Nova said. Some evil memory.

Then Sybille understood. She left the girl and hurried to the hearth, where the remainder of the lamb sat on a platter. One more sin on Olivier's account. But where could she have seen the burnings? Perhaps in Toulouse, or at any one of a dozen towns on the road between Fanjeaux and Montségur. Why had Olivier permitted her to watch? She stared at the charred meat congealing in its grease. Behind her, Nova was moaning.

"Mama?"

"I'm going out for a minute." Platter in her hands, Sybille pushed open the door and went out, not completely certain about what she planned to do. The rain had slackened. Halfway to the corner, she slowed, listening. There was a dog whining close by. She followed the sound, came to a dungheap, heard it scuffling soft in the frothy dark. She plodded forward and whistled. He came toward her, head bent low, eyes gleaming. She rolled the lamb into the mud. As she went back toward the house, she heard him howling his thank you.

On her pallet Nova lay in exactly the same position as Sybille had left her. "Mama," she said. She tipped up her eyes, lost as an infant foundling. "Are you coming to bed?"

The house still smelled of flesh and fat. Kneeling, Sybille put her arms around the girl. "Why didn't you tell me?" she whispered. But Nova would say nothing, only clung to her like the child she still was. That was the last time Sybille cooked meat. She and Nova ate vegetables and fish, like the heretics, which Sybille found ironic.

Throughout the spring, Sybille observed her daughter. On her last natal day, Nova had been sixteen, old enough to be wed, even though she scowled when Sybille mentioned the idea and insisted she wanted no husband. The fact was, the girl was a stranger to her, as alien as if they had just met. Nova and her father had the same hair color, but now it occurred to Sybille—and it was an alarming idea—that perhaps they shared the same melancholic disposition. Why does she act so hard? she wondered. Is it my fault? Did my absence cause it? Then she thought, What difference what caused it? Either way, she is maimed and I can see no gentleness in her, only the gutter toughness of someone who has learned the trick of survival. Like a rat. Nova, she decided, had no pity for anyone, least of all for herself.

Sybille's daughter had made a friend in the town. She was a fuller's apprentice. One Sunday Nova brought her to the house, with much nervous giggling and boisterous making of faces, making clear to Sybille that the girl was not important to her, and to the girl that her mother was not important. Opposite them at the trestle, Sybille smiled and piled stewed figs and carob cream in their bowls. They ate without looking at her.

"Do you like it?" Sybille asked to open a conversation.

The friend bobbed her head. Frowning, Nova leaned sideways to elbow her roughly in the ribs. "Stupid. Say, 'Yes thank you, lady.' " Her tone was pleasant, even helpful, but Sybille at once began to reprove her daughter and said she should use better language. It was not courteous to call people stupid.

Nova showed surprise. "But that's her name," she protested.

Sybille shook her head, disbelieving. "Of course it's not," she snorted. She turned her gaze on the girl. "What is your name, child?" When the girl only smiled, she said more sharply, "You haven't answered my question. You *do* have a Christian name."

The girl went on devouring the figs and licking clean her spoon after every bite. Finally she cleared her throat, swallowed, and said in a hesitant voice, "It's Gaillarde—I think."

"Indeed. Don't you know?"

"No. But I think people used to call me Gaillarde."

Sybille managed a smile. "Well, Gaillarde. You have a lovely name and you use it. Don't allow people to call you stupid."

"Yes, lady."

Gaillarde, in her crumpled bliaut and patched wimple, was a dumpling-plump girl with placid eyes, a perfect full-moon face, and an air of unmistakable passivity, in marked contrast to Nova. But there was something similar about the two of them. A lack of ordinary tact, Sybille speculated. Or simply an insensitivity to ordinary feelings.

When she asked Gaillarde the place of her birth, she said she had no idea.

"And your mother? Your father?"

Gaillarde gave a blank smile. Sybille retreated. She murmured, "Well, well, it's no matter."

"Her mama," Nova said, "went up in smoke."

Sybille bit her lip, profoundly horrified at the lack of care with which Nova was choosing her words.

"That's right," Gaillarde was saying. She turned to Nova and waved her spoon cheerfully. "She burned up and blew away." Sybille heard Nova telling Gaillarde, "My mother was pretty lucky. They didn't burn her."

"Nova, you thought they did, you told me the friars got her and roasted her. You say my mama will never come for me, but I think you could be wrong about that."

"Don't start that again, Stupid," Nova said. "She was dead long ago. Didn't you see her burning?"

"Yes."

"Eyes don't lie. She's gone. High time you realized it. Now with my mama, there was some question."

"Question?"

"She was in prison, I told you. So then it's up to the friars. They can let you kick the bucket or burn you. Whatever they like." Nova swabbed her thumb along the rim of her bowl.

"Lady," Gaillarde asked, "did you try to escape?"

Sybille said she *had* escaped. That was the reason she was there.

"Oh, I thought you were pardoned. So you escaped. That's great." Lifting the bowl to her face, she swabbed it clean with long laps of the tongue. "Did your mother help you get away?"

Sybille was thunderstruck. What had her mother to do with it? She could not follow the girl's reasoning. Perhaps something was wrong with her mind. Finally she said, "No. My mother is dead, God rest her soul."

Gaillarde nodded; Nova said briskly, "Well, you can't live forever, can you?"

Sybille wondered in what auto-da-fé Stupid's mother had lost her life. She guessed it must have happened some years ago, if the girl did not know her own name. And had her father been burned as well? She dared not ask.

* * *

Spring retreated slowly at Montségur. The seasons behaved queerly up there. On Ascension Day, when it was already hot in the lowlands, Sybille's yard was bearded with frost. Olivier did not visit again. Good, she thought. We don't need you. You're not worth a handful of mud. But then the meadows turned the color of mossy emeralds, and bluebells sprouted from every crack in every rock, and the air suddenly tasted of spiced wine and lust. She was surprised to notice her bitterness thinning. Oh Jesus, why can't I rein my temper? Now I have driven him away for good. Truthfully speaking, she wondered why she was so eager to forget his cruelty. You're a hopeless fool, Sybille. These last months have been good. Why spoil it?

Every day but Sundays and holy days she sorted and washed the wool, and she worked from terce until sunset. After the shearing time in May, Nova would come home at midday and help for a half hour. Occasionally Sybille's neighbor two houses up the lane would work an hour, in exchange for a few poges, but Na Roqua had her baskets to make, and Sybille had never become fully comfortable around the woman. She was truly hideous to look upon. Her skin, at least every inch that showed, was red, burn-scarred, and puckered into folds. On her face there were no eyebrows or lashes. Na Roqua never referred to her appearance, indeed seemed oblivious and went about her business as calmly, and as cheerfully, as any other person. She is one of those people, Sybille mused, whose history is writ upon her own skin. There was no need to ask—she was a woman who had recanted at the eleventh hour and had been pulled from the fire. Nova, flippant as usual, said of her, "She should have made up her mind ten minutes earlier."

Summer came. It got hot, and Sybille began taking a nap at midday. The town was packed now. Countless multitudes of pilgrims trudged up to the castle of Montségur, and on the outskirts of town the meadows were white with tents. At cockcrow, the lines began snaking up the southwest slope like long, creeping vines. The sick were carried on muleback, and the mortally ill remained to die. The well gawked about and heard a sermon if they were lucky; all received a blessing, and then by sundown they came back to the village. Unlike pilgrims to Compostela or Rocamadour, they were given no cockleshell or relic, for the Good Christians disapproved of such nonsense.

On Whitsunday Sybille took Nova and Gaillarde up to the summit. They must be, she told them, the only ones in town who had never been there, and anyway it was a good reason for an excursion. But this was an excuse. She wanted to see Corba de Perella, wanted to and did not want to, which was why she had procrastinated all these months.

That morning, it was cool and clear. A storm had blown up during the night, blown up, broken, and floated noiselessly away, so that by noon the sun was almost blinding. The lower slopes were smeared with golden butterflies. Sounds of cowbells undulated from the pastures, and from a distant invisible valley came the tinklings of sheepbells, vibrating like harps, and the cries of shepherds hallooing their loneliness from hill to hill. Overhead, eagles were plunging black shadows against the blankness of the day sky. Gaillarde whispered, "Everyone is being so quiet. Is it forbidden to talk?"

Nova laughed. She was in a merrier mood than Sybille had seen for many weeks. She hopped along the steep road like a hungry squirrel. "This mountain," she said to Gaillarde, "is supposed to be a holy place. You don't talk in church, do you?"

Gaillarde squinted up at the castle. "That's a queer-looking church."

"It's a queer-looking castle," Nova snapped, and they fell silent.

They were both right, Sybille thought. The architecture of the double god's fortress looked like none she had ever seen, and she vaguely recalled Raymond de Perella telling her once the castle was many centuries old. It had been built, he said, by the Good Christians of ancient days, and the position of the walls related in some complicated way to the rising sun, but Raymond could not explain exactly how. Now, staring at the walls, she felt her skin begin to tingle; she had the eerie sensation that the wide world was dropping away and she was crossing the border of some silent kingdom where time held its breath. When she gazed downward, she felt as if she were standing on the topmost crown of the world. But she pushed away these thoughts and said to herself, What idiot would think to build in this spot? It leads nowhere, it overlooks nothing. Except other mountains. Some chatelain with a passion for solitude, obviously.

They passed a mule cart laden with long, flat crates. Lances, Sybille guessed. Or perhaps crossbow bolts. Abruptly Gaillarde fell back and tugged at Sybille's sleeve. They were broaching the main gateway; they stopped to stare in amazement. Nova pointed. "Holy Jesus, look at that!" she shouted, and Sybille warned her to keep her voice down.

The archway was almost two yards across, wider even than the Narbonne gate in Toulouse, and it had no portcullis, no protecting tower of any kind. You could walk right in.

"What's that?" asked Gaillarde.

"A gate, Stupid," Nova said.

"It doesn't look like a gate."

"Don't worry, you can trust me. If I say it's a gate, it's a gate." She marched into the yard where fat doves were pecking, and Sybille and Gaillarde followed.

"We shall drink to our children," Corba said. "May they live and be happy when this war is over."

They were sipping clear white wine, sitting in a bare corner room on the upper floor of the keep. Turning, Sybille asked when this was supposed to happen, since she had heard the Inquisition had resumed after Lady's Day.

Corba leaned forward on the bench. She was neatly dressed in a gown of superior linen and kept tucking a long stray tendril into her wimple. She had the same sweet, womanly face, but her brown hair was flecked with silver now. "Doesn't Olivier keep you informed?" she asked.

"No," Sybille said. The sudden mention of Olivier's name unnerved her. She had been trying to tell Corba she had no contact with him, but as yet had not done so.

"Pierre-Roger?"

"Who?" Sybille shook her head.

"My son-in-law."

"I've not met him, alas." She was still struggling to orient herself; she remembered Corba's eldest daughter as a small child but had trouble imagining Philippa a grown woman, married to this Pierre-Roger de Mirepoix, who was apparently the garrison commander at Montségur. Corba's two younger daughters Sybille knew not at all, and she was surprised to hear of her having a son, Jordan, only five. The afternoon had been stuffed with a confusion of names and faces.

Corba sipped at her wine. "Imbert de Salas? Bérenger de Lavelanet?" Sybille, throwing up one hand, was becoming slightly impatient with Corba, who talked at top speed. "They are friends of Olivier's."

The names sounded familiar but not from any conversation with Olivier. It was Pons, at Cantal, who had spoken of Pierre-Roger and the others. And it was Daniel, at Garrigues' Garden. These were people her silence had protected.

Corba said, "I don't want to be too specific about their business. But I'm sure I don't need to be. You get my meaning, don't you?" A glint sparkled in her eyes.

Sybille got to her feet. She put the cup on a chest. "I know nothing of these matters. Because I work all day. Because I mind my own business. Because I've not seen Olivier in years and—"

Corba de Perella cleared her throat. "But he told me you were living in the village. He said you'd had a child together, yes and both of you would come to see me, but you never did. I couldn't understand it. I assure you, he talks of you whenever I see him. What was I to think?"

Sybille went to stand by the window. Glancing over the ledge, she saw there was nothing down there but air, and she reached out to clutch at the shutters. The floor seemed to rock beneath her. What a dangerous place to live, she thought. I would not wish to be up here, scraping the clouds with my head. What if one toppled out? She turned back to Corba. "You are at peace, my friend?" she said.

"This mountain is peace. I'm a free woman, with my lord husband, my children, my blessed mother. What more can I want? What can hurt me here?" She smiled a wide, beautiful smile. "Nothing. I'll sit up here where heaven and earth meet, and when the war ends I'll return to my house in Toulouse and give a great feast for my children and grandchildren. And then, when I have no further use for the things of this evil world, I'll withdraw and take the robe as my lady mother has done."

Sybille smiled mechanically but made no comment. Corba believed the war would end; she sounded confident, hopeful. But it was not ending, she thought, and that is the horror. People keep waiting for the day—they talk about it, imagine the circumstances, the date, the weather, the feasts they will hold. Then she sighed to herself because she thought, The irony is, it has ended several times. Didn't it end after Simon de Montfort's death? After the treaty of Meaux? But it always started up again. So it was never really over. The crusaders went home but they returned; the Preaching Friars came, left, returned, and now to imagine they would disappear one day was the biggest delusion of all. So the hope of an end was a mirage that kept disappearing and reappearing, like a speck on the horizon that got smaller and smaller.

The filament of sunlight on the wood floor faded. Sybille, eager to feel solid earth under her feet, became restless and spoke of leaving, but Corba insisted she first call on her aged mother, and Sybille had no choice but to assent.

With Nova and Gaillarde, she straggled down the cliff just below the fortress, where a number of noble robed ladies were living in huts huddled against the rock. Marquésia de Lantar might have been a queen. About her flowed an aura of extreme dignity and strength. Paradoxically, she did not look strong because her body had shriveled into the folds of her gown and her face resembled a November leaf, crisped and dusty-thin, in danger of imminent desiccation. But this fragility only enhanced the impression of strength and regality. No one could approach her without experiencing the urge to bow deeply. Nova and Stupid fell silent in her presence and sat on the threshold of her hut, holding their breaths.

With violet-marbled hands Na Marquésia poured water into wooden cups, and Sybille passed them around. The old woman smiled at the girls, studying them. At last she said, "You are lovely young women. It gives me joy to look upon you."

Eyes downcast, Nova and Gaillarde seemed afraid to speak. After a moment, Nova mumbled timidly, "Thank you, holy lady," and puckered her mouth shut.

Sybille, nervous, sat down near Corba's mother. This shelf of rock was making her feel even more dizzy than the castle above. It was gusty and unprotected, with no fence to hold back the wind.

"You are living in Fanjeaux?" Na Marquésia was asking her.

"No," Sybille said swiftly. "The friars took Cantal."

"Ah." She smiled. "Rue St. Bernard."

"No, lady. They took everything. We live in the village here." When Na Marquésia nodded, Sybille could think of nothing further to say.

"Life is a mixture of pain and awe. Do you still write?"

When Sybille said she had neither the time nor the parchment, Marquésia offered to supply the parchment but said Sybille must find the time. She repeated the word "must." Sybille did not want to talk about her work. In the silence that followed, Na Marquésia turned her gaze on Nova, who was biting her nails. "You must encourage your lady mother."

"I can't," Nova protested, like a child. "I know nothing about verse. I don't even like it."

Marquésia asked why not, and Nova, diffident, spoke of economics: She did not believe in words. You could not eat them or wear them, or use them to cover your head when it snowed, and they were therefore without value for her. She defended her ideas with assurance.

Saddened, Sybille watched Nova from the tail of her eye. Probably she was right. Can words be trusted? Should they be? It was growing late and she was thinking of making their farewells when Marquésia spoke again. She directed her words to Nova.

"It is the poets, not the chroniclers, who remember. Chroniclers lie. This has always been so." Nova stared out the door. "The poet bears witness to despair. This too has always been true."

Nova turned and began to say, "My mama—" but bit her lower lip. A look passed between the old woman and the young one.

"Your lady mother has seen what they have done. She must write." Marquésia hesitated, still staring at Nova. "If not her," she asked quietly, "then who?"

Nova stared back at the old woman but said nothing more, and five minutes later they were on the path to the village, walking quickly in the June twilight. They did not speak until they reached the elm in the main square, and then Sybille heard Gaillarde ask Nova, "What does that mean—bear witness?"

Nova glanced over, frowning slightly. "You like leek soup?"

"I like it fine."

"Come eat with us."

"All right."

On Sybille's bed that night, when she lay down in the light of the hearth, there was a flat brown packet tied up with cord. She sat up and turned it over in her hands, mystified as she could be. She called out softly to her daughter to ask where this parcel had come from.

"I don't know." Nova yawned.

Sybille clucked impatiently at the lie. Why could she never get a civil answer from the girl? "Nova," she said severely, "what is this?"

"Something I saved. It belongs to you."

"Mine?"

"Yes. From Cantal."

So Sybille unwrapped the package and discovered all the verse she had saved, from her previous forty-two years.

But it was Marquésia de Lantar and her gift of parchment who made it possible for her to record the poems composed at Garrigues' Garden. She picked at them like scabs, then changed her mind and left them as they had been originally conceived.

The shepherds came down from their summer pastures for the harvest feast. Sunburned as the autumn earth, they mingled with the townsfolk and pilgrims, and the streets echoed with laughter and the sounds of vielles. By sundown, when the trees blazed with torches and the cobbles seemed transmuted to gold, everyone was drunk. Except Philippe Cervel, who did not observe the Devil's holidays and shut himself in his workshop. Sybille followed Nova and Gaillarde through the crowds to the square, taking care to let them be alone with their young friends. They joined a game of hot cockles and she went on, lured by the sound of fiddles. Near the elm, she climbed on a bench to watch a jongleur singing one of William the Troubadour's songs:

> I'll write a song about nothing.
> Not about myself or other people
> nor about love or youth
>   nor of anything else;
> It just came to me one day
>   while I was sleeping on my horse.

A boy came up and shoved a cup into Sybille's hand. From Nova, he shouted, and she thanked him without turning her head. Her body was breathing with the rhythm of the strings. For a moment she lost herself.

After the fiddler had stopped, she stayed up there sipping the wine. It was raw and stripped her throat. Above the heads she picked out her daughter, caught her eye, waved. A minute later, a hand tugged at her skirt, and she heard someone calling her name. She glanced down. The boy was standing in the shadows, smiling at her. She nodded faintly, and he fretted her skirt again.

"What is it?"

He held up a cup. "More wine, lady?" he asked.

"I'll be drunk," Sybille told him. "I have work to do tomorrow." Her tone made it clear he should run along and join his friends.

"What does it matter?" He laughed. "Tonight is tonight."

She did not take the cup but gazed out over the heads of the crowd and waited for the dancers to start up. A woman in balloon trousers plastered to sweaty thighs held up her cymbals and sprang into the air. The music, indigo hot and sensuous, fizzed up. When Sybille next looked down, she was surprised to see the boy still standing there, watching her.

"All summer I've been wretched," the boy called cheerfully.

Startled, she answered without thinking. "Why?"

"I've been up in the passes."

"What's wrong with that?"

"Men and sheep." He made a face, and they both laughed.

Torchlight slicked his hair; it spooled like threads of black silk from the crown of his head to a place slightly above his shoulders. Sybille dropped to the cobbles alongside him. He stood a head taller than she did. Now she could see that his two eyes were as dark as his hair. His shirt was pleated and embroidered with tiny rosettes the color of blood. It was immaculate and smelled of soap. This one is his mother's young darling, she thought. He took the empty cup from her hand so that their fingers touched and replaced it with the one he had been holding, and she said nothing. Slowly she began to swirl the dark liquid in her mouth. She listened to him talking. He was the son of a sheep farmer whose flock numbered over a thousand. That makes his father very prosperous indeed, she thought. He told her he had spent the summer with one of his father's foremen and eight shepherds in a *cabane* up in the mountains and had learned to make cheese. He had had to share his bed with two others.

Listening, Sybille finished the wine. When he paused once, she asked his name.

"Jean-Pierre Constant," he told her. His father sold wool to Philippe Cervel. Which was how he had come to know Nova.

"How many years are you?" Sybille asked.

"Twenty-two. On St. Boniface's Day."

"How wonderful. To be so young and—"

He cut her off before she could finish. "Lady, I feel old," he said in an annoyed tone. "In three years I'll be twenty-five. That's very old." He sighed loudly.

Under her breath she laughed. The idea of being twenty-five distressed him; he had no concept of thirty or forty. After a few minutes she began to weave through the crowd, winding toward the winestall to leave the cup. She knew he was behind her, even though he had stopped talking. She put the cup on the counter and turned to the boy.

"I won six deniers dicing," he said and grinned.

"Well, I guess you're lucky." Sybille smiled. "Lucky in money, unlucky in love." He did not get the joke.

"Let me buy you a pasty."

"I don't think so."

"A honey cake?"

"It's time to go home," she said, avoiding his eyes.

"But it's early."

"Early for you, late for me." She moved away; Jean-Pierre Constant stayed at her side, his fingers webbed so lightly on her sleeve that she barely felt them. They started across the square. By matins the drunks would be snoring on the chipped cobbles. Once they reached the candler's shop, she stopped to face him. "Go back and drink," she said, pointing to the elm. A woman with a sleeping child in her arms jostled them.

"No, I want to stay with you."

"I'm tired. You're not. Your friends are waiting for you."

"You can be my friend. I like you."

Her laugh rang out sharp in the cool air. *IlikeyouIwanttosleepwithyou.* No, that was another man. Did all men use the same words? She asked Jean-Pierre, "What kind of a remark was that?"

He shrugged in surprise, either real or feigned. Sybille could not tell. He said, "What do you mean?"

"Come now. You're my daughter's generation. I'm my daughter's mother." They left the square behind and began to advance down Rue Château, but she was careful to go slowly so she would not lose him in the crowd. When he did not answer, she continued: "You know what I'm talking about."

"I know." He rubbed one hand over his chin, then said mournfully, "You want me to go away."

She looked squarely at him. He had young skin. "And you? You want to walk with an old woman when you could be with youngsters?" She smiled at him, and he smiled back at her.

He asked earnestly, "How old are you, lady?"

She smiled again and turned her face away. Tell him, tell him, she said to herself. Put an end to this nonsense. Ah Sybille, you are a bigger old fool than you imagined. What good can come of a sin like this? Think of the boy's mother. Who is probably younger than you. Instead, she said to him, "Laddie, don't ask women such questions. They don't like it." She could feel the tightness in her voice. When she turned into her lane, she decided, I will let him stay only until we reach my gate. After all, what is the harm in walking with him? He is only an overfriendly child. A mama's boy, no doubt. Or virgin.

"You like living in the mountains?" the boy asked.

"Oh, it's all right," said Sybille and walked slower. She liked the lowlands with its storms of molten light, its white-hot skies. No, she did not like the mountains. Now they were passing Na Roqua's house. Well, when they came to her gate, she would go inside and lie down to sleep, and he would go back to the square and drink wine with his friends, perhaps even with her daughter. And then at dawn, very drunk, he would go home to his mother. She wondered, Can he be thinking what I am thinking? Certainly not. This elation she felt was only the pathetic dreamings of an old woman whose flesh continues, alas, to gnaw deeply. And inappropriately. Coming down the lane toward them were a man and woman, and the man had his hand in the nook of her hip, possessive.

They had reached her yard, and she curved in without stopping or speaking to Jean-Pierre Constant. When we get to the door I'll send him away, she promised herself. She listened to him breathing behind her.

"This is a nice little house," he said.

"The roof leaks." He's so young, she thought.

"I'm sorry. I'm sorry your roof leaks."

She pushed open the door and stepped inside. He was still right behind her, and she could hear him shutting the door. In the warm darkness she turned to stare at him. His fingers silently touched her cheek. Her lungs filled with happiness. What if he is young? she thought. So she bruised her mouth hot against his.

"Put your arms around me," she said.

"I can't sleep like that."

"Why not?"

Jean-Pierre did not say anything.

"Then how must you sleep?"

"Only on my stomach," he told her. "Or I'm awake all night."

She rasped unhappily, "Oh, in that case—"

"Please, lady. Don't be angry."

"That's all right," she sighed. "If you must sleep on your stomach, you must. We shall not speak of it further." She lay alone, arms at her sides, and was careful to hold herself still. Someone was thrashing up and down the lane, sculpting the night with curses. "Kiss my heretic ass, you prick-faced priest, kiss my ass." Over and over. A crazy, Sybille said to herself, and did not think twice about it. She thought, All right, I can't get even the smallest things from men, and I don't ask much either. But even so, I'm lucky this boy is here. I must not expect too much. Men are all right if you do not ask anything of them, or want them to love you, or show them you love them. She remembered Olivier and the nakedness of his hunger for her and the way his breath was always so short before she gave herself to him. But then she had pleated her love into *Ieu Sui* and he had said, "What has this got to do with me?"

The boy was asleep now, sprawled face down, breathing steadily. Men, she decided, are not the same as other people. One thing I have never gotten from a man is love. This boy's body is hairless, his flesh hard under my fingers as half-green peaches on St. John's Day, and this awes me but he will not love me either. I have no illusions with this one. Suddenly the door opened and Nova came clopping across the floor. Sybille pretended to be asleep. Nova went into her corner and pulled the curtain. After a while it was quiet again.

Sybille remembered those long-ago June days when Simon de Montfort's troops were whirling heads across the ramparts. Folco was dead by then. The gun was hers. Bel Vezer, she had called it, and prettied it with a bright-blue ribbon. This youth at her side had been a boy of four when Bel Vezer had crushed Simon de Montfort's head into a thousand bleeding pieces. Just as she was trying to remember Olivier's face that summer, she fell asleep.

At daybreak he looked at her with sleep-filmed, sullen eyes. When she asked what was wrong, he was tongue-tied. He began wrenching on his shirt.

"I feel sick at my stomach," he said at last, not looking at her.

"Yes. Too much wine."

"And my left shoulder hurts me," Jean-Pierre grunted. "I've not slept well all week."

She tried to give him bread and milk, but he refused them.

"I must go home."

"Of course," Sybille agreed.

"I must see my father."

"Of course. You can eat first, can't you?"

He was not hungry.

"Take bread with you and eat later on the road."

He would not be hungry later either.

She sat down slowly at the trestle. The lad is eager to leave me, she thought, and the reality of this hurt her. Now it's daylight, he can see I'm old and he is sorry. She said gently, "Then run along. God be with you."

Once she had said that, he brightened. "If it pleases you, lady, I can come back some other day."

She hesitated. "Very well."

"When?"

"Sunday."

He nodded cheerily. Coming to her, he bent to kiss her mouth. Then he trotted to the door and headed out. Sybille sat there with her head masked between her hands. Behind the curtain, Nova was crinkling her clothes. Maybe this is a blessing, Sybille thought. If this boy were perfect and I truly loved him, he would cause me much grief.

Nova was taking a long time dressing. She will be late to En Philippe, Sybille thought. About the time she decided to tell her this, Nova emerged. Her face was cheesy white.

"How are you?" Sybille asked.

"Bad."

"Merry nights, sad mornings."

Nova neither replied nor looked at her. Then, without warning, she said to Sybille, "He could be your son." Her tone was freezing.

"Yes," Sybille agreed. "You're right."

"He could be my lover." With this, Nova turned toward the door, apparently planning to make a swift departure.

But just as swiftly Sybille got up and barred her way. She stood with her chin thrust grandly into the air. "Not everyone is a saint," she said. "You think I'm disgusting. I suppose you are right. Mayhap even I find myself a bit disgusting. Well, I won't argue with you. But he pleases me and I prefer to think of him as a gift from God."

Nova flared, "You don't believe in God."

Sybille let that pass and went on. "Yes, as a gift from God. And since God has never done me a favor before, I've decided to show my appreciation by accepting His gift." To herself she added, "God owes me."

Nova stood watching her with an incredulous look about her mouth, as if her mother were a stranger.

"You'd better go. Do you want to eat on your way?" Sybille asked.

"Yes, please," said Nova and went to the trestle. She nicked off a chunk of bread and a piece of hard cheese and put all this in her sleeve.

"Would you mind asking En Philippe how many bushels he has for me this week, or tell him I still have two left and they'll be ready tomorrow. He can decide what to give me."

In a few minutes Nova was gone. When Jean-Pierre Constant came into the yard late Sunday afternoon, Nova, by the window, called out to her mother, "Here's your marzipan," and gave her a look, amused and sweet as sugar candy. He had with him six or eight bright-colored marbles, which he showed to Sybille and she admired them. It was a warm, sunny day, the yard slippery with amber and orange leaves, like a Moorish tapestry. She took a bowl to the corner and then down Rue Château, but the dairywoman had no fresh milk to sell, and she started back, walking slowly. Na Roqua was sitting outside her house; her old goat, usually tied in the yard, had wandered into the lane. When Sybille shooed him home, Na Roqua said walls were thin and tongues wagged easily. Sybille said, alas, for he was a fine boy. Balls as firm as two Bordeaux plums. Na Roqua said the *consolamentum* wiped out all sins at death, so she may as well enjoy herself.

In the yard Nova and the boy had scratched a circle in the dusty leaves and were kneeling over the marbles. Sybille went inside to slice turnips for the soup. After an hour she looked out and saw they were still playing. Their expressions were rapt, at least the boy's was. When she called to them, Nova got up, but the boy did not stir. After she had called a second time, he came inside but she saw he would rather have stayed with the marbles. Under her breath she laughed in irritation but tried to conceal it. While he was drinking the soup, he talked excitedly about one of the marbles.

"You can't get those kind anymore," he said, clicking them in his palms. "They were made before the war."

Sybille buttered his bread for him. Nova asked where he had acquired his fancy marbles. From his mama, he answered happily. He had five younger brothers and sisters, but she did not buy them marvelous presents. He told them he fought plenty with his brothers and sisters, even sometimes with his father, but never with his mama; he loved her. Sybille, bored, only half listened. After a while Nova said she was going to visit Stupid, if Sybille would not mind. Sybille did not.

Jean-Pierre came around the trestle and sat next to her. There was a slight bulge under his breeches, she noticed. He nuzzled her ear, affectionate as a young cat, then kissed her mouth hard. Fumbling, she pried the marbles from his cupped fist and laid them on the trestle without looking.

"Really, this is silly," she whispered against his ear. "You are too young for me."

"Yes." He went on kissing her. After a moment he stopped and looked at her. "Are you worried?"

She nodded, pensive.

"Cheer up." He grinned at her. "There's nothing we can do about it, is there?"

He could do something; he could find a girl his own age. "I guess not." She smiled at him.

He tipped up her chin. "Lady," he said politely, "do you want to lie with me now?"

Later, beneath the coverlet, she understood why Nova had associated him with candy. He was as satisfying as a confection. Nova was being disrespectful, of course. But now Sybille repeated the name: Marzipan. It suited him perfectly.

Each Sunday, the marzipan appeared in the yard with his marbles. He played with his toys, ate supper, got into bed with Sybille at sundown, and went back to his mother the next morning. It became part of the week's routine, like washday.

Advent came. Winter winds tattered the flimsy plank walls of her house. The flat roof sank below a lip of snow. Far above the town, Montségur reared its ghostly humps. One evening just before Christmas, Nova mentioned that Olivier and another knight had stopped at En Philippe's shop. They were camped on the road to Morency, near the communal dairy farm.

For two days Sybille waited, hoping Olivier would come to her. Her mind tumbling with indecision, she finished drying a bushel of wool, baked an onion pie, started a poem about Douce, washed her hair, and refrained from questioning Nova, even though the questions were poised at the tip of her tongue. On the third night after supper, she decided Olivier had no intention of coming. She put on her cloak and told Nova she was going to visit Na Roqua.

"It's beginning to snow again," Nova said. "You should wear boots. Here." She got the boots and brought them to her mother.

Sybille had no trouble locating the camp, since it was the only one near the dairy farm. When she was still some distance off, she could see the tents and a bonfire splattering showers of bluish-orange sparks into the evening sky. At her approach the men squatting around the fire turned to stare, then one of them, who was fat, stood and walked out of the orange circle, unsteady. She hung back.

"Lady?" He was chewing on some kind of meat. He did not bow to her.

"Where is Olivier de Ferrand?"

He looked at her with curiosity. "Olivier? I'll fetch him." He turned around and sauntered into the largest of the tents.

Sybille leaned against a lone beech. If Olivier had loved her, she would not have been forced to degrade herself with the marzipan. It is his fault, she thought. That she, Sybille d'Astarac, could be thrown on her back by a good-looking child was what loving Olivier had brought her. The air was cloudy with smoke and snowflakes. Winter in Montségur. It would be like this until the middle of May, and there was nothing she could do about it. She watched Olivier step from the tent and squint. When he spotted her, he scuffed forward, and so did she, all her nerves screaming. He smiled at her and said, "Hello there, lady. It looks like you have a friendly expression on your face." He stooped, brushing a cold-warm mouth against her lips.

"Should it be unfriendly?" she managed to say calmly, even though the first words from his mouth had been deliberately provocative.

Olivier laughed. "It was spiky as a two-edged blade last time we met. I remember it quite well. A man could die from an expression like that one." He seemed pleased to see her, but with Olivier she never knew for certain. He offered a handful of walnuts. She shook her head, staring past him at the men sitting around the fire. Before she had a chance to ask about his companions, he was saying, "I thought of visiting you."

Sybille asked him what had stopped him.

"I was waiting," he said, studying her face.

For what? she wanted to know.

"To gauge the level of your anger," he said pleasantly.

Sybille could think of no comment. She watched the men's silhouettes fringed against the firelight. They were talking quite loudly, but the wind whirled their voices in the opposite direction. She looked up at Olivier. "You're looking well, my lord," she said in a small voice. "How are you?"

"The same." He gnashed a walnut between his teeth and spat the shell into the snow.

The same, she repeated to herself. That meant she should expect nothing, only more of what he had always given her. Her shoulders sank under her cloak. Turning her face toward the woods, she struggled to strain the bite from her speech. "Something has to be done about Nova," she said at last.

"She's all right."

"It's time she was wed. Perhaps you know of some knight—"

He broke in, bored, "I have no time for matchmaking."

Hearing that, she backed away a few steps. Damn him, she thought angrily. He has time for his cronies, none for his daughter. But she mastered her anger, and when she faced him once more, she had made her expression agreeable. She asked, waveringly, "Would you care to visit me?"

He threw her a glance, which she read as significant. "That depends."

"On what?"

"You, lady. On whether you're reasonable."

Cheeks flushing, she stared down at her boots. A wet wind was bunching her skirt around her ankles. She knew he was looking at her. Is he going to tear holes in me again? she cried silently.

"Sybille, I never hurt you." He said it gravely, as if he believed it.

His easy lies. She could not help groaning aloud. "It felt like pain to me," she replied.

"You felt wrong."

Straightening her back, she looked up at him, eyes steady on his face. His hair had thinned, thinned and faded, and there were white streaks along each temple. "Please come see me. I've missed you."

After a silence of some thirty seconds, he tilted his head. "Very well." She smiled. "Sunday. At sundown."

"Not Sunday," she said hastily and looked away. "Tomorrow."

"Well, all right. I guess I can come tomorrow."

They stood awkwardly, familiar strangers having nothing to say.

"Farewell," she said, suddenly excited.

"Bye-bye."

She trudged back to town. It was so quiet. The road was dark and the snow began dancing down in waves, wet, perishable. *Bye-bye.* Olivier had never learned to say farewell like a grown man. It was past compline when she reached the house. Nova was kneeling at the hearth, toasting a slice of bread, scorching it.

"I've been to see your lord father," Sybille announced. "He's supposed to visit tomorrow night." There was a hesitancy in her voice that invited backtalk, so she added in a firmer tone, "I invited him."

Silence. Nova cleared her throat. "You—what?"

Sybille shrugged. She shed her wet cloak and hung it near the fire. Avoiding her daughter's eyes, she went to her bed and put her back to Nova. She heard her say, "You're a fool."

Everyone can't be smart, she thought. "Don't be impertinent," she told her and stripped to her shift. She slid under the coverlet, thinking of Olivier and tomorrow night. I can do it, she thought. I can be with him a few hours and then say farewell. He can't hurt me now. I know everything about him, and he knows everything about me. He is hopeless, and since I know that, how can he hurt me? Then she laughed at the cunning way she gave herself permission to deceive herself. Oh, you are truly remarkable, Na Sybille; you'll go to your grave trying to convince yourself that cursed man loves you. She opened her eyes. The fire had gone out and Nova had gone to bed. After a while she closed her eyes.

Olivier sat at the trestle gulping down cup after cup of wine. Sybille shuttled between the table and the hearth, trying to drink along with him and poach a plaice and start a sauce. She had made a special effort for this reunion. The house had been scrubbed and the baskets of wool pushed against the wall. The fish was dear, as was the Spanish wine. At the far end of the trestle, darning her hose, Nova ignored her father.

Olivier called to Sybille, "Where's supper?"

"Soon," she said, careful to keep her voice neutral. "There is nothing to be gained by hurrying a mustard sauce." With a fork she poked at the plaice in its broth and tasted it. Not yet. Olivier's impatience was making her uncomfortable.

Nova said to him placidly, "Are you in a rush?"

"No," he said.

Over her shoulder, Sybille called out cheerfully, "Your father is a busy person. He doesn't care so much about food."

"There's your bitter tongue again," Olivier shot at her back, and she wheeled around, shocked at his touchiness.

When she protested she had intended no offense, he raised his hand to interrupt. "Don't try to honey it over. Another person would have said, 'Your lord father must be very hungry.' That's what you should have said. But you always spoil things." He directed his eyes to Nova. "She might have asked you to help serve me." He refilled his cup quickly.

Nova let a minute go by, then said, "Begging your pardon, but this isn't the Château de Pamiers and you're not the count of Foix."

"Peace!" Sybille yelled.

Looking up sharply, Olivier said to Nova, "I see you've got your mother's mouth."

"My mama works hard. Why don't you help her?"

"Yes, yes. Well, who's the guest here? Guests wait to be served. You could be pleasant to me, you know. I don't sit at your table very often."

"And whose fault is that?"

Olivier protested, "Nobody invited me. If I'd gotten an invitation to sup, I would have come." He sounded sincerely indignant.

Nova burst out laughing and went to stand beside her mother at the hearth. She nudged her and whispered, disgusted, "The Prince of Misrule here—what a pain in the ass."

"Shh." She thought, If I don't botch this, Nova will. She measured a cup of ale and poured it slowly into the mustard.

"Let me look at you, missy," Olivier called to Nova. He tapped his cup on the trestle top, but she did not turn. "Come over here. You're getting fat." He went on teasing his daughter, and when Sybille, tight-lipped, threw him warning glances, he ignored her. After five minutes Nova bumped to the wall hooks and snatched her cloak.

Sybille called to her, "We're going to eat in a minute."

"I'm not hungry."

"Nova! Where are you going?"

"Out." She slammed the door behind her.

Sybille said nothing, only sighed deeply over the saucepan. The girl could not tolerate teasing and Olivier should know better. While she carried the plaice to the trestle, he filled up their cups again and they began to eat at last.

Olivier spooned mustard sauce over his fish. "That snot-nose girl must be hard to live with," he said without raising his eyes.

"Don't call her names."

"She's mine too. I can call her whatever I like."

"She's not happy," Sybille said.

"Who is?" He dipped bread into the sauce, raised it to his lips, and sucked his fingers. He ate rapidly. Already half the fish on his platter was gone; there was no sense trying to keep up with him. "This is good," he said after a while.

"I'm pleased to hear that," Sybille answered. His table manners were still awful.

"Raymond Trencavel's plan is getting hot," Olivier told her.

"Plan? What plan?" This was news to her.

He stared. "Why, to rule Carcassonne again. Don't you know what's going on in the world? Of course the count can't help him directly. But Trencavel has plenty of followers. Every *faidit* will fight for him, everyone in the Sault district, the lord of Termes—"

She asked, "Do these men have money?" She sipped at her wine. "It takes livres tournois to fight a war. I've heard it said Trencavel hasn't a sou and King James gives him nothing but women and good Spanish wine."

Olivier laughed. "I tell you, when the time is ripe, he will have a thousand *faidits* with their swords and that will be enough."

Wiping his platter clean with bread, Olivier began talking of his friends, none of whom sounded impressive to Sybille. They were small-beer barons. Finally she asked if these companions of his were heretics.

He supposed so.

"Isn't that dangerous?" He shrugged. "Olivier, have you turned heretic?"

"Boobies." He laughed mockingly and refilled his cup. "Namby-brained dreamers. They have big enough holes between their ears, you could piss in them."

Reaching for the plaice, he scraped the rest of it on to his platter and put the dish back empty. So much for Nova's dinner, Sybille sighed to herself. Her gaze went to the hearth, to the baskets of fleece along the wall, back to the hearth. All evening the subject of Garrigues' Garden had been perched on her tongue; all evening she had forced herself quiet, thinking she must say nothing to agitate Olivier. But that was exactly what she proceeded to do. She began telling him about Daniel Marty, careful to present her experiences in general terms. Immediately she felt Olivier's withdrawal, but she plowed on just the same, unconsciously editing the most painful details. For some reason, he did not exhibit the reaction she expected. He seemed bored. After fifteen or twenty minutes, he asked if she had any apples, he felt like eating something sweet. She left the trestle without speaking and went to get the apples. When she returned, she said nothing more about the Preaching Friars. Olivier was gazing around the room. He glanced at the baskets and wrinkled his nose.

"That wool stinks up the whole place," he said.

"Yes. I'm accustomed to it now."

"En Philippe pays you fairly?"

"I told you, I get by." She had propped her chin on her fist and was watching him consume the apple. He had started at the bottom and was working his way up, chewing the core and seeds along with the pulp. The silence went on a long time. After he had finished three apples, she said quietly, "Have we nothing to talk about?"

"We never did," he murmured. "I'm not a skilled conversationalist but you never noticed. You were too busy talking."

She laughed at that and said, "I noticed. That and other things. I noticed you're not good with women—you don't know how to treat them."

"I'm an animal," he said, quick and flat.

She said perhaps he was right.

"Think of me as an animal. You can't expect anything from an animal."

She tilted more wine into her cup, drinking it as if it were water. "You snarl and try to tear me to pieces, and when I defend myself you say I'm unfair, I'm being cruel to you!"

"Lady, I never tried to injure you. I never treated you badly."

Didn't he? She smiled wearily.

"I am what I am. How can I be blamed for that? You can't help being what you are either."

Who says so? She smiled again, as if she understood and accepted his words as true. But the smile was a mask, to conceal her helplessness. He was so blind. He could not, would not, see that people are held accountable for their actions. All Olivier could do was deny, as though cause and effect was a law to which he had been granted immunity.

"I can't be a lady's truelove," Olivier went on. "You can invent one on parchment, Sybille. You did. In that *canso* you once wrote for me."

"*Ieu Sui.*"

"Yes, *Ieu Sui.* Little Lord Jesus! No such man exists. Really, Sybille."

"Hmm," Sybille said, which meant if none existed, he should.

The door swung open and Nova clopped into the house, still sulky. As she loped past her father, he slapped her bottom. "Don't!" she squealed. Olivier grinned at her back. Sybille watched her get the wool shears and sit at the hearth snipping raggedy ends from her hair. She had her back to Sybille and Olivier and did not speak to them. In the silence Sybille was waiting for him to rise and get his cloak, but he did not. He belched. Since she could not bear the thought of his leaving, she prayed he would do it quickly, get it over with. She stared into his eyes, into kisses in Corba's bedchamber high above the cloister of Daurade. Then she noticed Olivier pouring wine from his cup into hers, just a small gesture but it touched her.

Without saying good night, Nova went to her sleeping corner and drew the curtain. Sybille could hear her moving about, then it was quiet. Olivier said, "Soon it will be compline." She nodded. "Cold out even for a dog."

She held her breath. As yet he had not touched her, had kept the width of the trestle between them. Abruptly she got up, moved around to him, sank on his lap, slipping one arm over his shoulder. He burst out, "If I get into your bed, I'm not getting up. You're not going to lie with me and throw me into the cold like the others." He sounded angry and jealous.

Sybille gave a surprised laugh. "Are you asking to sleep here?"

"It's not a request—it's a proclamation."

She murmured above his ear, "I had hoped you would stay."

Immediately he said, "Don't start hoping," yet he said it gently.

She rose; he pulled off his boots. She cleared the trestle; he undressed and crawled into her bed, pulling up the coverlet just as if he slept there every night. Ten minutes later, when she joined him, he reached out and glued his body against hers. The house was still. Behind the curtain, Nova groaned in her sleep, sailing voyages of her secret heartaches.

Against Sybille's hair, Olivier said, "My teeth have been hurting."

"Gums or teeth?"

"Both."

"Did you try a poultice?"

"In Barcelona I saw this surgeon, some bloody Moor. Oh, woe is me! What a collection of torture instruments! Scrapers, files, some ghastly thing for pulling teeth."

"Ah, did it hurt?"

"Good heavens!" he sputtered in the darkness. "Do you think I let him? Do you think I'm a half-wit? He dipped a sponge in hemlock and wanted me to sniff it. 'I'll put you to sleep,' he said. I told him, 'Fuck your sponge, I'm too young to go to sleep.' "

"And your teeth still hurt? If it's your gums, a green salve is good."

"No, they're better now. Don't poke your knee in my belly—it hurts."

She flopped on her side; around her he spooned his long body, which was as soft and flat as her own, so she closed her eyes and fell into a light sleep. Early in the morning, before cockcrow, he awoke stiff and entered her without a word. Later she kissed Olivier's curls, the shaggy ones drooping at the base of his neck.

"A curl for every girl," he grunted.

"Don't be unkind now."

"I wasn't."

"You remind me of your lemans and say it's not unkind?"

"Lady, you've been with other men. I can tell."

The assertion hung between them under the coverlet. She did not want to deny or affirm it, and finally said smoothly, "You can't tell."

"You wriggle around more than you once did." He asked no questions, which she found curious. Then she reminded herself he had never desired her fidelity, only the opposite. Abruptly she got up and went to light a fire in the hearth to heat wine for his breakfast.

A half hour later, he was ready to go. "How long will you be in Montségur?" she asked, desperate to extract information.

"Don't know." As always, he was unwilling to reveal anything.

"What are you doing today?"

"What I usually do."

At the door, he turned to hug her. "Well, I have business." He added, "Not like some people who loll around all day writing verse."

She smiled at him. "That's right."

"Bye-bye."

She stayed in the doorway, watching him hurry down the lane. He did not glance back. She closed the door, still smiling.

Nova raised her face from her porridge. "You're in love again," she said gloomily.

Chapter Seventeen

For the fourth night the men camped in her yard and were drinking themselves to sleep. In Sybille's mind that spring was peaceful, although when peace resembles war it is foolish to make quick judgments. Raymond Trencavel's capture of Carcassonne had been shortly followed by his loss of Carcassonne, and the thirty-three priests murdered in the town's faubourg now seemed a questionable sin. Raymond of Toulouse, who had called the revolt premature, had chosen instead to observe his cousin's uprising without contributing a single siege engine, the old rivalries between their two houses not having been unlaced by time or catastrophe. He was obliged, nevertheless, to go up to Paris and have his knuckles rapped by Blanche, who made him promise to drive out the *faidits*.

Sybille stood behind the half-open shutter, trying to overhear Olivier and the knights whispering outside in the yard. They were his *faidit* friends, and to have him nearby she had to put up with them but she didn't like it. Or them. There was something about the knights, their predatory eyes, that made her think: They are hunting trouble.

The little yard was domed with pale, warm light, bright enough to see the four dark shapes lying down, the wooden cups and the wineskins, the evil glitter of the ax blades. The air smelled of apple blossoms in the trees. A horseman jigged up the lane, slowed as if he meant to stop, then rattled on toward Rue Château. Behind Sybille's back, Nova called out abruptly, "Why don't you go to bed?"

She turned away. "Too early," she whispered.

"Then why have you blown out all the candles. I thought you were going to work on the sestina tonight."

"Not so loud."

After a minute, Nova said, "What's Papa doing?"

"Drinking himself to death," she muttered.

"Still? Why—"

"Please keep quiet."

Nova kept quiet; Sybille listened. Earlier the wind had been slanting south, blurring some of their conversation, which mainly had concerned a new inquisitorial tour. It had not seemed especially important to Sybille. William Arnaud and Daniel Marty were making a circuit through the Lauraguais district. With them were the Franciscan Stephen de Saint-Thibéry, two or three friars, the archdeacon of Lézat (formerly a troubadour who wrote obscene verse), and several clerks and servants. So what, Sybille had thought. The Lauraguais is far from here. There was nothing remarkable about such tours. Last fall the Inquisitors had burned people at Lavaur and Saint-Paul de Caujoux, and nobody had marked it particularly. It had been small beer compared to the failure of the turnip harvest.

Now the wind had shifted direction, and outside the window every whisper was audible. The fat knight struggled to his feet and hobbled to the hedge. Sybille heard him urinating. When he came back, he lowered his bulk to the ground and said, "There is no armed escort, I tell you."

The knight with the wispy red beard, Pierre Laurens, laughed doubtfully. "They would be idiots to go around unguarded. They're not idiots." He flipped a wineskin toward the fat man.

"Oh well. Those whoresons may not be idiots. But they don't expect trouble either. Have they ever had trouble? They have not. I reckon they feel safe. Get my drift?"

"I guess so," sniffed Pierre Laurens.

"They think God protects them."

"I guess so," sniffed Pierre Laurens.

"Olivier," said the fat man. "My prong is boiling. What do you say we go plough some *cons*?"

"I say no," Olivier replied gruffly. "Do what you always do."

"I'll go blind."

There were giggles. Pigs, Sybille thought.

"We stay put," Olivier said. He sounded impatient.

"God's holy farts, we've been waiting four days."

"Four days is nothing. We'll wait four years if we have to."

There was silence. "Olivier," the fat man called again. "What if D'Alfaro can't find William."

"William's waiting at Bram. Don't bother me with these stupid questions."

Suddenly another voice squirted out of the darkness. It was shy young Giraud Massabrac, who had spent the last few days cozying up to Nova. He was a virgin, Sybille suspected, but ready to remedy the situation. "Well," he piped, "it seems to me everything is so vague."

"Vague to *you,*" Olivier grunted.

"To all of us."

"Giraud"—Sybille could see Olivier rubbing his nose in the moonlight—"Giraud, my dear little laddie, do you want to stay here?"

"What? No, my lord."

"Because there's nothing I'd like better. I'm telling you straight to your face. You give me trouble, I'll leave you home with the women. Got me?"

The others laughed, and the fat knight slapped his thigh. Giraud's head went down.

Sybille's ears were tingling. At first she had not understood half of what they had said, but now she realized some kind of raid was being planned. But from what she could gather about the operation, she was forced to agree with young Giraud. It—whatever "it" was— sounded immensely disorganized.

Pierre Laurens was pouring more wine. Sybille could see Olivier pulling off his boots. He threw them toward the pile of arms and stretched out on his back in a typical Olivier pose except he did not have his finger in his navel. What a waste of time, Sybille thought, eavesdropping on these fools. It must be nearly matins, and she could have been working on the sestina. Or sleeping. She was about to turn away when she heard Giraud say slowly, "Is the count going to be there?" and she realized she had been missing the point all along, this was not merely some half-cocked scheme of Olivier's.

Olivier hissed, "Keep your voice down, you fool. It's too danger-ous for him to show his face. But D'Alfaro has all the instructions. It's up to us now."

The rings on the fat knight's podgy hands gleamed in the moon-light. He swigged at a wineskin, drained it, threw it over his shoulder. Pigs! Sybille thought again. Nova will have to clean the yard tomorrow. Now they were going on about this man D'Alfaro: D'Al-faro was hotheaded, he could not keep a secret; no, D'Alfaro *could* keep a secret but he lacked intelligence and nerve.

Raymond d'Alfaro, as everyone knew, was the count's nephew; his mother had been the old count's bastard daughter. For five or six years now, he had been his uncle's bailiff at Avignonet, but Olivier often laughed about him and told Sybille that D'Alfaro was so inefficient the count might just as well have a puppy dog running the château.

Giraud was saying, "He can drug the wine, can't he?"

"I don't know," Olivier answered. "He didn't say. It's unlikely. If I were he, I wouldn't. We don't want them asleep."

"Not groggy either," said Laurens.

"That's right. We want them awake. Wide awake."

"Amen," said the fat knight grandly.

They were quiet then. Sybille waited for someone to speak again, but no one did. An owl screamed far off. As she was about to leave the shutter, she heard the fat man remark sleepily, "They're at Saint-Félix tonight, is that right?"

There was a murmur of assent.

"Well," he went on, "what if they don't go to Avignonet? They could change their minds."

Olivier laughed. "Then we'll light their fire someplace else. At Castelnaudary maybe. Don't worry."

"By that time," the fat man said mournfully, "half the Lauraguais will know."

Olivier laughed again. "What makes you think they don't already?"

Oh, how she longed to throttle him. So half the Lauraguais knew of this caper; then so must the Preaching Friars. Those idiots out there were preparing their own nooses and didn't have the sense to recognize danger. Instead, they were laughing. She moved away and went to bed, in disgust.

It was still dark. Nova was bending over her. A horseman had ridden up, but he had gone off again without dismounting. And now the knights were awake and Giraud had gone to get the horses.

Quickly Sybille got up and pulled on her gown. She swept to the door, opened it with a kick, and called to Olivier in her brusque way. "My lord, where are you going?" He came toward her. "Who was that knight?"

But Olivier had no intention of satisfying her curiosity, even though half the people in the Lauraguais district knew about it. When Nova hopped out and said, "Papa, don't get hurt," he began muttering about some knight named William who was on his way up to the château. Nothing he said made sense.

From habit Sybille glared at him, screwing up her chin to show she did not care what terrible things happened to him. She said to him, "Let's see if you can get yourself killed" and other abuse.

He moved away and Nova followed, plucking at his sleeve.

"Why can't you tell me what's going on?" she asked.

"I'll tell you why, my pet. It's none of your business."

"Papa—"

"Wait and see, wait and see." His voice was pitched high with excitement. "Get all the axes, Giraud," he called.

Sybille stood impatiently in the middle of the yard, gazing around at the knights. She turned to the fat man and fixed him with a stern eye. "Listen, turd," she growled, "you seem to think I'm some kind of fool."

"No, lady," he said amiably. "I don't think that."

"Where are you off to?"

"The square, I think."

"Beg pardon. What square?"

With his nose he pointed in the direction of Rue Château. As they were talking, Giraud came down the lane with the mounts. Olivier had come up behind her and the fat knight said to him, "What are we waiting for?" Sybille swung around to face Olivier.

He said, "Stop acting like a witch. This is men's business. Don't pry."

In the thin light she hesitated, saw Nova coming out the door with her cloak thrown over her shift, and she barked at Olivier, "Fuck yourself, my lord."

"Well," he drawled, "if that's the attitude you want to take—" and went toward the horses. Sybille stamped into the house and slammed the door behind herself. She poured wine into a cup and deliberately drank it down unwatered.

It was almost light when she heard them leaving. She ran to the shutters just in time to catch a glimpse of Nova bounding up the lane behind the horsemen. Sybille flung open the shutters. "Nova, damn you!" she shouted. *"Come back here!"* But she had already disappeared. That girl! Running about the village barefoot in her shift.

An hour later Nova was back. Breathless from running, she brushed past her mother and hurried to dress because she was late for the wool merchant. She said excitedly, "Papa waited under the elm until they got there."

"Who are they?" Sybille demanded.

"The lord of Mirepoix."

Sybille nodded. Pierre-Roger de Mirepoix, Corba's son-in-law, who commanded the garrison at the château.

"And lots of soldiers."

"How many is lots?"

She shrugged. "Fifty, sixty. Where's my other slipper?"

Without moving, Sybille said irritably, "Did you find out where they're going?"

Nova said, "Gaja, I think. Everybody was yelling. I couldn't hear."

Sybille picked up the wool shears. Nova said farewell and ran out. So everybody was yelling, Sybille grunted to herself. They would yell themselves into prison before they reached Gaja or wherever they were riding. She decided to try to put Olivier out of her mind.

The day passed. There was the rest of the wool to be cleaned and returned to the shop. En Philippe had said he wanted it finished today because tomorrow was Ascension Day. Sybille did not work on feast days, no matter how much Philippe Cervel grumbled.

Nova came home with Gaillarde, and they ate. Afterward, Sybille lit a candle and settled at the trestle with pens and parchment. In the yard the girls were sitting on a bench, talking about the feast day. She heard Nova say, "Of course I'm not going to mass because it's Ascension. I don't go any other day."

Gaillarde said obstinately, "But we could say a prayer."

"To whom?"

After a little, Gaillarde sighed. "Are you telling me there is no Our Father who art in heaven? That's stupid."

"No, I didn't say that. I reckon there might be. I reckon He might be up there shaking His head and saying, 'See what they're doing to each other now, those fucking fools.' And He just wants to cry or throw up."

The sound of their voices jarred Sybille's concentration. She pushed up and went toward the window.

Gaillarde said, "Nova?"

"What?"

"Don't you ever wonder about things? About God and dying, I mean."

Nova declared she did not. It did no good to wonder. Sybille closed the shutters and went back to the sestina about her mother. She had had no trouble choosing the six key nouns: cittern, sorrow, bell, rain, lavender, madness. It was not necessary to rhyme the sestina, only to use the six words in progression, the end word of one stanza becoming the last word of the first line of the next. And so forth for six stanzas.

The problem was she could not cram her thoughts into the five-beat meter. No sooner had she sausaged them into their casing, they popped back out again. Words are not meant to be enclosed, she thought. They want to be free. No rules, no meter, just words running ragged all over the page. That's my style, she mused. I enjoy creating chaos. I do it so well, and she thought of Olivier, and then of Jean-Pierre, who had stopped coming to see her.

Compline came, black and windy, and the girls wandered inside and lay down, giggling behind the curtain. The wind blew all night. Sybille got up once to fasten a loose shutter. It was cold. The blossoms on the apple trees were rippling madly. She thought, The trouble with writing verse these days is that nobody needs it. In the old times, when my lady mother was alive, a song was meant to express joy, and there were wonderful troubadours and *trobairitz*. Now they are all dead; their patrons were dead too, or they were *faidits*. She went to bed mourning the troubadours and wishing she had been born a century earlier.

In the morning, sleepy, she was in a bad temper. Nova and Gaillarde slept until terce. To them, holidays meant staying in their shifts until noon, and then slumping around the square begging poges from rich pilgrims. She was hoping they would sweep the yard, but Nova protested and promised to do it tomorrow. Finally they put on clean gowns, ran out, returned at vespers to say they were sleeping the night at Gaillarde's house. Sybille had spent nearly the whole day working on an envoi for the sestina. In six hours she wrote only three lines. It was strange not sorting wool on a Thursday; the day felt like Sunday. She had the urge to go to church, felt that if only she could kneel and pray, maybe Olivier would love her and she could write a decent sestina and Nova would behave as Sybille wished her to. Then she forgot about church and instead sipped wine and cold pea soup; it was a relief to be alone and get a little drunk.

When it grew dark, she lit a candle and picked up the pen, but the envoi still sounded inane, no matter how much she strained. It was cold again tonight, so she started a fire, sat down once more at the trestle, but her mind was blank. Near to matins, there were hoof-beats farther up the lane, and something made Sybille lay down her pen and rise to her feet. Listening—nobody in the lane owned a mount—she went to the window. The horse was slowing down. It stopped outside and then she could hear Olivier's voice. He was saying, *"Sanctus, sanctus. Benedicite. Hosanna in excelsis. Christie eleison."* When she ran to the door and peered out, she saw him tying his mount to the fence.

"Benedicite. He's dead. *Sanctus* and *benedicite."* It was almost a chant. When she called to him to be quiet, he charged forward. *"Benedicite* there, Sybille," he yelled. "As you see, I did not kill myself or fuck myself, and here I am again. It's your Galahad."

She stared as he pushed past her into the house.

"You don't believe in extravagant welcomes, do you, lady?"

In the candlelight the skin around his eyes was brownish with fatigue; his tunic and breeches were stiff-caked with mud. Then, looking at him closely, she clenched her fists because she saw his eyes were glazed, like those of a person who has taken fever and becomes slightly crazy. She dropped heavily onto a stool.

"They never suspected," Olivier shouted. He was stumbling back and forth between the trestle and the hearth. "Do you hear, Sybille? Never suspected. We break down the door and D'Alfaro goes in head-first. They're all in their nightshirts getting ready for bed, and when the boobies see us they fall on their knees. D'Alfaro yells, 'This is it, Brothers!' That's all he says: *'Va be, esta be!'* So they start the *Salve Regina,* and they're farting like a corps of horn players. *Benedicite, benedicite.* D'Alfaro rushes over to Brother William and drives a blessing through his belly. I go after Brother Daniel, who's showing me the back of his head, and I slice off a little piece, and then Mazerolles relieves him of an arm. We're all yelling and trying to spear anything that moves and they're just kneeling there chanting and this dog is barking his head off. I hear Mazerolles yell, 'Get the dog!' so I go after the dog. Where the hell he came from I don't know—"

He's crazed, Sybille thought, and she stared at him. At the trestle Olivier poured two cups of wine and drained both of them, but Sybille did not stir. She stayed on the stool and kept staring at his un-shaven face, at the moving of his lips, by the light of the candle. His speech was rapid, breathless, youthful, with no pause between sentences.

"—this dog is racing around looking for the door and I'm chasing him. He's no fool—he's not singing any *Te Deum*. Then Acermat notices Brother William still twitching and he amens his skull. Everyone is screaming like dervishes and slipping on the blood. I can still see it! What a fucking mess. You can't imagine what a shambles that hall was. D'Alfaro is turning the place inside out for the Inquisition registers and then we all start going through their things. William got a box of ginger, Acermat got a candlestick. And believe it or not"—he reached into his girdle and tossed something into Sybille's lap—"I got a little memento too." He laughed proudly.

She stared down at Daniel's relic bag, then shrank back.

"Oh, Mirepoix was in a fury. When we get back to Gaja woods, he runs out and he's rubbing his hands for joy. And Acermat yells, 'Friend, I did it—I killed Brother William!' That was a slight exaggeration but never mind. Anyway, Mirepoix can see that all Acermat has is a candlestick and he gets mad because he wanted Brother William's head. 'You stinking traitor,' he says to Acermat. 'Where is Brother William's cup?' and Acermat has to tell him he doesn't have it. 'Oh, Pierre-Roger'—peep, peep—'Oh, Pierre-Roger, it got broken.' So Mirepoix says, 'Why didn't you bring me the fucking pieces? I would have bound them together with a gold circlet and drunk wine from that cup for the rest of my days.' Christ Jesus, nobody could drink from that skull once we finished with it."

He paused for breath, and Sybille spoke at last. All she said was, "What about the dog?" and she had to choke it out.

"Dog?" Olivier blinked.

"You said there was a dog. What happened to it?"

"How do I know? Somebody destroyed it—Mazerolles or somebody. It doesn't matter."

For a moment there was silence. Then Olivier rushed on: When they left Avignonet, people rushed into the streets with candles and cheered them as if they had won a great battle. The next morning, at Saint-Félix, the church bells were chiming. Waiting to welcome them were the town priest and all the villagers, and there was a grand procession to the square, with women leaning from their windows and hurling bunches of broom. Olivier said the war was on again. Avignonet was the dawn of liberation, and this time they would win. Sybille looked at him and whispered his name once or twice, but he kept on gabbling.

He spoke of a white surcoat and the prior of Avignonet and a gold cross and eel pasties and a scapular and a palfrey and a green-haired woman. And other nonsense.

Then she shouted his name, and he stopped.

"Olivier," she said, "You've damned your soul. For such a crime as this—"

"You're not smiling," he cried angrily. "Why not? I did this for you, but you're not smiling!"

She turned away, remembering his father had been a monk. How could he have killed monks, no matter how evil? She told him he didn't do it for her—that was a lie.

"Fuck you!"

"You've damned yourself," she repeated. "They'll catch you and they'll kill you. And you'll go to hell."

Olivier had been at the far end of the room, near Nova's corner, but now he came forward and fumbled for the edge of the table, and he cried in one long great breath: "Fuck Rome and the pope and all his dumb asskisser bishops and saints. Fuck Dominic and Francis and Blanche and my old friend Raymond. Fuck mass, fuck Montségur, fuck sin, fuck crusades, fuck Christ and heretics and God and the Holy Booby Ghost and fuck going to heaven. Fuck the Devil! Fuck peace fuck dying fuck living and drinking red wine, fuck fucking fuck everything in this fucking rotten world, because I killed Daniel Marty and for once in my life I'm happy and I don't care what happens now!"

Gasping, he slumped across the trestle and said he was hungry, did she have any food? She went to get bread and cheese, and he ate without saying a word. Afterward, he went to take his mount to the stable, and when he returned he had calmed down and wanted to go to bed. "Throw your clothes into the fire," she said. He did not argue with her. When his head was turned, she flung the relic bag into the flames.

A while later, in bed, they lay side by side on their backs. It was very quiet. Sybille took his hand, and Olivier did not remove it. She told him, "This isn't good for you, you know."

"What isn't?"

"Killing."

"Go to sleep," he sighed. "You know nothing."

"And it was senseless." She moved a little closer. "You don't steal a few records, you don't croak a dozen friars, and expect evil to disappear. Is that what you expect?"

"It's a start, isn't it? Scores must be settled."

"Yes. But it doesn't bring back the dead."

He snorted, "You and your bloody female moralism."

"You and your bloody male heroics. Now you'll have to hide for the rest of your life."

"Don't bark in my ear. Why can't you talk softly?"

She remembered when Daniel had discovered a tick on Arnaud one morning and, screeching, ordered Friar Luke to get that thing off him. He always had that soft, buttery voice, although occasionally he hardened it. But that morning he was so horrified about the tick, and his pitch screaked up so high that he sounded almost womanish. Get it off, Brother. In the name of Christ, hurry. Daniel had paced around wringing his hands, while Friar Luke searched the dog's fur for the tick and Sybille watched, her head scratchy with lice. Daniel would not rest until Friar Luke swore the tick had been apprehended and removed, and then Daniel put Arnaud on his lap again.

"I think," she whispered aloud, "when an evil is that great, it can never be punished."

"We have to try. Christ, what else have they left us but murder?"

"I suppose."

"And if we don't punish them, who will?"

"God." She laughed bitterly. "They say God takes care of all that, remember?"

He hesitated. "Perhaps," he said. "Unless God is them."

Toward prime a dream woke her. She was running along Rue St. Bernard, into Saint-Sernin square. But it was not the square she knew. All around her rose a forest of immense castles, their keeps so tall they seemed to graze the clouds. She kept looking up. Overhead soared silvery-blue birds, metallic as icy steel. There were outlandish sounds so loud they hurt her ears—noises from the birds in the sky and on the ground a tangle of explosions and clanking. At the same time she dimly heard the distant trickle of music. It was someone playing a lute, so slow, so sweet, and it sounded ludicrous in this misshapen world where nothing on earth or in the heavens looked reasonable. Head throbbing, she ran toward the song as if it were some precious object she could catch in her two hands, but it receded before her like wisps of cloud.

She woke weeping for two or three minutes before deciding the strange sights in her dream were nothing but the world unsprung. And the melody, it was the last chord of the last song. It was something just this side of an echo. A recollection of yesterday, she thought, and went back to sleep.

For the rest of that summer and fall, the people in Languedoc assured themselves their hour of deliverance was near. Between Ascension and Lammas, Count Raymond reconquered the Minervois, Razès, and Termenès districts; he rode triumphantly into Narbonne and reclaimed his old title of duke. And after two years of plotting a coalition against the French crown with the kings of England, Castile, and Aragon, and even Emperor Frederick, his foreign diplomacy seemed about to yield results. The idea was to encircle France's possessions in the south and attack on several fronts simultaneously.

This plan was feasible but it failed, although through no fault of Raymond's. Within the space of two days, the French army crushed his allies at Saintes and Taillebourg, and King Henry of England had to beat a hasty retreat to Bordeaux. Suddenly Raymond found himself deserted on all sides. From that moment, he was beaten and he knew it.

He understood now he could continue to protect some of his subjects but not all. The heretics would have to be sacrificed. That was plain. Again he went up to Paris and saw Queen Blanche and her son. King Louis was not yet the saint he was destined to become; indeed, he was still very much a child under his mother's thumb, which was absurd in a man of twenty-seven. Raymond knew what they wanted and he knew exactly what would be demanded of him—the destruction of Montségur. It was the symbol of the resistance movement, the symbol of heresy poised to swallow God's Church on earth.

Those conversations in the gloomy tower alongside the Seine can be imagined. The Queen Mother with her fierce eyes, the docile young king, the count pretending to be a cooperative vassal. He was not, after all, a child-man like Louis; he was a man of forty-five, entangled in a war that had been dragging on for thirty-four years. At first he thought they might be moved to clemency by words, and he talked about history and what he had learned from it and said he would like nothing better than to persecute heretics, since that was what they desired. Only let him do it himself. Remove the Inquisition from his land.

But soon he saw they would not be swayed by any words of his. They listened to him and heard only the irritating buzz of a man still in temporary control of a French province. Their expressions were impatient; they wanted deeds from him, not words. The Church wanted deeds, not words. It was simple. Why couldn't he understand?

When Raymond returned to Toulouse, he summoned all the important bishops and abbots. He told them he was convinced heresy must be eliminated. There was no disagreement there. But he sincerely questioned the wisdom of this job being continued by the Dominicans. His people hated them, and since Avignonet, their monasteries had been plundered and friars killed who had nothing to do with the Inquisition. Let the order lay down this terrible burden and go back to preaching the gospel. There was no reason why he, Raymond, shouldn't be the one to shoulder their tasks.

The count expected the Dominicans to scoff at his idea. Instead, they were willing. They asked Pope Innocent to relieve them of their inquisitorial powers, which they said had caused them nothing but grief. They knew he would refuse, and he did.

In the spring at a Church council, Raymond sat opposite Archbishop Pierre Amiel of Narbonne, and when Pierre mentioned the Avignonet assassins were hiding at Montségur, Raymond said he knew this to be a fact. When the archbishop said the heretic headquarters must be destroyed once and for all, the count obediently nodded approval. And when it was suggested the French seneschal of Carcassonne, Hugues des Arcis, assemble an army to besiege the fortress at Montségur, Raymond assented almost before the words had left Pierre's mouth. This happened at Béziers in mid-April, in the year of our Lord, 1243.

So on the third Monday in May, Hugues des Arcis and six or seven hundred knights pitched camp on the Col du Tremblement at the foot of the rock. In the commander's tent, Des Arcis and his adjutants sat drinking Spanish wine and eating the season's first strawberries they had brought from Carcassonne. Des Arcis saw at once he couldn't surround a mountain of that size, not even with the reinforcements he had been promised. On the other hand, he didn't have to. All he had to do was rely on the elements and let the summer sun dry up the château's cistern. By the end of summer Montségur would surrender.

Everyone in Montségur village had expected this might happen. For years they had watched the wagonloads of arms and wheat going up the mountain. But now that the day had come, they found themselves bewildered by the reality. Why were all these soldiers walking their streets? There were thousands of them, and more arrived each week. Were there no men left in France to weed the vines?

Despite the soldiers, daily life went on much as usual. Indeed, for the shopkeepers it was an unexpected blessing. They were making more money than they ever could have imagined. When Sybille went over to the square, she saw the line waiting for garlic pies winding around the elm tree and down Rue Esclarmonde.

Philippe Cervel was wild. He saw drapers selling surcoats and blankets to French soldiers. This was outrageous, this was cutting their own throats because all the cloth people in Montségur were heretics. The thought of his wool warming those who wanted to destroy his church tormented him, and for a week he did not come into the workshop. He stayed upstairs in his bedchamber and knelt for hours, praying and weeping. Then he hurried around to the shopkeepers and begged them to stop selling to the French. He told them: Close down. This siege won't last forever. They said: We have to live in the meantime, don't we? So he went back to his shop and resumed shipments of carded wool to the weavers. It was a sin, he told Nova, for which he would have to pay in another life.

Olivier was up on the mountaintop, but that was not surprising. After Avignonet, he had joined the Montségur garrison, and Sybille did not object, feeling it was the safest place for him. She had gotten into the habit of having him nearby, and this routine was comforting. But now it was different. The week before the French came, full of fear and love she begged him to stay with her and he refused, and they had quarreled badly. It was suicidal, she warned him, to voluntarily trap himself in a besieged fortress where the French could grab him for the Avignonet crime. It was equally suicidal, he retorted, to remain in the village. Besides, Hugues des Arcis would never take Montségur. It was impregnable. This same argument was repeated several times, and still Olivier ignored her pleas.

It was another damp, chilly spring, with overcast mornings and rain often by nones. Then the weather would clear up for a few hours, and the sun lay wanly over the housetops. The air in Sybille's house smelled of mold. She forced herself out of bed in the mornings and then mechanically went through her usual rituals: cooking, sorting and rinsing the wool, writing after supper by candlelight. Then, when she could no longer sit up straight at the trestle, she fell exhausted into bed again. She was determined not to think about what the next day might bring, and certainly not the next weeks.

On Sunday she and Nova strolled to the square and then turned up the road toward the slope where the French were camped. Sybille stopped and stood looking at the men swarming over the Col du Tremblement like an open wound on the green landscape. She felt her legs shaking and wished Nova would stop chattering.

"How many of them?" Sybille asked. "How many do you think?"

"Mama, don't worry. They don't have enough. You can see that."

Sybille could see the field lacquered with men and horses, tents and cooking fires. It looked like they had enough, but she kept silent.

She circled around a big pine and climbed a rock, where she gazed at the bare open space between the French camp in the valley and the walls of the fortress rearing against the wide blue sky. There was no way the French could venture up that steep slope without being wiped out by the Montségur guns. Of course, there was the backside of the mountain with its perpendicular cliffs. No, they had to attack from this side or not at all. And she noticed they were keeping a safe distance. She could see what would happen if they tried to haul guns up that slope. They wouldn't get very far.

Walking home, Sybille told herself the situation was not as bad as she had imagined. We might win, she thought. We might.

The tenth day of the siege, Olivier came down to the house, as if the French army did not exist. Someone had given him a bad haircut. Otherwise he looked healthy, and he was in high spirits.

"The worst part is the crowding," he said. "You can't turn around without stepping on someone."

"How many are up there?" Nova asked.

"Hard to say. About two hundred robed heretics I'd guess. Then the garrison, another hundred and fifty. Plus some wives and children. You figure it out, Sister Nova." He grinned at her.

"Don't. I told you not to call me that."

"Listen here," Olivier said. "When this is over, I'm going to see you lose your virginity."

"I don't give a damn about my virginity!" Nova shouted at him.

"Unless you've already lost it," Olivier teased.

Sybille watched him at the trestle. He was grinding almonds. On the hearth, salmon was simmering in milk. They were all going to eat together, and Olivier was making a salmon stew.

He went over to peer into the saucepan. "This needs a few pomegranate seeds," he remarked gravely, "to give it the proper color."

Sybille clicked her tongue impatiently. It was just like him to worry about pomegranates when the world was falling apart. "My lord," she said, "don't be unpleasant to Nova. It's not her fault she's still a maiden."

"Yes, it is," he insisted. "I made quite a big effort with Jordan du Mas and she turned up her nose."

From the doorway Nova sniffed. "Wasn't that kind of you? He has bad teeth. Among other things."

She doesn't want a man like her father, Sybille said to herself. Not some knight who comes home once a month, if it occurs to him. She did well to reject Jordan. No, she wants a man like my father; she wants what no longer exists, and she will never get it.

Olivier said, "I might just throw in some dates."

He's going to ruin it, Sybille thought. But his presence made her feel so happy she didn't care. "I'm very glad to see you again, my lord," she burst out.

"That's understandable. Where's the ginger?"

"Behind the pepper. Olivier—" His head was bent over the pan. He was thinner, more fit-looking than he had been in a long time. Calmer too, she noticed. "Olivier, how did you get down here?"

"Walked." He was sprinkling ginger into the pan.

"But how?"

Des Arcis' blockage was a farce, Olivier explained. Day and night watches could not be kept on every trail. All week long, partisans had been hauling great quantities of corn to the summit. None of them had been challenged by patrols.

"But how can you tell if a patrol is friendly?"

"You can tell. This is done." He lifted the kettle from the fire and carried it carefully to the trestle. "Hie, Nova. Let's eat."

They seated themselves around the table, and Olivier dipped stew into the bowls and passed them around, and Sybille poured wine, just as they had done during the years at Cantal. There was the same feeling of being a family. This is not something he ever truly desired, Sybille thought, and the old anger returned for a second. "This is good," she said to him. "I guess you came down to get a decent meal."

He answered stiffly, "If I thought you would feel like that I wouldn't have come."

"Don't be silly," Sybille said, smiling. She put her hand on his arm. "Can't you tell when I'm teasing? You really are a marvelous cook. You always were."

"All right," he said sulkily. "Don't try to sweeten it with flattery. I know you by this time, lady. You make mean remarks and then claim you're joking."

There was some truth to that theory, but she would not give him the satisfaction of agreement.

"Papa," Nova said, "do you think it will be as easy going back?"

"Probably. Don't worry."

"When do you think the crusaders will leave?"

"When they run out of patience."

"People are saying you'll run out of water."

"We have plenty of water," Olivier said. "Plenty of food. The boobies can stay a year if they want to and it won't matter. They'll never get us."

"Stay here tonight, Papa."

"All right."

Gaillarde stared down at the trough of fuller's earth.

"Where is she?" Sybille cried out. "What has happened to her?"

Gaillarde would not look at her, but kept on staring down into the trough. "She went to see someone."

"Who?"

After a moment: "Her lord father."

"Olivier," Sybille said, confused. Her voice quavered. It was very hot and steamy in the fuller's workroom and she felt limp. "Where is Olivier?"

"Why"—Gaillarde gave a little laugh of surprise—"where he always is. Don't you know?"

"On the rock." She made a helpless cry in her throat. The fuller came toward her carrying a stool and told her to sit down.

"Thank you," said Sybille. She felt the walls liquefying, shimmying around her.

"A cup of water?"

"Thank you," she said to the fuller. She was trying to push the walls back into place.

"You're not going to faint, are you?"

"Of course not," said Sybille. The walls were going to crush her.

Nova had not gone to Philippe Cervel's yesterday; she had not come home to sleep last night. She was gone. Sybille tilted up her head and gazed at Gaillarde. "Why did she go up there?"

The young woman turned away. "She had her reasons, I guess."

"To kill me—" She stopped. "If you knew she was going, why didn't you stop her? And if you couldn't, why didn't you warn me?"

Gaillarde said quite calmly, "But she's coming back tonight."

The fuller returned with the water. It was cold, and the cup sweated. Sybille gurgled the water in her throat. "She wants to kill me," she repeated.

Behind her, the fuller said not to move until her strength returned. There was no sense fainting in the street. If she remained quiet the dizziness would pass.

"Yes," Sybille said. She slanted shut her eyes.

"No," Sybille said. "I don't understand." She felt a churning in the pit of her stomach.

"Isn't he my father?" Nova said. "I've got a right to see him."

Sybille cast out a hand to touch the waves of hair tangled with brambles. "You left me," she whispered. "You might have been killed."

Nova shrugged and freed herself, as if her mother's words were irrelevant. Sybille stared at her, at the man's shirt and breeches she was wearing. Her hands were bloody with scratches. A gaudy violet bruise rippled from ear to chin. She had gone up the trail in the dark, alone possibly, for she would not discuss it with her mother, while Sybille had slept in her bed.

"Can't I have some milk, because I'm thirsty?" Nova asked.

Sybille sighed and stood up. It was dawn outside the window. Chastising her would serve no purpose. "Have your breakfast now. Then you should sleep."

Her fear began to ebb, and she went to fill a cup with milk. Behind her, Nova declared, "They might take the rock—you never know. If they do they'll surely kill him. I would never have seen him again. You should go yourself. Go up and see him."

Sybille listened impatiently. "They'll never take it," she answered without turning, because that was what she wished to believe. She brought her daughter milk, wheat bread, and sweet white butter. "Eat," she said.

The rainy season came and passed, and then winter arrived in October, early even for the mountains. There were blizzards before All-hallows. Hugues des Arcis thought when he set up his blockade that this would be a siege of two or three months. He remembered Lavaur had held out two months, Carcassonne a fortnight. Even supposedly impregnable fortresses like Minerve and Termes had not been able to last more than four months; thirst had conquered them all. Montségur was only a tiny, overpopulated castle.

But after five months Des Arcis was just as far from capturing Montségur as the day he arrived, and it was with a sense of acute desperation that he signed on a detachment of Basque mercenaries. These tough mountaineers were not in the least intimidated by Montségur. In late October they headed along the ridge of the mountain, thrashed up the east face, and finally secured a foothold on a ledge only some eighty yards below the fortress.

Even so, the position of the defenders was by no means hopeless. True, the French could get crossbowmen and equipment up to the bridgehead, but this strip of rock was perilously narrow and offered no room for maneuvering. The garrison of Montségur had the protective advantage of the fortress, but the French had to camp on the ledge, crouched around their bows and guns and lashed by gales, snow, and the vicious cold. There was no shelter to be found, and everywhere they glanced there was nothing but space—leaden sky and that terrible void sifting slowly below them and a dull gray silence. It was a place where nobody felt safe, not even the Basques, and the men had to be relieved every day or two.

Des Arcis had his secret weapon hauled up on ropes. It was a stone-gun designed and built by the bishop of Albi specifically for the bombardment of Montségur. Pierre-Roger de Mirepoix took one look at the bishop's gun, assessed its danger, and sent to Capdenac for an engineer of his own. But before Bertrand de la Baccalaria could arrive, the French mounted their gun with wild yells and began battering the eastern barbican, the outpost tower lying a few score yards beyond the curtain wall. The engineer had no difficulty penetrating the blockade and getting up to the fortress. He set to work and soon rigged up a machine that could return the stone-gun's fire, shot for shot.

So all through November and December they lay there, besieger and besieged, Bishop Durand supervising the men on the ledge and Bertrand de la Baccalaria with the men in the barbican, and the two guns peppered each other with nearly continuous fire. On both sides there were casualties. The garrison lost twenty-five men, among them Nova's rejected suitor, Jordan du Mas. Nobody knew how many French soldiers lost their footing and their lives. And nobody really cared, because with seven or eight thousand men waiting below, the French could bring up relief forces whenever they liked. Pierre-Roger de Mirepoix also received reinforcements. Eight men in November, five in December.

Two days before Christmas, aware of the stalemate on the summit and figuring the fighting might slacken in respect for the Lord's nativity, Sybille announced she was going up to visit Olivier. In this decision her daughter encouraged her. The next noon, when Sybille had made arrangements for a guide to take her up and stood on the snowy threshold, breeched and booted and wearing a backbag plump with oranges and almond cakes, a feeling of terrible anxiety came over her. "Oh God, maybe I should stay. Tell me what to do. Knowing him, he won't care if I come. And once I'm there he'll find a way to make me miserable. So maybe I should forget the whole thing and stay with you. Nova, sweet heart, tell me what to do. You're a sensible person. What do you think best?" And so forth for ten or fifteen minutes.

She repeated, "Tell me what to do" so often that Nova's eyebrows began to knit into a frown. "Mama, please. Don't be so dramatic. You're not going to the Holy Land, you know. And you'll be back day after tomorrow. What's the point in changing your mind now? If you don't leave soon, you'll be late to meet William."

Still Sybille hesitated. She glanced at the trestle. Apples in a basket, sheets of parchment. Two sestinas were only half finished. "I don't like leaving you."

"Go anyway." Nova smiled. "I'll keep an eye on the verse."

She waited a moment longer, then embraced her daughter and went out.

"Friend, how far to the top?"

"Tired, lady?" the guide called without turning his head.

"Oh no," she lied. As she spoke, her breath plumed out upon the air like white smoke.

It was midafternoon and the snow lay banded across the trail like a cloisonné counterpane; the boughs over her head were bleached lace-white. For an hour she had been hiking along behind the guide, circling around to the far side of the mountain, and already the back-bag weighed like a boulder on her shoulder blades and she was making grunting noises.

Don't think about reaching the top, the guide told her. Think about something else. There would be a moon this evening, which would be helpful. Not necessary but helpful. His voice was cheerful.

The forest and the snow enclosed them. With bowed head, Sybille was careful to step where the guide had stepped. The easy route Nova had taken in the early summer was now patrolled by soldiers, who could not be relied upon to look the other way. This path, leading to the Porteil chimney, went up the northeast face of the mountain. It was, the guide mentioned, the last trail still open.

In the late afternoon, when the snow was smudged bluish, the guide stopped on a narrow ridge and threw down his ax and rope. From his bag he pulled meat and bread. They squatted under an overhanging rock, sharing the food, not speaking. When they had finished, he continued to sit there quietly. He picked up the coiled rope and began to run it meticulously through his fingers, inch by inch, and when this was done he replaced it at his feet. That he was in no rush to move on was obvious, and Sybille was too tired to question him. But after fifteen or twenty minutes, she asked, feigning casualness, "What are we waiting for? Soon it will be dark."

Then he smiled and said the darkness was precisely what he awaited. The rest of the way would be more difficult—it could be maneuvered by the experienced climber in daylight or by the novice in darkness.

"What do you mean?" she cried. He was making her nervous.

"Ever done any climbing before?" He smiled again and turned to her.

Sybille said, No, only ladders.

"And?"

"I felt—a bit dizzy."

"Right. Darkness is best."

"And if I should slip?" She stood, knees weak. "If I'd known it was dangerous, I wouldn't have come."

"Leave it to me, lady," he said, almost motherly. "I could take a blind man up this mountain."

Now the air was icy cold. In spite of mittens and three layers of stockings, Sybille's hands and feet were painfully numb, and she asked herself why on earth she had wanted to make this foolhardy journey. I am too old, she thought. A moment passed. Slowly the guide got to his feet and said they would be leaving the ridge soon to begin their ascent of the cliffs. At first the rocks would be fairly easy, then they would become steeper and more difficult. He would go up each one first while Sybille waited below. When he called down to her, she must begin to climb with the help of his rope. Did she understand?

She did.

Three times he looped the rope around her waist, then knotted it. Coupled together, they set off with Sybille ten feet behind him. Once she peered around but could see only the frozen moon hanging peacefully overhead. Pinpoints of light twinkled in the valley below. Crusaders' bonfires perhaps. Above her the mountain emptied its mysteries in an internal hemorrhage of hisses and hectic sighs. The wind penetrated her sleeves and seeped into the recesses of her bones; her feet were as heavy as stones. She said nothing to the guide because she was short of breath and worried about finding the strength to go on. With effort she narrowed her concentration to her feet. After a while, as she mechanically placed one foot in front of the other, the steps began to take on a rhythm: "Onward, onward, onward." It was like a prayer.

The guide halted and checked the knot of rope binding him to Sybille. The first cliff was a ten-foot grade with plenty of cracks and footholds, and Sybille scrambled after him with her arms outstretched, feeling for the cracks where he had placed his feet. Then the cliffs grew steeper and higher. The guide would go up and anchor himself, then call in a husky voice, "Now, lady." She followed the sound streaming down from inky space. Her fingers, legs, feet, elbows pried and grabbed and lifted, and all the while the taut rope was gently hoisting her body up and up, like a puppet on a string. "Good," he kept repeating. "Good."

She counted the cliffs. Then she stopped counting. Once she thought, That last one was nearly vertical. Panic foamed up, and she broke into cold sweat before quickly numbing her mind.

"How do you feel?" the guide asked.

"Very tired." She gasped the words.

"Rest for a minute."

Standing there, she suddenly had the sensation of being outside of her body, observing herself. She thought, There is a woman clawing up a cliff, isn't that absurd? Then she thought, God must be a gargoyle with motes in both eyes; destinies that are quite ridiculous are meted out at random, without reason or sensitivity. If this Creator had been a shade less maniacal, less chaotic in his thinking, Pons and I would be in Carcassonne with our children and grandchildren this Christmas Eve. And I, in a silk gown, might be in my bedchamber, taper-lit, writing verse about a woman clawing up a cliff on Christmas Eve. Then she smiled, because she knew such a theme would never have occurred to her.

"Let's go," the guide said.

Moving again, she felt even colder. There was no sensation in her feet, and she had to struggle against closing her eyes. Upward they went. Good, called the guide. Very good, lady. Now we move on. Good. Keep going. Good.

Noises crackled around her ears, the wind and a whacking sound that thudded hard at three- or four-minute intervals, but she paid no attention.

When they had been climbing silently for a long while, she heard the guide's voice ring out above her head. "Lady, lift your head. Look over to your left. That's right. What do you see?"

She craned her neck. Her vision was blurred. Something was glowing above them like a fiery tear in the darkness. "Light." She blinked. "It's a light."

"The summit, lady. Fifty yards to go, that's all."

At his words, the flesh seemed to drop from her bones, as if some frigid fire had seared her whole body and she weighed no more than a handful of ashes. She thought, I'm going to make it. She shouted to the guide, *"Kyrie eleison!* We're going to make it!"

"Lady," she heard him laugh, "this is simple. It's going down that's hard."

She climbed, looking neither to left or right, only keeping her eyes fastened on the reddish-gold warmth looming above her. Then a woman's voice trumpeted, "William! Is that you, William?"

"Hie, Arpais! It's me. Toss down the ladder, my love."

Ladders, more ropes, outstretched hands, and then at last Sybille was hauled atop the curtain wall. Torchlight dazzled her eyes. Every muscle screaming, she scrambled to her feet, hobbled a step, and almost fell. A woman with her hair in long braids caught Sybille in a hug. "Welcome to Montségur, my friend," she cried. She was smiling.

Chapter Eighteen

The courtyard was mobbed with people laughing and talking. For a moment, confused, Sybille stood on the wall gaping down at the tops of their heads. Then she twined one mittened hand around the arm of Corba's daughter and slithered down the steep stairs, into a pack of children bickering and toasting bread over a fire. A fiddler hunched over a vielle and shrilled out William Figueira's banned *sirventes*. A pair of women in embroidered red wimples bobbed and twisted to the music, and people clustered around watching and clapping out the beat. The yard looked like a village square on a feast day.

Sybille was still gripping the woman's arm; now she let her go and turned to watch the movements of the dancers' feet against the hard-packed snow. She was silent, then said, "Forgive me but I've forgotten—are you Arpais or Esclarmonde?" She breathed in wheezes, her voice barely audible above the racket.

"Arpais," the woman said. She tossed back her braids. "My name is Arpais and I'm married to Giraud de Ravat. They say I resemble my little sister, but she has black hair and she limps."

Surprised, Sybille moved her head around. "Why?"

Arpais shrugged. "She was born that way. Didn't Mama tell you?"

"No," Sybille said. They started off across the yard, with Arpais clearing a path for them with her elbow. A knight was opening a tun of wine, and people began to hurrah and come forward from the shadows with cups. Just then something whined in the air and crashed against the east wall, and Sybille drew in her breath sharply. She jerked to a halt. Her ears were ringing. Arpais's face, bathed in torchlight, was blank. Sybille asked, "Doesn't that bother you?"

"Not anymore," Arpais said steadily. A dog began to bark. "Come along, lady. Let me take you to my mother."

Around Sybille, the people in the yard were pretending nothing had happened. She noticed nearly everyone was young—garrison soldiers and their wives and children, and somberly dressed youths with pale cheeks who were probably still postulants, because Montségur was also a seminary. All of them appeared to be enjoying themselves. No one had even flinched when the missile hit the wall. This is queer, Sybille thought, and peered up at the sentries patrolling the walls. While she and Arpais were crossing to the tower, she began counting the minutes, trying to remember how long it takes to load a gun, hoist it into firing position, and so forth. Just as she decided it was time, the next stone hammered the night apart as it ripped into the wall. Before the sound had died away, Sybille heard the barbican gun firing back.

Inside the bare, whitewashed hall, the crowds were even denser, and the air reeked of sweat and wine. When Arpais snatched her hand and began shoving through the bodies, Sybille let herself be dragged along. She worried about the almond cakes getting crushed. Behind her shoulder, somebody said, "How do you know what the emperor will do?" Another voice, full of indignation, answered, "Oh, I know, Peyrepertuse. I know he's coming to raise the siege." The first voice drawled, "You don't know shit." Sybille turned her head, but saw nothing except backs and heads milling about.

She called out to Arpais, "Wait a minute. Do you know where I can find Olivier de Ferrand?"

"Olivier? He's busy now." Arpais glanced back.

"But do you think I can see him?"

"Not unless you want to go out to the barbican."

"But when is he coming back?" cried Sybille, shoulders suddenly hunching with tension.

"Soon," she said. "The watch changes in about an hour. It takes them only a few minutes to get back here. Unless there are casualties. Mama is over there."

As Sybille neared the hearth, Corba was saying to a girl seated on a stool at her side, "See how you twist my words around. It makes me feel terrible when you talk like that." The girl looked away. Then Corba saw Sybille and jumped to her feet.

"Hello, my friend." Sybille grinned and swayed forward. "Joyous Noel."

"What are you doing here? Oh God! Esclarmonde, look! It's Na

Sybille. But wait—oh, my dear, how did you get up here?" Tears gushed from her eyes, and she fell on Sybille's shoulder. "I can't believe my eyes. You didn't come up the Porteil chimney. Oh God!"

Over Corba's head she saw Esclarmonde cross her arms over her chest. The girl stared up, curious, but when she saw Sybille looking at her, she closed her eyes. Sybille gave a laugh. "This is a very nice feast."

"Oh, we're just ending our fast," Corba sniffled. She straightened, stepped back, and peered at Sybille's trousers. She burst out, "You're—you're quite wonderful!"

"No, I'm not. I'm crazy." She laughed again and shrugged off her backbag, letting it drop to the ground.

Sybille sat on the bench. Esclarmonde was staring at her. Sybille could see she had been quarreling with her mother. The corners of her mouth were locked into a fretful expression; she was full of childish suffering.

Corba had gone to get wine. Sybille turned to the girl and smiled. Their eyes met for an instant, then Esclarmonde jerked her gaze away. Hunting for a way to break the discomfort between them, Sybille said casually, "This place is like a beehive. Is there never any silence then?"

"The soldiers make it hell. When the soldiers leave it will be quiet again."

Sybille nodded. Esclarmonde pressed her lips together and looked past Sybille. Watching her there on the stool, Sybille thought it was impossible to know she was crippled. She was very pretty. In fact, lovely. Or would have been if her face and body had not shown such misery. Sybille tried again. "How old are you?" she asked.

"Fifteen."

That old, Sybille thought. She looks twelve. The heat of the flames was making her sweat, and she pulled off her outer tunic. "Look," she said to Esclarmonde, "it's not easy to be fifteen under any circumstances. Certainly not these." She jerked her head toward the window, meaning the siege. "But when this is over—well, then you can have pretty ribbons and gowns and you—"

The girl broke in sharply. "What makes you think I want ribbons? I want to be ordained, lady. I can decide what I want to do with my life, and my mother can't stop me—"

"I see," Sybille murmured. "And your mother wants you to do—what?"

"Have a husband," she blurted out, "and children and be like her."

Sybille smothered a sigh. "There's nothing wrong with that," she said mildly. "You can always be ordained later. Like your grandmother."

"I do not wish to be like my grandmother," she answered coldly.

Corba was squeezing through the crowd toward them, a cup in each hand. Sybille looked up at her, eyes full of pity.

"Just like a little goat!" For an hour Olivier had been drinking and eating oranges and marveling over Sybille's unexpected appearance at the fortress, and now Sybille was wearying of hearing him talk about her exploit. "On those stumpy little legs of yours, you marched straight up the cliffs—"

Sybille, shivering, crouched closer to the fire. He had not tried to conceal his pleasure—he had kissed her again and again, he had held her hand—but he could not break his habit of teasing her. He knew she had perfectly fine legs, how much it annoyed her to hear them called stumpy.

She sighed again and swept her eyes around the hut. "My house," Olivier had called it, although it was hardly worthy of the name. It was one of a dozen wooden hovels pitched on a steep slope below the keep. These cramped dwellings had once been occupied by pairs of goodmen and goodwomen, and only a flimsy palisade stood between them and the edge of the cliff. Now that the heretic ministers had moved into the fortress, senior officers of the garrison used them. Olivier shared this one, with Jordan du Mas before he was killed and now with Imbert de Salas, the sergeant-at-arms. "My lord," she interrupted Olivier loudly, "does this mean you're happy to see me? If I'd known, I would have come earlier."

He reared back his head and tossed an orange peel at the fire. "Well, let's not go to extremes. Only a genuine booby would come here now. And up the Porteil chimney! That guide was a madman to bring you. How much did you pay him?"

"Six sous. But that includes the return trip." Sybille sat up straight. It occurred to her that she had not seen the guide since she had been hauled over the wall. He had agreed to take her back the day after Christmas. Now she wondered if he had returned to the village or whether he would remain until Thursday. Better find out in the morning, she thought.

A knight plunged his head in the doorway and grinned at Olivier. Pierre-Roger de Mirepoix was seeking him. Olivier drained his cup. "No thanks, Imbert. Go along and tell him I'm busy tonight. I have a pretty drinking friend. *Ai! Ai!* My wife dropped in. This doesn't happen every day, you know. And see if you can get us another skin of wine."

When the knight had gone, they both began to talk at once.

"What an awful place this is! The door doesn't close properly and all that cold air blows in, and you might as well be sleeping outside—"

"Well, don't start criticizing because it's better than—"

"Don't get mad. I was just giving you my opinion."

"I didn't ask your opinion. Anyway, I'm lucky to have it. How is Nova?"

"Good, good. She's all right. I was furious last summer when she came up here. Never a word to me, never a thought that I might be worried. Oh, never mind—I guess there's no use talking about that now. I'm sure you were happy to see her. She—"

"You're getting a few gray hairs on that side. But it's amazing how young you look. You should climb mountains every day. Throw a few more twigs on the fire."

"I'll never understand Nova. Twenty-three and no interest in men. Most girls of Nova's age—well, no, I take that back. Look at Esclarmonde, have you ever spoken to that girl? Fifteen—and she hates her mother because Corba won't let her become a postulant."

"Her father won't permit it either. But nobody pays attention to Raymond anymore."

"These people up here are weird. Everybody is smiling and pretending there is no siege. What do you mean—nobody pays attention to Raymond? It's his castle."

"Didn't you see him? He's—I don't know—gloomy. Keeps to himself. Rarely talks."

"Ah, thank God somebody is sober up here, they're all acting bloody strange if you ask me. No, I don't care if it's good for morale. Aren't you going to put more wood on the fire? I'm freez—"

"Did you run into Fabrisse?"

"Fabrisse! Fabrisse! You mean my sister Fabrisse? Are you saying—damn it, what is she doing here?"

"How do I know?"

"Why didn't you tell me? She's really here! My own sister? What for?"

"Take it easy. What's the matter with you anyway? You've never liked her. And believe me, the bitch hasn't changed any."

"Olivier," she bristled, "I don't want to hear you call my sister names. Because Fabrisse is the only blood relative I've got in the world and I love her! Just because you never had any—"

They went on that way for another hour. When Imbert de Salas returned with the wine, they were huddled asleep under a fur with their arms around each other's heads, and the house reeked of oranges.

All night long the French stone-gun bumped the east wall. The missiles slapped steadily every four or five minutes, although in Olivier's house the sound was slightly muffled, like distant rumbles of thunder. It was nearly noon when Sybille stirred herself on Christmas Day.

She met Fabrisse in the afternoon. Sybille saw her in the women's dormitory stooped over a pallet, busy changing the linen.

The discovery of this chamber cleared up a mystery for Sybille—where these mobs of people were sleeping. It was an immense underground cave directly below the main hall of the fortress. There the ministers slept in shifts because despite its size there were not enough beds for each of them. The room had been partitioned with curtains into men's and women's dormitories, and there was always somebody snoring on the rows of pallets or meditating. At the far end of the room were kept crates of crossbolts and stones, and soldiers were constantly tramping back and forth, carrying the boxes up to the yard.

There were no windows. Two or three big standing candles burned day and night, but the place was gloomy and airless and smelled of burning wax and too many unwashed bodies. Apparently someone already had told Fabrisse of Sybille's arrival, because when she saw her she calmly lowered the sheet she had been unfolding and came around the pallet to give her the kiss of peace.

"Let me look at you," Fabrisse said. "So you climbed the Porteil chimney. Na Corba told me all about it. I was looking for you last night but I supposed you were with De Ferrand. You wouldn't have wanted to see me anyway." She laughed. "You're getting reckless in your old age, little sister. You could have fallen and broken your neck. Isn't it hard to pee with those breeches?"

"Are you doing all these beds?" Sybille asked.

"Certainly. When the emperor crosses the Alps and this is finished, we can go back to sleeping on the ground. But now we deserve pampering—at least that's what Na Corba says. I don't happen to agree."

Sybille went around the bed and stood opposite Fabrisse. Her sister's face glowed, pale and emaciated. "Let me help you, sister."

"No, no," Fabrisse murmured. "This is my task. Watch out you don't step on those pillows."

Sybille made a circuit of the row of pallets, came back to Fabrisse, and lowered herself painfully onto one of the unmade beds. Her legs were almost too stiff to bend. She forbade herself to become offended at Fabrisse's brusque manner. When had she ever been different? She was watching her sister and trying to decide how to begin a conversation, when Fabrisse said, "Of course the emperor will not come," and went on tightening a sheet across a pallet.

"Of course he will," Sybille said quickly. "Or the count himself will raise the siege. More likely the French will just give up and go home. How long have you been here?"

"Michaelmas."

"Michaelmas!" Sybille exclaimed. "You don't mean you came up here after the siege began!"

"Yes. That's what I mean, little sister."

"Why?" Fabrisse did not answer, only ripped the sheets from the next pallet and dropped them on the ground in a heap. Sybille repeated, "Why? Didn't you know it's dangerous here?"

"Oh, please don't, Sybille."

"Tell me why. It's important that I understand."

"I can't be anyplace else, because this is my faith and my faith is going to be destroyed. And when that happens I must share in its end—whatever that may entail." Sybille fell silent and stared into her lap. "Well, you asked me, didn't you? Don't look so sour now. How nicely the laundry does these sheets. Smell them, aren't they nice?"

"Don't try to change the subject. All that nonsense about your church being destroyed—there are still goodmen in every city in this land. There are a whole flock of them over at Queribus, aren't there? I'll tell you what I think—I think you're hoping Montségur will surrender so that they can put you in the fire and you'll be a—"

"You don't understand anything," Fabrisse interrupted. She gave

Sybille a brief smile, then went on. "All your life you've had nothing in your head but words and silly songs. You've never had the slightest concept of the real meaning of life."

"You're wrong. You don't know this, but I spent a year in a Dominican prison and I had plenty of time to think about meanings. Plenty." Her voice began to tremble. "I saw Brune Maurand burned and I saw them drag this corpse down Rue Méjane, this hideous thing they said was Mama, and they were going to burn her, but it wasn't Mama. It was some woman with black hair, thank God. The house in Rue St. Bernard they tore down. Cantal is probably gone too. But Fabrisse"—she was getting hot, seeing Fabrisse smiling that way—"the answer isn't to get yourself burned! I wish you'd listen to me. Fabrisse, put down those sheets. Think of Mama and Papa—they would die if they knew."

Fabrisse gave a little laugh. "But they *are* dead. Don't get so emotional."

Sybille struggled awkwardly to her feet. "Listen to me. When the guide takes me down tomorrow, you can go with us. You can go to Spain or to Lombardy. Those are safe places for your faith. And you can go on preaching. Sister, it's not necessary to die. You see? You can be more useful to your church alive than dead. Doesn't that make sense?"

Scooping up a bundle of soiled sheets, Fabrisse carried them to the end of the row and dropped them into a basket. Then she turned and counted on her fingers the number of beds still needing clean sheets. "I'm going to be two short," she said. "No, only one. Matheus says he hasn't slept in his bed for a fortnight, so I needn't bother with his."

Sybille tramped toward her, going carefully between the newly sheeted pallets. There is no need to get so worked up, she told herself. Chances are this place will never be taken, and Sister will have to go seek her pyre elsewhere. She's just exaggerating, saying things to frighten me like she always has. She doesn't really mean it. It's some crazy idea in her head— if she were actually faced with the fire, she would stop romanticizing death. Sybille called lightly to her, "You will consider leaving with me, won't you?"

"No," Fabrisse answered. She turned away to smile at Bérenger de Lavelanet, who was crossing sleepily to the stairs.

To her back, Sybille sputtered, "You care so little for life then?"

"I care a great deal, but I care more about my God. And my church, the church of love."

Sybille thrust out her chin. "Damn it, Fabrisse," she shouted. "I beg you. Why don't you listen to me?"

Fabrisse took a step and wheeled to face her. "Don't swear at me," she said without raising her voice. "People can hear you." Sybille stared at her down the rows of beds . "Go back to your *cansos* and your children and stop persecuting me. Please. Go on, go up to the hall. Na Corba will be wanting to see you."

Sybille stared a moment longer, trying to keep back the tears. "Have it your way," she said and went toward the stairs.

Later when she met Fabrisse in the hall at dinner, they both smiled politely and spoke of the corn soup. It was delicious.

It was getting dark. All day she had been halfheartedly looking for the guide, but no one seemed to know his whereabouts, and finally she had gone to the garrison commander. It was possible, Pierre-Roger de Mirepoix told her, that William had gone back to the village. But he was reliable—Pierre-Roger had known him for years—and surely would return for her if that was their agreement.

"So—keep cool, sweet heart." He smiled down at her and winked. He was a big man, a head taller than Olivier, with hair and beard the color of bright autumn foliage. His large, rough presence dominated Montségur. He gave the impression of being everywhere at once—jogging along the walls, cursing and hugging his men in the yard, dandling his and Philippa's sons—and his favorite oath, "By the cock of St. Peter!," reverberated through the fortress. Sybille never saw him without a cup of wine, either in his hands or nearby. She remembered the night Olivier had come back from Avignonet, when he had babbled so wildly about Pierre-Roger, who had wanted William Arnaud's skull for a drinking goblet.

Sybille, restless, did not know what do with herself. Olivier was on duty at the barbican; he would not return until matins. He would be starved and want to have his dinner and then drink half the night. She went down to Olivier's house and tried to take a nap, but found she could not sleep alone there. On the other side of the mountain, the guns rattled dully. She went back up to the hall, thinking to find Corba and talk, but Bishop Bertrand Marty was leading a prayer service.

Sybille stood there listening and yawning. It was very quiet in the hall, with everyone straining hard to hear the bishop's words. He was very old—close to eighty, Sybille guessed—and his once fine voice no longer carried. Five or six minutes slipped by. Bishop Bertrand was praying: ". . . for we are not of this world, and this world is not of us. We fear lest we meet death in this realm of an alien god . . ." Sybille turned away and got herself a cup of hot wine. She took it outside and went to stand by one of the bonfires. The wind had died down; it was not so cold that evening. There was nobody in the courtyard except a few soldiers, whispering and drinking, and the sentries pacing the wall. With each thud of the missiles, the torches on the walls seemed to leap up into the night as if human.

Soon afterward, Raymond de Perella strolled up to her and mumbled a greeting. The sight of his creased face saddened her. She wanted company, but he spoke to himself in whispers and groped for words until she found his presence discomforting, in fact utterly depressing. Standing beside her, his eyes fixed on the east wall, he wove nets of anguish around himself. He droned on and on about Count Raymond, explaining that periodically Pierre-Roger had sent messengers to the count to inquire how his affairs were prospering, and that Sybille must understand these were code words. Sybille, he said, would be interested to know the replies always came back in the affirmative.

Did these "affairs" mean the count was going to revolt again and raise the siege? Sybille wondered, or did they refer to surrender? If Montségur gave up, what would happen to the heretics? To the garrison, many of whom, like Olivier, had been participants at Avignonet? Would their lives be spared? When she interrupted Raymond to ask these questions, he did not answer them, only ground on about the count's "affairs" in his misty voice. At last, nervous and bored, she sighed and broke in impolitely: "My lord, what news of Pons? Is he well? Have you seen him in recent years?"

"Why? Haven't you seen him?"

"Of course not. What gave you an idea like that?"

"I don't know. I just thought—oh, he's all right. Fine, in fact."

"Is he still preaching in the Albigeois?"

"Maybe. Maybe not."

He doesn't trust me, Sybille thought. Probably he is right not to trust me. "Why are you so suspicious? I didn't tell Daniel Marty what I knew of Pons. Why would I inform on him now?"

Raymond sighed. "One can never tell what one might do. I was thinking of your welfare, Sybille. Things you don't know you can't repeat. Am I not right?"

She thought, At least Pons is still alive. That is all I wanted to know anyway. She finished the wine in her cup and observed the relief watch straggling out from the barracks. Olivier should be back soon. The men crossed to the postern gate in the northeast wall, yawning, shoulders hunched, and one by one padded into the night.

The service had ended, and the congregation began spilling out into the yard. Sybille thought of the trip back. The village, her house, and the wool, even Nova, seemed strange and far away now. Within twenty-four hours this mountaintop had become more vivid to her than her own life. The guide had said going down was more difficult, but she pushed away that thought nervously. Then she thought that once she returned home, she would be alone again, without Olivier, and she pushed aside that thought too. She had started to move away, but Raymond stopped her. He pointed. Bertrand de la Baccalaria, the engineer, was coming in the postern gate and behind him was Olivier. She watched him swing toward her, grinning.

"Hie! Sybille!" he called out. "I want an orange! Go get me an orange!" As he passed one of the ministers, he gave him a friendly tap on the shoulder. "Hie! Matheus. Drinking wine again, and you call yourself a goodman. You should be ashamed of yourself. What you need is an orange. Here's Sybille who can give you oranges."

When he flung his arms around her shoulders, Sybille smiled and said, "We finished them last night—remember?"

Olivier sagged heavily against her, until her legs began to sway under his weight. "Ah, woe is me! No oranges." Over her shoulder he must have caught sight of Raymond de Perella's son, because he began teasing him. "Ho! Jordan. Go get me an orange, boy! What do you mean you can't? What kind of an answer is that?" His voice blazed with excitement and good humor, and he began to imitate a money-mad Spanish farmer, pushing his mule up the Porteil chimney, determined to sell oranges to the besieged. Olivier's mimicry, his dialogue between the farmer and his mule, were truly hilarious, and Jordan screamed with laughter, and Jordan's dog, on his rope, barked wildly. Sybille's sides ached from laughing. He is unusually happy tonight, she thought, and she hoped it was because of her.

Still laughing, she pushed him away, and he stopped clowning and walked over to Pierre-Roger. Suddenly his voice was pitched low.

She could not hear what the two men were saying; probably Olivier was giving him a report on the night's fighting because the commander was crossing his arms over his chest and nodding his head. Watching them, she sank down on her heels by the fire and rested her cup on the snow.

From the ramparts a sentry called out. Pierre-Roger stiffened and lifted his head. The soldier called again. Pierre-Roger turned and headed for the wall stairs, taking them three at a time. Sybille picked up her cup and went over to stand beside Olivier. "What is it?" she asked, but he did not answer, only kept his eyes on Pierre-Roger. The people in the yard began to quiet down, curious. Above Sybille's head another sentry choked out a high yell. "On guard!" Suddenly she saw Imbert de Salas sprinting toward the steps, cramming on his helmet as he ran. When she looked around again, the sentries on the east wall were dousing the torches and Pierre-Roger de Mirepoix was leaning out over the parapet, neck thrust forward, and he was peering into the night.

"Peyrepertuse!" he bawled toward the barbican. "Laufre, Laufre, can you hear me!" Without turning, he yelled over his shoulder, "Kill that torch, Acermat." Then: "Peyrepertuse, this is Pierre-Roger. Speak to me! Hello, hello—"

There was not a sound from the people in the yard. All of them had halted dead in their tracks, with their arms and legs held frozen in various poses. The dogs had stopped barking. Pierre-Roger went on shouting: "Peyrepertuse, Peyrepertuse!" There was no reply. The mountain was utterly silent. Even the guns have stopped firing, Sybille thought, and then her heart began to pound wildly. The stone-guns were quiet! Pierre-Roger wheeled around and came flying down the steps, crossed to the postern gate, and rushed out. In the stillness she could hear his footsteps crunching on the snow. Then, like a hum in the air, like a bee singing in a corked jug, a voice stirred in the darkness. It came from the direction of the barbican, and the words were French. *"Joyeux Noël,* friends." Silence. "Greetings from Queen Blanche."

Pierre-Roger came back to the yard with Raymond Peyrepertuse and laid him down flat on the cobbles beside a fire. The knight did not move, and Pierre-Roger dropped to his knees and bent his ear close to the man's face. After a minute, Olivier and Imbert and some of the other officers shuffled forward and stood in a semicircle just above

Peyrepertuse's feet. Sybille rammed her hands into the sleeves of her tunic.

People began hurrying forward, crowding toward the soldier on the ground. Olivier came to Sybille, walking slowly. Flippantly, he said, "They got our best bowmen."

"What happened to the rest of them?" She stared at him.

"Dead," Olivier said in a different voice. "They're dead." His head slumped down.

She put out her hand and clawed at his sleeve.

"They've got our gun."

She shook his arm until he looked at her. "What happened? How did they get up to the barbican?" It was impossible. There was no way to climb to the barbican from the ledge where the French were; it was sheer rock face.

"There must have been some steps chipped in the rock. Somebody guided them."

"Who?" she asked in his face.

"Peyrepertuse and the others heard them coming. They let them come up." His voice was raw. "Because they recognized somebody's voice, because they thought he was a friend."

"Who?" she repeated.

"Who. You keep asking who. Your guide friend, William, that's who. I need a drink." He spun away into a group of goodwomen.

From the dark came muffled shouts. "Come on over, heretics! Come and suck our pricks! Come onnnn! Anybody coming?!" There was a rumble of laughter. "We're waiting for you!"

On the height of the wall, a sentry's arms pumped. He bellowed back, "You'll have a long wait, you fuckers!"

By sunrise Bertrand de la Baccalaria's gun was ripping away at the east wall, and by the end of the day the French had dragged up the bishop of Albi's gun to the barbican, and the two guns alternated until they seemed to blur into one endless roar. The Frenchmen were so close you could smell their cooking fires and the aroma of roasting meat. The kitchen at Montségur did not of course prepare meat, or fowl, or any dish requiring milk or eggs, because they were impure foods. Sybille imagined the men's suppers and found her mouth watering.

Now that William had betrayed them, there was no way she

could leave. The realization hit her like a boulder. It was hard to believe. She paced back and forth in the yard, watching Bertrand de la Baccalaria and his crew rigging up a new gun. A stone boomed against the wall, hurting her ears. When she had asked Olivier why the guide had betrayed them—it was incomprehensible to her—he let out a humorless laugh and said no doubt William had been handsomely rewarded for his treachery. No doubt Queen Blanche had promised him a château in Anjou with a view of the Loire. She still did not understand it. She stood there a moment longer, watching the engineer's face. His eyes were ploughed with dark furrows, but otherwise he appeared to be unperturbed. Then Sybille turned and went into the hall.

The French brought up reinforcements. Those few ministers still living in their huts on the southern and western slopes were now in range of the missiles and had to be evacuated in a hurry; the tower was so crowded one could barely find space to sit or stand, and the yard stank of urine. They went on living their lives while the noise of the firing went on, endlessly. The east wall, luckily, was unusually thick. In spite of the battering it was getting, the French could not knock it down. Pierre-Roger de Mirepoix chafed with frustration. The narrow space between the barbican and the fortress offered some protection for Montségur's defenders but left no room for offensive action. He wanted to throw the French out of the barbican. He groaned and boiled and cursed restlessly for nearly two weeks, and the end of it was that one of the goodmen, Matheus, volunteered to go down the Porteil chimney and see if he could find reinforcements.

Matheus was a tiny young man with a thatch of straight black hair framing his squarish face. He wore a quilted orange tunic and bright-green breeches and looked like part of a jongleur's troupe because he had lost his black robes making a hasty exit from Carcassonne and had never gotten around to requesting another. His traveling companion, the deacon Pierre Bonnet, would not allow him to go alone, and so the two men together left the castle on January sixteenth. To Sybille's surprise, they had heavy bundles strapped to their backs, and when she questioned Corba later about this, Corba said the bags contained money.

"Livres tournois?"

"Yes, and gold and silver bullion."

There must be a king's fortune in those bags, she decided. Corba explained that Matheus needed the funds to hire mercenaries, but Sybille did not believe her. She suspected that Matheus and Pierre were removing the church's treasury. If that were the case, Bishop Bertrand must have decided the fortress was no longer safe.

Time passed. The stoning went on. The wall held. On the evening of the twenty-fourth, the French crept up to the postern gate, but the garrison beat them off without much trouble and without the loss of a single man. Three days after that, Matheus and Pierre returned with two crossbowmen from Usson. Pierre-Roger greeted the bowmen enthusiastically. He kissed them on both cheeks and called for wine, and he looked happy. But once Imbert had taken them off to the barracks, Pierre-Roger's face sagged with disappointment, and he was heard to mutter that two were better than none, he supposed.

Montségur's situation actually was not as hopeless as it seemed; not only had Matheus smuggled up the two soldiers but he was bursting with news that fired morale in the fortress. Count Raymond wanted to know if Pierre-Roger could hold on until Easter. Admittedly Matheus had not spoken to the count himself, but he had gotten this from a knight in Usson and this same man, Bernard d'Alion, was going to save them. He knew a certain Aragonese mercenary captain, a man named Corbario. With two hundred men under his command, each of them skilled in every aspect of warfare, Corbario could chase the French from the barbican and set fire to their gun. Bernard d'Alion was arranging a meeting with Corbario that very week.

At once confidence soared. Despite the bombardment, everyone brightened, and the mere mention of Corbario's name made them smile. Matheus made a second trip down the mountain to meet Corbario, and a contract was drawn up. The Aragonese captain agreed to bring twenty-five men to Montségur. They settled on a price: fifty livres, which was steep but not unreasonable. With the garrison's support, Corbario saw no problem in driving out the French from their forward position in the barbican. Even without the garrison's help, he could do it. Matheus gave him twenty-five livres in advance; the third day of February was set as the date of Corbario's arrival.

Matheus, triumphant, returned to Montségur the next afternoon. Sybille went out into the yard and mingled with the crush of people waiting to greet and congratulate the little minister. She could not get near him and finally turned around and made her way back to the hall. Corba came up smiling, and Sybille put her arms around her and kissed her hair. Corba took her up to the De Perellas' private apartment on the top floor of the tower and sent her maid for wine. In the past few weeks, once Sybille knew she was unable to leave, she had worn one of Corba's gowns. It was made of Spanish wool in a deep-burgundy color, beautifully sewn, and wearing it made Sybille feel happy and fashionable. Her hair was tucked into a white silk wimple.

Standing by the door, watching Corba bending over a mirror and smoothing rouge on her cheekbones, Sybille gazed around at the tapestries, the Damascus carpets, the featherbed with its ivory knobs, the pallet where Esclarmonde slept. Hard sunlight sheeted the cushions and bounced off Corba's mirror.

The maid came back with a tray of goblets, and Esclarmonde limped in softly at her heels. She wore red silk ribbons in her braids. "Mama," she said in a high voice, "I was talking with Bishop Bertrand. He says there's no reason I can't go to the seminary at Foix, there are other girls my age and—"

"Oh," Corba grunted. She put the mirror in her lap. "The bishop is a dear man but he's wrong to encourage you. I don't think he realizes the feelings of your father and myself on this subject."

"Arpais says—"

"Arpais is wrong too," Corba said irritably. "Tell her I said so."

Backing away, Esclarmonde threw herself on a stool. The maid passed around the wine and swept out. Corba picked up the mirror again and reached for the kohl, her expression grim. To Esclarmonde she said, "I am your mother and you must obey me."

Head bobbing over her goblet, Esclarmonde said quietly, "I owe you obedience in all matters, except in the matter of my faith. So"— she made her voice harsh—"there I cannot promise to obey you."

Sybille, standing a little way off, bent her head over the wine but she did not drink. She thought of Nova. Esclarmonde was staring at Corba's back. Sybille put down her goblet on a chest and went out, unnoticed. She walked slowly down to the hall where she had last seen Olivier. Her hem caught on the leg of a bench. Carefully she freed it and went up to him, took his arm, and pulled him toward the door. "Do you think Nova is all right? She must be worried sick."

Olivier said, "She knows you can't come back now."

"Isn't there some way I can send her a message? Maybe next time Matheus goes back down—"

He shook his head. "Come on, Sybille. Matheus can't deliver personal messages. Besides, I don't think he plans another trip. What for? Once Corbario gets here—"

"I just want her to know I'm not dead."

"She knows. Don't worry."

The third of February came. The besieged kept an all-night vigil in the yard, waiting for the Aragonese. Fires blazed. People hung on the battlements and craned their necks. Pierre-Roger paced along the top of the wall. Hands crossed over his chest, he looked like a giant priest reciting his prayers. In the morning, with the sun slowly climbing, he slouched off to bed for a few hours and left Olivier in command. The same scene took place again that night and the next. And the next. On Sunday, after dark, Matheus plunged over the wall and started down the mountain. He was back long before prime. There were soldiers everywhere, he reported. The trails were swarming with them. It was clear Corbario had not yet been able to break through the lines.

Pierre-Roger exploded in a bombardment of oaths that could be heard all over the yard above the hammering of the guns.

His knights and men-at-arms went on patrolling the walls and firing stones and bolts at the barbican, and picked off an occasional crusader. Storms blew up twice in February and dumped two and three feet of snow into the yard. The Good Christians began their Lenten fast and ate only bread and water on Mondays, Wednesdays, and Fridays; an elderly goodwoman opened a vein and bled to death. By the end of the month, there was still no sign of Corbario and his mercenaries. Pierre-Roger would wait no longer. Meeting with Raymond de Perella and Bishop Bertrand, he persuaded them it would be illogical to assume help would come now. It was obvious they were cut off from the outside world and that meant they must rely upon themselves. If they did not win back the barbican, they would all perish sooner or later.

Night fell, the last one of February. The moon did not shine. Almost half the garrison lined up at the postern gate with axes, knives, and crossbows, and silently began plowing their way along the white-crusted ridge just below the summit. They hoped to skirt the barbican and take the French by surprise. The snow was deep, the hillside steep, with a sheer drop on their left hand. As they curved toward the round stone tower, there was not a sound from the men in the snow. Through the trees loomed an island of light: torches and fires and the bishop of Albi's gun bulging its tall, dark shadow over the battlements. In a lull between firing, they could hear the gunners gossiping.

"Did you fuck Marie, Lord Geoffrey's wife?"

"No, but she—"

Pierre-Roger raised his bow, aimed, and yanked. A sentry fell back screaming in pain and a few seconds later men began rushing from the barbican.

"Get inside!"

Sybille wheeled and ran toward the tower. A sentry screamed. Somewhere outside the wall, voices exploded and echoed in the dark, drumming closer and closer to the postern gate. Another sentry shrieked, then another, and abruptly they began snapping around their bows, pointing them down into the yard.

"Go on!" Arpais shoved Sybille from behind. When they got to the tower door, Sybille turned to look back. Suddenly the yard was full of men running, limping, dragging the wounded behind them like sides of slaughtered meat. Sword in hand, Pierre-Roger raced across the yard, and Sybille saw Olivier pumping behind him. Inside, she pushed her way along the side of the hall until she reached a window. Breath caught in her chest, she pushed someone aside. Bernard Roainh ran by the window. Near the well, he slumped to his knees on the black snow. He scrambled up, a bolt in his chest. The front of his jerkin was a shiny bubble of dark blood. There were French bowmen in the postern gateway, firing bolts again and again.

Sybille crouched there dazed, and she thought, The raid must have failed. There would not be Frenchmen in our yard if it had been successful. Pierre-Roger said this could happen, that some might be killed. It was impossible to recapture the barbican without someone being hurt. But he did not mention the French coming up here to kill us.

Behind her, a man's voice boomed, "Get back from the windows, get back!" But Sybille did not hear him. All she could hear were swords cracking and the screams of the wounded and the frenzied singing of the crossbolts in the air. She saw Bernard Roainh lying on his back near the well. Next to him knelt the bishop. His long white hair was in shadow, but torchlight rippled on his pale hands, which were cupped lightly on Bernard's forehead. Then he lifted his hands and began crawling to another man, who also lay sprawled on the snow. He began to give him the last rite. Sybille thought, The bishop is too old to take such risks. He might be killed. Then she noticed Olivier running up the steps to the ramparts, a crossbow slung over his arm. She watched him hurrying along the top of the wall, looking down into the yard. His bow, raised in the air now, was pointed into the mass of men rattling below. Sybille turned and started shoving herself toward the door.

Outside in the air, she glanced up at the sky once, then raced past the storage sheds, past the barracks, going as fast as she could toward Olivier but keeping close to the buildings. Her chest suddenly exploded with pain, but she did not stop. When she got to the stable, she heard him calling to her.

He was shouting. "Go back, booby!"

She paused, gasping for air, waiting for the stabbing hurt in her chest to go away. A bolt whirred close to her ear and splintered the doorway. She dropped down. A minute later she lifted her head. She was crouched almost directly beneath Olivier, and she looked across at the steps leading up to the wall and at the twisted body of Jordan de Perella's dog lying limp and still on the bottom step. Sybille lunged out and staggered up the steps, heaving herself over the dog.

They stayed up on the wall until midnight, and then when the last Frenchman was dead or chased back into the night, they crept down into the yard and flopped on the cobbles near the barracks, sweating heavily. Pierre-Roger, lips tight, was counting the dead. The walls rose up around them, as unsubstantial now as if they had been made of marzipan.

Sybille put out a hand to Olivier. "Will they come back to-night?"

"Who knows."

People were milling around. Jeanne de Vensa, whose husband's body lay now at the bottom of a ravine, was bleeding her woe. "I don't feel well," she was saying over and over, "I don't feel well."

"I think," Sybille said to Olivier, "we have lost a great many men tonight."

"Obviously."

"Speak to me," she said. "Are we going to surrender? Tell me what you think." She rocked against his shoulder.

"I think we will wait and hear what Pierre-Roger has to say. Don't lean on me. I'm tired. Pierre-Roger will decide. He'll do what he thinks best."

Sybille moved away and sat upright. I am Sybille d'Astarac, she said silently. I am forty-nine and I'm still alive. "At least half the garrison must be dead," she said steadily.

"At least," said Olivier.

Chapter Nineteen

When her eyes opened, she was in Olivier's house, rolled up in a knot under the furs. Through the smokehole she saw blue mist. She stretched her legs, bumping against something metallic—axheads or a clutter of cups. Her temples were throbbing. She touched her hand to her head. The wimple. It was gone. She thought, My pretty wimple.

"Olivier?" she called. She could hear someone breathing close by and raised her head quickly, peering at the bundled shape near the door. "Olivier—"

Imbert groaned and rolled on his back. "Lady," he growled. "Olivier's in the barracks. You're all right. Go back to sleep."

"Imbert, what happened?" She squirmed free of the fur and sat up. The house smelled of sour wine.

For several minutes he ignored her, and when she repeated the question, he yawned and said, "Pierre-Roger has gone down to talk to them. He'll see what he can do." She burst out crying. "He went up on the wall first thing this morning and sounded the horn. He— Are you listening?"

"Go ahead. I'm listening." Tears were streaming down her cheeks.

"Then he got his mount and rode out the front gate. Just as cool as custard." Imbert's voice was furred with admiration.

"All alone? He rode down all alone?"

"No—Bérenger and Giraud went along." Imbert was staring up at the roof. Suddenly his lips parted in a crooked smile.

"What are you laughing about?" Sybille said hoarsely. She wiped her nose on the fur. "It's surrender. That's what it means. We're done for." And Olivier and Acermat, even Pierre-Roger himself, all the men who had been at Avignonet, would be executed. They'll kill Olivier, she moaned to herself in silent terror, they'll kill Olivier! She untangled herself from the furs and stood shakily. Stumbling over to Imbert, she saw him smiling up at her, not moving. His face was gray with exhaustion.

"Well," he drawled sideways, "Pierre-Roger has his conditions for surrender. If he doesn't get them, we'll go on fighting. You worry too much, lady."

She could not speak for a while. Then she said grimly, "Pierre-Roger is signing his own death warrant. Is that anything to laugh about?"

"He's going to ask for pardons. Try to find me some wine, will you?"

She blinked at him in the murky light. "Pardons for what? Defending Montségur? For what?"

"Everything," Imbert said. He struggled to sit up, scratched his nose, fell back.

"Avignonet?"

"Yes."

"And the Christians. What about them?"

"Freedom for all."

Sybille scowled at him. "He's dreaming." Imbert shrugged. "He's stupid. To imagine that Des Arcis—"

"He can ask, can't he? No harm in asking, I say."

Turning away, she dragged herself past him to the door and opened it a crack. It was surprisingly mild outside, and she noticed the snow melting a little on the path. Her head pounded and her throat was parched. She wanted water. Her back to Imbert, she muttered, "He's crazy."

"Shut the door. There's a draft."

Sybille went out into the sunny air. "He's crazy," she said, shutting the door. She stood there a minute, listening. The guns were no longer firing. Then she trotted along the footpath through the puddles of thawing snow, yawning, holding her head in one hand.

The yard was tidy. The dead had been collected and washed and wrapped in hides, and now they lay patiently near the barracks door. People stood around in small groups, drinking water and talking in whispers. Now and then someone would cross to the hall or the well, or edge back and sidle off to another group. Nobody knew how to behave without the racket of the guns. The hush was disturbing. One of the preachers laughed; everyone started and the sound splatted nervously into the far corners of the silent yard.

Olivier and Jordan de Perella were standing on the southwest wall, looking out between the battlements. Jordan was straining his neck and from time to time he would point at something in the valley. Then Olivier would nudge him and point in a different direction. Their two heads, one fair and one dark, were thrown together in relief against the clean blue sky and the midday sun. Only yesterday the air had been freezing. Overnight, it seemed, winter had left, and now everything smelled wet and fresh. This too was disconcerting, perhaps even more than the absence of the gunfire.

When Olivier spotted her, he waved. She crossed to the steps at the front of the yard and climbed up. Jordan called, "Na Sybille, they're coming back!"

Olivier shook his head. "Come on, boy. They won't be back for hours yet. You're seeing things."

Sybille went around and stood next to Olivier. The mountainside spread below her and dipped straight down to the valley, a sheet of glistening silver crystals. Far below were the French camp and the smoking chimneys of the village. Vaguely she could make out tracks in the snow where Pierre-Roger and the others had gone down the road.

Jordan was saying, "Look there, En Olivier—see those spots. That's them!"

Suddenly Olivier was pushing him aside and staring, although he did not confirm the boy's words. When he finally spoke, his voice was bulky with disbelief. "I see something. But—"

Farther down the wall, somebody yelled, *"Aiii!"* Then Sybille heard Matheus's voice ring out. She twisted toward Olivier, but he was already on his way down the steps and Jordan was spinning after him.

Fifteen minutes later Pierre-Roger was climbing on a barrel at the far end of the yard. Two more barrels had been turned upside down and placed on either side for Bishop Bertrand and Raymond de Perella. But they did not mount them, only waited on the cobbles and gazed up at the sky. The yard was jammed to its farthermost corners, and people stood on the steps and along the top of the wall. Somewhere ice was melting and dripping noisily against a stone.

"All right, friends," Pierre-Roger announced. "Let's get down to business." His expression was calm. Glancing down at the bishop, he stooped, spoke a few words, straightened again. He scanned the crowd, then glanced at a folded paper in his right hand. "As you know," he said, "Bishop Bertrand and En Raymond and myself—we talked last night and we agreed to try and treat with the French and see what would happen." He stopped to clear his throat. "We had three conditions for surrender. First, pardon for political crimes. Second, liberty for both military personnel and noncombatants. And third, the bishop's request for the right to remain here for another fifteen days. In other words, a two-week truce before we actually surrender the castle."

Sybille, standing between Corba and Olivier, held her breath.

Pierre-Roger went on: "All right. Now I'm going to tell you what Des Arcis was willing to grant. But first I'd like to mention something. My discussion with Des Arcis and Bishop Durand was extremely brief—I'd say less than an hour, maybe forty-five minutes. And the reason was that much of the groundwork for negotiations had already been done by Count Raymond. So I believe we have a great deal to thank him for. Now"—he wiped his brow and glanced at the paper in his hand, then lifted his head—"now this is it. First, we can stay here until March sixteenth, provided we give them six hostages by Wednesday. They specified several individuals by name, but I'll get to that in a minute."

The people around Sybille were all craning their necks to watch Pierre-Roger. Behind her, someone painfully butted her in the back with an elbow but she did not turn. She kept her eyes on Pierre-Roger.

"On one of our chief demands—amnesty for political crimes—they are agreeable." Sybille let out her breath with a weak little cry. "Full pardon for all, uh, so-called crimes, and that includes Avignonet. Every man-at-arms here, every knight, will be permitted to leave with his arms and baggage. Men, at some future date you'll have to see the Inquisitors and confess your sins. But absolutely no prison sentences—the most you'll get is a light penance. They've promised. I think they were extremely lenient."

Sybille looked over at Olivier. His head was tipped to one side, so she could not see his expression. Then she turned to Corba, who smiled at her.

Somebody called out, "What about the Christians?"

"Wait, wait." Pierre-Roger raised his left hand. "I'm getting to it. Everyone else is also free to leave. Same terms as the garrison—appear before the Inquisition, make your confession, get a mild penance. But only"—he paused no more than ten seconds before plunging on—"if you abjure religious beliefs contrary to the Catholic faith." His voice boomed in the silent yard, then his chin dropped.

Nobody moved. Sybille reached over for Corba's hand. It was cold.

Pierre-Roger lifted his head. He said in a choked voice, "Those who recant will be spared. Those who do not recant will be burned." Then he cleared his throat twice, loudly, and hurried on to name the hostages: Jordan de Perella, Bishop Bertrand's brother, Pierre-Roger's uncle. . . . The castle of Montségur, he said, would pass into the hands of the French crown and the Roman Church. The folded paper was still clutched in his hand. Jumping off the barrel, he gave it to Raymond de Perella without a word and began making his way through the crowd.

Olivier went back to his house and slept until vespers. Sybille, dazed, let the crowd jostle her into the hall, where bean soup was being ladled up. She got herself a bowl and two pieces of bread, still warm from the oven, and looked around for Corba. While she was eating, Fabrisse came up carrying a cup of water. "How are you, sister?" she murmured.

Sybille did not know what answer to make and finally replied honestly, "I have a terrible headache."

"That's easily remedied. Take some lady's mantle or lavender. Go see Raymonde de Cuq—she has all kinds of herbs. She'll fix you up."

"I'll do that," she said stiffly. "Thank you."

"Not at all," Fabrisse said cheerfully. She sipped the water slowly. "I'm glad to help you." She began swiveling her neck, gazing around the hall.

Between swallows, Sybille stared at her sister staring at the people moving back and forth with cups and bowls. When she had drunk the last of her soup, she held the empty bowl in her hands. Fabrisse, allowed unlimited bread and water, had taken only a single cup of water. Suddenly Sybille said, "Did you decide what you're going to do?"

Fabrisse did not look at her. She said, "There is nothing to decide. You know that."

Sybille got up and took her empty bowl to the trestle. All through the afternoon, the fortress was calm. Sybille found the good-woman with the herbs and watched her crush lavender leaves in a wooden cup and mix them with wine. She choked it down, trying not to grimace, listening to the woman chatter about diets for asthma and gout. People were doing ordinary things: talking to their friends, sewing, reading. In the yard, motionless as tree trunks, oblivious to the sun, sat a row of holy women meditating. Sybille did not hear anyone mention the sixteenth of March. Even Bishop Bertrand, when she passed him on the dormitory stairs, smiled at her and said the weather was nice and springlike. He was tired of the snow, the long, dark days.

The weather continued pleasant and fair. In the late afternoon, Imbert de Salas put on a clean jerkin and strolled down to the barbican to talk to the French soldiers. He was gone about an hour, and when he came back he had a smoked ham in his hand. He announced, pleasantly defensive, that this was the first ham he had seen in nine months and please forgive him, friends, if he did not offer to share it. He sat down on the wall steps and ate, then carefully licked the grease from his fingers. He threw the bone to the dogs, so nothing would go to waste. Olivier and Sybille passed him, and climbed up to the top of the wall and leaned against the battlements, as they had earlier in the day.

One of the goodmen had given Olivier a bag of walnuts. He laid the bag on the ledge between them and dug in for them, nut by nut, and loudly cracked the shells with his teeth. Without looking at him Sybille held out her hand, palm up.

Chewing, she asked idly, "Where did you get these?"

"Amiel Aicart. People are already starting to share out their things."

"Already?" she murmured unsteadily, trying to hide her horror. I am becoming like these people, she thought, pretending everything is fine. Still, they, who will burn, can pretend, and I, who will not, find it impossible. She said aloud, "Fabrisse—" then closed her lips.

He made no answer, but from the corner of her eye she watched him shrug. He threw a handful of shells over the embrasure. She stood very still. Olivier grunted, "What did you expect? None of them will recant."

"Olivier," she said, "it's a miracle Des Arcis agreed to the two weeks. I've never heard of such a thing."

He said quickly, "It's not a miracle. They want to end it. Des Arcis is tired. We're all tired. I'm not surprised."

"And the Avignonet reprieve?" She rubbed her nose. We can go back to the village, she was thinking. Live in my little house with

Nova. Be like other families at last. "You can't deny the reprieve isn't a miracle."

He snorted. In the dark she could not see his expression. He crunched a walnut. Rain began to fall in whispers. She pulled the bag of nuts under the edge of her borrowed cloak. The air was wet around her ears. They went down the steps and across the yard, where a fire was sputtering damply. Inside the hall the Good Christians were praying. On the footpath to Olivier's house, they passed Bérenger and his wife, Guillelme, pressed together, feeding on each other's necks; they did not look up. The rain began to pour down, and Olivier dragged her on. He opened the door of his house and lit a fire.

Side by side, they sat on the furs. Olivier asked, "Are you sleepy?"

She shook her head. "Olivier, what's going to become of us now?" She meant their land. "Is there any hope?"

He twisted around to stare at her. "Don't waste your time hoping," he said. "There's nothing left to hope for." He said a few more things, but she did not wish to listen and told herself he was deliberately trying to make her sad.

Finally she spoke in a low, scratchy voice. "I don't think it's possible to live—without hope."

"Oh, it is, it is, " he insisted. "Hope. What does that mean? It means the unknown. Probably one fucking sorrow or another. But hopelessness, that's something else. That's my friend."

She sighed angrily and told him he did not mean that.

"I do." He lay back and propped his head on one hand. "I know hopelessness." He said hopelessness was his reason for living. He remembered how unsatisfying hope had tasted. But once he had discovered hopelessness, he had found it as filling as good bread. All moral dilemmas were automatically resolved. No more did he have to worry about right or wrong. He just went about his business and let hopelessness make all his decisions. Then he stopped talking and buried his head in her lap. Sybille folded her hands over his bald spot. He closed his eyes. "It's late," she said. "I love you."

The mild weather held. On the lower slopes the sun melted the snow. The guns were silent now, the walls bare of sentries. Jordan de Perella, leaving to be a hostage in the French camp, wept as he parted from his mother. Sybille roamed from the tower to the yard, back and forth, like a caged bird, and the silence alternating with the prayers and sermons put her nerves on edge. The Good Christians gave away all they had. The gifts were of little value because none of them had any possessions to speak of. Corba's old mother, Na Marquésia, gave Sybille a candle stub. Bishop Bertrand presented Pierre-Roger with pepper, wax, and a piece of green wool. Olivier got a pair of boots and some salt.

On Easter Day, everyone stood in the great hall. Hundreds of white candles were lit. Bishop Bertrand bestowed the *consolamentum* on all who wished to be initiated into the church. Seventeen people, one by one, came forward for the laying on of hands. Eleven were garrison soldiers, and among them were the two crossbowmen Matheus had brought up in February.

The rest were women. Three were married to men who had just converted that evening; they did not wish to be separated from their husbands. Another was Esclarmonde de Perella. And last of all was Corba. Sybille and Olivier edged forward, craning their necks to catch a glimpse of her. The hall was stifling; a child coughed and coughed at the back. Corba was standing hidden somewhere in the midst of the congregation, but they could hear her voice. The bishop, following the regular service, spoke of the ascetic life Corba must now lead, a life of danger and persecution. Knowing that, was Corba willing to surrender herself wholly to God? Did she promise never to eat meat, eggs, or cheese? Never to lie or swear, never to touch a man, never to kill, never to eat without saying the Lord's Prayer, never to sleep naked, never to betray the faith? Corba did.

The hall was utterly silent. Stepping forth from the crowd, going toward the bishop, Corba paused three times to kneel and say, *"Benedicite."* She seemed dazed, especially her eyes, and moved like a person asleep. After the bishop had given her the gospels to kiss, he touched the book to her shoulder, then grazed her elbow with his own because she was a woman and he could not give her the kiss of peace. The congregation pressed forward to touch Corba's shoulders or place their hands on her head. Sybille ground her mouth against the sleeve of Olivier's tunic. He slid his arm to her waist. The ceremony was over. They went forward with the rest to congratulate Corba because it was customary.

A sound outside the door jarred her out of sleep. When she groped for Olivier, he was gone. Sybille kept her eyes closed, but at once her thoughts began hopping around crazily. Corba's decision was so unreal Sybille could not even begin to grasp its meaning. Corba had wanted to go back to her house in Toulouse and give a great feast. She should have recanted like her husband would, but instead she had condemned herself to death and apparently was allowing Esclarmonde to do the same. The service the previous evening was incomprehensible to Sybille.

When Olivier scuffed in, Sybille half sat up. "Where were you? It's not time to rise yet."

From just inside the doorway, she felt Olivier staring down at her. "I'm leaving. We drew lots and I won." She could hear him drinking from a cup.

Confused, she struggled to her feet.

"Pierre-Roger has a plan," he said. "There are some documents and holy books the French musn't see. He said, 'The Church has to go on, go on.' So three Christians are going to escape." He began to speak rapidly. "Get the sacred stuff to Queribus or someplace. Get the rest of the money out so the French won't have it. Dig up the gold Matheus buried in the woods at—"

Sybille rushed up to him. "What has this got to do with you?" Olivier had left the door open, and she went around him and banged it shut. "Three of them are getting away. What do—"

"Why are you so stupid, Sybille?" He laughed. "Those nambies can't protect themselves. They need—"

Over him she said sharply, "Someone to kill anybody who gets in their way."

"That's right. The senior officers drew lots and I won."

She gripped his arm so tightly the wine spilled over the edge of his cup and dribbled down the sleeve of her gown. "You can refuse. Why are you doing this to me?"

"I can't refuse!" he shouted. "Why do you always think of yourself? This is a serious mission. It's a privilege to escort these people." Olivier's voice was high-pitched and manic. It was the same voice he had used before Avignonet. In fact, he was talking now like Pierre-Roger. "By St. Peter's cock, what an honor! History will remember my name—"

"History!" she cried. "History is a joke. History will remember Hugues des Arcis as a hero and the rest of you as criminals. Nameless criminals." She laughed bitterly and went back to sit on the fur. Olivier emptied his cup and squatted on his haunches opposite her. He was looking at the door, not her. Puffed up with importance, he began telling her about the escape plans. The three heretics were to be Amiel Aicart, his companion, Hugo, and a postulant named Jean the Poitevin. Before dawn the four of them would be lowered on ropes to a secret cave directly below the dormitory. There they would wait until after the surrender in the morning; then, while the French were busy with the auto-de-fé, they would continue on down the mountain.

Sybille said dully, "It's a violation of the truce."

He said, "So what? Nobody will know until afterward. And then it will be too late." His mouth was set.

"But what about you?" she asked. "Once the mission is over—if you aren't dead, that is—what's going to happen to you? Olivier, look at me." It was too dark to see his face, but she could sense him blinking at her, in mock innocence.

"I'll be back. Probably things will be hot for me for a while. I may have to go over the mountains. But if I do, I'll come back. You stay in the village with Nova. Try to find her a man."

If he returned from Spain, they would seize him for this crime. She thought, There is nothing I can do. She asked, "What kind of holy books?"

"I don't know. I think one is the book with the story of the fool and the hanged man."

"That's important?"

Olivier shrugged. "Must be. The bishop is cutting it up—each of us gets a bunch of pieces. Just in case somebody is caught." He threw down the cup and came to stretch out alongside Sybille. She leaned back into the circle of his arms. Gently his fingers grazed her cheeks. He told her to sleep, he would not be leaving for two or three hours. "Don't worry," he was saying. "I've got my sword and a knife. I'm taking wine. Why don't you give me some of those walnuts? I can eat them down in the cave." Her dread began to evaporate, dissolving into bone-weary exhaustion. Her eyes closed. He stroked the hair curling around her ears.

"Olivier," she breathed. "Take all the nuts."

"They are gone," Pierre-Roger said, furious. In the gray light just before dawn, he shoved her away and stalked toward the barracks door, and she lurched after him. Over his shoulder he hissed, "Olivier never should have told you. By God, I gave him orders not to."

"Have you no feelings? I know I'll never see him again. We didn't say goodbye."

He wheeled around at the barracks door. "There are more important things than farewells, lady. I could not endanger four lives so you can have your farewell."

Sybille dropped her hands to her hips, and the bag of walnuts dangled helplessly at her side. Oh, why did I fall asleep? she cried to herself. I've let him go without a last glance, a last kiss. Olivier, I know you don't like goodbyes. But you should not have played this trick on me. I should not have let you. She said to Pierre-Roger, "When did they go?"

"About an hour ago. Say nothing of this to anyone, hear me. Swear it. You mention this to anyone and I'll kill you."

"What do you take me for, a traitor?" Sybille replied.

She looked away. The tower was still shrouded in darkness, but candles glowed in Corba's window and in the entrance to the hall. The yard remained empty. The Good Christians seemed not to know this was a special day. She said, "He was always running, Pierre-Roger. Thirty years and he never stopped running from me. You don't know how sad it made me. I wrote him a *canso* to show how much I cared for him and he called me a sly little fox." She lowered her eyes. "He said I was trying to crucify him."

Pierre-Roger coughed and said, "He didn't mean that."

"Yes—he did. That's what is so strange. He did mean it. He could not love anyone, not even his child. He told me that at the beginning, sat in my father's hall in Rue St. Bernard and said, 'Lady, I can't love.' How did I know he was speaking the truth?"

She rambled on for another five minutes, and Pierre-Roger did not stop her. He nodded his head as she spoke. Then he slouched into the barracks, and Sybille stuffed the bag of walnuts into her sleeve and went away.

The Bishop of Albi, at first invisible among the impatient horsemen crowding through the main gate, came up with Hugues des Arcis' party. With him were two Preaching Friars and a gaggle of young assistants and clerks and scribes. It was another mild day, and a mob of French knights cantered up to have an unofficial look, but Des Arcis chased them down again. He said he had not realized how crowded it was up there. The sky turned from dark gray to white, and then the sun poked through the clouds. The churchmen ordered a trestle and stools brought out from the hall and set up in the farthest corner of the yard, near the east wall steps. They sat down behind the trestle, and the scribes briskly spread out their ledgers and unstoppered their ink jars. Sybille stood alone on the wall opposite, watching them. Earlier she had made an attempt to see Corba, but had been unable to push her way upstairs through the crowd. So she had come back out again.

Bishop Durand was pacing near the trestle, waving his arms. When he caught sight of Pierre-Roger de Mirepoix, he beckoned him over and laid his hand on the knight's shoulder. The two men moved their mouths gravely and nodded, and then the bishop patted Pierre-Roger's shoulder two or three times. The rings on his fingers flashed. A few minutes later, one of the bishop's clerks dashed up, and the friars also got up and came out from behind the table. One of them had an apple in his hand and he finished it as he walked toward the bishop; he flicked the core under the table.

Imbert started up the steps and came to stand next to Sybille. She asked, "What are they doing?"

"Figuring out a way to interrogate everyone."

"Oh, that's impossible," she muttered. If that's what they want to do, she thought, this might take days. She was thinking nervously of Olivier below in the cave.

Imbert scratched his chest. "Where's Olivier? In the house?"

"Olivier? I don't know. I think so. He's probably drunk." She snapped her glance away.

"He'd better get his ass up here, so he can get his reprieve."

Sybille did not answer. When next she swept her eyes over the yard, Pierre-Roger was standing on the trestle. His face was white.

"Friends!" he rasped. "Friends, give me your attention. The Reverend Brother Ferrier has asked me to announce—"

Sybille peered down. "Which one is Ferrier?" she asked Imbert, but he only shrugged. People were leaning out the tower windows, making a lot of noise. Pierre-Roger raised his voice. "The tribunal has asked me to say—let everyone please come out and stand in the yard so the reverend brothers may speak to you."

Someone yelled, "Louder. What did you say?" Pierre-Roger repeated the request, then jumped down and stood next to Bishop Durand. Five minutes went by. Soldiers began to straggle into the yard; some dozen Christians ambled out of the tower and stood near the door with their hands clasped behind their backs. The rest stayed inside. The bishop frowned. Friar Ferrier stuffed his hands into his sleeves. At last he climbed on the trestle, looked around, and waited. People began to quiet down. Face flushed, the friar began to talk about the upright God and how He would forgive the errors of the most ignorant person and grant him a place among the workers in His vineyard, giving latecomers no less payment for their labors than the first arrivals—if he showed himself sincerely repentant. He went on talking that way for ten or fifteen minutes, repeating himself, before asking people to line up.

Sybille saw Pierre-Roger tugging on the friar's sleeve. He bent, listened to Pierre-Roger, then straightened. He said awkwardly, "In the interests of efficiency—I mean, since it is so crowded here, let those who wish to confess their errors and return to the Church, uh, let those people form a line in the yard. Those who do not may remain in the hall. Thank you." He lowered himself to the cobbles.

"Imbert," Sybille called. He was scuffling away from her, starting down the steps. She ran after him.

He did not stop. "Come on," he mumbled. "This is no time to hang back, is it?"

"Does that mean they aren't going to question everyone?"

"I guess. I guess it would be a waste of their time."

They went to the back of the line, behind Bertrand de la Baccalaria. "Well, Bertrand," Imbert said, "you're finally getting off this bloody mountain."

The engineer grunted over his shoulder. "Not today. Mark me, we'll be lucky if we get down by Wednesday." He let out a string of curses.

Sybille stood in the line almost half the morning. The yellowish morning light edged higher and higher in the sky over the east wall, over the Preaching Friars' white robes, the stable and the green-painted barracks, the smoke in the air, the two little girls playing with their dolls, the hooded well. Every three or four minutes the line went forward. Three or four minutes seemed to be the time in which it took to be questioned and have one's name recorded in the scribes' registers. It occurred to her that was fairly fast; the friars could not be asking much more than superficial questions. Now they were talking to Bertrand de la Baccalaria. Tensing her ears, she folded her fingers together over her waist and listened.

Bishop Durand had raised his head sharply when he heard Bertrand's name. In fact, all the tribunal were staring at him with a kind

433

of admiration, certainly with curiosity. "Did you build the gun?" the bishop barked.

"This is true," said Bertrand, his voice firm.

"Did you come up here in October? From Capdenac? Were you sent for?"

"This is true."

"Did you come for the express purpose of constructing a gun that would enable them to keep up the siege?"

"You might say so," the engineer replied. "Yes, this is true."

The bishop of Albi went on asking professional questions about the gun, and finally Friar Ferrier broke in. He wondered if the engineer wished to be restored to God's Church on earth, and Bertrand said this was true, he did. When he had been dismissed and Sybille broached the table, the friars were still whispering about the engineer. Friar Ferrier quickly asked her name and residence. A clerk came up with wine, and the friar drank thirstily before setting the cup on the trestle. Then: Did Sybille wish to recant?

She licked her lips. "I am a Catholic," she said. "I am not a heretic."

He frowned and fingered the cup. "Then how came you to be in this place?"

Sybille said her husband had been an officer of the garrison, but he had been killed, and now she wanted to return to her home and family.

"Fine," said the friar. "Next." Imbert stepped up, treading on Sybille's heels.

The next two or three hours were peaceful, and there were no more interrogations. The French were preparing for the auto-da-fé. On the southwest face of the mountain, less than three hundred yards below the fortress, soldiers were heating pitch and putting up a palisade of stakes that was large enough to enclose two hundred persons. They marked out a square area with pieces of timber, trees they had axed down near the crusaders' camp. They split the trees and dragged them up the muddy slope and hammered them together. Inside the palisade the ground was being carpeted, and workmen sprinkled a layer of fagots and twigs. When that was done, they covered the fagots with straw, and then they went around with buckets and carefully poured out pitch. Sybille, standing on the wall, could gaze down into the empty pen and see the men tipping the buckets.

She was hungry, and she ate two of the walnuts. Finally she went down into the yard and crossed to the tower. The hall was hushed, with people standing in small groups and talking softly, making their farewells. Corba was upstairs in her chamber washing off her rouge and kohl. The room was packed with robed women. When Corba saw Sybille, she threw down the soapy cloth and stood. She smiled as she took Sybille in her arms. "Courage," she said. "God is with us."

Sybille could not speak.

"Goodbye, my friend. Don't cry. Pray God we will meet again in a happier life."

"Yes," she said quickly, wiping away her tears. She hoped it was true. For a few minutes she stood in the room and listened to Corba and her daughters and the other women talking, and then she shuffled downstairs. On her way she passed Raymond de Perella going up and wanted to speak but did not know what to say. Imbert and two other knights were in the entranceway eating and drinking. Sybille stood with them. They all had wine and fish pies, which the dark knight named Del Congost had begged from a French soldier. No one said much. There was the feeling that time was racing forward and there was nothing anyone could do to slow it.

Sybille remembered Corba's last words, about meeting again in another life. Perhaps all of them—Corba and herself and Olivier—would return someday. Perhaps even Daniel Marty and Simon de Montfort would be reborn and have a chance to redeem themselves. She thought: If I am born again, it will not be in this land, not if the choice is up to me. And then she had a curious thought: Suppose I am alive again some very great distance in the future, five hundred years or a thousand. Will I recognize Corba? Or Olivier? How? And will I remember this day at Montségur? She decided the answer must be yes: Never would she forget this day, not in a hundred lifetimes. Suddenly she heard her name and spun around.

Fabrisse was standing wearily, like a tired child calling impatiently for her mother. She is going to be a martyr, Sybille thought. She has been preparing for this day a long time. And then she thought: This is my sister. How can they burn my big Fabrisse? It is not possible.

Sybille went over and put her arms around her neck. Fabrisse kissed her, and while she kissed her, Sybille knew that her sister was not thinking of her. Fabrisse's neck and shoulders were shivering. She felt like a skinny little girl.

Fabrisse moved back a step. "Are you all right?" she asked.

Sybille said she was.

"Good," Fabrisse said. "Patience. It will be over shortly."

"I know."

"You and Olivier will be going. Your daughter will be waiting for you."

"Nova is her name."

"How pretty."

"Yes, it is very pretty." Sybille's voice was steady.

Fabrisse said, "Mama and Papa's only grandchild. They would be happy if they knew." She gave Sybille the kiss of peace, broke away, and hurried into the hall. Sybille went back up on the wall.

An hour before vespers, several dozen French soldiers came riding up the road. Chains in their hands, they went into the hall and began binding the condemned together, as if they were dogs who would go scampering off across the mountain if left unleashed. Then this escort dragged them into the yard and out the front gate, hurrying them along with the tips of their lances and swords. There were some, the elderly, the ill, who tripped on the chains and fell, but they were pushed and dragged along with the rest. Jordan de Perella, standing in the yard with his father, looked at his mother as she passed. He called to her, and she turned her head and looked at her husband. Everyone, Bishop Bertrand, all the black-robed deacons and ordinary ministers, the garrison soldiers who chose death, all the young women who were postulants or ministers or garrison wives, were shoved down the road toward the palisade while their friends and kin watched and wept and screamed.

As Sybille watched, she wondered if God were watching. She didn't think this with any bitterness or anger—it was only an idle thought. To Sybille, the disinterest of the Lord was a fact she took for granted. Perhaps Nova's idea was right, that God had no control over them and evil was something He permitted in order to teach them lessons. But what, Sybille wondered, is the lesson of all this? And who among us is wise enough to recognize it, let alone profit?

It was no longer afternoon but not yet evening. People began coming up on the wall. On either side of her, they stood silently, heads bowed, silhouettes between the battlements. For a few minutes the wind carried the sounds of chanting, the priests singing their psalms in Latin, and then the wind moved and the chanting drifted away. Soldiers, torches in their hands, lit the four corners of the palisade. Once the flames had caught and were sucking, the soldiers moved back.

The low rays of light were leaving the sky. Sybille stared out and down. The fortress and the rock, the trees, the patches of snow, the mountain itself, had vanished. She stood in space. Nothing was there but emptiness and, lower, farther down, the red glow—the flesh and blood of two hundred women and men burning in the darkness. Then thick smoke began to spread out across the mountainside, down to the valley where Nova was and up to the walls of the château. After an hour or so, Sybille walked slowly all the way around the top of the wall, to the place where Olivier and the others had been lowered to the cave below. She threw herself down flat with her face pressed against the stone walk. "I will love you forever," she whispered into the rough stones. Oh, Olivier, are you still there? Have you started down the mountain yet? Don't wait. You must go quickly now. No one is looking. "Bye-bye, bye-bye," she said over and over. "Bye-bye, my sweet lord."

She pushed herself up and groped her way down to the yard and out the gate. The door of Olivier's house was open. She lit a candle. Methodically she began to collect his things—a few shirts, a purse, a small vial of salt, a gold ring, a leather jerkin. All his earthly possessions. She tied them up in one of the shirts, snuffed the candle, and went out. Closing the door behind her, she staggered back up the path to the tower.

Inside the great hall, near the hearth, she went and sank down next to Pierre-Roger and Philippa. They sat in silence. Sybille laid the bundle in her lap.

Tomorrow, she was thinking, tomorrow they will take us off to Pamiers. Pierre-Roger believes they will ask us many questions, keep us in prison a little while. But, Olivier, they cannot hold me there forever. With luck, I will be free by summer and get my little penance and perhaps a yellow cross, and I'll go home to Nova. I just wish I had been able to say goodbye to you properly. But when I'm back in my house with my parchment and ink, I'm going to write a *canso* for you. Not one like *Ieu Sui,* not some story of a romantic knight. But a *canso* about you, as you truly are and what your life has been. Yes, and you will like this *canso,* my lord. I promise.

After the early morning haze the day had turned hot and golden, and the daisies near the sides of the road flamed saffron and blizzard-white above the weedy underbrush. Over her head the sky also was white, but she did not look up. Once, perhaps an hour earlier, she had stopped and turned to glance back at the walls of Pamiers. But the glance had lasted five or six seconds, no more, and then she had turned forward, shifted her bundle to the other hand, and gone on. She was thinking, With luck I might reach Les Pujols by midday, and she felt the sun falling on her head and she smiled. She was in a hurry, and she was not in a hurry; she slowly walked quickly.

The traffic ahead and behind was steady—an endless procession of merchants and farmers with their oxen and mules and sleek mounts. There were not many châteaux on this road, but a great number of farmhouses and children weeding in the fields, and she passed a small, dusty village where men were drinking wine and between the houses wet laundry hung limp on ropes. Sybille constantly swiveled her head from side to side, as full of wonder as if seeing such sights for the first time.

After she had passed the village, a cart slowed down and the driver turned to stare back at her. She had been hoping someone would offer her a ride, and when the farmer jerked his mules to a halt and motioned to her, she hurried forward. She smiled and called out, "Good morning, friend. Would you like company?"

He was a local man, she decided; the cart was filled with baskets of apricots and atop one of the baskets lounged a cat, gray, with long, shaggy fur. As she scrambled up, the farmer asked, "Where are you bound, lady?"

She hesitated to mention Montségur, in case he might mistake her for a heretic and make her get out. "The mountains," she answered. "Lavelanet or thereabouts." She squeezed herself in between the baskets. On the floor of the cart she made a cushion of her bundle and sat on it. As they began to move, she said to the man's back, "And you? Where are you going?"

"Not that far south," he told her. "Laroque d'Olmes. But if that is a help—"

"Close enough," she said. "That's fine. Thank you most kindly." She smiled at the cat, who was observing her with a certain amount of peevishness.

She settled back. It was a strange feeling, rocking along with the fields moving slowly past her and the smell of the ripe apricots in her nose.

The man said, over his shoulder, "So you're a mountain woman. Bad trouble up there lately."

From his tone she could not tell if he were Catholic or heretic, so she said, noncommittal, "Yes." Then quickly: "I'm not a mountain woman—I'm a Toulousan."

He faced her for a minute. "Oh?" he said, sounding interested. "I was there once." His voice was that of a country man who has seen one big city and sees no reason ever to visit another. "City or faubourg?"

That was the usual question. "Faubourg," she answered. In a way she was eager to talk, to make ordinary conversation about nothing, but the words came slowly. "I lived in one of the little streets behind Saint-Sernin—Rue St. Bernard. That was where I grew up."

He nodded. "Oh, yes, Saint-Sernin. I went there. And to Saint-Etienne. Very beautiful. And the houses"—he shook his head in remembered awe—"the houses and mansions in Toulouse are very fine."

That made her think of Douce's bedchamber, with its tiles—not the usual tiles but white marble cut in squares—and the deep windows set with Poitou glass and shaded by pale-blue curtains. That reminded her of the way the afternoon light had painted the tiles and the whole room bluish, how peaceful she had felt being in that room. The man was still talking about the houses in Toulouse. She did not answer for a while, then she begged his pardon for not replying, and he finally said, "Forgive my chattering, lady. I can see you've been ill. We don't have to talk."

"I'm not ill," she protested. "Well, I was sick about six weeks ago but now I'm fine. I feel strong now."

They clattered through Les Pujols, continued along the Mirepoix highroad for another half hour. Then late in the morning they turned into the trail going south, where there was much less traffic. They had begun to talk. She found it took no effort to converse with the farmer. He was a simple young man, respectful and courteous. He had a good deep voice, and she could see he liked to laugh, even though there was something soft, even grave, about his laughter. She could tell he also took things seriously. He gave her bread and cheese, and she ate eagerly.

"Try some of those apricots, lady," he called back. "They're very good."

"Your orchards?" she asked.

He nodded. "Yes. My father's. Take some. As many as you like."

She reached out for an apricot, sucked slowly until the sweet juice began to roll down her throat. The cat fussed at her elbow. "Wonderful," said Sybille with her mouth full. "Ah, it's been a long time since I've eaten such delicious apricots. What luxury!"

The farmer laughed and leaned back to stretch. "For myself they are not so extraordinary," he said. "But I can see why others like them. They have truly excellent flavor." He stopped and laughed again. "Listen to me—boasting too much about my fruit. But I know you understand."

They had left behind the flatlands and the wild flowers. Now the trail began to wind into the hills. The country was drier here, with barren slopes and scrubby pines. They puffed up the hills and rolled down, and the road curved and zigzagged, and the mules were working hard. Within sight of the road there was a stream, and sometimes, for a short stretch, it followed the road. Growing along the water's edge were touch-me-nots and daisies and weedy flowers whose names Sybille did not know, but as soon as the trail veered away, the vegetation was brownish again.

The farmer asked her, "Are you sleeping, lady?"

"No. Just resting. This is so nice. What was that last village called?"

"Vira."

"Vira," said Sybille. "You know, I feel so happy today. I'm going to see my daughter. It was before Christmas when I left her, and now it's June. How I long for the sight of her face. Frankly, I've been very lonely without her." And Olivier, she added silently. He will return soon. That will be a joyous day.

The farmer said thoughtfully, "I had imagined the older one gets, the less lonely one feels. I mean, I thought we learn how to be alone."

"That I've never learned," she said quickly and smiled. "Other things—"

"What things?"

She grinned at his back. "To talk less and listen more. When I was small, I was as noisy as an April rain. Swoosh, swoosh. Constantly chattering. My lady mother was always saying, 'Child, you're giving me an earache.'" Then for no reason, she added, "My mama was the most beautiful woman in Toulouse. Everyone said so. That was before the war, but you weren't born then."

"No," he said.

A little farther on, two more streams suddenly joined the one they had been following, and they had to cross a wooden bridge. The sun sang gently on Sybille's cheeks and hands. Sinking back between the baskets, she stuffed the bundle under her head and stretched out her legs. The cat curled its warm fur over her ankles. Beneath her head the earth was heaving and rolling like waves flowing to an unseen shore. The farmer began to whistle a *sirventes*—some tune by two Tarascon knights. She could not recall their names, but she knew the song. It had been one of Olivier's favorites. She stared straight up at the unmoving trees, at the clouds so white they hurt her eyes. For a moment she slipped one hand over her eyes, then let it drop and surrendered herself to the sky. Everywhere were clouds in snowdrifts, dissolving, reassembling, imprinting themselves upon the deep-blue bowl. I regret nothing in this life, she thought. I've loved a man and a child, and I wrote some decent verse. If a woman can love and write, there is nothing to regret.

She heard the man talking to her, but she did not answer. She was still watching the clouds and the sky. She thought about the color blue and the color white. Then she thought of a ribbon she once had had, about her mother who had given it to her. That's right, she thought. It was made of watered silk, blue like that sky, and it was sewn with little white pearls. Mama, it's so pretty. Again she heard the farmer's voice. He was wondering if she were thirsty. He certainly was. They would stop at the next town. At Dun there was a well with good cool water.

She thought: Very well. I'm ready to stop.

When she made no reply, the farmer turned briefly, noticed her eyes were closed, and was not surprised. He himself would be glad to halt for a rest soon, and he went on whistling, only more softly.

When he came to the square at Dun, he reined in the mules under a tree. "Lady, wake up," he called back. He jumped to the ground and went around to the side of the cart. The cat sprang onto his shoulder, clawing his shirt. "Lady?" he said again. He peered among the baskets and saw she was still asleep. Hesitating, he shook her shoulder lightly. Then he saw she was not asleep. She was dead.

He walked through the light over to the people around the well. A woman was giving her small son a drink and trying to hold back her dog, which she had tied to her wrist with a woven cord. Behind her stood two workmen talking, and the farmer went up to them.

All of them walked back to the cart. For a few minutes they stood looking down at Sybille, then the farmer and one of the workmen lifted out her body and laid it in the dust at the side of the road. A crowd began to gather. Someone went to find the priest, and while they were waiting for him, the villagers began asking questions, one after another. The farmer, whose name was Giraud Lafitte, was tired, and he was extremely upset. He had not expected the old woman to die. Nor could he answer their questions. He knew nothing about her, not even her name.

When he remembered she had been carrying a bundle, someone went to fetch it. On the ground they untied it and fumbled with the faded shirts; they rubbed the leather jerkin and opened the vial and announced it was salt. Then they searched the girdle and sleeves of the shabby gown Sybille was wearing. There was nothing. The priest came, hurrying in his dusty robe and predictably annoyed. He had been playing tables with the blacksmith and drinking wine. Stooping, he peered at Sybille's face for a minute or two and declared she must have been a heretic. Her face was too pale. He wanted nothing to do with heretics, dead or alive.

Wait, the farmer said. She spoke of once having lived in a big house in Toulouse and of hearing mass at Saint-Sernin. Also, she had told him she was recovering from an illness. There was no reason to assume she was a heretic. The young man spoke well, and the priest relented, although reluctantly. Bring the wretched woman to the church, he grumbled, and he would find her a place in the paupers' burying ground.

While they were preparing the grave, Giraud Lafitte sat under an olive tree with the cat in his lap and watched them dig. By the time the body had been put in the ground and the earth heaped over it and the priest had mumbled his prayers, the sun was going down and the air was cooling. Giraud Lafitte stood by the grave, head slightly bowed. The priest asked if he were sure the dead woman had had no money. The farmer said he was sure.

Giraud Lafitte crossed the square, had a drink at the well, washed his face in the aching-cold water, and then climbed back onto his cart and put the cat across his knees. If he hurried, he could make Sautel by dark.

Epilogue

They waited at Marseille five days. The first three days it had rained heavily, and after that the air was balmy and soft but still no ships could leave the harbor. But finally one evening after supper, the master mariner sent a boy to their inn, saying they must come quickly. He had a tide and a good wind. The ship would sail at midnight.

Their chests and boxes were already in the ship's hold. They gathered the few remaining things in the room. The man swung the satchel over his shoulder, and the young woman carried the bird in its cage and the parcel, which she had wrapped in hide and bound tightly with cord. There was no reason she could not have packed it in her chest. There was plenty of space among her gowns and chemises, and the package was not very big. Some forty or fifty pieces of parchment, that was all, but she told herself it was best she carry it with her, in case the chest somehow was swept overboard into the ocean. In truth, it made the woman happy to keep it in her hands.

They went quickly to the quay and up the ship's gangplank. The man walked aft and began speaking to one of the pilots in English, and the woman stood near the forecastle and put the birdcage at her feet. All around her in the torchlight there was noise and movement. The seamen climbing over the vessel were barefoot and naked except for their breeches and the little snood caps tied under their chins, and they were busy jerking ropes and tightening shrouds, and then they yanked the gangplank up over the side. All the while they shouted to each other in great bursts of noise, and the woman did not understand a word.

When the man came back, she was staring up at the mast, watching the sailors fasten the lateen sail. He went around to stand behind her, with his hands resting on her shoulders, and they watched together. The wind struck fiercely against the sail and their faces. Feeling her shiver, he took the hood of her cloak and pulled it up around her ears and over her hair. At last the anchor was hoisted and the ship began to move steadily and slowly out alongside the long, dark jetty. The man pulled her against him, wrapped his big cloak around both of them, and held her tight in his arms.

"What do you have there?" he asked and patted the package she was hugging close to her chest.

"Verse. Only words." She knew that everything is perishable: human lives, families, wealth, love, art. Even God, from whom all blessings are said to come, can Himself be destroyed by men. She knew that parchment might be used for kindling fires, for wrapping cod, but she also knew her mother's words must somehow be made to survive, so that what had happened in her time and place should not be forgotten.

The man was smiling down against the top of her hood. "It is a long voyage to London. Do you plan to hold it all the way?"

"Perhaps. I may." She laughed softly and was happy. "Richard?"

"Yes, my love."

"What is that word I saw painted on the hull?"

"The name of the ship."

"Yes. But what does it mean in my language?"

He said, "Why—justice. It means justice."

The lateen caught the wind and pulled them away from the jetty, farther and farther out into the black, salty water. The lights of Marseille faded, until Nova could see only a lighthouse beacon flickering in the darkness. In a short time she could not even see the beacon. They sailed on.